LEN DEIGHTON

Faith

HARPER

Harper
An imprint of HarperCollins*Publishers*
1 London Bridge Street,
London SE1 9GF

www.harpercollins.co.uk

This paperback edition 2016
1

First published in Great Britain by
HarperCollins*Publishers* 1994

A catalogue record for this book is
available from the British Library

ISBN: 978 0 00 812504 2

Set in Ehrhardt by Born Group using Atomik ePublisher from Easypress

FAITH

Len ghton was born in 1929. He worked as a railway clerk befo ing his National Service in the RAF as a photographer atta to the Special Investigation Branch.

his discharge in 1949, he went to art school – first to the St in's School of Art, and then to the Royal College of Art on a olarship. His mother was a professional cook and he grew up an interest in cookery – a subject he was later to make his in an animated strip for the *Observer* and in two cookery boo He worked for a while as an illustrator in New York and as art ctor of an advertising agency in London.

iding it was time to settle down, Deighton moved to the Do gne where he started work on his first book, *The Ipcress Fil Published* in 1962, the book was an immediate success.

Si then his work has gone from strength to strength, varying fro espionage novels to war, general fiction and non-fiction. Th BBC made *Bomber* into a day-long radio drama in 'real tim Deighton's history of World War Two, *Blood, Tears and Fol* , was published to wide acclaim – Jack Higgins called it 'an abs lute landmark'.

s Max Hastings observed, Deighton captured a time and a m d – 'To those of us who were in our twenties in the 1960s, his b ks seemed the coolest, funkiest, most sophisticated things we'd ev read' – and his books have now deservedly become classics.

By Len Deighton

FICTION
The Ipcress File
Horse Under Water
Funeral in Berlin
Billion-Dollar Brain
An Expensive Place to Die
Only When I Larf
Bomber
Declarations of War
Close-Up
Spy Story
Yesterday's Spy
Twinkle, Twinkle, Little Spy
SS-GB
XPD
Goodbye Mickey Mouse
MAMista
City of Gold
Violent Ward

THE SAMSON SERIES
Berlin Game
Mexico Set
London Match
Winter: The Tragic Story of a Berlin Family 1899–1945
Spy Hook
Spy Line
Spy Sinker
Faith
Hope
Charity

NON-FICTION
Action Cook Book
Fighter: The True Story of the Battle of Britain
Airshipwreck
French Cooking for Men
Blitzkrieg: From the Rise of Hitler to the Fall of Dunkirk
ABC of French Food
Blood, Tears and Folly

Cover designer's note

As Bernard Samson is now on an assignment in Poland I searched through my collection of photographs for a suitable image that would evoke that part of the world, and Bernard's involvement with the women in his life.

I remembered that, while on location for one of my documentaries in Poland, I had come across a window with a lace curtain adorned with a pair of ladies; the image of this would now provide a subtle visual analogy for the Iron Curtain.

I discovered that by placing a larger than life photograph of Samson in the window it created a rather surreal effect. Rather like Kong peering in at an unsuspecting Fay Wray, Bernard looms behind the curtain, an unwilling outsider ostracized from domestic comfort.

For a further reference to the two women in Bernard's life, the back cover displays a heart-shaped traditional Polish Wycinanki, an intricate design carefully cut from folded paper. Here, the heart is torn in two, separated by the sword of a KGB badge. You will note that the Western half features a very elegant gold wedding ring.

At the heart of every one of the nine books in this triple trilogy is Bernard Samson, so I wanted to come up with a neat way of visually linking them all. When the reader has collected all nine books and displays them together in sequential order, the books' spines will spell out Samson's name in the form of a blackmail note made up of airline baggage tags. The tags were drawn from my personal collection, and are colourful testimony to thousands of air miles spent travelling the world.

Arnold Schwartzman OBE RDI

Introduction

'Is this going to go into a book, Len?' my friend asked. He was a close and trusted friend and also an important functionary of the communist government. But he was armed with a healthy scepticism for all authority and this provided a bond and, at times, much merriment. I can't remember which year it was; sometime in the mid-nineteen sixties probably. We were sitting on a bench in what had once been the site of the Sachsenhausen Concentration Camp near Berlin.

'I don't know,' I replied.

'Because when I read your books I suddenly come across a description of something we have seen or done together and it brings it all back to me.'

To write these introductions I have been reading my books and this has revived many memories. Some memories have been happy ones but some are painful and now and again I have had to put the book aside for a moment or two. It is only now, with this re-reading, that I see how much of what I wrote was based on people, facts and experiences. I have often claimed that my books were almost entirely created from my imagination but now I see that this was something of a delusion. Now, as I read and recall events half-forgotten, brave people and strange places come crowding into my memory. Many of these people and places no longer exist. I can't offer you the past world but here is a depiction of it; here are my impressions of that world as I recorded it.

I had asked my friend to take me to the Sachsenhausen site, which was in the 'Zone' thirty miles from Berlin and outside the limits of its Soviet Sector. We went in his ancient Wartburg car with its noisy two-stroke engine that left a trail of smoke and envy. For even this contraption represented luxury to the average citizen in the East. Since neither of us had permission to enter the Zone we enjoyed the childish thrill of breaking the law. Sachsenhausen had been the Concentration Camp nearest to Berlin, and for that reason it was haunted by the ghosts of Hitler's specially selected victims. Eminent German generals had been locked up here before being tortured and executed for participation in the 'July 20th' attempt to overthrow the Führer. Some notable British agents passed through these bloodstained huts including Best and Stevens, who were senior SIS agents and whose capture and interrogation crippled the British Secret Intelligence Service for the whole war. Peter Churchill, an agent of the British SOE, was brought here. Martin Niemoller was imprisoned here too, so was Josef Stalin's son and Bismarck's grandson. Paul Reynaud, the PM of France, the prominent former Reichstag member Fritz Thyssen, Kurt Schuschnigg the Austrian chancellor and countless other anti-Nazis were locked away here. So were the Prisoners of War who escaped from Colditz, German Trade Union leaders, Jews and anyone who stepped out of line.

The camp had been set up in 1933 by Hitler's brown-shirted hooligans, the *Sturmabteilung*, but the 'Night of the Long Knives' had seen fortunes reversed; the SA leaders were murdered by Himmler's SS 'Death's Head' units, which took control of the camps and of much else. It was while under SS control that the camp installed a forgery unit for Operation Bernhard, for which imprisoned printing and engraving experts were sought from camps far and wide. These prisoners forged documents of many kinds and produced counterfeit currency

– notably British five-pound notes – that even the Swiss bankers could not distinguish from the authentic ones. But more horribly, this camp was notorious for the systematic murder by gassing of many thousands of innocent Jews. My friend, in an official capacity, had interrogated one of the camp's Nazi commanders during his postwar captivity, and recalled the chilling way in which he had spoken of the killings without remorse or regret.

After the war, the Sachsenhausen camp was used by the Russians. Called 'Special Camp No. 1', they imprisoned here anyone they considered to be enemies of the Soviet occupation authorities or anyone who opposed the communist system of totalitarian government. After the Wall fell, and the Russians departed, excavations revealed more than 12,000 bodies of people who died during the period of Soviet control.

In fact, I never did use my visit to the Sachsenhausen-Oranienburg camp complex in my books but it was another lesson in my attempt to understand Germany and the Germans. German history has always obsessed me and in my writing a well-researched historical background provides a necessary dimension to the Berlin where Bernard Samson has lived since childhood. Although my asides about German history are subordinate to the plot and to the characterizations, they are researched with care and attention. And the story is not confined to Berlin. *Faith* quickly moves into Magdeburg, which the German secret police and their Russian colleagues made the centre of their operations. My brief aside about Adolf Hitler's mortal remains being held there was based upon reliable evidence. Despite what is widely written, Hitler's body was not completely consumed by flame in a shallow trench outside the Berlin bunker. The amount of gasoline used could not ignite a fresh corpse, so much of which is water. When the Soviet Russian Army arrived in Berlin, the army's secret police seized what remained of Hitler's body as a macabre trophy, and have held on to it ever since. After Magdeburg this collection of dried flesh and scorched bone was taken to Moscow where, as far as my research can discover, it remains, kept in a glass-sided cabinet like the revered body fragments of medieval saints.

Discovering facts or a sequence of events that others have missed is the great joy of research. Some such discoveries can be confirmed given a little digging, some cross-references and some whispered confidences. Even such well-turned over soil as the Battle of Britain revealed to me some remarkable revelations and in *Fighter* became a cause of argument and anger. Now, however, the 'surprises' in my history books have been accepted as facts. But some research brings surprises more difficult to confirm. Even when I am quite sure about the truth of them I have abstained from declaring them as history. But 'fiction' brings an opportunity to say things that are difficult to prove. That's how it stands with the revelations about the Russian Army's electronics and hardware being stolen and shipped from Poland in exchange for CIA money. There were historical finds, too. I discovered that, during the Nazi regime, all extermination camps were situated just outside the German border so that the insurance companies could avoid payment to the relatives of people murdered in the camps, but I failed to find written evidence. Other than the maps that showed how deliberately systematic the siting of the camps was, proof was beyond me. My recourse was to use that undoubtedly true discovery in *Winter* together with other lesser-known facts of history.

I work hard to make each book of the Samson series complete, and I contrive a story that does not depend on knowledge of the other books. The story of *Faith* continues directly from *Sinker*, which is devoted mainly to the events seen through the eyes of Bernard's wife, Fiona. Fiona's secret assignment was to establish financial links between London and the Lutheran Church in the German Democratic Republic, i.e. communist Germany. It was an important task and a notable success. Of the 20 million people living in communist East Germany about ninety per cent remained members of the Christian Church. As Bret remarks, they provided a 'powerful cohesive force' that would eventually break down the Wall.

But the plot, and the strategy of the British intelligence service, is not the most important thread in the series. The characters were at the heart of my labours. The social exchanges of *Faith* demonstrate Bernard's painful dilemma when Fiona confronts Gloria, and the love affair which Bernard stumbles into when he believes that he will never see his wife again. The reactions of both women, and such events as Dicky Cruyer's dinner party which both women attend, is vital to the development of the plot and the interaction between all the major characters.

Writing ten books about the same small group of people is a strange and demanding task. I am a slow worker and I don't take regular vacations or set work aside for prolonged periods. Ten books meant about fifteen years during which these people, their hopes and fears and loves and betrayals were constantly whirling around in my brain. They disturbed my sleep and invaded my dreams in a way I did not always enjoy. Because the story line was such a long one, the characters became well-defined and were not easily bent to the needs of the plot. Unlike the content of my other books, Bernard Samson and his circle became imprinted in my mind and remain there today. I confess to you that I find this unremitting concern for these fictional people disturbing. That long period of concentration seemed to be a brain-washing. Do other writers suffer the same problems? I don't know; not many writers produce ten books about the same people so it is not easy to find out.

Len Deighton, 2011

1

'Don't miss your plane, Bernard. This whole operation depends upon the timing.' Bret Rensselaer peered around to spot a departures indicator; but this was Los Angeles airport and there were none in sight. They would spoil the architect's concept.

'It's okay, Bret,' I said. He would never have survived five minutes as a field agent. Even when he was my boss, driving a desk at London Central, he'd been like this: repeating the instructions, wetting his lips, dancing from one foot to the other and furrowing his brow as if goading his memory.

'Just because Comrade Gorbachev is kissing Mrs Thatcher and spreading that glasnost schmaltz in Moscow, it doesn't mean those East German bastards are buying any of it. Everything we hear says the same thing: they are more stubborn and vindictive than ever.'

'It will be just like home,' I said.

Bret sighed. 'Try and see it from London's point of view,' he said with exaggerated patience. 'Your task was to bring Fiona across the wire as quickly and quietly as possible. But you fixed it so your farewell performance out on that Autobahn was like the last act of *Hamlet*. You shoot two bystanders, and your own sister-in-law gets killed in the crossfire.' He glanced at my wife Fiona, who was still recovering from seeing her sister Tessa killed. 'Don't expect London Central to be waiting for you with a gold medal, Bernard.'

He'd bent the facts but what was the use of arguing? He was in one of his bellicose moods, and I knew them well. Bret Rensselaer was a slim American who'd aged like a rare wine: growing thinner, more elegant, more subtle and more complex with every year that passed. He looked at me as if expecting some hot-tempered reaction to his words. Getting none, he looked at my wife. She was older too, but no less serene and beautiful. With that face, her wide cheekbones, flawless complexion and luminous eyes, she held me in thrall as she always had done. You might have thought that she was completely recovered from her ordeal in Germany. She was gazing at me with love and devotion and there was no sign she'd heard Bret.

Sending me to do this job in Magdeburg was not Bret's idea. I'd caught sight of the signal he sent to London Central telling them that I was no longer suited to field work, particularly in East Germany. He'd asked them to chain me to a desk until pension time rolled round. It sounded considerate, but I wasn't pleased. I needed to do something that would put me back in Operations; that was my only chance of being promoted and getting a senior staff position in London. Unless my position improved I would wind up with a premature retirement and a pension that wouldn't pay for a cardboard box to live in.

I nodded. Bret always observed the niceties of hospitality. He had driven us to Los Angeles airport through a winter rainstorm to say goodbye. They could watch me climb on to the plane bound for Berlin, and my assignment. Then he would put Fiona on the direct flight to London. The Wall was still there and people were getting killed while climbing over it. Now Bret was just repeating all the things he'd told me a thousand times before, the way people do when they are saying goodbye at airports.

'Keep the faith,' said Bret, and in response to my blank look he added: 'I'm not talking about timetables or statistics or training manuals. Faith. It's not in here.' He tapped his forehead.

'It's in here.' Gently he thumped his heart with a flattened palm so that the signet ring glittered on his beautifully manicured hand, and a gold watch peeped out from behind a starched linen cuff.

'Yes, I see. Not a headache; more like indigestion,' I said. Fiona watched us and smiled.

'They are calling the flight,' said Bret.

'Take care, darling,' she said. I took Fiona in my arms and we kissed decorously, but then I felt a sudden pain as she bit my lip. I gave a little yelp and stepped back from her. She smiled again. Bret looked anxiously from me to Fiona and then back at me again, trying to decide whether he should smile or say something. I rubbed my lip. Bret concluded that perhaps it was none of his business after all, and from his raincoat pocket he brought a shiny red paper bag and gave it to me. It was secured with matching ribbon tied in a fancy gift-wrap bow. The package was slightly limp; like a paperback book.

'Read that,' said Bret, picking up my carry-on bag and shepherding me towards the gate where the other passengers were standing in line. It seemed as if it would be a full load today; there were women with crying babies and long-haired kids with earrings, well-used backpacks and the sort of embroidered jackets that you can buy in Nepal. Fiona followed, observing the people crowding round us with that detached amusement with which she cruised through life. With one phone call Bret could have arranged for us to use any of the VIP lounges on the airport, but the Department's guidelines said that agents travelling on duty kept to a low profile, and so that's what Bret did. That's why he'd left his driver behind at the house and taken the wheel of the Accord. Like other Americans before him, he had exaggerated respect for what the people in London thought was the right way to do things. We reached the gate. I couldn't go through until he handed over my carry-on bag.

'Maybe all this hurry-hurry from London will work out for the best, Bernard. Your few days chasing around East Germany will give Fiona a chance to get your London apartment ready. She wants to do that for you. She wants to settle down and start all over again.' He looked at her and waited until she nodded agreement.

Only Bret would have the chutzpah to explain my wife to me while she was standing beside him. 'Yes, Bret,' I said. There was no sense in telling him he was out of line. Another few minutes and I'd be rid of him for ever.

'And don't go chasing after Werner Volkmann.'

'No,' I said.

'Don't give me that glib no-of-course-not routine. I mean it. Whatever Werner did to them, London Central hate him with a passion beyond compare.'

'Yes, you told me that.'

'You can't afford to step out of line, Bernard. If someone spots you having a cup of coffee with your old buddy Werner, everyone in London will be saying you are part of a conspiracy or something. God knows what he did to them but they hate him.'

'I wouldn't know where to find him,' I said.

'That's never stopped you before.' Bret paused and looked at his watch. 'Be a model employee. Put your faith in the Department, Bernard. Swallow your pride and tug your forelock. Now that London Central's funds are being so severely cut, they are looking for an excuse to fire people instead of retire them. No one's job is safe.'

'I've got it all, Bret,' I said, and tried to prise my bag away from him.

He smiled and moistened his lips, as if trying to resist giving me any more advice and reminders. 'I hear Tante Lisl has had a check-up. If she's going to have a hip replacement, or whatever it is, trying to save a few bucks on it is dumb.'

4

That was his way of saying that he'd pay old Frau Hennig's doctor's bills. I knew Bret well. We'd had our ups and downs, especially when I thought he was chasing Fiona, but I'd got to know him better during my long stay in California. As far as I could tell, Bret wasn't a double-crosser. He didn't lie or cheat or steal except when ordered to do so, and that put him into a very tiny minority of the people I worked with. He handed over my bag and we shook hands. We were out of earshot of Fiona and anyone else.

'This Russkie who's asking for you, Bernard,' he whispered. 'He says he owes you a favour, a big favour.'

'So you said.'

'VERDI: that's his codename of course.' I nodded solemnly. I'm glad Bret told me that or I might have arrived expecting an aria from *La Traviata*. 'A colonel,' he coaxed me. 'His father was a junior lieutenant with one of the first Red Army units to enter Berlin in April '45 and stayed there to become a staff officer at Red Army headquarters, on long-term political assignment at Berlin-Karlshorst. Dad married a pretty German fräulein, and VERDI grew up more German than Russian … so the KGB grabbed him. Now he's a colonel and wants a deal.' Having gabbled his way through this description he paused. 'And you still can't guess who he might be?' Bret looked at me. Surely he knew I wasn't going to start that kind of game; it would open a can of worms that I wanted to keep tightly shut.

'Do you have any idea how many hustlers out there answer that kind of description?' I said. 'They all have stories like that. Seems like those first few Ivans into town fathered half the population of the city.'

'That's right. Play it close to the chest,' said Bret. 'That's always been your way, hasn't it?' He so wanted to be in London, and be a part of it again, that he actually envied me. It was almost laughable. Poor old Bret was past it; even his friends said that.

5

'And your girlfriend,' whispered Bret. 'Gloria. Make sure that's all over and done with.' His voice was edged with the indignant anger that we all feel for other men's philandering. 'Try to hang on to both of them and you'll lose Fiona and the children. And maybe your job too.'

I smiled mirthlessly. The airline girl ripped my boarding pass in half and before I went down the jetty I turned back to wave to them. Who would have guessed that my wife was a revered heroine of the Secret Intelligence Service? And with every chance of becoming its Director-General, if Bret's opinion was anything to go by. At this moment Fiona looked like a photo from some English society magazine. Her old Burberry coat, its collar turned up to frame her head, and a colourful Hermès scarf knotted at the point of her chin, made her look like an English upper-class mum watching her children at a gymkhana. She held a handkerchief to her face as if about to cry, but it was probably the head cold she'd had for a week and couldn't shake off. Bret was standing there in his short black raincoat; as still and expressionless as a stone statue. His fair hair was now mostly white and his face grey. And he was looking at me as if imprinting this moment on his memory; as if he was never going to see me again.

As I walked down the enclosed jetty towards the plane a series of scratched plastic windows, rippling with water, provided a glimpse of rain-lashed palm trees, lustrous engine cowling, sleek tailplane and a slice of fuselage. Rain was glazing the jumbo, making its paintwork shiny like a huge new toy; it was a hell of a way to say goodbye to California.

'First Class?'

Airlines arrange things as if they didn't want you to discover that you were boarding a plane, so they wind up with something like a cramped roadside diner that smells of cold coffee and stale perspiration and has exits on both sides of the ocean.

'No,' I said. 'Business.' She let me find my own assigned place. I put my carry-on bag into the overhead locker, selected a German newspaper from the display and settled into my seat. I looked out of the tiny window to see if Bret was pressing his nose against the window of the departure lounge but there was no sign of him. So I settled back and opened the red bag that contained his going-away present. It was a Holy Bible. Its pages had gold edges and its binding was of soft tooled leather. It looked very old. I wondered if it was some sort of Rensselaer family heirloom.

'Hi there, Bernard.' A man named 'Tiny' Timmermann called to me from his seat across the aisle. A linguist of indeterminate national origins – Danish maybe – he was a baby-faced 250-pound wrestler, with piggy eyes, close-cropped skull and heavy gold jewellery. I knew him from Berlin in the old days when he was some kind of well-paid consultant to the US State Department. There was a persistent rumour that he'd strangled a Russian ship's captain in Riga and brought back to Washington a boxful of manifests and documents that gave details of the nuclear dumping the Russian Navy was doing into the sea off Archangel. Whatever he'd done for them, the Americans always seemed to treat him generously, but now, the rumours said, even Tiny's services were for hire.

'Good to see you, Tiny,' I said.

'Hals und Beinbruch!' he said, wishing me good fortune as if dispatching me down a particularly hazardous ski-run. It shook me. Did he guess I was on an assignment? And if news of it had reached Tiny who else knew?

I gave him a bemused smile and then we were strapping in and the flight attendant was pretending to blow into a life-vest, and after that Tiny produced a lap-top computer from his case and started playing tunes on it as if to indicate that he wasn't in the mood for conversation.

The plane had thundered into the sky, banked briefly over the Pacific Ocean and set course northeast. I stretched out my legs to their full Business Class extent and opened my newspaper. At the bottom of the front page a discreet headline, 'Erich Honecker proclaims Wall will still exist in 100 years,' was accompanied by a smudgy photo of him. This optimistic expressed view of the General Secretary of the Central Committee of the SED, the party governing East Germany, seemed like the sincere words of a dedicated tyrant. I believed him.

I didn't read on. The newsprint was small and the grey day-light was not much helped by my dim overhead reading light. Also my hand trembled as it held the paper. I told myself that it was a natural condition arising from the rush to the airport and carrying a ton of baggage from the car while Bret fought off the traffic cops. Putting the newspaper down I opened the Bible instead. There was a yellow sticker in a page marking a passage from St Luke:

> For I tell you, that many prophets and kings have desired
> to see those things which ye see, and have not seen them;
> and to hear those things which ye hear, and have not heard
> them.

Yes, very droll, Bret. The only inscription on the flyleaf was a pencilled scrawl that said in German, 'A promise is a promise!' It was not Bret's handwriting. I opened the Bible at random and read passages but I kept recalling Bret's face. Was it his immi-nent demise I saw written there? Or his anticipation of mine? Then I found the letter from Bret. One sheet of thin onion-skin paper, folded and creased so tightly that it made no bulge in the pages.

'Forget what happened. You are off on a new adventure,' Bret had written in that loopy coiled style that characterizes

American script. 'Like Kim about to leave his father for the Grand Trunk Road, or Huck Finn starting his journey down the Mississippi, or Jim Hawkins being invited to sail to the Spanish Caribbean, you are starting all over again, Bernard. Put the past behind you. This time it will all be different, providing you tackle it that way.'

I read it twice, looking for a code or a hidden message, but I shouldn't have bothered. It was pure Bret right down to the literary clichés and flowery good wishes and encouragement. But it didn't reassure me. Kim was an orphan and these were all fictional characters he was comparing me with. I had the feeling that these promised beginnings in distant lands were Bret's way of making his goodbye really final. It didn't say: come back soon.

Or was Bret's message about me and Fiona, about our starting our marriage anew? Fiona's pretended defection to the East was being measured by the valuable encouragement she'd given to the Church in its opposition to the communists. Only I could see the price she had paid. In the last couple of weeks she'd been confident and more vivacious than I could remember her being for a very long time. Of course she was never again going to be like the Fiona I'd first met, that eager young Oxford-educated adventurer who had crewed an oceangoing yacht and could argue dialectical materialism in almost perfect French while cooking a souffle. But if she was not the same person she'd once been, then neither was I. No one could be blamed for that. We'd chosen to deal in secrets. And if her secret task had been so secret that it had been kept concealed even from me then I would have to learn not to resent that exclusion.

When the flight attendant brought champagne and a liver compound spread on tiny circles of toast I gobbled everything down as I always do, because my mind was elsewhere. I still couldn't help thinking about Honecker and Bret and the Wall. It's true that things were slowly changing over there; financial loans and political pressure had persuaded them to make the Stasi dig up and discard a few of the land-mines and automatic firing devices from the 'death-strip' along the Wall. But the lethal hardware remaining was more than enough to discourage spontaneous emigration. I suppose Western intelligence was changing equally slowly: people like me and 'Tiny' were no longer travelling First Class. As I drifted off to sleep I was wondering how long it would be before that professional egalitarian Erich Honecker found himself adjusting to the rigours of flying Economy.

'Did you manage to sleep on the plane?' said the young Englishman who met me at the airport in Berlin and took me to his apartment. He put my luggage down and closed the door. He was a tall thin thirty-year-old with an agreeable voice, a pale face, uneven teeth and a certain diffident awkwardness that sometimes afflicts tall people. I followed him into the kitchen of his apartment in Moabit, near Turmstrasse U-Bahn. It was the sort of grimy little place that young people will endure in order to be near the bright lights. As a long-time resident of the city I knew it as one of the apartment blocks hastily built in the ruins soon after the war, and nowadays showing their age.

'I'm all right.'

'I'll make some tea, shall I?' he said as he filled the electric kettle. I reached the teapot from the shelf for him and found on its lid a sticky label with a message scrawled across it in a feminine hand: 'Don't forget the key, Kinkypoo. See you at the weekend.'

'There's a message here,' I said and gave it to him. He smiled self-consciously and said: 'She knows I always make tea as soon as I get home. That reminds me – I was told to give you something too.'

He went to a cupboard, found a box and got from it a slip of paper with typed dates, times and numbers. It was a good example of the bullshit that the people behind desks in London Central wasted their time with: radio wavelengths.

'Okay?' said the kid, watching me.

'Typed on a 1958 Adler portable by a small dark curly-haired guy with a bandaged middle finger.'

'Are you kidding?' said the kid, reserving a margin of awe in case I was serious.

I tossed the paper into the kitchen bin, where it fluttered to rest among the dead teabags and accumulated strata of half-eaten frozen TV dinners, their seams marked by the azoic ooze of brightly coloured sauces. This was not a place to stay on full pension. 'If we get into trouble over there,' I said, 'I'm not going to be wasting a lot of time trying to contact London by radio.' I opened my suitcase and laid my suit across the back of the sofa.

A large fluffy cat came in to investigate the kitchen garbage, sniffing to make sure that the discarded message was not edible. 'Rumtopf!' said the kid. 'Come over here and eat your fish!' The cat looked at him but forsaking the fish strolled over to the sofa, jumped up on to its favourite cushion, collapsed elegantly and went to sleep. 'He likes you,' said the kid.

'I'm too old for making new friends,' I said, moving my suit so it didn't pick up cat hairs.

'There's no hurry,' said the kid as he poured tea for us both. 'I know the route and the roads and everything. I'll get you there on time.'

'That's good.' It was still daylight in Berlin, or as near daylight as it gets in winter. It wasn't snowing but the air shimmered with snowflakes that only became visible as they twisted and turned, while dark grey cloud clamped upon the rooftops like an old iron saucepan lid.

He looked at my red eyes and unshaven face. 'The bathroom is the door with the sign.' He pointed at an old enamel Ausgang sign, no doubt prised from one of Berlin's abandoned railway stations. The apartment had many such notices, together with advertisements and battered American licence plates and some lovingly framed covers from ancient *Popular Mechanics* magazines. There were other curious artifacts: strange weapons and even stranger hats from far parts of the world. The collection belonged to a young German art director who shared the rent here but was temporarily living with a redheaded Irish model girl who was depicted in a large coloured photo doing handstands on the beach at Wannsee. 'London said I was to give you anything you needed.'

'Not just tea?'

'Clothes, a gun, money.'

'You don't expect me to go across there carrying a gun?'

'They said you'd find a way if you wanted to.' He looked at me as if I was something out of the zoo. I wondered what he had been told about me; and who had been telling him.

'Half a dozen different identity documents for you to choose from. And a gas-gun, handcuffs and sticky-tape and restraints.'

'What are you talking about?'

'We won't need any of it,' he hastened to assure me as he prodded at the discarded list of radio wavelengths to push it deeper into the garbage. 'He just wants to talk to someone he knows; someone from the old days, he said. London thinks he'll probably offer us paperwork; they want to know what it is.' When I made no response he went on: 'He's a Stasi colonel … Moscow-trained. Nowadays we can be choosy who we take.'

'Restraints?' I said.

'London said you might want handcuffs and things.'

'London said that? Are they going crazy?'

He preferred not to answer that question. I said: 'You've met this "Stasi colonel"? Seen him close up?'

'Yes.'

'Young? Old? Clever? Aggressive?'

12

'Certainly not young,' he said emphatically.

'Older than me?'

'About your age. Medium build. We talk to him in Magdeburg. And check the material if he has anything to show us. But if he arrives panting and ready to go, London said we must have everything prepared. It is prepared – a safe house and an escape line and so on. I'll show you on the map.'

'I know where Magdeburg is.' It was useful to know that I was now officially in the 'certainly not young' category.

'A back-up team will take him from us. They'll do the actual crossing.'

'Have you had a briefing from Berlin Field Unit? What does Frank Harrington say about all this?' Frank Harrington ran our West Berlin office, doing the job my father once did.

'Frank is being kept informed but the operation is controlled directly from London Central.'

'From London Central,' I repeated softly. It was getting worse every minute.

The kid tried to cheer me up: 'If there is any problem we also have a safe house in Magdeburg.'

'There's no such thing as a safe house in Magdeburg,' I said. 'Magdeburg is home town for those people. They operate out of Magdeburg, it's their alma mater. There are more Stasi men running around the Westendstrasse security compound in Magdeburg than in the whole of the rest of the DDR.'

'I see.' We finished our tea in silence, then I picked up the phone and dialled the number for Tante Lisl, a woman who'd been a second mother to me. I wanted to pass on to her Bret's message of encouragement, and if surgery for her arthritis was going to prove costly I wanted to see the hospital and make my own financial arrangements with them. Meanwhile I planned to buy a big bunch of flowers and go round to her funny little hotel to hold her hand and read to her. But when I got through,

13

someone at reception said she had flown to Miami and joined a winter cruise in the Caribbean. So much for my visions of Tante Lisl expiring on a couch; she was probably playing deck tennis and winning the ship's amateur talent competition with her inimitable high-kick routine of 'Bye Bye Blackbird'.

'I'll shave, shower and change my clothes,' I said as I sorted through my suitcase. To make conversation I added: 'I'm putting on too much weight.'

'You should work out,' he said solemnly. 'The older you get the more you need exercise.'

I nodded. Thanks, kid, I'll make a note of it. Well that was great. While I was nursemaiding this kid he was going to be second-guessing everything I did because he thought I was out of condition and past it.

The bathroom was in chaos. I'd almost forgotten what the habitat of the young single male looked like: on a chair there was draped a dirty tee-shirt, a heavy sweater and a torn denim jacket – he'd obviously donned his one and only suit in my honour. Three kinds of shampoo, two flavours of expensive after-shaves and an illuminated magnifying mirror to examine spots.

I went to the bathroom window, an old-fashioned double-glazed contraption, the brass handles tightly closed and tarnished with a green mottle as if it had not been opened in decades. Along the bottom ledge, between the dusty sheets of glass, lay dozens of dead moths and shrivelled flies of all shapes and sizes. How did they get inside, if they couldn't get out alive? Maybe there was a message there for me if only I could work it out.

The view from the window brought mixed feelings. I had grown up here; it was the only place I could think of as home. Not so long ago, in California, I had continually ached to be back in Berlin. I had been homesick for this town in a way I had never thought possible. Now that I was here there were no feelings of happiness or satisfaction. Something inexplicable had happened, unless of course I was frightened of going once more to the other side, which once I'd regarded as no more demanding than walking to the corner store for a pack of cigarettes. The kid thought I was nervous and he was right. If he knew what he was doing, he'd be nervous too.

Down in the street there was not much movement. The few pedestrians were wrapped in heavy coats, scarfs and fur hats and walking head-bent and hunched against the cold east wind that blew steadily from Russia's vast icy hinterland. Both sides of the street were lined with cars and vans. They were dirty: caked with the mud and grime of a European winter, a condition unknown in southern California. On the glasswork of the parked cars, frost and ice had formed elaborate swirling patterns. Any one of these vehicles would provide a secure hiding place for a surveillance team watching the building. I regretted letting the kid bring me here. It was stupid and careless. He was sure to be known to the opposition, and too tall to be inconspicuous; that's why he'd never last as a field agent.

After I'd cleaned up and shaved and changed into a suit, he spread a map across the table and showed me the route he proposed. He suggested that we drive through Charlie into the Eastern Sector of Berlin and then drive south and avoid the main roads and Autobahnen all the time. It was a circuitous route but the kid quoted all London's official advisories to me and insisted that it was the best way to do it. I yielded to him. I could see he was one of those fastidious preparation fanatics, and that was a good way to be when going on a venture of this sort.

'What do you think?' the kid asked.

'Tell me seriously: did London Central really say I might want restraints to drag this bruiser out even against his will?'

'Yes.'

'Do you have any whisky?'

As is so often the case with frontier crossings that inspire a nervous premonition of disaster, passing through Checkpoint Charlie went smoothly. Before driving out of the city I asked the kid to make a small detour to call at a quiet little bar in Oranienburger Strasse so I could get cigarettes and a tall glass of Saxony's famous beer.

'You must have a throat like leather to actually crave East German cigarettes,' said the kid. He was staring at the only other people in the bar: two youngish women in fur coats. They looked up at him expectantly, but one glance was enough to tell them that he was no proposition and they went back to their whispered conversation.

'What do you know about it?' I said. 'You don't smoke.'

'If I did smoke, it wouldn't be those coffin nails.'

'Drink your beer and shut up,' I said.

Behind the counter Andi Krohn had followed our exchange. He looked at the girls in the corner and stared at me as if about to smile. Andi's had always been a place to find available women for a price: they say it was notorious even as far back as before the war. I don't know how his predecessors had got away with it for all these years, except that the Krohn family had always known the right people to cultivate. Andi and I had been friends since we were both schoolboys and he was the school's most cherished athlete. In those days there was talk of him becoming an Olympic miler. But it never happened. Now he was greying and portly with bifocal glasses and he took several minutes to recognize me after we came through the door.

Andi's grandparents had been members of Germany's tiny ethnic minority of Sorbs, Slavs who from medieval times had retained their own culture and language. Nowadays they were mostly to be found in the extreme southeast corner of the DDR where Poland and Czechoslovakia meet. It is one of several places called the Dreiländereck – three-nation corner – a locality where they brew some of the finest beers in the world. Strangers came a long way to seek out Andi's bar, and they weren't all looking for women.

We exchanged banalities as if I'd never been away. His son Frank had married a pharmacist from Dresden, and I had little alternative but to go through an album of wedding photos and make appreciative noises, and drink beer, and a few schnapps chasers, while the kid looked at his watch and fretted. I didn't show Andi pictures of my wife and family and he didn't ask to see any. Andi was quick on the uptake, the way all barmen become. He knew that whatever kind of job I did nowadays it wasn't one you did with a pocketful of identification material.

Once back on the road we made good time. 'Smoke if you want to,' the kid offered.

'Not right now.'

'I thought you were desperate for one of those East German nails?'

'The feeling passed.' I looked out at the landscape. I knew the area. Forests helped to conceal the military encampments, row upon row of huts complete with chain-link fences and coils of barbed-wire and tall watch-towers manned by men with guns and field-glasses. So big were these military camps, and so numerous, that it was not always possible to be sure where one ended and another began. Almost as abundant in the first fifty miles of our journey were the open-cast lignite mines where East Germany obtained the fuel to make electricity and to burn in a million household stoves and create the most polluted air in Europe. Winter had proved capricious this year, tightening and then loosening its grip on the landscape. The last few days had seen a premature thaw and had left snow patches to shine in the

17

moonlight, marking the edges of the fields and higher ground. The back roads we'd chosen were icy in places and the kid kept to a sensible moderate speed. We were within fifteen miles of Magdeburg when we encountered the road-block.

We came upon it suddenly as we rounded a bend. The kid braked in response to an agitated waving of a lighted baton of the sort used by German police on both sides of the frontier.

'Papers?' said the soldier. He was a burly old fellow in camouflage fatigues and steel helmet. 'Switch off the engine and the main beams.' His country accent was perfect: something to put into the archives now that all East Germany's kids were talking like TV announcers.

The kid switched off the car headlights, and in the sudden quiet I could hear the wind in the bare trees and subdued pop music coming from the guard hut. The man who'd spoken handed our papers over to another soldier with Leutnant's tabs on his camouflage outfit. He examined them by means of a flashlight. It was the very hell of a place for a lengthy delay. A bleak landscape of turnip fields until, right across the horizon, like tall-stacked cruisers of the Kaiser's coal-burning battle fleet, there stood a long line of factory chimneys, puffing out clouds of multicoloured smoke.

'Get out,' said the officer, a short slim man with a neatly trimmed moustache and steel-rimmed glasses. We got out. It was not a good sign. 'Open the trunk.'

When it was open the Leutnant used his flashlight and groped around the oily rags and spare wheel. He found a bottle of Swedish vodka there. It was still in a colourful fancy box they use for overpriced booze in airport duty-free shops.

'You can keep it,' the kid told him. The Leutnant gave no sign of hearing the kid's offer. 'A present from Sweden.' But it was no use. The Leutnant was deaf to such bribes. He looked at our papers again, holding them close to his face so that the light

18

reflected on to his face and made his spectacle lenses gleam. I shivered in the cold. For some reason the Leutnant didn't seem interested in me. Maybe it was my rumpled suit with its unmistakable East German cut, or the pungent smell of Andi Krohn's rot-gut apple-schnapps that had been repeating on me for the last half hour and was no doubt evident on my breath. But the kid was using a Swedish passport, and the identification that accompanied it described him as a Swedish engineer working for a construction company that was about to build a luxury hotel in Magdeburg. It was plausible, and anyway the kid's German was not good enough to pass him off as a German national. The Swedes had made a corner for themselves building hotels to which only foreigners with hard currency were admitted, so it was a reasonable enough cover. But I wondered what would happen if someone started questioning him in Swedish.

I stamped around to keep my circulation moving. The trees were tormented by the wind and the skies had cleared enough to bring the temperature drop that always accompanies a sight of the stars. I didn't envy these men their job. As we stood there on the country road the wind had that cruel bite that dampness brings. It was more than enough excuse for becoming bad-tempered.

The two soldiers circled the old dented Volvo, looking at it with that mixture of contempt and envy that Western luxuries so often produced in the Party faithful. Then, with the boot open, the two soldiers went back to their hut, leaving us standing there in the cold. I'd seen it all before: they were hoping we would get back into the car so that they could come back and scream at us. Or that we would close the trunk or even drive away, so that they could phone the back-up team at the next checkpoint and tell them to open fire at us. It wasn't anything to take personally. All soldiers are inclined to get like that after too much guard duty.

Eventually they seemed to grow weary of their game. They returned and examined the car again, wondering perhaps if it would be diverting to tear the upholstery out of its interior and then make sure there was no contraband hidden inside the tyres. The Leutnant stayed close to us, still brandishing our papers, while the old man climbed into the back seat and prodded everything proddable. When he'd completed his examination he got out and looked again at the back. There was a loud bang as he slammed the trunk. When he returned he was carrying the vodka. The Leutnant gave us our papers. 'You can go,' he said. The older man hugged the fancy box to his chest and watched our reaction.

We got in the car and the kid started up the engine and switched on the lights. I turned my head. Just visible in the darkness the two men stood watching us depart. 'We'll be late,' said the kid.

'Take it very slowly,' I said. 'And if they shout "Stop", stop.'

'You bet,' said the kid.

'Militia,' I said as we pulled away.

'Yes,' he said, suddenly turning testy now that the danger seemed past. 'The accountant and one of the men from the packing shed playing soldiers.'

'They have to do it.'

'Yes, they have to do it. They started tightening up on the factory militias eighteen months ago.'

'We were lucky.'

'It usually goes like that nowadays,' said the kid.

'I thought we'd be sitting there all night,' I said. 'They like company.'

'Not lately. It's beginning to change. Lately they just like vodka.'

We were in the outskirts of Magdeburg, and running twenty-five minutes late, by the time he spoke again. 'I screwed up,' he said suddenly, and with that knotted anger that we reserve for our own errors.

'What?'

'Do you think we'll be back by tomorrow?'

'I don't know,' I said truthfully.

'I forgot to leave the key for my girlfriend. She won't be able to feed the cat.'

I felt like saying that Rumtopf had more than enough body fat to sustain itself over a few foodless days, but people can be very unpredictable about their pet animals, so I grunted amiably.

'This colonel, this VERDI, says he knows you. Is he working for us?'

'Because he has a cover name? No. They all have those if we deal with them on a regular basis, or mention them in messages. Even Stalin had a cover name.'

'VERDI says he owes you a favour; a big favour.'

I looked at him. 'What's he supposed to say?' I'd had enough of this crap from Bret without more from the kid. 'Is he supposed to say that I owe him a big favour? That would really get their attention in London Central, wouldn't it?'

'I suppose it would.'

'Of course he's going to say that he owes me a big favour. That's the way these things are done: the person making contact always says he's trying to repay a favour: a big favour. That way no one in London is likely to suspect that I'm going over there to bend the rules and do all kinds of things that the boys behind the desks have inscribed in their big brass-bound no-no book.'

'I didn't think of it like that,' said the kid.

'He's a bastard,' I said.

'VERDI? SO you do know him?'

'He thinks I owe him a favour.'

'But you don't? Is that what you mean?'

I thought about it. 'He tossed an arrest certificate into the shredder instead of putting it on the teleprinter.'

'That's a favour,' said the kid.

'He had other reasons. Anyway favours done for the opposition are like money in the bank,' I said resentfully. And then, before he thought it was a currency I stocked up on, I added: 'For guys like that, I mean. They like being able to call in a few.'

The kid shot a sudden glance at me. I'd gone too far. I had the feeling he'd heard in my voice that note that said that I was under some kind of obligation to the bastard. And that was something I'd not until then admitted even to myself. 'What's your guess?' the kid said. 'Do you think he wants to talk?'

'We all talk,' I said. 'Opposing field agents all talk. You bump into these guys all the time; at airports, in bars and on the job. Sometimes we talk. It can be useful. It's the way the job is done. But we never ask questions.'

'But if VERDI wants to go on the payroll we can start asking him questions. Okay, I understand now. But will he know something we need to hear?'

'There is usually something worth hearing if they want to be helpful. If he gives us a few good targets; that would be valuable.'

'What are good ones?'

'Cipher clerks who gamble or borrow money,' I said. 'Department chiefs who drink, analysts who are screwing their secretary, translators who sniff. Vulnerable people.'

'This one knows you. He'll talk only to someone he knows.'

'Yes, you told me. But I'll take a lot of convincing he's on the level.'

The car had slowed and the kid was looking at the street signs. 'I know the house,' he said. 'I delivered a package here last month. Money I think.'

'You live dangerously,' I told him.

'All this won't last much longer,' he said. 'I want to get a little excitement while I can. I want to be able to tell my kids about it.'

He must have been talking to Bret. 'You can have my share,' I told him, and smiled. But such highly motivated youngsters

22

worried me: so did these people who thought it was so nearly all over. There was once an old chap at the training school who started the very first day's lecture saying: our job here is to change gallant young gentlemen into nervous old ladies. This kid needed that lecture badly.

2

Magdeburg, where we were headed, is one of the most ancient German cities, a provincial capital tucked into the most westerly bend of the River Elbe at a place where the river divides into three waterways. Its commanding site at the edge of the North German plain has always made it a target for plundering armies. Devastated by the Thirty Years War, it was razed again by the Second World War and even more thoroughly by the Soviet-style city-planners and architects who came after it.

Magdeburg has been a home to men as choosy as Otto the Great and Archbishop Burchard HI and the more refined members of the house of Brandenburg. So great was the power vested here that when they came to build the railway joining Paris to Moscow they diverted the line through Magdeburg. More than a century later, in the postwar race for growth, the city was hastily transformed into one of the world's most polluted industrial regions, where the proletariat choked on untreated chemical waste and more than half the children were suffering from bronchitis and eczema. Now, as the Marxist empire shrank and its privileged ruling class felt threatened from all sides, the Stasi, the Party's Moscow-styled secret police and security service, had chosen Magdeburg to make a fortified compound where its most secret and highly treasured documents and artifacts could be guarded and hidden. Even the mortal remains of Hitler and Goebbels had been secreted away in the compound.

'Do you know where the Smersh compound begins?' I asked him as we drove through the centre of town.

I'd almost forgotten how dark and bleak East German towns became after dark. There was little traffic, fewer pedestrians and no advertising signs. Two cops standing under a street light watched us pass with interest.

The kid glanced at me and smiled. 'So they really call it the Smersh compound? I thought that was just something invented by the newspapers.'

We passed slowly along a wall of billboards around a building site. At least two dozen huge posters affirmed with typographic bombast the DDR's loyalty, obligation and friendship to the mighty USSR and the even mightier socialist brotherhood. We passed the cathedral for a second time. 'One side is the Westring, I remember that,' I said, as we came to the billboards again. 'It's a long time since I was here.' Traffic signals brought us to a halt, and then he made a turn and said he knew where he was.

The kid had the car window down and was staring out into the shadowy moonlit streets. 'Our man lives off to the left.' He slowed and having spotted Klausenerstrasse – onetime Westendstrasse – signalled a turn and we were in a quiet street, paved with neatly arranged cobblestones and darkened by mature trees. These large comfortable houses had miraculously survived the RAF night bombers, the American day bombers and all the artillery fire that came afterwards.

It is a curious paradox that Hitler's Third Reich and subsequent communist governments had preserved East Germany as the last remaining European country with domestic servants. Only in the DDR were such grand old households functioning in the old-fashioned way. Senior officials of the Stasi, and lucky detachments of KGB liaison officers like VERDI, had readily settled into this sort of bourgeois comfort, and now this unassailable elite occupied choice tree-lined streets of German towns complete with gardens, garages and quarters at the rear for attentive maid-servants, chauffeurs, cooks and gardeners. Only recently had chipped paintwork, untrimmed hedges and cracks in the glass signalled some tightening of the economy.

'This is the house where VERDI lives,' said the kid, reducing his voice almost to a whisper. 'He shares it with two other officials and their families.' The wrought-iron gates were closed. He parked at the kerbside and we got out. It was a big house: two storeys, with some of the upper rooms granted access to a long decorative balcony by means of french windows. There were no lights to be seen anywhere, but that might have been a tribute to the heavy curtains.

The front garden of the old house was protected by a more recently installed six-feet-high chain-link fence. It was anchored to stone gateposts and a pair of ancient and elaborate gates. The kid shone his flashlight on the brass plate which bore the house number. Above it a more recent white plastic sign indicated which of two bellpushes should be used by visitors and which by delivery men. It was that kind of house.

He unlatched the gate and we went inside without pressing either bell. In the air there was the smell of burned garden rubbish. 'We're only half an hour late,' said the kid. 'He'll wait.' It was very quiet in Magdeburg. There was not even the sound of traffic, just the hum of a distant plane droning steadily like a trapped wasp. In the silence every movement seemed to cause unnaturally loud noises, our footsteps crunching in the gravel like a company of soldiers marching through a bowl of cornflakes.

Three stone steps led up to a wide entry porch where a panelled front door with a fanlight was flanked by two small wired-glass windows that provided the residents with a chance to make sure that the delivery man was not using the wrong entrance.

'Are you all right?' said the kid, looking at me strangely.

'You've been here before?'

'They always leave the front door unlocked. It's all right.' As if to demonstrate this familiarity he pushed the heavy door open and stepped inside. I followed him. The house was in darkness, and only silky moonlight through the fanlight enabled us to see. A wide staircase with a carved wooden rail descended to a grand hall tiled with large black and white squares. Against one wall a longcase clock stood still and silent, its lifeless hands clasping the number twelve. Occupying the greater part of the opposite wall hung a towering oil-painting: a life-size depiction of a Prussian general stared serenely at the artist, while smoking cannon roared and a bloody mayhem of men and mounts provided a colourful background. The overall effect – of the family home of some nineteenth-century nobleman – was marred only slightly by a pungent smell of carbolic and scented polish that intruded an institutional dimension.

I heard the sound of the kid clicking the light switches, but no light came. 'Power failure,' he pronounced after several tries. 'Or maybe it's switched off at the main supply.'

For a moment I thought he was just going to stand there until something else happened, but he gathered himself together and went to the door of one of the front rooms and opened it slowly, as if half-expecting a shouted objection from inside.

I followed him. The moonlight coming through the tall windows revealed a big room with over-stuffed armchairs and sofas, and some antique furniture that had seen better days. There was an ornate stove and a large mirror that made the room seem double its size.

'Look!' said the kid.

But I'd already seen him: a man sitting on the sofa and toppled slightly to one side, canted at an impossible angle like some discarded doll. The kid directed his torch at the figure.

'Douse the light. It might be seen through the windows.' I went to the sofa. The man was dead. It was obvious just from the awkward posture. The moonlight made everything colourless, but the big dark patch on his chest was blood and there was more of it on the sofa and on the carpet too. His head was thrown back and his face was a horrific mess: his skull cracked open like the shell of an egg. 'Keep still a minute,' I said.

'Where did you get the Makarov?'

'Keep still. It's just a toy,' I explained, but the long silencer made the damn thing as conspicuous as a frontier Colt.

I quickly went through the dead man's pockets. The body was still warm. The blood was wet and becoming tacky. I sniffed the air but there were none of the smells of oil and burned powder that gunfire leaves. Still it was obvious that the shooting had taken place just before we arrived. I was no expert, but it would be foolhardy to think the killer must have left the vicinity.

'From the guy at the bar,' said the kid, as the explanation of where I got the gun occurred to him. 'I should have guessed you didn't want cigarettes … He gave it …'

'Shut up,' I said. It was the sort of stupid carelessness that got good men into trouble. 'Pull yourself together. Check the windows and the hallway.'

He must have realized what he'd blurted out, for he looked around as if he might spot a microphone or wires. It was his nervousness about being overheard that caused him to spot the broken window. 'The shot came from outside,' he said. He was holding the window curtain aside and pointing at a large round hole in the glass pane. It was at about the right level for a prowler to shoot a man sitting on the sofa.

'Get away from the window – pull the curtain closed. Can the power be switched off from outside?'

'Yes. The fuses are on the cellar steps.'

28

'Close the curtain.' The kid was still at the window looking at the garden. Then without warning I heard him retch deeply, and then came long and splashy vomiting. Oh boy, that's all I needed. 'Let's go, Kinkypoo,' I said bitterly as he coughed, spat, and wiped his face with a handkerchief. I could hear him follow me as I went to the hallway and opened the front door. I looked around the garden. There was no sign of movement, but enough big dark shadows for a battalion to be concealed.

'Run for the car. I'll cover you as best I can. Get into the back seat: I'll drive.' I suppose it was my way of ensuring he didn't depart without me, but by now I had the nasty feeling that a reception party would be waiting by the car.

'I'm sorry,' he said. I didn't reply.

'Go,' I said.

He ran across the grass, dragged open the wrought-iron gate and dashed out into the dark street. I followed him, flattening myself against the wall as I got outside. The trees were being shaken by the wind and making shadows on the cobbles. There was no one to be seen in any direction: just silent parked cars. Reassured, I climbed into the driver's seat, closed my door and started the engine. The kid slammed his door with all the force he could muster, making a noise that could be heard for two or three blocks.

'What's the matter?' he asked anxiously.

I was covering my face with both hands, seeking a moment of darkness to gather my wits. I understood the anxiety I heard in his voice. When I was young I'd seen some of the old wartime field agents resorting to that sort of gesture, and I'd written them off as burned out and useless. 'I'm okay,' I said.

Gently I revved up and pulled away. I swung my head to get a look at him in the back. The kid had stains and marks down the front of his coat. He looked at me and wiped his mouth self-consciously. He smelled strongly of sour vomit.

29

'What a foul-up. Poor VERDI. Are we going to be all right?' he asked.

'You stay there in the back seat and watch the road behind us. They'll probably tail us and arrest us at the Checkpoint. It's the way they like to work. They'll want to see what we do.'

'What's the score?' he said. 'Who killed him?'

'How do you know VERDI lives there?'

'As opposed to meeting me there? I don't know. I just assumed it.'

'Always in that same room?'

'Yes, always in that room. I guess they were on to him. They let him go to the rendezvous and then killed him.'

'Maybe.'

'Maybe they spotted me last time,' said the kid. Then in a sharper voice: 'There is a car …'

'I can see it.'

'A big dark Mercedes. He turned when we did at the signal.'

'Keep an eye on him.'

I didn't want to make a mistake. It's easy to think you're being followed. What percentage of the cars driving through the middle of the city were heading towards the Autobahn ramp? A lot of them I would say.

'Go around the block,' suggested the kid.

'That will tip them off that we've spotted them, and it makes it look as if we are running away.'

'Slow down and stop.'

'I don't think so. Let's see what they do.'

'Slow down to walking pace.'

'So that they can overtake us and block the road in front?'

'You're right,' said the kid. 'What are you going to do then?'

'I want them to think they have the wrong car. I want to be very innocent … very law-abiding.' Even as I said it I realized that it sounded like a plan based upon despair; and it was.

30

'They're still behind us. Still at about the same distance.'

We were out of town now, driving through moonlit country-side. It was a lousy situation. It was after midnight. Out here among the turnips was not the place to be. You could lay down an artillery barrage and bring in a couple of bulldozers to bury the bodies without the danger of attracting any witnesses.

'I'm going to choose a suitable stretch of road and have a showdown,' I told the kid. 'When I stop the car and get out, I want you to scramble over the seat and get behind the wheel in the driver's seat. Keep the engine ticking over but don't rev it. Keep your head well down. When I shout go: burn rubber … Would you be able to do that for me?'

'You bet I would.'

'I'll stop. Then I'm going to walk back towards them, shining a flashlight into their eyes and behaving like a lost tourist. Slightly drunk. If they are the kind of people I think they might be, they will get out of their car.'

'Why?'

'You can't shoot accurately through windscreen glass. And leaning out of a car window and shooting a gun is something that only Humphrey Bogart learned how to do.'

'You're going to stop and go back and talk your way out of it?'

'Watch me and don't wait too long.'

'Okay.'

'And don't take the Autobahn route. See that hill on the skyline in front? I'll come to a stop near the bridge at the bottom. When I shout go, you be in a low gear … and swing and swerve as you pull away – got it?'

'I'll be all right,' he said.

The road was narrow. When we reached a stone bridge over a stream, I slowed down and stopped there, positioning the car so that there was no room to pass it. They stopped too. I hid the pistol in my raincoat pocket and then with as much noise

31

and fuss as I could manage I swung open the car door and stood up and squinted into their headlights, and waved an arm like an innocent traveller who had strayed off the Autobahn and wanted to ask the way to Helmstedt, the crossing point to the West. There was ice underfoot, but the water in the stream was still trickling: I could hear it even over the sound of the car engines.

The driver of the other car jumped out of his seat immediately. I could see that there was someone in the back seat but the rear doors remained closed.

Walking back towards them, illuminated in the full headlight beam, I called out: 'How many kilometres to Helmstedt?' in a shrill Austrian accent that would not have fooled many people sitting under the trees in the Wiener Wald but here amongst the 'Prussians' would probably be convincing enough.

My question was framed to cause momentary confusion, and it obviously did, for the driver bent down to say something to the passenger in the back seat.

Close enough now to see what I was doing, I dropped flat on my belly and fired at the nearest front tyre, aiming so that the round's entrance and exit would rip out a big enough chunk of tread to deflate even the most fancy of puncture-resistant tyres. Like all Russian pistols, what the East Germans call the Pistole M is a crudely designed piece of machinery with a simple blow-back system and a butt angle like a letter L, but its Soviet designers gave it a legendary reliability which in tight corners makes up for all other shortcomings. Bang! The noise was deafening, the ancient silencer providing no sound reduction at all. Too late to remove it now. I squeezed the trigger and there was that stiffening that precedes a jam. I cursed and pulled harder on the trigger – it must have just been lack of oil, for the gun fired, and I saw a piece chopped from the second tyre.

The sound of escaping air seemed to go on for ever. I jumped up and ran back to my car. The kid revved the motor.

The shots had brought the back-seat passenger out of the car, and now he was bending down, trying to see the tyres. The driver was still in the same position: standing, feet apart, watching me as if petrified by the sudden events. I stood up and, to make them keep their heads down, I aimed a final shot to go over the driver's head. But my hand was not steady and what was intended to be a frightener dropped him. The poor sod spun round and fell, clutching at his chest, then he rolled around on the ground groaning and kicking and rocking face-down, pressing himself to the icy road as if that might ease the pain.

'Shit!' I said. 'Go, go, go.' I threw myself into the front passenger seat. The car leaped away before I'd closed the door and as I slammed it my head banged against the window glass with a sharp crack. The kid heard the sound and glanced round to see if I was still conscious. But I had a thick skull; it is one of the few qualifications needed for the work I do. 'Floor it!' I told him. The engine screamed in pain as he jammed his foot on the pedal and we went roaring up the hill in low gear.

'The passenger is climbing into the driving seat. He's following us,' called the kid.

'Keep your eyes on the road,' I told him.

The second man was making a plucky attempt at chasing us, despite the sparks that came off the road surface as the tyres flapped around the wheel rims.

As the Volvo breasted the hill the kid changed gear. I looked back to see the Mercedes slewing across the road out of control with black snakes of rubber following it as the tyres were ripped to pieces. Despite the driver's desperate efforts the Merc slowed, hesitated and then slowly rolled backwards until it hit a ditch. The car tilted up so that the main beams shone into the sky. Beyond it, at the bottom of the hill, I could see the other man still writhing on the ground clutching his chest. But even as I watched his movements slowed. Then the hilltop closed off my view of the horrible little cameo.

'You were fantastic!' said the kid in high excitement. 'Un-bloody-believable! You got him.'

'Yes, clever me. It was exactly what I was trying to avoid.'

'Trying to avoid? What?'

'They'll not forgive us for that one,' I said grimly. 'And there's a witness still alive. These are sure to be Moscow men, not Germans. You don't know the lengths they'll go to get even with us.'

'You want to go back and kill him?'

I wet my lips. For a moment I was going to say yes. It was the logical, sensible thing to do, even if it was the kind of solution they glossed over at the training school. But at that moment I wasn't sure I was up to killing him in cold blood. I was drained, and experience told me the kid wouldn't be able to do it. 'Keep going,' I said.

We sped through the night like drunken bank-robbers, the kid taking the bends in narrow country roads at dangerous speeds. He was flushed and excited and driving beyond his abilities. Suddenly he said: 'What say we give the Autobahn a try?'

It was tempting of course. We were close to the major route that ran from Berlin to the bright lights of freedom. On the Autobahn there would be lots of 'Westies', commercials and trucks trundling through what we used to call 'the Soviet Zone' on their normal route between the West Sector of Berlin and West Germany. But such a short cut was too tempting, too logical, too convenient to be safe. 'No. That's the first place they'll block off.'

'I have extra papers,' said the kid. 'In a little box welded to the underside of the car.' He was Mr Ultra-efficient.

'No,' I said. 'And slow down. That flea-bitten moggie of yours will be all right for a day without food. Forget the Autobahn. It's not worth taking a chance. Even the traffic computer on the

34

western end picks up drivers for five-year-old unpaid parking tickets in their home town.'

'You're right.' He sobered a little.

'Stick to the plan,' I told him.

'The plan is shot. VERDI is dead: one of the opposition is dead … maybe two of them. We don't have any escaper needing false papers and transportation.'

'Stick to the plan,' I said. 'Assume the dead man wasn't VERDI; assume VERDI is on the run.'

'You're crazy. We're sticking our necks out for nothing.'

'Maybe I am crazy. You've never been out there where we all go crazy, or maybe you'd be crazy too.' I remembered so many times when things had gone wrong for me. The field agent always desperately hopes that the operation can be salvaged. You hope like hell that the men assigned to meet you won't just cut their losses and run. 'We'll go to the safe house and wait for an hour until the Stasi alert teams have done their preliminary checks. Driving in these rural parts in the small hours of the morning makes me feel very conspicuous. Any time now they'll have a chopper overhead.'

'It's a village church about eight miles from here. The pastor is one of our people; an experienced man.'

'Let's do it,' I said. 'Let's get off the road and come back on it when the commuter traffic starts. We're too bloody visible out here in the sticks in the night.'

Before the war this village had been neat and prosperous, a dazzling prospect of whitewashed walls, flowers and well-kept farms with the church its cherished heart. Now it was a miserable little huddle of houses. Its ancient church had been destroyed, along with half the village, by a jettisoned RAF bomb-load in 1944. After the war ended the Red Army garrison commander had permitted the villagers to build a hut on the same site and continue to hold services. The postwar German communist politicians were more actively hostile to the Church than the Russian troops had been, and now that temporary structure – patched and propped – was still the villagers' only place of worship.

We parked the Volvo alongside a rusty tractor in the barn and the kid found some keys hidden in the bowels of the tractor's engine. Under the temporary hut the crypt of the old church had been restored to use. He took me down a flight of stone steps and when he switched on the lights the whole crypt, an extensive vaulted subterranean area, was revealed. One section had been divided off and made into a chapel with a permanent altar and a strange assortment of chairs that had probably been collected over the years, donated by the congregation. A large austere altar and a candelabra looked as if they had been salvaged from the wreckage of the razed church, repaired and restored to become the centre-piece of this improvised sanctuary.

The pastor arrived five minutes after we got there. Jumping out of bed fully alert in the middle of the night is a part of the job for a good pastor just as it is for a field agent, fireman or cop.

The old pastor seemed strangely familiar: weathered face with wrinkles and old-fashioned steel-rimmed glasses. I remembered having seen him a couple of times in Berlin, at the houses of mutual acquaintances. Now he displayed unlimited energy as he strode about switching on lights and tidying up misplaced coffee cups and pamphlets, prayer books and dried flowers with that dedication that neurotics display when they need time to think. A woman in a sleeveless floral-pattern house-coat arrived and without a word brewed a jug of foul-smelling coffee for us, while the pastor kept up small-talk about his village and masterfully restrained any temptation to ask us questions.

'We lost contact,' the kid told him as we drank our coffee. 'Our man is unlikely to have revealed – or even been told – that this was our first stop, but I wanted to go through the motions.' He turned to include me in his speech, as if I might otherwise contradict him and tell the pastor that our man was dead on a blood-soaked sofa in Magdeburg. And that we were fugitives who'd murdered a government official, probably bringing retribution hard on our heels.

'Poor devil,' said the pastor with convincing concern. He turned around fully now, as if the time had come to give us his full attention. 'If he's out there with a general alarm ringing in his ears, I hope God is watching over him.' I wondered how much the pastor had been told. Draped upon a chair I noticed a dark suit and outer clothes, smelling strongly of moth-repellent. If these were intended to disguise our missing escapee the pastor might have been told quite a lot, right down to VERDI's shoe size.

The kid said: 'Someone was killed – it might have been our contact who was killed … And we had trouble on the road. You should be prepared for house-to-house searches.'

'It's not often that things go according to plan,' the pastor said, remaining almost unnaturally calm in the circumstances. The only sign of anxiety came in the way he took out a packet of cigarettes and lit one with that steady determination that is the mark of the addict. He blew smoke. 'It's in the nature of under-cover work that the unexpected so often happens. You plan for three different eventualities but the fourth occurs.' He grinned and reached for the coffee jug. 'Moltke said it: he said it about war.'

'No more coffee for me.' I put my hand across the top of the china mug.

'This is a war that is going on here,' he said. 'It's no use denying it. Men are always at war. We are always at war because every man is at war with himself.'

'Is that another of Moltke's sayings?' I asked him.

He'd been looking at me quizzically and now – jug in hand – he ventured: 'We met. Remember? Some sort of celebration in a private house in Köpenick … No; wait: a hotel off the Ku-Damm and a fancy-dress party. I know your wife?'

It was framed as a question. 'It's possible,' I said warily.

'Yes, I worked with her. She is a great woman.' He said it with a depth of reverence and awe that startled me.

'Yes,' I said.

Perhaps my subdued response prompted him to tell me more: 'She started us on our first steps to freedom. We have a long way to go of course, but it was your wife who taught us that we must fight. We had never fought. It was a hard lesson to learn.'

I must have looked puzzled. It was no longer a secret that my wife had defected to the East in an elaborate and successful scheme that had encouraged widespread grassroots opposition to the communist rulers. I'd heard other people speak of my wife's profound achievements and I'd always nodded it through. This time I didn't. 'What did she do?' I asked him.

He smiled. He had one of those rubber-mask faces that relax naturally into a grin. It was an old-fashioned face: the sort Hollywood used to cast as a priest who plays the harmonica and says wise things to Bing Crosby.

'You've got to understand how it has always been for the Church in Germany,' he said. 'Countless small principalities, the religion of each of them decided by its ruling prince or bishop. That ensured that the Church and State were indivisible. Even in Nazi times, the State's tax-gathering officers collected Church dues from every citizen and paid them to the Church. Little wonder that we churchmen found it so difficult to confront the Nazis, and then after the war even more difficult to resist the institutionalized anti-Christ of communism. We became dependants of the State. But your wife told the

Churches of all denominations that if this monstrous regime under which we suffer is ever to be resisted and overthrown, the rallying places must be sanctuaries offered by the Church: the German churches.' He sipped his coffee. The kid and I were silenced by this display of emotion. The pastor added: 'Lenin said "Whoever controls Germany, possesses Europe." This will be the last place the communists yield.'

His passionate speech had made me uneasy, but such deeply held feelings were needed by anyone confronting the communists in their police-State. For lately the politicians here had seen what was happening to their fellows – the communist crooks who were running the neighbouring countries – and were beginning to identify the Churches as their most dangerous enemy.

'I say a prayer for her,' said the pastor. 'All my flock say a prayer for her. Cherish her.'

'Yes,' I said.

'It will be getting light,' said the kid. He'd been shuffling about as if made uncomfortable by this high-flown talk.

'You are too young to understand,' said the pastor gently. 'Only old men know enough to cry.'

Suddenly I remembered where I'd last seen the pastor. He'd been at a big fancy-dress party at Lisl Hennig's hotel in West Berlin. It was the night when everything seemed to go wrong. My wife was brought out of the East that night. We were involved in a stupid gun battle on the Autobahn and I saw Tessa my sister-in-law murdered. That night I left Germany and solemnly vowed I would never come back here. Never. 'Yes, I remember you now,' I told the pastor. 'That party in the hotel near the Ku-Damm.' Amid that frantic collection of revellers, in his dark clerical suit and dog-collar, I had taken the pastor for just another guest in fancy dress. Perhaps his presence there that night supplied one of the missing pieces of the jigsaw puzzle that was still far from complete.

'Yes, I was there that night,' he admitted. He'd been about to add something else but now he stopped suddenly as we heard the sound of vehicles coming along the road. Several of them. They slowed and turned into the cobbled churchyard where we had left the Volvo in the barn. I hoped they wouldn't search the premises, for the Volvo with its West licence plates would make them start tearing everything apart.

'Pray!' said the pastor and dropped to his knees. I heard them more clearly now. Two vehicles: one heavy diesel and one petrol. There were loud squeaks and the hiss of hydraulic brakes. A car door opened and slammed. That meant one person. It was a bad sign. I had no doubt that the heavy truck contained an armed assault team of barrack-police who were now sitting silent and alert and waiting for orders. 'Pray!' said the pastor again, and I sank down on my knees before him, as did the kid and the woman who'd made the coffee.

The pastor began a droning litany of prayers as metal boot studs sounded on the stone steps. With a stifled groan of pain the woman got to her feet, rubbed her arthritic knee, and went to receive the visitor with a soft and deferential greeting on her lips and a cup of hot coffee in her hand. 'Is something wrong?' she asked him.

'Yes,' said the cop without explaining further. He sipped the coffee.

'A night of continuous prayer,' she said, and explained our presence as bereaved parishioners from a neighbouring town. She had a strong local accent and as the explanation continued I could follow it only with difficulty.

Out of my half-closed eyes I could see the policeman standing feet apart staring at us. His uniform revealed him as a local cop, sent no doubt to lead a team of outsiders from Magdeburg – draftees perhaps – who didn't know the country districts. Impatient toots of a car horn made the cop look at his watch.

Then there was the sound of another car door and the hurried clatter of boots. 'You haven't got time for cups of coffee,' came a shout from the top of the stone steps. The unseen commander – disconcertingly accurate in his guess about the coffee – had a voice that was hard and Berlinerisch, the accent that educated urbane men use to command those they regard as country bumpkins.

Jolted by the accusation the cop pushed the coffee cup back into the woman's hand. 'All is in order here, Captain,' the policeman shouted, and started back up to join his commander. The German Democratic Republic – more realistically an undemocratic dictatorship run by the Soviets – was changing. Out here in the country districts some of the more cautious officials had begun hedging their bets against the day when the unthinkable happened, and their beat became part of a truly democratic republic with all the dangerous consequences such a turn-round could bring to those in rural isolation.

'You need not pretend to pray any more,' said the pastor when the sound of the two vehicles had dwindled to nothing.

'I wasn't pretending,' I said. The old man looked at me and rose to his feet.

There was just a thin line of purple along the skyline as we got back on the road. The kid was driving: I wanted to look around.

'The pastor is a decent old man. His family had a big estate here. They were landowners since goodness knows when. He volunteered for the U-boats,' said the kid. 'After the war, when he was released from the POW camp in England he came back and found that the family estate had been confiscated without compensation. It was rotten luck. The Russians only seized farms larger than 250 acres and theirs was only a few acres larger than that.'

41

'Then he found God,' I said.

'No, that's the funny thing. He became a fervent communist at first. It was only afterwards that he went back to the Church and then started working against the regime.'

'It happens.'

'He said he used to think that Karl Marx was an economist. It was when he realized that Marx was a moralist that he began to see how deeply the theories were flawed.' When I made no response to this he said: 'Have you read Marx?'

'Karl Marx was a nut,' I said. 'He should have kept his mouth shut like Harpo.'

'We'll be in Berlin early. Do you want to return the gun to your friend?'

'Didn't I tell you to forget about the gun?'

I'd let my anger show. 'Sorry, boss.'

'I must get rid of it. I'm glad you reminded me.'

'Is it the shooting you're worried about?'

'Who said I was worried?'

'You did everything exactly right,' he said, with an exuberance calculated to cheer me up. 'It was terrific.'

'But it smells all wrong,' I said. 'Who were those bruisers?'

'In a shiny new 500 SEL Merc? They were Stasis or left-behind KGB or something. They weren't innocent peasants on their way to church, if that's what's worrying you.'

'They did nothing except drive along a public road. I shot holes in them.'

'You can't be serious?'

'They didn't shoot back, that's what's worrying me. This is their territory. In a car like that they always stow all manner of weapons … and heavies like that get their shots in first.'

'But …?'

'I have a feeling we were set up. I have a nasty feeling that – apart from my shooting that driver – we did everything the other side wanted us to do, right from the moment we were stopped at that militia checkpoint.'

'Well if you are right, we sure put a spanner in the works.' He was not to be deprived of his gleeful satisfaction.

'And don't mention Krohn's bar or that damned handgun in your report.'

'You can rely on me, old-timer.'

'And you can leave out the old-timer, Kinkypoo.'

3

'I have your report,' said Frank Harrington. 'I read it very carefully.' Frank Harrington was Head of the Berlin Field Unit. Because the Russians call their equivalent outfits rezidentura he was usually called the Berlin Rezident, and that had passed into official use. Frank, although no longer young, had a soldier's bearing, a pale face and blunt-ended stubbly moustache, so that he was frequently mistaken for an officer of the British garrison. He'd been one of my father's best friends.

I didn't respond. Dicky Cruyer, Controller of German Stations and temporarily in charge of Operations in London, had come hurrying to Berlin. Presumably he wanted to be here when VERDI arrived. Now he stood by the window peering through the louvred window shutters to see down into Frank Harrington's extensive back garden, sucking on the end of his Mont Blanc fountain-pen and trying not to interrupt. Although these days it was growing more and more difficult to distinguish soldiers from anyone else, a soldier was not the first guess one would make about Dicky Cruyer's occupation. His curly hair was too bushy and he favoured faded designer denim, and the sort of tall elaborately decorated cowboy boots that he was wearing today.

In another part of the city, the Berlin offices were temporarily hidden behind a cocoon of scaffolding, and enjoying a long-overdue redecoration. To get away from the mating cries of construction workers, the regular clang and jangle of metal rods dropped from a height upon pavement and the pungent smell of paint, Frank was staying home and using the office he'd established in one of the upstairs rooms of his grand old Berlin mansion in Grunewald. None of the room lights were lit, and only a thin melancholy daylight filtered through the window shutters. The sombre light in the domestic surroundings, the stillness, and the silence into which the two men had fallen, produced a feeling that they shared some almost overwhelming sorrow into which I found it difficult to break. And now I waited for one or the other of them to speak.

I looked around. This was the mansion provided to Frank in his capacity of Rezident, and I had known this room since my father occupied that coveted post. There was the same buttoned leather bench, scarred, whitened and worn but as familiar as an old friend. The wall was adorned with the horned heads of various fleet-footed quadrupeds. It was difficult to believe that Frank had actually shot any of these mournful beasts, for Frank – despite his wistful attitude to the profession of arms – had always showed a curious antipathy for guns. Getting him to issue any sort of handgun was such a struggle that most of the field agents found it simpler to provide their own. Amid the trophies of the hunt there was a formal sepia-coloured portrait photo of the Queen. It hung immediately above a camphor-wood military chest upon which Frank Harrington's ancient typewriter was enshrined; a totem of the ascendant role of paperwork in service to the Crown.

Unforgettably, it was also the day that the heating of Frank's mansion suffered a failure that defied all the efforts of three determined heating engineers and now caused all three of us to be wearing our overcoats. The antique stove, six feet tall, standing in the corner clad with lovely old blue pattern tiles, had been coaxed into use for the first time in many decades. The comfort it gave was entirely illusory. Despite the efforts of Frank's servants with bundles of kindling and screwed-up pages from *Der Spiegel* followed by the more inflammatory sheets of *Die Welt*, there was no sign of flame through its dull and discoloured mica door, but the distinctive aroma of burned paper made my nostrils twitch.

'Your report is a masterpiece,' said Frank, speaking as if this verdict was the result of long and deep reflection. He was sitting before the stove, stiff-backed on a small bentwood chair, wearing a smooth woollen herring-bone overcoat of such beautiful material and cut that, had I not known Frank so well, I might have suspected it as a reason for turning off the heat. 'It will be incorporated into the lectures at the training school and some future Director-General will quote pages of it from memory.' Such heavy sarcasm did not come naturally to Frank, who was avuncular, and by nature a healer of wounds rather than one to rub salt into them.

The ensuing silence was broken only by the sound of Dicky tapping his expensive fountain-pen against his still more expensive teeth. I recognized that look on his face: Dicky was thinking; lost in a world of dreams, plans and ambitions. Feeling that a reply was expected of me, and with Dicky's recent promotion – albeit temporary – a living reminder that the Department was inclined to value effort above result, I said: 'I spent a long time writing it.'

'I'm certain of that,' said Frank with a snort. 'And I spent a long time reading it. The first time I read it, I marvelled. Here was a report seemingly reasoned, acute and reflective and informative.'

I said nothing. With a self-tormenting perversity that I suspected to be a product of his public school years, Frank, who was trying to give up smoking, was toying ceaselessly with the bright yellow oilskin pouch that contained his favourite tobacco and pipe.

'I read it two or three more times,' said Frank, as he stood up and dumped the pouch on the table. 'To see the extent to which the whole thing is evasive, ambivalent and noncommittal.'

'I try to be empirical,' I said.

'Imperious I would have said. Even when you meet a Lutheran pastor you call him "a man in clergyman's clothes". At what stage does cautious observation become evasion?' Just because a large measure of Frank's irascibility was due to the torment caused by his renunciation of tobacco, it didn't make being the target of his bitter comments any more appealing. I looked at him with polite attention and said nothing.

Frank said: 'Yes, I know you have been away. I know you feel you've been badly treated by the Department. That you resent not being told everything about the decision to send your wife across there as a double …'

'Anything,' I corrected him mildly. 'I was not told anything.'

Dicky had been staring down into the garden and giving no sign of following Frank's questioning or my responses. Now Frank paused long enough for Dicky to swing round and say: 'For God's sake! Need-to-know! That's the essence of the business we're in.' He was wearing a short black leather overcoat, a double-breasted design complete with lots of buckles and buttons and shoulder straps. As he moved, the lining of bright red silk was revealed. It looked brand-new. I guessed he'd just bought it in one of those swanky men's shops in the Ku-Damm; every visitor found time to visit them. 'You're supposed to be a secret agent, Bernard. How can you complain about the way secrets are guarded?'

I saw Frank make a paddling motion with a limp hand that was hanging at his side. It was a signal to Dicky to shut up and let him handle the situation. Frank said: 'You are still *judging* us, Bernard. It's not healthy.'

'Not unless you would prefer being permanently behind a desk somewhere,' drawled Dicky. Just in case I recognized that as the threat it was, he added: 'You know what they are like in London,' as if he had no say in postings and assignments.

'I wish you would be a little more explicit,' said Frank to me.

'It was a set-up,' I said.

'Why not put you in the bag?'

'Surely that's what they were trying to do?' I said.

'The men in the car you fired the pistol at? Umm.' Frank rubbed his chin as he thought about what I'd written. 'Not a very serious effort unless you've missed something out.'

'Oh, no? What could they have done to make their effort more serious?' I asked, without letting my irritation show. Neither of these two desk men had ever heard a shot fired in anger, so I didn't take easily to their dismissal of an action of the sort that, on the rare cases when it's happened to other more senior men, has been marked by flowery commendations and promotions. I smiled.

'The monitor service heard nothing: no orders to block off the Autobahn exits, no instructions to Berlin checkpoints, nothing.'

'Their car slid back into a ditch,' I said. 'Maybe they ended up unconscious and were put into hospital.'

'Perhaps that's it,' said Frank, in a tone that indicated that it was not high on his list of possible explanations. 'But VERDI ... why did they wait outside and shoot him through the window? Why not inside? Why not somewhere more private?'

'I didn't say they did shoot him through the window,' I said.

'I noticed that,' said Frank. He let the pages of my report flutter in the warm draught that was coming from a fan heater that one of his servants had placed so that the air warmed his feet. 'Why?'

'The hole in the window wasn't made by a bullet.'

'Can you be sure?'

'Yes,' I said. 'It's something you learn to recognize. I won't go into the details.'

'Go into the details,' said Dicky, joining the conversation suddenly. 'I'm interested in how you can be so categorical about it, and still leave it out of your report.'

I looked at Frank. Frank raised an eyebrow.

I said: 'A high-velocity missile going through glass, a round from a hand-gun for instance, produces radial fractures and several concentric fractures. In this case there were none. Furthermore the hole made by a bullet produces a powdering of glass around the actual hole. A low-velocity missile, such as a stone, knocks a piece out of the glass leaving a neater smoother edge.'

'Are you snowing me, Bernard?' said Dicky, shaking his head to stress his disbelief. Frank looked from one to the other of us, adopting his favourite role of unbiased adjudicator. 'Is this just your own theory or something out of a home-repairs manual?'

'Surely, Dicky, every schoolboy knows that glass is a super-cooled liquid which, under impact from a fast-moving missile, bends until it fractures in long cracks radiating from the point of impact. It continues bending for a long distance until eventually it makes a second series of cracks concentrically from the point of impact. Also a high-velocity missile makes a quite different type of hole. It fragments or powders the glass as it exits, and this reveals the direction of the missile. The degree of fragmentation usually gives a rough idea of the likely range from which the shot came; the closer the range the heavier the fragmentation.'

Frank smiled.

'Okay, you clever shit,' said Dicky. 'So why didn't you say the killer definitely was not waiting outside? You didn't say they weren't waiting outside did you?'

'Because the killer might have fired through a hole in the glass that was already there,' I said.

'You didn't say that either,' he complained.

'I can't be sure what I said.' If proof was needed to tell me I was slipping, my ill-timed lecture about fracturing glass was it. In the

49

old days I would have taken more care when kicking the sand of science into the face of a prima donna like Dicky, especially doing it in the presence of Frank, an old-timer everyone respected, or claimed to. 'The fact is that I didn't stick around to find out.'

Dicky had been to Oxford University and come away with an undisputed reputation for cleverness. That reputation had stuck. Cleverness was not measured and quantified in the way that passing exams or rowing strenuously enough to become a blue was on record. Cleverness was a vague characteristic not universally respected by Englishmen of Dicky's class; it suggested cunning and the sort of hard work and determination that marked the social climber. And so Dicky's cleverness remained a threat ever present, but a promise still unfulfilled. He looked at me and gave a sour grin. 'But why cut and run, Bernard? You had a good man with you.'

'An inexperienced kid.'

'Fearless,' said Dicky. This suggested to me that the kid might be one of Dicky's protégés, some amiable graduate he'd met on one of his frequent bibulous visits to his alma mater. 'We've used him on a couple of previous jobs: utterly fearless.'

'An utterly fearless man is more to be dreaded as a comrade than as an enemy,' I said.

Frank laughed before Dicky had absorbed it. In Frank's hand, along with my brief account of our unsuccessful mission, I could see the report the kid had submitted. In yellow marker I spotted a sentence about me firing the gun. There was some lengthy comment pencilled in the margin. They hadn't mentioned the gun I collected from Andi. I still had that to come.

Dicky said: 'This dead colonel – this VERDI – asked for you. What's this about someone owing someone a favour? What favour did the poor bastard owe you?'

'They always say that,' I explained. 'That's the standard form when they are seeking a deal with the other side.'

'When did you last see him?' said Dicky.

'I know nothing of him. His asking for me was just a gimmick.'

'Try and remember,' said Dicky in a voice that clearly said that he didn't believe me. 'He knows you all right.'

'More to be dreaded as a comrade than as an enemy,' said Frank, as if committing it to memory, and chuckled. 'That's a good one, Bernard. Well, if you can't remember VERDI maybe we'll leave it at that. You'll want to get back to London and see your children. Your wife is joining you there I heard.'

'That's right,' I said.

Dicky shot a glance at me. He didn't like the way that Frank was letting me off the hook, and I thought for a moment he was going to mention Gloria, the woman I'd been living with during the time I believed my wife was a defector working for the East. 'Then why is there a seat reserved for Samson on the flight to Zurich?' Dicky asked.

I got to my feet. 'Samson's a common name, Dicky,' I said, without getting excited.

'Field agents are all devious.' Frank smiled and waved a languid hand in the air. 'It's the job that does it. How could Bernard be so good at his job without being constantly wary?'

'Who do you know in Zurich?' Dicky asked, as if knowing someone in Zurich was in itself a sinister development.

'My brother-in-law.' Frank looked at Dicky as if expecting some reaction to this, but Dicky just nodded. 'He moved there after his wife was killed. I will have to see him eventually … there are domestic affairs that will have to be settled. Tessa assigned property and her share of a trust to Fiona.'

Frank smiled. He knew why I was going to Zurich of course. He knew I would be cross-checking with Werner Volkmann everything the Department had told me. Dicky knew too. Neither of them liked the idea of me talking to Werner, but Frank was rather more subtle and able to hide his feelings.

51

Dicky had been pacing about and now he turned on his heel and left the room, saying he would be back in a moment.

'He gave a little party last night at a new restaurant he found in Dahlem. Indian food apparently, and he suspects the bhindi bhaji has upset him,' Frank confided when Dicky had gone. 'Do you know what a bhindi bhaji is?'

'No, I'm not quite sure I do, Frank.'

Frank nodded his approval, as if such knowledge would have alienated us. 'Did Bret Rensselaer tell you to see Werner in Zurich?'

I hesitated, but the fact that Frank had waited for Dicky to exit encouraged me to confide in him. 'No, Bret told me to stay away from Werner. But Werner gets to hear things on the grapevine long before we get to know them through our channels. He might say something useful.'

'Dicky has staked a lot on having VERDI sitting in London spilling his guts to us. VERDI dead means all Dicky's planning dies with him. He'll be casting about for someone to blame; make sure it's not you.'

'I wasn't there,' I explained for what must have been the thousandth time. 'He was dead when we got there.'

'VERDI's father was a famous Red Army veteran: one of the first into Berlin when the city fell.'

'So everyone keeps telling me.' I looked at him. 'Who cares? That was over forty years ago and he was just one of thousands.'

'No,' said Frank. 'VERDI's father was the lieutenant commanding Red Banner No. 5.'

'Now you've got me,' I admitted.

'Well, well! Berlin expert admits defeat,' said Frank smugly. 'Let me tell you the story. In mid-April 1945 – as they advanced on Berlin – the 79th Rifle Corps got orders from the Military Council of the Third Shock Army that a red flag was to be planted on top of the Reichstag. And Stalin had personally ordered that it should be in place by May Day. On April 30th, with the deadline ticking, our man and his team of infantry sergeants fought their way up inside the Reichstag building, from room to room, floor to floor, until they climbed up on to the roof and with only four of them still alive, completed their task with just seventy minutes to go before it was May Day.'

'No, but I saw the movie,' I said.

'Make jokes if you like. For war babies like you it may mean nothing, but I guarantee that communists everywhere would have been devastated at the news that the son of such a man – a symbol of the highest peak of Stalinist achievement – would come over to us.'

'Devastated enough to kill him to prevent it?'

'That's what we want to know, isn't it?'

'I'll find out for you,' I said flippantly.

'Don't go rushing off to Switzerland to ask Werner,' said Frank. 'You know Dicky; he is sure to have asked the Berne office to assign someone to meet the plane and discreetly find out where you go. Treat Dicky carefully, Bernard. You can't afford to make more enemies.'

'Thanks, Frank,' I said and meant it warmly. But such assurances left Frank unsatisfied, and now he gave me a penetrating stare as if trying to see into my mind. Long ago he had promised my father that he would look after me, and he took that promise seriously, just as Frank took everything seriously, which was what made him so difficult to please. And like a father, Frank was apt to resent any sign that I could have a mind of my own and enjoy private thoughts that I did not share with him. I suppose all parents feel that anything less than unobstructed open-door access to all their offspring's thoughts and emotions is tantamount to patricide.

Frank said: 'As soon as Dicky knew that VERDI was dead he said someone must have talked.'

'Dicky likes to think that people are plotting against him.'

'Can't you see the obvious?' said Frank with an unusual display of exasperation. 'They haven't sent Dicky here as a messenger. Dicky is important nowadays. Whatever Dicky thinks will inevitably become the prevailing view in London.'

'No one talked in London or anywhere else. It's absurd. They'll eventually discover their mistake.'

'Oh no they won't. The people in London never discover their mistakes. They don't even admit them when others discover their mistakes. No, Bernard, they'll make their theories come true whatever it costs in time and trouble and self-delusion.'

I pulled a face.

Frank said: 'And that means that you'll be put under the microscope ... Unless of course you can take Dicky aside and gently persuade him that he's wrong.' He prodded his oilskin tobacco pouch as if resenting the torment it offered him. 'Werner's contract was ended and he was hounded for no real reason except that he seems to upset someone on high. From what little I hear he's feeling damned bitter about it all. But he's not working for us. Don't let him persuade you he is.'

'You know what us field agents are like,' I said.

'I'm not sure I'm getting through to you.'

'Tell me again, Frank.'

He had the oilskin pouch in his hand. Now he swung it around. 'Admit it. Someone talked, didn't they? It wasn't just a coincidence that you arrive in Magdeburg and there is a warm corpse waiting for you.'

'About VERDI?'

'Don't be so stupid. Of course. They set him up and killed him. Had they squeezed him before killing him they might have got you too.'

'And that's what Dicky thinks?'

'You have a different theory?' He had the tobacco pouch in his hand, holding it up as if to admire its lines but also keeping it within olfactory range.

'It's one way of looking at it,' I said grudgingly.

'Yes, it is,' said Frank, sniffing at the tobacco pouch. 'Someone preferred VERDI dead, rather than alive and over here talking to us.'

'Maybe.'

'How long were you held up at that militia checkpoint outside Magdeburg?'

'About half an hour.'

'And would you say that when you arrived VERDI had been dead for about half an hour?'

'What are you getting at? Are you suggesting that the delay was arranged so that VERDI could reach the rendezvous and be intercepted and killed before we got there?'

'It all fits together doesn't it?' said Frank.

'No.' He looked at me and I yielded a little. 'It's possible. But there is no evidence whatsoever to support that theory. Unless you have some evidence to add.'

'Or … looking at this business and pretending that we didn't know the agents involved …' Frank's voice trailed off. 'Do you see what I mean, Bernard?'

'Yes, I see what you mean all right. You mean that if I and that kid invented the hold-up at the checkpoint we could have got there and killed VERDI ourselves.'

'Using that pistol that came from nowhere,' added Frank for good measure. 'It could look bad if someone wanted to throw mud at you.'

'Ask the kid. He's Dicky's man isn't he?'

'Very much Dicky's man,' agreed Frank amiably. 'He wants to please Dicky; Dicky says there might eventually be a place for him in London.'

'He's a decent kid. He wouldn't tell lies. He'd tell an inquiry the truth, and blow Dicky's theory sky-high.'

'I'm glad you are so confident about that,' said Frank. 'That settles my mind. But of course one can't guarantee anyone a job in London. Nowadays a young chap like that one can find himself posted to some God-forsaken place in Asia or Africa. Some of them are out of touch for years.' He opened the door of the stove and prodded the burned paper delicately with a poker. For a moment I thought he was going to throw my report in there. Such dramatic gestures by Frank were not unknown. But instead he tried again to light the fire using small pieces torn from a newspaper. He was rewarded by a sudden flame and pushed a piece of kindling into it.

'Point taken, Frank,' I said.

He looked up and gave a fleeting smile, pleased perhaps at his success with the fire. 'Of course I've kept this business very need-to-know. Dicky, me, you, and of course what's-his-name: this youngster who went with you.'

'Plus secretaries, code-clerks and messengers – any one of them might have leaked it,' I added, joining in the silly game in an effort to show the absurdity of his conspiracy theory. 'And there's VERDI too. He knew we were coming, didn't he?'

'Of course he did. And who knows who else got to hear? I've no intention of starting a witch-hunt, Bernard. That killing might have had nothing to do with him wanting to defect. A man like that – deep in the secrets of the KGB and Stasi too – is sure to have made plenty of enemies. For all we know the reason he wanted to come to us was because his life was in danger from whoever murdered him.'

'Exactly,' I said. I got up to go.

'I know I can't stop you visiting Werner,' said Frank, 'but you'd better guard your tongue when you are with him. If London gets to hear that you've been sharing Departmental secrets with him – even low-grade ones – they will throw the book at you.'

'I'll be careful, Frank. I really will.'

As I was going to the door, he undid the pouch and put his empty pipe into his mouth while fingering the tobacco. The smell of it reached me as he grabbed a handful of it. I watched him, thinking he was going to fill the pipe, but he didn't. He opened the door of the stove and thrust the entire contents of the pouch into the fire. The tobacco flared and hissed and a snake of pungent grey smoke coiled out into the room. 'I'm determined this time,' said Frank, looking over his shoulder at me, his eyes wide and birdlike.

I was outside the door, and about to push it closed, when Frank called out to me and I looked back inside.

'The pistol, Bernard. I haven't asked you about the pistol.' He pursed his lips. In Frank's view anyone using a gun betrayed the Department and all it stood for. 'You shot the tyres out, it said in the report. But where did the hand-gun come from?'

'I thought the kid told you about that,' I said warily.

'No, he was as puzzled as we were,' said Frank, watching me with great interest.

'I found it on the body,' I said.

'Fully loaded?' said Frank formally, as if he was about to write it down and ask me to sign.

'That's right, fully loaded. A Makarov – German manufacture: a Pistole M to be precise – I put it in my pocket and that's what I used when they chased us in the car.'

'I don't remember anything of that in your report.'

'I thought the kid would have covered those sort of details.'

'Write the whole thing again,' suggested Frank. 'Fill in a few of those missing details … the Pistole M, how glass bends and so on. You know what those people in London are like. They might think you collected the gun from one of your East Berlin

57

cronies. And then they won't give me any peace until I find out who it might have been.'

'You're right, Frank,' I said, wondering how quickly I could close the door and get out of there without offending him, and how soon Dicky would return with a thousand more questions.

'Smell that tobacco,' said Frank, wallowing in the smoke coming out of the stove top. 'I'm beginning to think it's better than smoking.'

4

'You just leave it to me, Mr Samson,' said the cheerful ordnance lieutenant.

The army is always there when you need it. My father's loyalty to the army remained no matter how long after his army service he worked for the Foreign Office. And Frank Harrington's devotion to the army was renowned. The army looks after its own and was always ready to take under its wing those who understood the obligations this entailed. And now it was a young army lieutenant who, without any up-to-date paperwork or even a telephone call, had put me into the cab of one of his trucks heading down the Autobahn. The soldiers were posted back to their depot. They were in convoy for Holland, and the ferry to Harwich in England. But I was on my way to Switzerland.

'We're getting near to the place you're wanting, sir,' said the driver without preamble. 'You'll hitchhike south from there.' He had a Newcastle accent you could cut with a knife, and my German upbringing had left me unable to comprehend the more pronounced British regional voices. 'Going home,' he added, doing his best to make me understand. 'We're all going home.'

'Yes,' I said. You could see the joy of it written in the faces of all these soldiers.

'What about you, sir?'

59

'Yes, I'll soon be going home too,' I said mechanically. The truth was I had no home; not in the sense that these men had their homes in Britain. My English parents had brought me up in Berlin and sent me to the neighbourhood school, frequently reminding me how lucky I was to have two languages and two countries; two lands in which I could pass myself off as a national. But as I got older I discovered just how tragically wrong they were. In fact even my most intimate German friends – boys who'd been close chums at school – had never regarded me as anything except a foreigner. While the British – not the least those men who sat behind the desks at London Central – regarded me as an unreliable outsider. I had none of the credentials essential for anyone who wanted to join their ranks. I wore no school or university tie, nor that of any smart regiment. I rode with no hunt, loitered in no Jermyn Street club, had no well-known tailor chasing me for payment. I couldn't even name a seedy local pub where I regularly played darts and could get a pint of beer on credit.

'You'll need money,' the corporal warned me. 'Hitchhikers are expected to pay their fare nowadays. It's the way things are.'

'I've got enough.'

'You should have bought a couple of bottles of duty-free booze. That's what most of the boys do. Do you understand me?'

'I understand,' I said. 'I wish I'd thought of it.'

The army in Germany – squeezed tighter and tighter by a German prosperity that shrank the pound sterling – had learned a great deal about saving money. The driver knew all about picking up a lift from one of the endless streams of heavy trucks that head south from Holland through Switzerland to deliver their freight to the Euro-Community warehouses in Italy. 'Good luck,' said the corporal. 'And persevere. It won't be easy. They'll think you are a soldier, and these fat civvies all despise squaddies until there's a bomb needs defusing or their plane gets hijacked. Keep asking; you'll get a lift eventually.'

It was a frosty night with a wind that cut through the moth-eaten lining of my old trenchcoat. I regretted for a moment leaving all my personal baggage – shaving kit, linen and change of clothes – behind in the kid's apartment, but it was a necessary part of giving the Berlin office the slip. My airline seat reservation would keep them content until morning: they were endearingly simple souls in the Berlin office.

The night was cold and dark. The sky moonless, starless and unremittingly black. 'It's good weather,' the corporal added. 'You'll be in Italy in no time. But get yourself cleaned up; you'll never get a lift if you're scruffy.' I suppose it was good weather from a driver's point of view. A dry road, without the prospect of ice or snow, and visibility as far as the headlight's beam stretched.

The corporal had dropped me off at what he said was his favourite interchange: two great cross-Europe highways meeting and intertwining in a desolate reach of rural Germany. The complex was lit like a football stadium, the ferocious glare illuminating a white haze of diesel pollution that wound in and out of the gas pumps and buildings like skeins of silk. From a distance the interchange looked like some huge and malevolent inter-planetary vehicle forced-landed upon the empty black German countryside. But upon arrival it proved no more than a plastic oasis, a limbo land occupied by drowsy downcast Gastarbeiter. No one lived here, no one slept here, no pedestrian would be mad enough even to attempt to get here. It was simply a 'stop'; a place where cramped and weary travellers paid extortionate prices for the basic essentials of the travelling life – fuel, hot food, cigarettes and aspirin – before resuming their trip.

After buying soap, a disposable plastic razor, toothbrush, clean underclothes and a tee-shirt in the silent fluorescent-lit

61

shop, I purchased a shiny plastic shoulder bag emblazoned, for reasons known only to the tortuous minds of the merchandising experts, with a crudely drawn skyscraper and the words New York New York. I went and shaved and changed. Then, following the corporal's advice, I walked into the special canteen reserved for long-distance truck drivers. It was a cheerless place, with long plastic-topped tables for men in dirty coveralls who wanted to keep an eye on the floodlit truck park to be sure their cargoes were safe.

Here at the self-service counter, East met West. An identical array of spicy flour-thickened stews was saved from anonymity only by the exotic labels promising Madras curry, Hungarian goulash, Irish stew and Mexican chilli. With no wish for journeys into the culinary unknown, I took a bowl of noodle soup and a cheese sandwich before moving from table to table soliciting a ride. Eventually I was lucky. After half a dozen negative responses a wavy-haired Dutchman signalled to me from across the room with a barely perceptible beckoning finger.

'Where are you headed, stranger?' His use of American vernacular was awkward and unconvincing. He was a muscular man with a puffy face and fair skin reddened at the cheeks and nose by the wind and weather. His neat moustache and eyebrows, like the wavy hair on his head, were blond, so that from a distance he looked like a plump angel who'd fluttered down from the loft of some baroque church. Under his battered brown leather jacket he was wearing what I recognized as a very expensive rainbow-striped silk shirt. On the table in front of him, aligned as if for inspection, there were a bunch of keys, a leather bag, a flashlight and a red plastic folder containing a batch of manifests, registrations and customs documents needed for him to take his truck and cargo across 'frontierless' Europe.

'South. Switzerland. Anywhere in Switzerland,' I replied.

'After that you'll pay your way?' he asked mockingly.

'I'll pay you,' I offered, 'if it's not too much.'

'Keep your dough in your pocket. Take the weight off your feet. My name is Wim. I'm transporting cars to Milan. I can do with the company; rapping keeps me awake.'

I sat down opposite him and drank my soup and ate my sandwich while he finished his steak. 'I'm not permitted to take hitchhikers,' he said with a furtive glance over his shoulders. 'Plenty of big-mouths in here tonight. Better you wait by the exit from the truck park.' He tore a bread roll in half, wiped the plate using the crust, and then stood up to drink the final mouthful of his coffee. On his hand there was a heavy gold signet ring and a tattoo that artfully incorporated his fingers into its continuous design, and gave emphasis to his gold wrist-watch. Driving long-distance heavy trucks was a well-paid job. It was not unusual to find such nomads spending their wages on personal luxuries rather than equipping the homes they seldom saw.

He stood up, flicked crumbs from the front of his shirt and picked up his flashlight after putting the rest of his belongings into his leather bag. 'Let's go,' he said. 'Let's get the show on the road.' It was the smooth American-style accent that those brought up speaking Dutch and German often assume. I was to find that his whole education and experience was derived from Hollywood films. From them he could quote episodes and dialogue with the effortless assurance of a preacher summoning Bible texts. I guessed he was going to use me as an English-conversation lesson, but that seemed a fair exchange. 'You leave now. You'll spot me all right. I'm driving that rig with the brand-new Saabs on it.' He was toying with the flashlight and he switched it on to be sure it worked. He did it automatically, more a neurotic habit than a test of its batteries.

The vast car transporter swayed and groaned as it came across the car park to where I was standing at the exit. It stopped with a squeak of brakes and I got in, slammed the door and looked around. This was Wim's world, and it came complete with air-conditioning, embroidered silk cushions and pin-ups. He ran through the gears and spun the steering wheel with one finger, grinning at me as we sped along the ramp and slid into the stream of traffic heading south. I need not have worried that he would interrogate me or want to be entertained with the story of my life. This fellow Wim wasn't like that: his idea of entertainment was having an audience for the story of his life.

It was the sort of yarn to be heard in the bars of almost every big town in the modern world. With difficulties in reading, a self-confessed truant and thief, he was well able to manage his spoken English, and German and Italian too according to what he told me. He handled his huge transporter truck with the same casual ease. Sentenced to three years in prison for large-scale car thefts and an armed assault upon a policeman, he had served seven months before being released on a technicality and his police and prison records erased. Thirty-one years old, he had five children by two different mothers: 'a ready and willing piece of ass in Stockholm and another in Turin' was how the unrepentant Wim described his present situation. One of them he'd married, but Wim gave no money to either family, for he thought it was the government's duty to provide for all. Didn't he pay his income tax? he asked rhetorically. 'She can give a heart-wrenching plea about money to feed the kids. I said: "Give 'em canned dog-food, at least they'll have good teeth and hair."' He laughed as he remembered this response. 'Never get married,' he advised. 'Once you're married they demand everything; never a word of gratitude whatever you do. Girlfriends expect little or nothing. And it's love and kisses when you bring them a box of chocolates.'

I listened, head lolling against the seat and dozing off during his long asides about the failings of society to look after its victims, among which Wim numbered himself. His droning voice was soporific but his caustic jokes jolted me awake from time to time. Despite my reservations about almost everything he said, he was an engaging personality; I could see why so many women had fallen under his spell. And yet his diatribe brought a growing realization of how much I had changed since that fateful night I left Germany for California. I had never cracked, the way the doctor there had warned me I might, but the enforced tedium of my days there on the far side of the Western world – and the pitiless repetitions of my debriefings – had deadened my mind and slowed my reactions, as I'd seen happen so often to those who survived psychoanalysis. Worse, I was taking life day by day … taking things as they came. I'd always despised people who took things as they came.

Frank Harrington had recognized the change in me of course. I could see it in his eyes as soon as we exchanged hellos. The shift I'd seen in Frank's attitude to me during the uncomfortable interview I'd just had in Berlin had its roots in some new and inadequate something that Frank detected in me.

And Wim's domestic predicaments were not without an echo in my own consciousness: 'You live in London but you're heading south?' he'd remarked, using that animal instinct which informs such street-wise semi-literates.

Perhaps the look on my face revealed something of the confusion in my mind.

'Running from one wife to another?' he said. 'Or running away from them both, like I am?'

I responded with a soft derisive laugh, but in a way he was right. Perhaps I was going on this excursion to Zurich in order to get vital information from Werner. Perhaps I was going there in order to put off that terrible time when I would be in London and forced to start sorting out my personal affairs. What did I have left of my relationships with two women I loved – with Fiona, my wife, and with Gloria who had patiently pieced together a new life for me when I was at my lowest? And what of my relationships with my two children, who were doubtless as confused as any of us?

'Be a real man,' urged Wim, flexing his arm in a lewd signal of machismo. 'The man makes the decisions; women wait for him to make up his mind. That's what nature intended. It's the way life is.' He offered me a swig from a bottle of Old Jenever that he had tucked into a toolbox behind his head. I declined and he smiled and put the gin away. 'Drinking and driving don't mix,' he said, with that smug air of accomplishment with which we all use cliches in a foreign tongue.

It was beginning to rain. Big droplets hit the glass and then moved sluggishly downwards, flattened by the air flow into wavy patterns. He switched on the massive wipers, which slid across the windscreen with a thirsty slurp and a contented whine from the motor. The weather had changed. It was no longer good weather for driving, for hitchhiking or for anything else.

The heating was switched fully on in the cab of the transporter. I became drowsy and, eyes closed, I found it difficult to respond to Wim's commentary and his occasional questions. Perhaps he was also succumbing to the warmth, for when I asked him what time he thought we'd cross the Swiss frontier he said: 'Go back to sleep, it's a long way yet.' He changed to a lower gear for the long incline ahead. 'At the next chance I shall pull over and check the load. I think I hear a rattle. Sometimes the car doors come open. It will take me only a minute or two.'

He slowed as he spotted a likely place and pulled the transporter into one of the wide spaces provided for emergency stops on the Autobahn. He switched off the engine. It was dark, the rain beat upon the road and ran in torrents from the tall fir trees, beating noisily on the roof of the cab like impatient fingers. 'Stay in the dry,' he said, and tugged his arms into a short plastic coat with a hood. He opened the door and climbed down, cursing all the while. I saw the flashlight beam and heard him making a circuit of the long vehicle, checking that his six brand-new Saabs were well secured. Eventually he climbed back into the driver's cab, waved the flashlight and switched it off and gave a sigh of content.

I felt a draught of cold air and flicks of water as he took off his coat. Eyes half-closed, I was slumped in the corner with my head resting against the seat back as Wim leaned across me as if to check that my door was safely locked. It was the tension and sudden movement of his arm that caused me to move my head. I rolled aside and the blow that should have knocked me unconscious only tore my ear lobe off. The heavy metal flash-light he wielded spent most of its force against the upholstered head-rest, landing with a loud thump.

'You bastard!' shouted Wim, whose rage I had long since figured could be directed against anyone who stood between him and his immediate wishes. I lashed out to defend myself as he came at me again. He was right-handed, and from his posi-tion in the driving seat, on the left side of the cab, this proved a disadvantage. I brought my right fist round and hit him as hard as I could. Then hit him again. But in the confined space move-ment was difficult. The first punch hit only his shoulder and the other did little beyond grazing my knuckles on his earring. We were both aiming wildly as we thrashed around in the confines of the cabin, punching, pushing and grappling like wrestlers. Twice I tried to pin his arms, but he was strong and I could hold him for no more than a moment before he wrenched himself free. He butted at me but I was ready for that, and brought my fist up and gave him a jab full in the face which made him snort and shake his head.

As he rolled back from the punch I saw his bloodied face and eyes shiny and demented. He swung round at me, this time bringing the flashlight right across his body from his left shoulder and delivering a blow that landed. It made my head sing and paralysed me with shock. I heard a distant scream of pain without at first realizing that it came from me. Anger took over. I struck out at his silly face. My fist connected but he was a tough street kid and had reached that stage of fighting madness where such blows meant nothing to him. Wim had done all this before; that was obvious by his confident persistence.

I reached out to grab his throat. 'English bastard!' he said, and managed to get a grip on my jacket, holding the bunched fabric tight, so that he could give me a good decisive blow with the flashlight. Made of heavy metal it was a vicious weapon, but within the confines of the cab, and impeded by the big steering wheel, he couldn't bring his arm back far enough to put lethal force into it. I deflected a second blow with my upraised arm and chopped at his throat with the edge of my hand. But already he had turned his head far enough for the neck muscle to shield the windpipe. For a moment we both paused, overcome by our exertions. He was breathing heavily and noisily, and there was a pattern of blood on his temple and more running from his nose. His mouth was half-open and a line of frothy spittle had formed on his lips. What wouldn't I have given for the 9mm Makarov pistol that I had dumped into an East German ditch only twenty-four hours previously.

The first extravagant exchange of blows was over and I had survived. He was cautious now, and determined to make no more errors of judgement. He used the flashlight as a prod, lunging to jab at my face. Twice I deflected it, and as I dodged around I looked for something to use as a weapon but there was nothing in sight. As he came at me the third time I struck at the flashlight with anger and reckless disregard, and hit it hard enough to knock it from his hand. It clattered to the floor and rolled under my seat, where neither of us could get to it

68

without becoming totally vulnerable. He wiped the blood from his mouth with the back of a hand and gave me a fleeting grin.

I slid my back away from him to get into the corner, where I curled up into a ball. My posture – knees drawn up to my chin and arms crossed on my chest – told Wim that I'd given up hope and resistance. Perhaps that's what had happened with his other victims – they'd simply cowered away, pleading for mercy – but Wim wasn't the sort who dealt in mercy. 'I'm going to kill you,' he shouted at me, and despite the anger that was boiling up inside me, it was easy to imagine the way that kind of threat had effectively removed all resistance from some wretched girl or skinny kid who were no doubt the sort of victims he looked for.

He came at me with his hands extended and fingers splayed. He intended to strangle me. There was no big spilling of blood with a strangulation. And if the body was disposed into the scrub and ferns at such a lonely section of road, who would ever guess where the victim had disappeared to, or what had happened? Only Wim would know, and in his pocket he'd have cash and any other valuables that a hitchhiker might carry.

'Help!' I called in a strangled voice, and with a note of terror that was easy to simulate.

Wim grinned widely. He was a sadist, and the prospect of a victim terrified and paralysed with fear was exactly what excited him. I put my elbows back and braced myself against the seat. My whimpering was enough to relax the tension that had racked his bloody face. I needed him nearer, and nearer he came. He whispered: 'There's no one here to help you, mister.'

He didn't complete the sentence, for at the last word I kicked out, kicking harder than I had ever kicked before, even harder than I'd kicked for the football team my father had organized for the German kids and drafted me into. The sole of my heavy East German shoe – with its metal heels – hit Wim full in his grinning face. My timing was right and so was my judgement of distance. He went hurtling back, his spine hit the steering wheel and his head hit the glass window with a bang loud enough to make the metal cab ring with the sound.

Then I was on to him. I scrambled around to find the metal flashlight from where it had rolled under my seat, and, taking all the time I needed, I hit him across the side of the head. I suppose I went mad for a moment. The release of the fear I'd suffered made me lose all restraint. At the second blow his eyes closed as he screamed out with pain. I didn't stop. I hit him again and again until his cries became whimpers and then silence and his body slumped down with his knees on the floor of the cab and his body skewed sideways on the seat, arms trapped in the steering wheel like a man at prayer.

I stopped myself then and sat back on my seat to collect my thoughts. What was happening to me? Everything I'd ever learned had been abandoned in that moment of rage. The last thing I needed was a murder investigation on my heels. I took the Dutchman's arm: his pulse was weak but steadying. He would probably come round eventually; it was hard to judge how long it would take. His face was bloody, his jaw broken, he'd lost teeth and was badly cut. I touched him carefully, avoiding getting blood marks on my clothes.

I opened the driver's door. Using my foot, I slowly pushed his unconscious body through the door until it overbalanced and crashed on to the ground. Then I went through his pockets to find his keys. I took them and made sure that all the doors of the cab were firmly locked, and the thief-alarm on, before tossing the whole bunch of keys into the undergrowth as far as I could throw them. They would not be easy to find unless the cops brought a metal detector into use.

I searched his other pockets. There was a billfold at his hip. In it I found a couple of driving licences, a few Dutch, German and Italian currency notes, a handwritten letter in Dutch, four snapshots of different undressed women – Wim's recent conquests no doubt – and some plastic credit cards. I removed everything that might reveal his identity and buried it in the mud. The money I pocketed: motive robbery. Then I pulled off Wim's jeans and leather jacket and silk shirt, bundled them all up and hid those too. When I came back he stirred but did not recover his wits. I dragged him off the tarmac and into a cold muddy puddle.

Having done all I could to delay Wim's return to the real world, I put the bag over my shoulder and went out on to the road and began to signal passing cars and trucks with the flashlight.

The rain soaked me to the skin, and passing trucks and cars sprayed me with muddy water without even slowing at the sight of me. I began to believe that I would stand there for ever. Fighting Wim off, and the narrow escape from death, had shaken me. The cold rain beat down upon my head and my resolve dwindled and was gone. I was bruised and battered; my head was still singing from the blows with the metal flashlight. Even worse was the near-mortal blow that had been delivered to my self-confidence. How could I have been so easily caught off-guard by a muscle-bound bird-brain like Wim? Only a year or so ago I would have recognized such a thug at first sight, and knocked him cold before he could raise a hand against me.

For perhaps the first time in my life I saw Bernard Samson as so many others had always seen him. I'm not talking about any kind of symbolism: my despair was practical, not philosophical, just as my joy had always been. But I was only in this predicament because I had gone out of my way to disobey orders from London Central about contacting Werner. I'd beaten Wim more ferociously than was necessary to escape him, and no doubt left enough evidence for an energetic police inquiry to trace me back to the ride I got out of Berlin. Worse was the fact that I had no one to turn to for help. Who at London Central would risk their career covering for me? Not even Frank would go that far. The two women in my life had nothing to thank me for, and Werner seemed to have gone to a great deal of trouble to make contacting him difficult. I was totally alone, in deep trouble and friendless. But I must get to Werner nevertheless: he was the only person who would understand my predicament. The fact that he was in no position to help me was a secondary consideration.

The nudges and winks, the hints and outright slanders I'd heard over the past few weeks, about Werner's sudden departure from the Departmental payroll, had not fooled me. If any of those stories, about Werner embezzling money or otherwise upsetting the applecart, were true, the Department would have put out a worldwide alert, found him and punished his misdeeds. But they had not done that, they'd left him in Switzerland to wither on the vine. That suggested one thing above all others. I knew only one sin that London would temporize, compromise and negotiate about: betrayal. Werner must have let something slip when he was over there on one of his business trips. It was easy enough to do. I would hate to be called into account for all the times I had sailed close to the wind. But for the time being Werner was in no position to help my career, even if he had the inclination to do so.

Rain washed my bruised and bloody face and squelched inside my shoes. The highway was completely silent and the sour stink of diesel fumes grew fainter as it was washed away by the rain. At this time of night even long-distance drivers are tempted to find a spot on the road to shut their eyes for an hour or so. I had no alternative but to wait, but so much time was passing that I walked back past the slip road which led to Wim's transporter. Several times I fancied I saw him walking around under the trees there, but they were no more than shadows conjured up by my troubled imagination. All the same, not wanting to take the

72

risk of Wim spotting me at the roadside, I walked farther along the road, back the way we'd come. I was still walking when a car caught me in its main beams and slowed to pick me up.

It was a dented Audi with a middle-aged German in a damp raincoat sitting at the wheel. As he wound the window down cigarette smoke billowed into my face. 'What are you doing out here at this time of night?' he said in a quarrelsome tone.

'I had a breakdown,' I said. 'Could you take me to the nearest town?'

'Get in,' he said.

I didn't get in. It was at that very moment that my mind suddenly exploded, and the events of the last hour or so assumed a new and terrifying pattern. How could I have mistaken Wim for a psychopath who killed skinny kids and foolhardy girls for kicks, or to get his hands on their meagre cash and belongings? My narrow escape had been from an assigned hit by a KGB professional. Wim had been sent to kill me. It all fitted together. He had been waiting in the right Autobahn interchange at the right time and selected me in the driver's canteen. He had beckoned me, and when getting me aboard had stopped at the ramp, a place where he made sure that no witnesses were around to see him picking me up. It had all been carefully planned: the offer of a swig from his gin bottle, and the heater turned fully up to make me drowsy. No firearms: bullets would leave bullet holes and too much blood.

I shuddered. It was a narrow escape. Had my luck not prevailed Wim would now have just finished burying me in a shallow grave by the roadside, where a body could lay undiscovered for years, maybe for ever. Wim was not some homicidal maniac; he was a professional killer.

The driver of the Audi was looking at my well-worn coat and the cheap bag with the skyscraper on it. 'Do you want a lift with me, or are you waiting for a Rolls-Royce?'

I suddenly became aware that I was standing in the heavy rain and looking at him blankly. 'Yes. Yes, thanks,' I said.

'Get in,' he told me again, and I threw my bag into the car and climbed in after it.

'I thought no one would ever stop,' I said.

He didn't reply. He was about forty, overweight, with slicked-back hair and a neatly trimmed moustache. 'You're not German,' he said accusingly.

'Yes, I am.' My hands were trembling as I thought about Wim and the men who might have sent him. Had I not been thinking of something else I would not have claimed to be German. It would have been easier to be a British soldier on leave.

'Maybe. So where did you get the accent?' he said, examining my face carefully. Over-confident, I'd been careless. He'd heard some false note and one false note was enough. He narrowed his eyes: 'Don't I know you from somewhere?'

'No, you don't know me. I've been away in Canada,' I said. If Wim had been positioned to pick me up and kill me, he would have a back-up to support him. If the site chosen for his attack was prearranged, why not have this toughie sweep up along the road to make sure that it had all gone according to plan? If it hadn't gone according to plan, if I was still alive, the back-up could stop and offer me a ride and make sure of me.

'Bullshit,' said the man. 'Canada; bullshit. And what the hell have you been doing? Fighting?' Despite the darkness he could see my face and its bruises and marks. One of my eyes was getting so puffy that it was impeding my vision.

'But I've lived in Berlin most of my life,' I said. I was working hard on my accent now. I knew he was listening to my voice and examining every syllable with the precision of an oscilloscope.

'What's the real story? Why are you trembling? You didn't have a breakdown. There was no car.' It was the gruff voice of a heavy smoker.

74

'It's damned cold out there, that's why I'm trembling.'

By this time I'd had a chance to look around his car interior – battered two-way radio, ashtrays brimful of ash and butts. This guy was a cop, a plain-clothes cop! One sight of this car, and the neglect it had suffered, should have been enough to identify it as an unmarked police vehicle. But that didn't rule out him being the back-up to Wim's attempt to kill me. 'No, it wasn't a breakdown,' I admitted. 'A driver … A long-distance driver dumped me out on the road.'

'Why?'

'It's a long story.'

'I've got plenty of time.' Without taking his eyes off the road he got a cigarette packet, put one in his mouth and punched the lighter.

'He wanted money,' I said.

'And you wouldn't give it to him?' He stole another glance at me. His red-rimmed eyes were beady, black and suspicious. The lighter popped out and he lit his cigarette.

'I'd given him two hundred marks already.'

'Was he a homosexual?' He was not the sort of man who spoke in euphemisms. 'Is that the story?' And then another thought struck him. 'Are you a prostitute?'

'Do you want a punch on the nose?'

'No, I guess you are not.' He looked at me and blew smoke. 'Or I wouldn't have stopped for you. I can spot a homosexual at one hundred metres. I hate those perverts, and they don't cross my path twice I can tell you. You're a Berliner you say?'

'Originally I went there to avoid the draft,' I said. 'I stayed on.' It wouldn't endear me to him, but I would never be able to stand up to questions about compulsory service in the Bundeswehr.

'Draft-dodger.' He hammered a fist against the heater outlet.

'I suppose that's what I am,' I agreed, flustered by the way he was punching at the car. 'It's a long time ago. Sometimes I wish I'd gone into the army. Were you in the army?' I swung the questioning to him.

He didn't answer. Like a furnace burning in the forest, a segment of dark red sun drew a line along his profile. He brought a handkerchief from his pocket and wiped condensation from the inside of the windshield glass. 'Something's happened to the climate,' he said, as if trying to start a quarrel. 'We usually have a metre of snow hereabouts by this time of year.'

'It's not testing those bombs that's doing it.'

'Very funny. One of these ban-the-bomb fanatics are you?'

'No, I like bombs.'

'Ummm. Why don't you grab some sleep?'

'I'm not tired,' I said.

He took a drag at his cigarette, blew smoke, coughed, beat his chest and then looked at the butt as if trying to read the trade mark. 'Have you got something on you … something to make a long journey shorter? Something to smoke, know what I mean?'

'Yes, I know what you mean,' I said. 'But I don't use dope, crack, smack or any of that kind of shit. Neither am I carrying an Uzi submachine gun or a half-kilo of Semtex. We never met before. I'm not selling my arse. I'm not anything except a hard-working son of a bitch who is trying to get a ride south. So back off! Okay?'

For a long time we drove on in silence. The sun turned orange and then yellow as if setting fire to the whole wooded landscape. This illusion was heightened by the way my companion's chain-smoking had by now filled the car interior with a choking haze of acrid blue smoke.

'I'm a cop,' he said suddenly and without preamble. 'A police inspector.'

'Is that so?'

'There's a long-distance bus station near where I'm headed. I'll drop you there.' He said it as though he was reluctantly

76

forgoing the alternative course of taking me to the police station and beating the life out of me. 'From that point on you're on your own. But let me tell you this: if one of my boys picks you up for loitering, soliciting or pestering drivers for a free ride, they'll bring you in, and I'll make you damn sorry you ever passed this way.'

'Okay,' I grunted.

'Speak up! Was that some kind of thank you, or was it just a drunken belch? I'll be going half a mile out of my way to take you to that damned bus station. Jolted you did it; me being a detective?'

'Yes,' I said. 'You seem too soft-hearted to be a police inspector.'

5

There was a time when Zurich was my back yard. Collecting bags of gold sovereigns from the army cashier's office in Hanover, and carting them to a private bank in Zurich under diplomatic cover, was one of the first official jobs my father allowed me to do. Werner and I would stroll into this magnificent bank on Bahnhofstrasse and slam the gold on to the cashier's counter to pay it into the deposit account of Madame Xavier. If they wondered why two scruffy youngsters would be contributing so handsomely and regularly to Madame Xavier's resources, the bank staff were too Swiss to reveal their feelings. It was not my place to point out that Zurich had gold in abundance: bankers can never have enough of it. I loved Zurich in those days. It was an island of peace and plenty in a Europe impoverished and exhausted by six years of war. A place alive with bright neon signs, where cream cakes contained cream, girls laughed without payment, and the dangers men faced were mostly in the stock-market.

I was twenty-one years old, and a wide-eyed habitué of the famous Café Odéon, where Lenin and Trotsky had sat planning to dethrone the Tsar, where Mussolini had sat hatching his 'march on Rome', where James Joyce sat writing *Ulysses*, and where now I could sit watching strip-tease, a form of entertainment forbidden in most cantons of Switzerland at the time.

It was wonderful while it lasted, but inevitably the men in London found a more convenient, more practical and presumably equally clandestine method of paying field agents, and our expenses-paid jaunts to Zurich ceased.

Since those far-off days, Zurich and I had irretrievably changed. For both of us, dignity, refinement, reticence and leisurely grace had been abandoned in favour of an undignified scramble for a plastic livelihood. The Matterhorn has been climbed ten thousand times, and Zurich has become an overnight stop for cheap package-tour groups on the way to somewhere else. When I arrived this time it was early afternoon and Zurich's Hauptbahnhof was as bustling as an oriental market. I pushed my way through groups of backpackers in well-worn anoraks and past elated school parties and bronzed glacier skiers clad in brightly coloured futuristic gear. Outside I got a ticket from the machine and swung aboard a No. II streetcar just as its doors were about to close. We rumbled along Bahnhofstrasse past banks, stylish shops and department stores and more banks. There was Carl Weber's famous toy shop where my son Billy fell off the mechanical rocking-horse. It always happens to Billy; why is that? And is it something he inherited from me?

Rippling silken lingerie and severe Chanel suits, Hermes handbags and thin-soled crocodile shoes – the big names went clattering past. At the end of the street the tram turns to where the luxury hotels squat along the River Limmat, which opens out suddenly to become the cold grey Zurich-see, and we crossed the Quai bridge to Bellevue and another Zurich where the attire is less voguish, the shoes are sturdy, and you eat your paper-wrapped würstli standing in the street, and suffer the cruel and constant wind that blows across the icy water.

The streetcar pushed on up the hill from Bellevueplatz, climbing gently to the suburb at Balgrist where little antique shops sell

79

dusty modern chinaware at museum prices. The sun was low as I alighted from the streetcar and crossed the road, careful to avoid the high-powered Mercedes cars driven by moneyed medicos who swarm in and out of the expensive Klinike nearby. Everything from 'radiated mud-baths' to second-hand hearts is available here, and the world's wealthiest invalids bring their hope from afar, like pilgrims to a shrine.

This was the place I wanted. Men such as Werner Volkmann do not depend upon post office boxes or forwarding addresses. They trust instead to a network of acquaintances to whom they confide the sacred knowledge of their whereabouts. Café Ziegler. It was a dark little place, smelling of dark-roasted coffee, tobacco smoke and warm cheese. There were about a dozen small tables, with red cloths, and on the window-sill some potted flowers struggled to contest a thin beam of watery sunlight. The only bright light was over a table at the far end of the room where four elderly men sat under a blackboard, upon which the luncheon menu had been scrawled. They were playing cards and drinking beer and smoking so that the cone of yellow light was crawling with serpents of tobacco fumes. I have never mastered the game of Tarok, but it involves a great deal of shouting and laughing and is always punctuated by the crack of cards snapped edge-on against the table-top. The men were speaking Schweizerdeutsch, not the simple variety that is spoken in the restaurants and banks down-town but a rapid tongue-twisting variety that was beyond my comprehension. At my intrusion they looked up, and the shouting and laughter died abruptly.

'We're closed,' said the oldest of the four. 'Open again at six-thirty.' I recognized him. Benjamin was Zurich born and bred, as his thick accent proclaimed. We'd met once or twice: that was over a decade ago when this man – whom we used to call Benny – had played middle man in a transaction that got one hundred specially made rifles for a syndicate of wealthy Canadian hunters. Only later was it revealed that the 'rifles' were really machine pistols and that explosives, detonators and radio fuses were a part of the deal. There was a tip-off of some kind, a raid on a lakeside house that came to nothing, and a critical report of official ineptitude in the local newspaper. The Canadians – who later turned out to be a shell company in the Bahamas owned by Colombian drug dealers – vanished, as did the 'rifles' and the money, except that Benjamin quietly retired and became the proprietor of this little café.

'I'm looking for a friend of mine,' I said. 'Werner. I've come from Berlin and I need to talk to him.'

'I don't know anyone named Werner,' said Benjamin in a bored voice. He didn't look up, and played a card as if the Tarok game was all that mattered to him.

'My name is Bernd,' I said. In such circumstances family names are never offered or demanded. I stepped closer to the pool of light so that he could see me and look at my face. He closed his fan of cards and stared at me but gave no sign of recognition. Identification was an essential element of the procedure. An inquiry on the phone would have got nowhere. Such men exposed their friends only to other known and identified friends. 'Bernard from Berlin?' he said.

'That's right,' I agreed.

The other three men were looking at the cards as if they could not hear us. 'Very well, Bernd-aus-Berlin. I'll ask some people I know. Come back tomorrow about this same time.'

'Thanks,' I said.

'Where are you staying?'

'I've booked a room at the Savoy.'

'The Savoy!' He raised an eyebrow without looking up at me. 'That's classy, Bernd-aus-Berlin!' When I said nothing he added: 'I doubt if I will be able to help you. But I'll ask around the district.'

Back in the street it was almost dark. The grey stone Klinike were pierced with blue rectangles of light, like a hundred TV screens where doctors and nurses and patients acted out their bloody dramas. The No. II streetcar arrived. Its brightly lit interior revealed a boxful of passengers packed absurdly tightly together like inebriated guests at a cocktail party. Together with a dozen other people I shouldered my way inside. The doors closed and we rattled off down the hill. I looked forward to luxuriating in a hot bath at the hotel and nursing my bruises, but found myself wondering how many times I'd have to go up the hill to Café Ziegler before Werner finally came out of the woodwork.

I got off at Paradeplatz, a streetcar junction just a few steps from the Savoy. As I was crossing the road only yards from the hotel someone called: 'Bernard!'

A woman's voice. I looked around. 'Zena!' Of all the people I might have met while looking for Werner Volkmann, his first wife, the irrepressible Zena, was the furthest from my thoughts. I hadn't seen her since the two of them had separated. She hadn't changed much: pale-complexioned with intense eyes, emphasized by discreet use of mascara, a little shadow in just the right places and carefully made-up lips. The little pointed nose was still the same too: sometimes I found myself looking at her and wondering what sort of nose-job she could have and how it would change her. She was wearing a full-length golden-coloured fox-fur coat, but even in sacking – and with or without a nose-job – Zena would have been a stunning-looking woman.

'What a coincidence! But what have you done to your face?' She was looking at my cuts and bruises with the sort of dispassionate inquiry one encounters when buying Band-Aids in a pharmacy.

'I fell into a xylophone,' I told her.

'I think I heard the chimes,' said Zena, and gave a soft nose-wrinkling snigger that under other circumstances might have been captivating. We'd never liked each other. It was too late now to have second thoughts, but we had long since agreed a mutually convenient armistice; bows, handshakes and eyes meeting with the polite restraint that the Koreans perfected at Panmunjom. 'Come and have coffee.' Suddenly a foxy limb reached out, and her elegant leather-gloved hand plucked at me. Everything that was predatory about Zena was exemplified in that gesture. 'Have you just come from Berlin?'

'No,' I said.

'And how is Frank Harrington these days?' Zena flatly ignored my denial and asked after the sprightly womanizer who not so long ago had painfully fallen victim to her charms.

'You're looking well,' I said.

'You'd better come and talk, Bernard.'

I looked at her. She didn't have to say more than that. I knew from the tone of her voice and the look in her eyes that Benjamin had already spoken with her. She had lost no time in acting on whatever he'd told her. I'd mentioned the Savoy and, while I'd been waiting for the streetcar and lumbering along the rails, she had driven down here to head me off.

'Whatever you say, Zena.'

'There is a wonderful café across the road,' she said. 'And I know your weakness for patisserie, Bernard.'

Seated in the café, across coffee cups and a selection of cream-laden mille-feuilles and éclairs, I could get a better look at her. She had slipped her magnificent fur coat off her shoulders and let it fall back over the chair in such a way that the label was displayed. Under it she was wearing a striped shirt-style

83

blouse with a gold and jade brooch and matching necklace. In any other town it might have been considered a bit over the top, but not in down-town Zurich. She hadn't changed much in the couple of years since I'd seen her in Mexico City. The Zenas of this world know their priorities, and Zena's number one priority was herself. She was twenty-six years old, and when she did her wide-eyed little girl act she could pass for a few years younger even. A strict regime of facials, work-outs, hair treatments and all the other sorcery seemed to have paid off. I admired her restraint. If only I could mutilate my cream cakes without eating them, the way Zena did it, I would be in better shape too.

'We're back together,' she said triumphantly. She knew how I felt about the shabby way she'd treated Werner, and that was a part of her triumph. 'The poor darling simply can't manage without me.' She looked at me and her eyes narrowed, as if she was about to smile, but the smile never came. 'At least that's what he tells me.'

'Where is he?' I asked.

'You realize that I was on the payroll?' A quick look over her shoulder. 'That London Central had me on the payroll?'

London Central had Zena on the payroll! Like hell I knew. I felt like leaping over the brass rail into the shop window and thrashing about in the meringues. But I did everything I could to conceal my surprise. 'Yes, I heard something about that.'

'I was monitoring Werner. They never fully trusted him, I'm sure you know that London never trusted him?'

She was right about that at least. That was what bugged me about the situation. London Central had never fully trusted Werner. All right: but how could anyone there have put their trust in Zena? She'd consistently demonstrated her powers of self-preservation and her devil-take-the-hindmost philosophy. Who could have considered her as a suitable Departmental employee? 'Is he here in Zurich?' I said. 'I must talk to him. It's official.'

'Official?' She laughed and drank some coffee. She drank double-strength coffee: as black as treacle and almost as heavy. 'You will have your little English jokes, Bernard. Werner has been fired. Kicked out in the most vindictive way those bastards could arrange it. Don't pretend you don't know that?'

'I must see him, Zena. It's very important for both of us.'

'Both of us? You and me, you mean? Or you and Werner?'

It was the sort of cat-and-mouse game that Zena most enjoyed. She knew how to keep Werner under wraps. If she was determined to keep him away from me, Werner would stay away rather than upset her. Zena's tempers were talked of in hushed tones by anyone who'd lived through one. 'All of us,' I said evenly. 'An agent has been killed. I want to talk to Werner before I go to London and talk to them about it. It could save a lot of trouble if we all agree about what we are going to say.' I kept it a bit vague, not being sure whether Zena's employment by London Central was still continuing.

'VERDI, is that it?' she said calmly. 'Well, that's all over and done with.' My God, the woman knew everything. Who else knew? No wonder we'd arrived in Magdeburg to find a corpse.

'Better I talk to Werner,' I said.

She took her time about replying. She finished her coffee, consulted her diamond-studded Carrier watch and looked at herself in a tiny mirror she took from her crocodile handbag. 'I'll go and get him,' she said, snapping the mirror closed and putting it away. 'You wait here.'

'Thanks, Zena,' I said.

'And wipe that blob of cream off your chin,' she said. She was always the nanny.

'Was it Frank Harrington who put you on the payroll?' I asked her.

85

'He's a sweet man,' she said.

'And did you file false reports and get Werner kicked out of Berlin?'

'Of course not,' she said, but after a moment she smiled.

'So that you could be with him here?'

She turned away from me. 'If you say anything like that to Werner, I shall tell him never to speak to you again.'

I waited in case she denied the accusations, but she didn't.

'And Werner will do as I say,' she added, as if I didn't already know it.

'How long will he be, Zena?'

'He's waiting in my car. And I don't want him to eat any cakes. I shall be angry, tell him.'

'I'll tell him, Zena. Sugar in his coffee okay?'

'You've got to have the last word, haven't you, Bernard? You can never learn when to hold your tongue.'

Just because Werner Volkmann allowed Zena to manipulate him so completely did not mean that Werner was in any way a weakling or a wimp. The people who made that mistake about him learned the truth at their cost. Except for his relationship with Zena, Werner was entirely his own man. He was stubborn and methodical. Trying to persuade him to do anything against his will was a futile exercise, even if Zena could twist him around her little finger. But when he arrived in a dark blue business suit, spotted tie and soft black cashmere overcoat with a black fur collar I felt quite sure that Zena had chosen everything he was wearing. Perhaps the silver-topped walking cane was not her idea: that elaboration smacked of Werner.

'You might have dropped me a line, Werner,' I said after he'd hung up his magnificent coat and seated himself. Fresh coffee had arrived, and I was biting into my second cream éclair.

He took a small Filofax sheet from his leather wallet and wrote a phone number on it with a silver pencil before passing it to me. 'I needed time to think,' he said defensively. 'Don't you ever feel you need time to think?'

'No I don't, Werner,' I said. 'If I start off thinking about everything – everything I say and do, and the stupid orders that I sometimes have to obey – high-pressure steam would start coming out of both ears, and I wouldn't know how to stop it.'

'Is that what happened last time?'

'Last time I started thinking? Yes, that's right.'

'I'm sorry Bernie. You're right, I should have written but I was staying away from everyone, not just you.' He was still the same old sleepy-eyed Werner; jet-black bushy hair, straggling eyebrows and strong Berlin accent. The son of a dentist, Werner was born at a time when the Nazis were energetically sending Jews to the death camps. Werner was his 'name for the outside'. I was born the same year as Werner, we went to school together and grew up together. Werner was as near to being a brother as I would ever get, and he measured everything I did or said with that godlike and superior impartiality with which brothers judge each other.

'I went in to get VERDI,' I explained.

'I heard.'

'They wasted him before he could talk.'

'How is Dicky taking that?'

'Dicky Cruyer?'

'VERDI is his baby, isn't he?'

'Not especially.'

'Not especially? How long have you been away, Bernie? Don't you know that VERDI is a big man these days?'

'VERDI was a big man, you mean.'

'Do I? Okay – was a big man, then.' He brought out a handkerchief and wiped his nose. I thought for a moment he was going to serve me up with all the rigmarole about Banner Party No. 5 scaling the heights of the Reichstag, but he mercifully passed over that episode and gave me what sounded more like the real cause of Dicky's distress. 'VERDI went to work in Moscow some time back. When he returned to Berlin he was put in charge of communications security – protection of KGB communications. Not just Stasi ones. You're listening?'

'I'm listening, Werner.'

'A job like that brings a man into contact with codes, cryptographic machines and all the other gimmicks and gizmos.'

'Well, he was never much good at the sharp end,' I said, remembering VERDI and a couple of noteworthy bungles of which I'd taken advantage when he was in the field.

'Yes, well don't let it go to your head, Bernie. VERDI's job as communications supremo made him a hundred times more important than you or I ever could be.'

'And enrolling him was Dicky's baby?' I mused aloud as I thought about the tangled knot of frustration Dicky's face had been during that meeting in Frank's study.

'No, I think the offer came from VERDI originally, but you know how these things are. It's difficult to know how they begin. London was all set. The rumours are that they'd already sold-on some participation to Washington.'

'Everything's got to be run on businesslike lines nowadays, Werner,' I said sarcastically. 'Even London Central.'

Werner gave a small close-lipped smile. He liked lighting the fuse and watching me explode. 'What did you do to your face?'

'I fought off a KGB hit man on the way down here. The son of a bitch nearly killed me.'

'What was he using, this hit man: his handbag or his high-heel shoes?'

'Very funny, Werner. He gave me a lift and waited until I was dozing.'

Werner indicated an almond slice with his fork. 'Do you want that one?' he asked.

'No, you have it,' I said.

Had Werner showed a little more concern I might not have been tempted to tell him in detail about the assault I'd suffered, but with him sitting there eating the almond slice and smiling like a brass Buddha I described exactly what had happened.

'You think he was a KGB hit man?' asked Werner at the end of my story, showing neither sympathy nor alarm.

'Or Stasi.'

'You're crazy, Bernard. They're not recruiting from the football hooligans; not yet anyway. That truck driver was nothing like a professional hit man; you know that if you are honest with yourself.'

'Why?'

'Who did we ever know who would flap and flounder around like that? Tell me one example of the other side sending some muscle-bound lunatic to take out an experienced field agent. A pro with a gun could have got rid of you in one minute.'

'And left holes in his cab?'

'So he tells you to get out ... or maybe uses a prussic-acid vapour-gun, and the coroner would swear you died of a coronary. You know these people, Bernie. They are not like this weirdo you're telling me about.'

'So who was he?'

'How do I know who he was? My guess is that you crossed the path of a madman. There are plenty of them about these days: pathological killers who just want to maim and murder at random and for no real reason.'

'You think that's the answer?'

'Yes, I do. The Autobahnen are dangerous for hitchhikers. Don't you ever read the newspapers?'

'I need Valium before I can face the newspapers these days. Is Zena coming back here?'

'She had to go to the beauty shop or somewhere.'

'Can you spare me some Swiss money?'

'The hairdresser I think it was,' he said, and looked over his shoulder furtively before taking out his wallet and putting a dozen or more 100-franc bills on the table.

'Thanks, Werner. Can you wait a week? I'll send you a cheque.'

'You think I'm a fool, don't you?'

'Your personal life is none of my business, Werner.' I picked up the money and put it in my wallet.

'Be honest.'

'You seemed happy running the hotel with Ingrid. You seemed to suit each other. You told me you were in love with her, and Ingrid loved you, didn't she?'

'I told you I loved Ingrid?' His voice rose in incredulity.

'Don't hedge, Werner. We came back from London together. You told me then.'

He thought about it. 'Perhaps I was in love with Ingrid at one time. I still like Ingrid. But Zena understands me. Isn't it better to have a woman who understands you?'

'No,' I said. 'Certainly not. It's the worst thing that can happen to any man.'

'You're a bastard,' he said. 'What are you going to do about those two women of yours? Are you going to divorce Fiona?'

'Fiona is still not fully recovered,' I said, remembering the way she bit me when we said farewell. 'I thought she was going to have a complete nervous breakdown. Everyone thought that, even the doctor. She doesn't want a divorce. She wants to give marriage another try and so do I. In California we got along just fine. I'm reluctant to abandon her: Fiona can't handle rejection.'

'And Gloria can?'

'Take it easy, Werner.'

'You'll have to face it.'

'Gloria is younger and sexy. Men are lining up to marry her; they always have been. She doesn't have to worry about that.'

'How convenient for you,' said Werner. 'More coffee?'

'No.'

'If you ask my advice, you should stop worrying so much about Fiona and start worrying about yourself.' I looked up. 'Have you looked at yourself in a mirror lately? You look like you've just been rescued from the Atlantic Ocean after ten days in a lifeboat. Never mind about Fiona almost going down with a nervous breakdown. Why don't you go and have a complete physical check-up? Because my guess is that you need attention.'

'I'm all right.'

'You're worrying about your kids. You're worrying about your job. You're worrying about your women. I wouldn't be in your shoes … not for anything.' Werner flagged down a waitress and ordered two more coffees. He was like that. He turned to study me again and said: 'You can't face going to London, can you? You only came here in order to put off the moment of facing those two women of yours.'

'Crap! And I wish you wouldn't keep calling them "those two women of yours", they've got names.'

'So why did you come here then?'

'I wanted you to tell me if the VERDI deal was on the level.'

'What do you mean?'

'They were waiting for us in Magdeburg. When we were on a convenient stretch of road they got nasty.'

'And you think they set all that up for you?'

'Or for anyone else that London Central sent to make contact.'

'But VERDI asked for you.'

'Did he?'

'You said he did.'

'I didn't say that VERDI asked for me.'

'But he did?'

'As a matter of fact, yes he did. But that might have been set up too.'

'And when they don't get you the first time, they send this Dutch lunatic after you?'

'It's possible isn't it?'

'You're getting old and paranoid, Bernie.'

'You weren't there, Werner.' The coffee arrived. 'I shouldn't have any more coffee; it gives me indigestion.'

'Coffee didn't used to give you any problems,' said Werner.

'What do you want to hear me say: that I'm getting older?' I pushed the sugar in his direction and he automatically grabbed it and spooned a lot into his coffee.

'London Central have put out an alert for you.' He looked at his watch. 'At noon today.'

'How do you know?'

'The alert said you were expected in London and didn't arrive.'

'Dicky Cruyer knew I was coming to Zurich. He checked the airline passenger lists.'

'Did you do that again?' Werner laughed. 'And Dicky fell for it? That Dicky never learns, does he? No wonder he got mad and put out an alert.' He laughed again. My subterfuge seemed to put him in a better mood. It was more like the Werner I'd known in the old Berlin days.

'Let's not personalize it,' I said. 'Maybe it's just the computer. It's like that in London nowadays: clocks tick, chips do whatever chips do, and the computer issues an alert or an arrest warrant, airline ticket or a medal or a month's leave with full pay.'

'An all-stations alert,' said Werner grimly. 'Dicky is mad and he's shitting on you.'

'Maybe.'

'You fouled up the VERDI contact and Dicky's getting even.'

'I didn't foul up anything. I had one of Dicky's dumb protégés with me. It was all over long before we arrived there.'

'See it the way Dicky sees it.' He was tense. He poured cream in his coffee, risking Zena's wrath.

'Dicky knew I was coming here.'

'Don't drag me into it,' Werner said. 'I'll help you all I can – you know I will – but don't use me to clobber Dicky.'

'You think VERDI was a genuine offer?'

'You know what I think.'

'No, I've just heard you avoid the question.'

'You've been away too long, Bernie.' Werner alined his coffee and hunched over it to watch the cream swirl around. Without looking up at me, he said: 'The KGB and the Stasi are undergoing agonizing times: re-appraisals and re-evaluations. All the most cynical, ruthless, ambitious roughnecks who clawed, backstabbed and sometimes murdered their peers and superiors to get important jobs and high ranks are exactly the ones who are now prepared to destroy their peers and superiors to become rich and successful working for the West.'

'So you think VERDI was for real?'

'How do I know?'

'And that's why they killed him?'

'What's the use of sitting around guessing, Bernard?'

'Let me know if you hear anything new.'

'Sure I will. Has Gloria got a fax machine in her apartment?' he said archly.

'Lay off me, Werner. We've both got woman troubles, haven't we?'

For a moment I thought he was going to deny it. 'Would you like me to pay for the coffees?'

'I haven't got small change, Werner, you know that.' He gave a prim smile, looked at the bill and put some coins on the table.

'That was hard on Fiona,' he said. 'Losing her sister like that must have been devastating.'

'That's the word, all right.'

'I was in my car on the Munich Autobahn when they told me Fiona had been killed,' said Werner. 'That's what they told me, at first. It was ages afterwards that I finally discovered that Fiona was with you in California. Everyone was saying that you'd run off with Tessa. People were even saying you'd been seen together in Australia and so on – you know how the rumours circulate in our business.'

'I saw Tessa killed,' I said.

'The DDR people misidentified the body? Is that what happened?' Werner was sounding me out.

'You know how slowly they work over there.'

'But that suited London, I suppose,' said Werner archly. 'It gave them time to use Fiona's secret material, while the Stasi thought the secrets had died with her. And Dicky too. In those first few hours they were saying that Dicky had been shot.'

'Dicky! I wish someone had shot him! It was all his fault. He took Tessa to Berlin. He shared a hotel room with her and registered in my name.'

'But Dicky wasn't at the shoot-out?'

'No. It was another London man. A fumbling amateur. The whole thing was a typical London Central balls-up,' I said.

'Or a very artful plan,' said Werner.

He got up and paid. We both put on our overcoats and in silence pushed through the doors and out into the cold street. 'It's going to snow,' I said.

'How are you going to handle Dicky Cruyer?' he said as we began our walk back towards the hotel.

'The hell with Dicky,' I said.

'You still don't get it, do you?' said Werner, and stopped walking.

'Get what?'

'Look,' said Werner, almost bursting with suppressed vexation. 'London Central sends you to contact VERDI. You go back to Dicky and Frank, and tell them he's dead. What are they supposed to think?'

'Think?'

'My God, Bernie, but you are *dumm*! They are going to think that you killed him or at least arranged the killing.'

'Of VERDI?' It was of course exactly what Frank had warned me about, but I'd dismissed it as just another manifestation of Frank's paternalism.

'And then you come to Zurich to find me and talk to me. Didn't you know that London Central are telling the world that I'm a double, working out of Berlin and selling London's secrets?'

'No one believes that, Werner.'

'Dicky does, Frank does. All those coordination and research zombies in London do. They all think I'm a double. And now they'll think you're a double too.'

'Because I've come here to talk with you?'

'Well ask yourself. They'll say I'm your case officer and you came to be debriefed. It all fits together, doesn't it?'

'Not to me it doesn't.'

'Well you're not working in London Central.'

'But I will be,' I said.

'Don't count on it, Bernie,' said Werner sadly. 'Dicky has been dreaming of the day he'd get rid of you, and you've served him every excuse he needs on a silver platter.'

'Why would I want to murder VERDI instead of bringing him back? There's no motivation, Werner.'

Werner gave an angry grunt and said: 'Save those stories for Frank and Dicky, and all those desk-bound schlemiels in London. I was there that day when they brought you in, Bernard. That day in Berlin. Remember?'

I didn't say anything.

'VERDI is the cold-blooded creep who had you thrown out of the Warsaw–Berlin Express. You're not going to deny it, are you, Bernard?'

'Better we don't resurrect old mishaps.'

'Mishaps? I was there when they brought you in. Your dad almost went berserk. The surgeon was asking one of the nurses to find out what religion you were, and get hold of a priest.'

'You always exaggerate, Werner. There's no conclusive evidence that VERDI had anything to do with that. And if London Central start thinking he had, they'll really start believing I might have wasted him.' He didn't reply. I slapped him on the back and said: 'See you around, Werner.'

I left him at Paradeplatz, standing at the roadside like a forlorn bear watching Goldilocks stealing off with his bowl of porridge. Although the traffic signals were against me, I hurried across the road, glancing back to give him a final wave. I was almost on the pavement when some stupid kid on a little motor bike came roaring around the corner and brushed close enough to make me lose my balance as I jumped to safety. As I straightened up, I shouted after the man on the motor bike, who shouted back and turned out to be a shrill and angry young woman. Then I smoothed my coat and pushed my hat into place and looked back in the hope that Werner had not witnessed the incident.

'They keep trying,' Werner called, and grinned at me. It seemed to amuse him that I'd almost been knocked over. Had I not known him so well I might have thought he was gloating. But that was never Werner's style, and our partnership went back too far for that: from the time that we were children. But there was no mistaking the fact that Werner's stance, the burly figure, feet apart, and one hand deep in overcoat pocket and the other holding his walking stick, showed reserves of power and

confidence in a way I did not remember. I had always dominated our partnership. I had always been the forceful one, with
Werner cautious, temporizing and needing me as a nursemaid.
Now I was chagrined to find it the other way round: Werner
was calm and amused and calling the tune, and I was anxious
and asking advice and narrowly avoiding getting killed in the
traffic.

6

'So – here is pain?' I felt the dental probe touch the molar.

'No,' I said.

'This is all then,' said the dentist. 'Nothing wrong!' He held the probe aloft for a moment, like a conjuror with a wand, before placing it back on the tray with a serried array of other instruments. Then he swung the illuminated magnifier away from the dental chair. 'Now you will rinse the mouth.' The girl, with that mask of professional inscrutability that nurses wear at work, stretched out a hand to give me a paper towel, a pink one that doesn't show the blood.

I had no desire to rinse the mouth but I did so dutifully, as his Swiss patients no doubt rinsed when commanded. Zurich dentists seem to enjoy full appointment books; this one had only agreed to see me because I said it was an emergency. And in the middle of the night, in the hotel room, it had seemed like an emergency. I awoke in panic unable to remember where I was. My jaw had ached and I thought all my teeth were about to fall out. 'I'm sorry to have bothered you,' I said, remembering the scowls and glares from the patients in the waiting-room as I was admitted to the surgery ahead of them.

'The teeth are in good condition,' proclaimed the dentist as he washed his hands. 'Cleaning and scaling needed, yes. Also two old fillings that must soon be made again.' He nodded to his nurse and said in Swiss-German: 'Who's out there?' Thus dismissed, I climbed out of the dental chair and held out my billfold in an age-old gesture of repentance.

'Frau Mettler is next, Herr Doctor; the hairline crack.'

'How did you have this injury, Mr Samson?' he asked.

'I was mugged,' I said.

'I will not charge you,' he told me, looking first at my face and the bruise that had now turned black and purple and spread across my cheek almost to my ear, and then at Werner's money.

'Doctor, I'm sure …'

'You have been listening to too many stories about Swiss dentists, Mr Samson. I regret you have such a bad experience in my country. Have a good vacation.'

'Thank you,' I said. 'But it happened in Germany.'

'In that case one hundred francs,' he said.

From the dentist's reception I phoned the travel agent again, but my position on the waiting list had not changed. I was still confirmed on the last flight to London. I phoned Fiona and told her to expect me late.

With a day at my disposal I decided to go in search of my brother-in-law, and thus substantiate the explanation I'd given Frank Harrington for my visit to Switzerland.

It was not a long journey south along the lake, but the taxi-meter clicked and the fare grew to alarming totals as I had him drive down side roads that dead-ended at the lake so that I could see along the waterfront. Finally I spotted the place I was looking for: a neat modern house and, tied to a distinctive pier, the sleek cabin cruiser of which George was once so proud.

When I rang the buzzer my brother-in-law answered the door and registered surprise.

'On your own?' he said.

'What were you expecting, George, an American Express tour group?'

He didn't answer for a moment. He was looking over my shoulder watching the road, and didn't speak again until the taxi that brought me had turned round and driven away. 'No one with you?'

'What's wrong, George?'

'What happened to your face?'

'A misunderstanding,' I said.

He nodded and decided not to pursue it. 'How did you get this address? Did I give it to you?' He seemed disturbed that I had found him, and his flat cockney accent emerged now and again from his posh English.

'I don't know the address. I remembered that framed photo of the house you had on the wall of your office. Are you going to invite me in?'

'Come in, Bernard,' he said mechanically. 'Office?'

'The office in Southwark.'

'Oh, that dump. Did I have a photo of this house on the wall?'

'A big framed colour photo.'

'Of course.' He snapped his fingers: he was much given to snapping his fingers. 'I've often wondered where that picture went.' He scratched his head with a fingertip as if to demonstrate the wondering. 'That idiot of a manager must have left it behind when we moved.'

'Yes,' I said.

George was a short energetic Londoner of Polish extraction. He had heavy horn-framed glasses that he liked to prop on the end of his nose. His greying hair was wavy and always beautifully cut, as were his suits and shirts. For George was one of those enviable people for whom the secret of making money was no secret.

'You found the house by remembering that photo?' I could see he didn't completely believe me.

'It wasn't too difficult, George,' I said. 'I'd seen it in your holiday snapshots as well as that framed aerial photo. Your green mansard roof, and your boat and pier, were easy to spot from the lakeside. And with your garage doors open, your Rolls, with its British registration plate, is visible from the street.'

'I forgot you were a bloody detective,' he said with a bitter smile. 'Don't just stand there. For heaven's sake, take off your coat. Have a drink? You didn't phone? Whisky? Gin? Vodka?'

'A cup of coffee?' I asked as he took my old coat from me and gave it to a young girl in a servant's apron who appeared from nowhere.

'Sure,' said George. 'Two cups of coffee, Ursi. Can you work that new machine, dear?' She said she could. 'I've just bought a big espresso machine,' he turned to me to explain. 'I thought; here I am every morning, climbing into that damned motor car and driving seven kilometres to get a decent cup of coffee. I'll buy a proper machine, like the ones they have in hotels. Saves time; saves money.'

'And it's better for the environment,' I said.

'For what?' He frowned, as if suspecting that this was a comment on the pretty blonde maid. 'Oh yes, pollution, the car exhaust.' He relaxed a little. 'You're right. Sit down, Bernard.' He was thawing a little now, but he was still searching for a reason behind my unannounced appearance.

George and Tessa Kosinski had owned this house for several years, but until recently it had been a place for their holidays. Now George had left England for good and had announced his intention of spending all his time here. We were in a large room, one wall of glass giving a panoramic view of the lake and the pier where George's motor launch was tied. The furnishings were modern, coarsely woven linen and brightly coloured rugs upon a beautifully maintained parquet floor. The only visible connections with his previous life were some items of antique furniture that I'd seen in the Mayfair flat he had vacated immediately after his wife's death.

There was a fireplace where a shiny brown log, like a neglected cigar, had one end turning into grey ash perfuming the air with smoke as sweet as incense. Over the fireplace there was a large oil-painting: a modernist impression of the Alps in large hurried strokes that exactly matched the colours in the carpet and curtains. Two angular leather sofas, covered in imitation zebra skin, were placed each side of a large inlaid coffee table where magazines and books were arranged in fan patterns. I sat down and offered my hands to the fire. George was striding around the room, but I was used to his displays of surplus energy, which I suppose was what he channelled into action in business deals when he wanted to make money. At least that's what Tessa had once said of him when complaining of being neglected.

'You took a chance?' he said. 'Took a chance that I would be at home?'

'Yes, that's right. I'm booked on the evening plane. I went to the dentist this morning, and when he said I didn't need treatment I thought I'd come and seek you out.'

'I'm not officially resident,' he said. 'I've applied to the canton but it's not so easy becoming a resident here these days. They want to be quite sure you're not a drugs baron or a terrorist.'

'Sounds reasonable,' I said.

'So they told you my phone is bugged did they?'

'No. Is it? Who do you mean? Who would tell me that?'

'The crowd you work for. That's why you didn't phone, eh?'

'This visit's nothing to do with the people I work for,' I said. 'They don't know I'm here.'

'You didn't tell them?'

'Well, I did mention it as a matter of fact.'

'Why?'

'Your name came up. I was looking for an excuse to come here and didn't want to tell them the real reason.'

The maid arrived and put a tray on the table. George stopped his restless striding to inspect the milk frothed high upon the espresso coffee in his fine china. He cut the froth with a spoon to test its texture. Then he picked up one of the Brunsli, the little spicy chocolate biscuits the Swiss eat in the winter, and bit a piece from it. Satisfied, he dropped his weight into the leather sofa opposite me and stretched out his legs to put his hand-sewn Ferragamo moccasins upon the low table. 'Thanks, Ursi,' he said, without turning his head to her, and with such gruff indifference that I wondered if the exchange was for my benefit. 'Since two weeks after I got here,' he said accusingly with his hands clasped behind his head. 'You can hear the clicks.' He popped the rest of the biscuit into his mouth. 'Help yourself, Bernard.'

'Maybe that's not the reason, George. Clicks on bugged phones were eliminated a decade or more ago. And the Swiss are not the sort of people who use outdated technology. Did you notice the pistols they issue to the soldiers and the cops: SIGs? It's the Rolls-Royce of hand-guns. The US Army went down on their hands and knees asking for them as replacements for their Colts, but Uncle Sam bought Berettas instead, at a quarter of the Swiss price. No, you won't hear any clicks if the boys from Berne are tapping your phone.'

He wasn't to be distracted by such ploys. 'I know what's happening, Bernard. If it's not the Swiss then maybe it's the Russians or the Germans or your lot. But someone is listening in.'

'And I'm party to it?' I said, betraying enough amusement to annoy him.

'Well, are you?'

'Of course not.'

'Do you know how long I waited before anyone told me Tessa was dead?'

'Believe me, George …'

'A month. Over a month: thirty-two long miserable days. Even then they wouldn't say where she died, how she died, or who did it.'

'She died in East Germany, George. On the Berlin Autobahn. The communists do everything at a snail's pace. The inquiries are probably still continuing. That's not in itself sinister.'

'They hinted that Tessa had run off with you. Did you know that?'

'I do now,' I said.

'Someone else said she went to Berlin with that fellow Cruyer. I'll get to the bottom of it if I have to spend all my life and every last penny doing it.'

'George,' I said. 'Don't say that.'

'I will say it. I vow it. I'll run them down, whoever is responsible, I'll find them. If you've come here to dissuade me you are wasting your time.'

'I didn't say don't do it, George. I warned you not to go around saying you're doing it.' I let that sink in. George picked up his cup and, holding his other hand to protect his sea-island cotton shirt from drips, sipped his coffee reflectively. I drank my coffee too.

'Have you eaten lunch?' said George. There was no missing the significance of this question. It was an armistice. I had got through to him.

'I weigh nearly one hundred and ninety pounds,' I said. 'I'm cutting down.'

'Ursi will make us something non-fattening: home-made muesli with grated apples and oat flakes – Ursi's mother's recipe … Or a sandwich made from some of the lousy tinned ham my local shop sells. You won't eat too much of that, believe me.'

'That's very considerate, George. Ham. Thank you, yes.'

'Ursi!' he called loudly. When her voice came in reply, he told her to fix us some sandwiches, and after that she could take the Honda and have a couple of hours off duty.

104

'Better we eat here,' said George. 'Can't talk in my local restaurant, nor in any eating place round here. People eavesdrop all the time. In these little communities everybody wants to know a newcomer's business.'

We drank our coffee and talked about how good the froth was, how long it took him to get to the airport, what the weather had been like and how well we were both looking. We listened to the sounds of the electric can-opener and the electric bread-slicer and the toaster and the microwave where the butter was softened. When the food came, we continued to exchange small-talk while we chewed our toasted ham sandwiches. I wanted to look at him. I wanted to know how he was taking the death of Tessa.

'Goodbye,' shouted the maid.

'It's not what you think,' he said, after we'd watched the Honda narrowly avoid hitting the gate, turn on to the road and drive away with the brake lights shining. 'Me and Ursula. It's not what you think.'

'I haven't come to spy on you, George.'

'Then why did you come?'

'Fiona is back in London. We both want to thank you for letting us have the place in Mayfair.'

'No thanks to me. That was Tessa's bequest to her sister.'

'You bought the lease,' I reminded him.

'I gave it to Tessa as a birthday present. It was hers to dispose of as she wished. I took the pieces of furniture that were my own possessions.' Then suddenly he added: 'Anyway I like you having it, Bernard. I hope you and Fiona will be very happy living there.'

'That's generous, George. Fiona is planning to keep one of the rooms solely for your use when you come to London.'

'Don't do that, Bernard.' He was so alarmed that he leaned forward as if about to stand up, but then relaxed to lean back

105

into the sofa again. 'No. My accountant would have a fit. I've left England for good. I'm not allowed back there – tax-wise I mean.'

'Fiona's father wants to call a family meeting to discuss Tessa's trust fund. You, me, everyone.'

'I know. I spoke on the phone with him. But I can't go to England.' He leaned forward and said: 'The day after the official notification finally arrived he sent a lawyer to me at Mount Street, demanding that I tell him where Tessa was buried. I said: What do you think I've been asking the bloody Foreign Office every day, with a dozen follow-up letters, and more phone calls than I can count? Go round and do your demanding to those Foreign Office bastards, I said. He gets my goat. But it's no good shouting at a lawyer.'

'I suppose the old man was beside himself,' I said in mitigation, although my own feelings about our mutual father-in-law were as vehement as George's.

'All he was concerned with was formal certification of death. I suspect he's put Tessa on the boards of some of his fake companies and all kinds of other capers: you know what a crook he is. I hate him, but he came round to seeing things my way in the end.' As George was saying this I noticed that his hand was trembling. He put down his coffee, but not without spilling some in the saucer.

'Take it easy, George,' I said.

'Don't tell me to take it easy.' His eyes were fixed on me, glinting and half-closed in anger. 'You haven't lost anything or anybody. For all I know you've been promoted. What did I do to deserve having her taken from me? I spent my whole life working hard, and all I ever got was trouble.' He wiped his lips with his linen napkin. 'She jumped into bed with everyone she met,' he said, and I realized that I was still not eliminated from his list of suspects.

'I thought we'd settled all that, George,' I protested. 'There was never anything between me and Tessa. Never.'

106

'And when I finally brought myself to believing that her betrayals were at an end, she was taken from me.'

I had never seen my brother-in-law so distressed. 'You must look to the future,' I said, hoping that a few platitudes might help him recover his equilibrium. 'You can't spend the rest of your life grieving for her.'

'I can and I will,' he said. 'And so will the others.'

'Others?'

'Fiona and the old man.'

'Fiona?'

'That's not why you're here?' said George, and for a moment we floundered in mutual confusion.

'Fiona?' I said.

'You didn't see the letters?'

'What letters?'

'Fiona has agreed to help me track down the murderer. We've exchanged long letters about it and we are keeping in touch by phone. I spoke with her this morning, and she will be keeping her father informed now that she's back living in London.'

'Wait a minute, George. You spoke to Fiona this morning? Do you mean that Fiona is encouraging you in this crusade to avenge Tessa's death?'

'Crusade?' For a moment he seemed as if he was going to take offence, but then he said: 'Very well. Crusade. Yes, let's call it a crusade. She's Tessa's sister, isn't she? When you said you weren't here officially, I thought Fiona had sent you with a message. That's why I got rid of Ursi.'

'No one sent me. I told you that.'

'The old man is putting one hundred grand into the hat.'

Persuading my father-in-law to contribute such a vast sum to a project without prospect of financial return was an amazing feat. Now I was even more confused. 'As a reward?'

'Reward; bribe; lobbying; other types of political pressure. Money will be needed. We must try everything. Her death was no accident. The authorities will not come clean unless they are pressed. You know that, Bernard.'

'Who are you approaching?'

He didn't hear me. 'Yes, Fiona is as keen as I am.' He paused to reflect upon that extravagant claim. 'At least she's not putting up a lot of objections.'

'But how are you tackling it?'

He suddenly became wary. 'I can't tell you any names or other details, Bernard. You'll understand that, I'm sure. But we have a reliable lawyer working for us in Berlin. Fiona gave me the contacts and I eventually found an experienced man and started the ball rolling. I've promised him a fifty grand bonus if there is a witness, named culprit and convincing evidence.'

'You're playing with dynamite, George. How do you know you won't be swindled?'

'Fiona knows what's what. She worked in the East, didn't she? We're using a man she's worked with.'

'A man she worked with? I hope not, George. I've spent my whole life dealing with these people – the KGB and Stasi and all those other hoodlums. They play rough, George. It's no game for an amateur to get into.'

He smiled. 'I know, Bernard. I've seen it on the movies.'

'Yes, but these guys don't use stunt men with tomato ketchup.'

'I was brought up in the East End of London, Bernard. I know how to look after myself.'

He brushed a hand along his head as if smoothing his hair, which was not out of place. He was calmer now, but I knew it was no good trying to make him see sense. 'I should be pushing along,' I said. 'Can you call a taxi for me?'

'No problem.' He dialled for a cab. 'Five minutes,' he told me. 'Do you want a plaster on that bad cut?'

'I heal quickly,' I said. 'Look, if things go sour, call me. I plan to be in London for the next few weeks.'

'Thanks, Bernard. And since Fiona seems to have been taking me literally, about not telling anyone, perhaps you'd wait until she breaks it to you.'

'Yes, it's probably better like that.' I looked at him and worried. 'And forget what I said about the clicks, George. Maybe you are right.'

'I'd already forgotten, Bernard. Anyway, on the day after tomorrow I'm getting an electronics expert in to check the line.' He laughed. Talking about his plans seemed to have a salutary effect upon him. He was very cheerful now, very relaxed and confident, but in his circumstances that was the very worst way to be.

7

Fiona loved to go to bed ridiculously early and then spend hours reading. In the old days I remember countless times when I arrived home late to find her sound asleep: propped up in bed, lights on, head lolling, clasping some heavy tome of tedious official material that her conscience had demanded she read. So when I got back from Zurich, late at night, I was quite prepared to find her tucked up in bed. But I could not have been more wrong; I had never seen her more animated.

Not having a key to our new luxurious home in Mount Street, I had to ring the doorbell. Fiona opened it wearing a white chef's apron over a bright cobalt-blue acrylic vee-neck and dark blue pleated skirt. On her feet she had pumps, and her hair was clipped back in a severe style that I'd seen her apply when working in East Berlin. But there any resemblance to the woman I'd seen in her communist office ended, for tonight Fiona was radiant and bubbling over with joy.

'It's bliss, Bernard,' she said. 'Pure bliss. Two floors. I'd forgotten all the rooms upstairs. It's vast.'

We embraced and kissed. 'I missed you,' I said. I knew she'd noticed my bruised face but she didn't remark on it. She knew I would talk about it when I was ready: we understood each other very well.

110

'I so wanted us to sit down and dine together,' she said. 'But you probably had dinner on the plane.'

'What can I smell: not ossobuco?' I put my coat on a hook and looked around at our new home.

'You'll think me an imbecile, Bernard,' she said, breaking away from me while still holding one of my hands. 'It's such a heavenly kitchen that I simply had to cook something. Can you truly eat again?'

'Yes,' I said. Fiona never got excited in the frenzied way her sister did, but I could see that being in London and in this flat had had a powerful effect upon her.

'We must give a party here,' she said. 'A house-warming. Look at the dining-room. George replaced the dining-table that he took away with a far superior one.' She slid back the door to reveal the tiled dining-room where I'd enjoyed more than one spectacular dinner party. There were two places set, as for a formal dinner.

'He took the old table because it belonged to his parents,' I said. 'It holds memories for him.'

'I couldn't resist using Tessa's lovely china. Shall we eat here?'

'Wonderful idea.'

'Open a bottle of wine,' she said. 'There's a mysterious wine cupboard with a temperature control. George left six cases of wine and spirits, and masses of lovely linen and lots and lots of china.'

I followed her into the kitchen. She snatched hot bread rolls from the double oven, dropped them into a basket and gave it to me. 'Take these, and put one of those tiled stands on the table for the hot casserole.'

'What timing.'

'I phoned the airport. I knew you'd landed.'

While I opened a bottle of George's Barolo Riserva Speciale and poured it, she opened the second oven and using kitchen gloves pulled out an orange-coloured iron pot from which came

111

a rich aroma of veal and lemon and anchovy and all the other exotic ingredients of which Fiona's special recipe was composed.

She put it on the metal pot-stand on the table and sat down. 'Do serve it, darling,' she said, and picked up a glass of wine and sipped some. As I began, she used a concealed switch to dim and douse the lights in the adjoining drawing-room, so that the only illumination came from the tiny spotlights over the table. 'More romantic,' she explained, and leaned over to kiss me on the cheek. I saw us reflected in the big mirror at the far end of the darkened drawing-room; it was like a few frames from a movie that used to be our life.

'What a surprise,' I said, looking at her shining eyes. 'If I'd known how happy it would make you, I would have bought you a luxury Mayfair apartment years ago.' I used a large silver spoon to serve the veal knuckle slices. One each. 'Wow! How long since I tasted this?' I served the rice and cabbage too.

'How many years have we wasted, darling?' she asked rhetorically. She tasted a forkful of veal, but seemed more interested in studying me as I ate, as if her enjoyment was gained entirely from my pleasure, as a mother might feed a favourite son returning home after a long absence.

'I saw George,' I said. 'I had to be in Zurich so I dropped in on him.' I drank some of the beautiful wine. George always served expensive wine. It was going to be a major let-down when we finished the bottles he'd bequeathed us.

'Dear George,' she said. 'He's such a dedicated Londoner; I can't imagine him ever settling down in that funny little house in Switzerland.'

'He has his consolations,' I said.

'In what form?'

'In the shapely form of a twenty-year-old blonde named Ursula.' In response to Fiona's raised eyebrows, I said: 'He swears she's just there to stir his muesli.'

'But you don't believe him?'

'I think he's dipping into her fondue,' I said solemnly.

'I hate you,' she said and offered a playful clout at me, but she laughed while doing it. 'Seriously,' she said. 'Is George all right?'

'No. He says he's fine, but anyone can see he's taking it badly. Very badly.'

'He's a passionate man,' she said. 'But his religion must be a comfort for him.'

'He didn't mention religion.' I was remembering George's unrestrained vows of vengeance. 'Did he write to you?' I asked her.

'George? Oh, yes.'

'About Tessa?'

'Of course.'

'There was some wild talk about pursuing some kind of vendetta.'

'Tessa was so young, Bernard. Not in years perhaps, but so very young in her ways. She made everyone feel protective.'

'George is swearing to track down her killers.'

'Poor man,' she said. I looked at her but failed to see into her mind. Did she think that one of the rounds I fired that night killed her sister? Or were some of her memories pushed away beyond recall?

'He said you are helping him,' I prompted.

'Of course I am,' she said mildly. 'I would do anything for him. After all he's my brother-in-law.'

'Yes, well, he's my brother-in-law too,' I said. 'But I draw the line at encouraging him to declare war on Moscow single-handed.'

'He'll be all right.'

I looked at her hardly able to believe my ears. Here was Fiona, one of the most mature people I'd ever met. I'd seldom seen her anything but professional and composed, reticent and cautious. This was the woman who was constantly being spoken of as a possible Director-General, and now she was condoning some wild unlawful caper by a disturbed man who knew nothing of the hazards he faced. 'Look, Fiona, have you put him in touch with any of those KGB people we both know?'

'Do stop fussing, Bernard. Your dinner is getting cold.'

'It's delicious,' I said, dabbing my bread into the gravy.

She was giving all her attention to tearing her bread roll to pieces. Soon there were tiny fragments of bread arranged all around the rim of her plate. 'What do you expect me to do?' she said suddenly. 'Tessa was my sister.'

'Grieve for her, darling. We all do. But there is no sense encouraging George in his bizarre ideas.'

'Give him time,' said Fiona. 'I hope you didn't make him more agitated. It's better to let him think he can get revenge. He'll simmer down, I know him better than you do.'

'I hope you do. He scared the life out of me.' We continued to eat our dinner in silence after that. I was reassured to see the way she ate it all. 'That was wonderful, darling,' I said when I finished, and gave her a kiss. 'Have you been crying?'

She touched her cheek with a finger and smiled bravely: 'My eyes? It was the onions.'

'Ossobuco takes hours to cook. How long ago were you chopping onions?'

'Oh for God's sake, Bernard. I'm not going to sit here and be interrogated.'

'I worry about you. Perhaps this flat is not the best place for you to be.'

'Because of Tessa, you mean?' She took one of the fragments of bread and reaching over began dabbing it into the gravy in the bottom of the iron pot. 'Yes, before I arrived here, I worried. I thought the idea that everything here was hers – her furniture, her pictures, everything – would perhaps be more than I could bear.

114

But it wasn't like that. The first night I stayed awake of course, but then I told myself that I had nothing to fear from Tessa's ghost. She wouldn't come back and harm me, would she, Bernard?' Having dabbed the bread into the gravy unnumbered times, she put it in her mouth and chewed it in a distracted manner.

'Of course not, darling,' I said and smiled, not sure how much of all this metaphysics was a sign that Fiona was coming apart.

'Her ghost is here of course. I see her everywhere. She's watching me. I heard her laugh even …' Fiona frowned.

'There is nothing to fear, darling,' I said.

'I told her that,' said Fiona.

'But she wouldn't want George going off on a crusade on her behalf, would she?'

'Why not? You don't know Tessa as I do. That's exactly what she would want. Think about it. Do you believe she'd ever rest if her death went unavenged?'

'Wait a minute, darling,' I said. 'Tessa is dead. She's dead and we can't do anything to bring her back to life again. We can't hear her laughing, or know what she wants in the way of vengeance. She can't hear us, and we can't hear her. You've got to accept that as a fact.'

'But she can, Bernard.'

'Being alone in a place like this can play tricks with the imagination,' I said. 'It's quite old, this building. There are always strange noises. Hot water systems cool, the woodwork creaks and so on. It can be very deceptive. Let Tessa rest in peace.'

Fiona got to her feet. 'But that's just it, Bernard. Until she's avenged she cannot rest. That's exactly what George said to me and I agree with him.'

I said nothing. She went to the kitchen to get a bowl of fresh fruit.

'Did it all go well for you?' Fiona asked when she returned with it.

'It was a shambles,' I said. 'The man we were supposed to collect was dead. They're still picking up the pieces. And I got a kick in the face.'

She looked at me and nodded. 'You must see a doctor in the morning.'

'I saw a doctor: I'm fine.'

'I knew something must have gone amiss,' said Fiona. 'Dicky arrived in the office breathing fire and saying that someone had betrayed the operation. He saw you in Berlin but you slipped away, he said. What happened?'

'When Dicky has to face the consequences of his own incompetence, he always roars around shouting that he's been betrayed.'

'He immediately set up a conference. He went bursting into a meeting of the estimates committee in the big conference room, and told them there was an operational emergency and threw them out. They had to hold their meeting in the D-G's ante-room. That was the only place available. They were spitting mad.' She related this story without focusing on Dicky. She spoke about him as if he were someone she hardly knew. And yet I was sure she blamed Dicky for taking Tessa to Berlin. If Tessa had stayed at home with George she'd still be alive. Fiona had told me that more than once.

'When did you first go into the office?'

Fiona turned and looked at me. 'Bernard, you must speak to her.' I didn't have to ask. She meant Gloria Kent, with whom I'd been living until I discovered that Fiona's defection to the East was all part of a long-term deception plan which had never been confided to me.

'You know I'm going to do that, sweetheart,' I promised once again.

'I thought she was going to university.'

'The Department let her down. They promised to continue paying her while she was studying and then changed their minds.'

'There must be all sorts of other scholarships,' said Fiona wistfully.

'I'm sure the present situation … with you being there, is just as difficult for her,' I said.

'She's waiting for you to marry her,' said Fiona with a brave smile that she had trouble holding on to.

'Of course she isn't. She knows I'm married to you.'

'If Daddy hadn't collected the children from her …' She stopped and I filled in the spaces. She was thinking of how she might now be asking Gloria if she could visit her own children. She'd probably spent a long time thinking about it.

'Don't be ungrateful, darling,' I said. 'What would have happened to the children if Gloria hadn't looked after them?'

'Daddy wanted them all along.'

I clenched my lips tight. The truth was that David Timothy Kimber-Hutchinson, Fiona's father, had been his usual autocratic uncooperative self when I'd asked for his help with the children. In any case, if Fiona would only admit the truth, she would have to say that any choice between having one's children under the care of Gloria Kent or exposing them to the long-term influence of her mischief-making old fool of a father was no choice at all. 'He could have done worse than leaving them with Gloria.'

'He said they were running wild.'

'I doubt that. She was trying to work in the office and look after the children too,' I said calmly and mildly. 'She did the best she could.'

'Is that what she told you?'

'I haven't discussed it with her, you know I haven't. Once I heard that your father had swooped in and grabbed the children there was nothing to discuss.'

117

'Swooped in and grabbed them,' she repeated. 'We're indebted to Gloria for looking after them, I notice, but when Daddy rescues them – and gets them a place in a good private school at short notice, pays their fees and does everything – he is said to have swooped in and grabbed them.'

'Don't let's argue about the children,' I said. My face was aching again, I suppose it was something to do with the bruising and the blood circulation. 'We both only want what's best for them.'

'So does Daddy.'

'Yes, of course,' I said. Fiona looked at me. She knew I was bursting to add that Gloria also wanted only what was best for them. I counted to ten and then said: 'But you must admit, it was you who left the children. It wasn't me or Gloria who created the problem.'

'How dare you say I abandoned them? You had them in your care. It was you who gave them to a stranger.'

Both of us were crippled with that English inability to discuss anything truly important. Perhaps I should have been more brutal and told her that now she would have to live with the consequences of her heroic escapade, even if it meant being a stranger to her children. I put my arm round her shoulder but she stiffened. 'We'll sort it out,' I said. 'When we go and see the children at the weekend we'll sort it out.'

She sipped some wine and then wiped her lips. 'I'm sorry, Bernard. I spent all day telling myself that when you arrived we mustn't get into a squabble about Daddy and the children.' She stood up and began clearing the table, collecting the plates and cutlery.

'Everyone means well,' I said. 'Everyone is trying to help.'

'I can't work alongside her,' said Fiona. 'And I won't.'

'You won't have to.'

'Suppose they assign me to the Hungary desk?'

'Yes, well Hungary is the place where it's all going to happen,' I said. 'If we can get the Hungarians to open their border, the DDR would have to fortify that entire frontier to prevent their people crossing over. That might prove the last straw for the regime.'

'It's a big if,' said Fiona, who was determined not to be cheered up. 'And meanwhile Miss Kent is running the Hungary desk.' She put down the plates and cutlery and stood there as if she'd forgotten what she was about to do.

'Not …?'

'No, she hasn't actually got the desk; she's just working there. But she speaks Hungarian like a native. What chance do I have working in a department with a chief already established, and Gloria a living encyclopedia on Hungary and everything Hungarian?'

'Tell Dicky you want to work somewhere else,' I said. 'He's Ops supremo for the time being: he could put you anywhere you want.'

'I asked for Northern Ireland, but Dicky said that was out of the question.'

'Why? It's up for grabs I hear.'

'You know why. It's the old boy network. It will go to some boozy someone with drinking companions in the army and "Five" and the RUC. Belfast is reserved for political nominees these days.'

'Maybe it's just as well. I wouldn't like to see you embroiled in all that Irish mess and mayhem. Belfast is too dangerous for a woman.'

'You sound like Dicky.'

'Dicky has to get it right once in a while, just by the law of averages.'

'Yes. And I wish you would try harder to see that. You make trouble for yourself by openly displaying your contempt for him. It undermines his authority.'

'I'll talk to Gloria tomorrow,' I said. 'I promise.'

'She'll be in the Data Centre. They are working hard burying their mistakes inside one of those very very thick reports for the Minister, in the hope that he'll not have time to winkle out the bits they need to conceal.'

'Wherever she is, I'll find her and talk to her. I promise.'

'She visits the children every week. Every week! She takes them presents and sends them cards. Sometimes her father goes too; the children call him "Uncle".'

'She goes to your father's home to see them?'

'Daddy won't hear a word said against her,' said Fiona. 'She's won him over completely.'

'Well, well.' Fiona's father always became totally gaga in the presence of any nubile girl, but it was easy to understand why Fiona felt isolated.

'Just tell her it's all over. Thank her for looking after the children and all that. But make sure she knows it's all over. You're happily married. Married to me. And I don't want her visiting my children.'

I nodded. Fiona's stories about Tessa's ghost may or may not have been passing delusions, but her feelings about Gloria were unmistakably heartfelt and chronic. 'Tell me something, darling,' I said. 'When Tessa made her Will assigning this flat and its contents over to you, you were in Berlin working for the DDR. What would you have done with an apartment in London?'

'Sold it, I suppose,' said Fiona, eyeing me warily.

'And thrown George out?'

'Perhaps Tessa knew George wouldn't want to remain here if anything happened to her. Perhaps they discussed it. Or perhaps some lawyer framed the terms of the Will. Anyway, who could have guessed Tessa would predecease George and me?' Fiona offered me the fruit bowl. 'The pears are ripe. Shall I give you a clean plate?'

'No thanks,' I said. 'So did you tell Tessa that your defection was all a stunt? Did you hint to her that eventually you hoped to return to normal duty and life in London?'

'But didn't tell you my secret? Is that what's troubling you?'

'Well, did you?' Changing my mind, I took back my meat plate from where she had stacked it and took a pear and started to peel it with the knife I'd used for the veal.

'You need a clean plate and a fruit knife.' Having left two small plates ready, she now reached for them and gave me one, together with a fruit knife. She took the pear from my hand and put it on the clean plate, and then removed the meat plate. Fiona was a careful planner, and she stuck to her plans; whether it was pears on fruit plates or anything else. She looked at me. 'Of course not. Almost no one knew. It was the closest-guarded secret the Department ever had. I wish you wouldn't keep brooding about it.'

'I'm not brooding on it – nor on anything else,' I said, masterfully restraining myself from asking why I mustn't keep brooding about her betrayal but she could keep brooding about its outcome.

'Oh, there are some letters for you.' She got them from a silver toast-rack on the sideboard which George had always used for mail.

'Who knows this address?'

'Don't be so secretive.'

'I've not given this address to anyone,' I said.

'Open your mail and perhaps you'll find out,' she said, and began to clear the table.

The letters were a collection of circulars and bills for telephone and gas, and a chatty letter from an uncle in Chicago. Unremarkable except that I had no uncle in Chicago.

'Good news, darling?' she asked as she took the dishes away to the kitchen and began filling the dish-washer.

'Yes, they are going to cut off the phone.'

'I paid,' said Fiona's voice from the kitchen.

I looked at the letter from Chicago. After two pages of banal chit-chat there were two lines of phone numbers. The handwriting was cramped and angular, to disguise the identity I suppose, but I had guessed what it was even before I'd got to the lists of numbers. 'I think I'll take a bath,' I called. 'Is the water hot?'

'Help yourself. There are mountains of lovely new towels and I bought a razor and shaving cream for you in case you arrived without your bag.'

'You think of everything.'

'Uncle' was of course Bret Rensselaer. The bogus phone numbers provided a message. He'd used the crudest code of all and yet, like so many crude devices – from home-made bombs to the three-card trick – it could be effective enough to defeat a great deal of sophisticated effort. The first number was the page, the second number the line and the third number showed which word it was. All you needed to read the message was the same edition of the same book that the sender had used. Since the code was based upon words, rather than letters, it provided no letter-frequency, which cracks most amateur codes wide open. In an age when there was an infinity of printed books available such codes were not easy to break. I had the right book: Bret's Bible. I'd carried it with me just as Bret had urged me to do. I suppose some instinct had already told me it would be needed.

I felt somewhat foolish running my bath in a steam-filled bathroom while I counted my way through the tiny Bible with its thin, almost transparent, pages. I hadn't decoded a coded message since I left the boy scouts. Or was it the training school: there's not a lot of difference.

Each page of the ancient little Bible was in two columns, but I soon realized that Bret was using only the left-hand column. I flipped the pages and the words emerged one by one in a strange sequence, giving me the eerie feeling that Bret was speaking from beyond the grave: as if the words were a spiritual communication coming by Ouija board.

UNKNOWN DEAD NEVERTHELESS REVEALED 4 WIFE'S SERVANT

I imagined Bret scouring his Bible for the words he wanted. It would be a frustrating task, and the names of people and towns were unavailable. It was typical of Bret that, having lavished a 'nevertheless' upon his text, he eventually grew impatient enough to use a numeral instead of 'for'.

'Don't phone me,' my uncle said in his letter. 'I won't be home.' But I rather thought that was a reminder that Bret's phone was not completely private. Poor old Bret. The last of the old top-floor warriors, he'd never give up his hopes of getting back to active duty in London.

'Is the water hot?' Fiona yelled from the other side of the door.

'Yes, and I'm in it,' I said feelingly, and flushed Bret's cryptic message down the toilet.

8

Dicky arrived at work only thirty minutes after I did. He'd been arriving earlier since getting temporary control of Operations. Which elements of his daily routine, of jogging across Hampstead Heath and returning home for breakfast, had been abandoned I don't know, but he was steadily putting on weight. I suppose the early arrival was part of his campaign to get the Ops appointment made permanent.

'Come in, Bernard,' he said brusquely as he came into the ante-room, hurrying past his secretary while extending a hand to grab the batch of opened mail she held aloft for him.

He went into his office where his lion-skin rug was stretched, limbs extended, mane tangled and glass eyes glinting malevolently. Dicky avoided stepping on his lion, I'd noticed that before, and went around to stand behind the polished rosewood table he used instead of a desk.

Set close together, and occupying a large section of the wall behind him, there were neatly framed black and white photos in all of which a smiling Dicky was clasping hands with someone rich and important. On the other wall there stood a reproduction Chippendale glass-fronted case containing books which Dicky had bought because of their impressive leather bindings. He kept it locked because closer inspection revealed them to be such volumes as *Glorious Days of Empire* and incomplete histories of the Crimean War and of Vickers Armstrong. The only one I'd seen him open was a battered old copy of *Who's Who* which he used in order to look up the antecedents of people he met at parties. 'Ah ha!' He shuffled quickly through his mail before dropping it into a tray. Then he pulled off his brown leather replica WW2 fighter pilot's jacket, and tossed it across the room to the waiting arms of his assistant. He stood there while I admired his knitted sweater; the grass-green one with a pattern of life-size apples, oranges and bananas across its front.

Arrayed before him on his bright red blotter there was a tumbler of water and half a dozen pills of various shapes and colours. Still on his feet, Dicky began picking up the pills one at a time, gulping each with a mouthful of water. 'Do you take vitamins, Bernard?'

'No,' I said. He sounded a little short of breath but I didn't remark on this.

'I have to take vitamins at this time of the year.' He popped a large red pill into his mouth.

'What debilitation strikes you down at this time of year?' I asked with genuine interest.

'Social commitments, Bernard. Dinner parties, Whitehall ceremonies, banquets, official gatherings, staff booze-ups and so on. It's very demanding.' This time he popped a flecked orange cylinder on to his tongue. 'B_{12},' he explained.

'It's tough,' I said. 'I never realized what it was like at the top.'

'It's all part of the job,' he said philosophically. 'It's the work behind the scenes that keeps this Department going.' When the last pill had been swallowed he finished the water and shouted very loudly: 'Coffee, slaves. Coffee!' In the ante-room beyond the door I could hear the unfortunate girl who worked there beginning the frenzied business of making Dicky's coffee. He forbade them to grind the coffee in advance; he said it lost the essential oils.

He sat down behind the table. 'Take the weight off your feet, Bernard, and have some coffee.' He seemed to be practising the charming smile and servile manner that he usually reserved for the Director-General. An invitation to join Dicky for coffee was not extended impulsively, so I knew he wanted something. 'Have you brought your revised report?'

'No,' I said, and sat down in the Charles Eames chair. Now that Dicky had taken delivery of a remarkable new 'posture' chair he'd seen advertised in *House and Garden*, the Eames was relegated to seating visitors. I sank deep down into the soft arm-chair, and as he watched me settle he focused on my face. The bruises had lost their initial dark purple hues and were streaked with crimson and orange, like a sunset. 'What in hell happened to you?' he said in an awed voice that made me think my bruises were worse than they were.

'A drunken idiot tried to rob me.'

'Where?'

'A stube in Kreuzberg.'

'You should keep away from greasy spoons like that,' said Dicky. And, with commendable concern for the affairs of the nation, added: 'Suppose you'd been carrying Category One papers?'

'I was,' I said. 'But I swallowed them.'

After a tight condescending smile he said: 'Frank told me you'd withdrawn the previous dissertation and were bringing a replacement.'

'I only got back late last night.'

'Back from where, old chap?' It was all mockery of course. He was showing me how good he was at keeping the lid on his anger while allowing a little of it to blow steam and dribble down the outside of the pot.

'I went to Zurich.'

'To Zurich. What pressing business took you there?' I knew then that Dicky's stringers in Berne had failed to locate me in

Switzerland, and I got an infantile pleasure from having outwitted him and his snoopers.

'I was talking to Werner.'

'Werner? Werner Volkmann? I wish you hadn't done that, Bernard, old sport.'

'Why, Dicky?'

'Your old sparring partner is persona non grata with us all at this moment in time.' There was the sudden whine of a distant electric coffee-grinder. He looked at the door, raised an arm and screamed: 'Coffee! Coffee for God's sake!' in the feigned rage that he claimed amused his staff.

'It was a domestic matter,' I said. 'I took two days from the leave owing me, and paid my own fare. There were other things I had to attend to there.'

'Your brother-in-law. Yes, I heard he'd become a tax exile.' Then the coffee arrived. The drinking of coffee was a ritual that provided for Dicky one of his most treasured moments of the day. It was not just any old coffee; it was a choice import that was brought from the shop of Mr Higgins, the famous London coffee merchant. It was conveyed at high speed by one of our official motor-cycle messengers and ground in Dicky's ante-room only minutes before brewing, using a special electric grinder Dicky had found in Berlin. It was all worthwhile of course. Dicky's coffee was renowned. There was no question of him being reprimanded for using the messengers for his personal errands. All the top-floor staff, even the old D-G, would come hurrying along the corridor to share Dicky's coffee. Now he put a strong cup of it before me and watched contemptuously as I poured cream into it. 'Ruins it,' he pronounced. 'These are the finest coffee beans you can buy. The flavour is as delicate as a good claret. And do you know, I'm beginning to think I can distinguish from one plantation to another.' After he'd poured his own coffee, he didn't go back round the table;

instead he propped himself against the table's edge and looked down at me quizzically.

'Amazing,' I replied. 'Even the plantation, eh?'

'I've always had this delicate palate.' He watched me. 'Really fine coffee like this is completely spoiled by cream or sugar.'

'Sugar. Yes, good. Have you got sugar?'

He reached behind his back and found the sugar on the tray without looking for it. He'd known what I was going to say. 'Here you are, you barbarian.' Perhaps I would have taken my coffee sugarless and black, as Dicky drank his, except that it would have deprived him of his chance to explain what a fine palate he had.

'You'll have to go back again, Bernard,' he said. 'You'll have to go and see what's happening.'

'I've only just arrived in London,' I complained. 'There's so much to do here.'

'I've got no one else.'

'What about that kid I took along?'

'Not for this one.'

'Why?'

'I'll tell you why, Bernard. Because you aren't telling me the whole truth, that's why. You are playing games with me.'

'Am I?'

'Frank thinks you are reluctant to tell us what you really think happened last week. Who were those people in the car that chased you? I know you have a theory, Bernard. Share it with me. Let's not waste time equivocating. Who were they?'

'It's possible that one of them was VERDI.'

'In the car behind you!' I knew my suggestion would ignite Dicky and I was not disappointed. He put down his coffee, his excitement causing him to spill some of it. Then he looked at me, gave a broad boyish smile, and smashed a fist into his open palm. 'VERDI!' Then he went to the window and looked out. 'So the dead man was someone else?'

'We should keep an open mind.'

'Was it something you found in the pockets?' he said hurriedly. 'I noticed that you didn't list what you found in the pockets of the dead man.'

'There was nothing in his pockets.'

'Nothing?' All the fire puffing Dicky up cooled suddenly and he deflated, and began gnawing at the nail of his little finger for solace. 'Nothing at all?'

'That's what I thought so damned odd,' I said.

A couple of nods. 'He was still warm but someone had found time enough to completely empty his pockets,' he mused aloud.

'Difficult to do that, Dicky,' I said, guiding his thoughts gently. 'More likely the mysterious someone made him empty his pockets first.'

'Then shot him. Yes, of course.'

'It's all negative,' I admitted, and tried to think of something else to please him. 'But it troubled me at the time. It's something I can't remember before: there's always something in an old suit … ticket stubs, a tiny coin, a pencil, a handkerchief …'

'Unless someone has taken a lot of trouble to make sure there is nothing,' growled Dicky, the flame in his heart now burning bright again. 'Yes, indeedy. And the dudes in the car?'

'They didn't shoot back,' I said.

'Perhaps they weren't armed?'

I smiled. 'You've never been over there, Dicky, or you wouldn't seriously suggest that possibility.'

He frowned as he tried to think of some other explanation. 'They don't shoot; so it's VERDI?'

'It's not conclusive, Dicky. Of course not. But you don't shoot at the other side when you are negotiating to defect.'

He didn't smile, but this line of thinking pleased him and he was ready to acknowledge that. 'You're not just a pretty face, Bernard.'

I wondered if perhaps I'd gone too far with my improvisation, although among London Central's minions there was a theory that in bending reality to please one's superiors you could never go too far. 'This is only a hazy suspicion, Dicky. It's not a theory we should act upon. That's why I didn't want to put it in writing.'

He was lost in his thoughts. 'Yes, that's why they shot him in the head. No identification. Then VERDI chases after you. You think he's ... and you shoot at him. It all fits together.'

I didn't want to say No, it doesn't all fit together, because that would have marred Dicky's obvious satisfaction. But once anyone began tapping this fragile hypothesis with the fingertip of reasoning, it would fall into a thousand brittle fragments. But at present my theory was the only thing that was keeping that smile on Dicky's face, and I needed his good will to get into the Data Centre. 'We should keep this notion just between the two of us,' I said. 'If it does eventually prove to be flawed, we don't want to be left with egg on our faces.'

'Don't worry, Bernard, old son,' said Dicky, patting my shoulder in an uncharacteristic gesture of support, and chuckling at what he thought was the reason behind my apprehension: 'I won't steal all the credit for your theory.'

'I wasn't worrying about that, Dicky,' I said. 'You are welcome to the theory, but I think we should keep it to ourselves for the time being.'

'I'm sorry about putting you into that little box-room with all those filing cabinets,' said Dicky, with what almost sounded like genuine contrition. 'We'll find you something better – somewhere with a window – when they confirm me in Operations.'

'It makes no difference,' I said, although it was difficult to ignore the fact that not only was Dicky's two-window office, with its view across the park, one of the largest in the building, but he'd annexed the grand office next door as an ante-room for

130

his secretary, with an extra partitioned area where visitors could kick their heels waiting for him to receive them. No chance that on the floor of my little sanctum I'd have a lion-skin rug like this one in Dicky's office, for the simple reason that my room was smaller than an average-sized lion could stretch its legs.

'No other insights, I suppose?'

'Not right now, Dicky.'

'What's next then?'

'I'd like to spend a couple of hours in the Data Centre,' I said.

'What for?'

'I'd like to try something on the computer.'

'About VERDI?'

'Yes. It could have a bearing on it.'

'Very well, Bernard. My secretary will give you a chit for the Data Centre. Our time over there is being rationed nowadays. I suppose you heard that?'

'Yes, I heard.'

'More coffee?' It was a signal for me to depart.

I got to my feet. 'No, it's exquisite but one cup is my ration.'

He smiled. His capacity to drink gallons of strong black coffee was something Dicky liked to boast about.

When I got to the door and opened it, Dicky came striding after me. He seized the door and pushed it closed in a gesture of confidentiality, although there was no one behind it to eavesdrop. 'What you don't know,' said Dicky, 'is that what you've just told me fits in with what I know already.'

'What do you know?'

'As far as the opposition is concerned, VERDI has completely disappeared. We've heard nothing about anyone being shot in Magdeburg and VERDI has not responded to any of our signals.'

'That's hardly confirmation, Dicky.'

'Don't be silly, of course it is. We've looked after this man like a cherished possession: we've assigned goodbye codes, drops and safe houses. He only has to raise an eyebrow. Until now he's ignored it all.'

'Am I allowed to know why VERDI is so important to us?' I asked. 'Does he have some special knowledge or what is it?' I opened the door, but Dicky took a grip on it and closed it again. When determined he could muster considerable strength.

'Yes,' said Dicky earnestly, 'VERDI has very special knowledge. He's bringing a lot of data with him. We need to keep him alive and all in one piece because he'll have to unravel it all. We have special plans for him. The big brass is asking me how long it's all going to take.'

'And what do you tell them?' I asked, as I suspected that whatever Dicky was promising the big brass, someone like me was going to be struggling to deliver.

'I don't promise them anything, Bernard.'

I breathed a sigh of relief. 'The only sensible thing to do is to wait until VERDI feels safe enough to make contact again.'

'Hah!' said Dicky, as if I'd tried to trick him. 'And we'll still be waiting for him at Christmas.'

'Don't push him, Dicky. You might be prodding a hornet's nest.'

'I'll give him a couple of days,' said Dicky, as if driving a bargain with me. 'Then someone will have to go and track him down and see what's happening.'

A couple of days! My blood turned to water. 'Lovely coffee, Dicky,' I said, finally wrenching the door open. 'But they say too much of it makes some people very tense.'

'Not me,' said Dicky, biting into a fingernail. 'I'm used to it.'

The money to build the London Data Centre had been voted through when the USSR was at its most bellicose. Various sums had been suggested as the cost of it; five hundred million pounds was one of the more modest guesses.

The 'Yellow Submarine' occupied three recently dug levels below the cellars of Whitehall. The entrance was in the Foreign Office, so that it was difficult for outsiders to spot or film those who made regular visits to the big computer. I handed in my duly signed chit to the guard in the security room. Nowadays not only did he have to identify me as an authorized user by calling up my computerized photo and description on the video screen, he also had to book me in, so that my time in the Centre was charged in hours and minutes to the Department's allotted time.

'Been on holiday somewhere lovely, Mr Samson?' said the guard as the video screen pronounced me persona grata and he waved me through.

'No, we won a sun-lamp at bingo,' I said.

I pinned on the big red plastic badge displaying my photo, its bright red surround announcing my right to be in the third, deepest and most secret level. From the lobby I took the shiny new lift past the mainframes, past software storage and down to secret data access. I got out and blinked at the fierce and unrelenting blue glare that came from the concealed ceiling lighting. There were offices all round this level. Access to them was from a corridor formed by a clear glass wall. Through the glass wall there was a view of an open area where sixty work-stations – buzzing, humming and clicking – were arranged in waist-high bull-pens, each pen just tall enough to provide privacy for anyone seated there. Almost all the bull-pens were occupied, their status signalled by the tiny red lights that shone from the top of each occupied console when its computer was switched on.

I walked along until I spotted Gloria. She was occupying one of the best pens – the ones at the corners – and had made it into a den. She was perched on one of the primitive typist chairs that the accountants insisted were good for the spine, although they didn't use them themselves. The chairs in the cashier's department were all soft, expensive and bad for you.

On her lap Gloria balanced a couple of printed reference books and a notebook garlanded with yellow flags. Her waste-bin was overflowing with discarded print-out and there were memos, reports, paper coffee cups, Coke cans and ballpoint pens scattered around as if she'd been working here non-stop for a week.

It was the first time I'd seen her for many weeks, and now I looked at her and remembered. She must have felt my eyes on her for she looked up suddenly. Burdened by her books she raised her arm and waved her hand, rippling her fingers in a gesture that hit me with a sudden pang of recognition.

I walked over to her. 'Gloria. Hello,' I said diffidently. As I said it, a movement in the next row of machines revealed the inquisitive and unfriendly eyes of a man named Morgan peeping over the top of the bull-pen. Morgan was a malevolent denizen of the top floor who was working on a PhD in gossip.

Gloria put her books on to the floor and stood up. 'Bernard! How wonderful. I was hoping … I heard you had arrived.' The greeting was warm but her manner was reserved. But then she softened a little: 'Your poor face. What did you do, Bernard?' She leaned forward and touched my bruises tenderly, bringing our faces very close so that I could smell her perfume and feel her breath and the warmth of her body. 'Is it awfully painful?' Must she lean so close like that? Was it some kind of test of my passion? Or was she testing her own self-control? Still unde-cided about her motives, and knowing that Morgan was watch-ing us, I compromised by giving her a brief brotherly kiss on the cheek. She smiled and touched her cheek where my lips had been. Her fingers were slim and elegant, but there was ink on the fingertips to remind me of the sixth-form schoolgirl she'd been only a short time ago.

'You're looking well,' I said. It was a stupid thing to say but I doubt if she heard me: everything that was happening between us was going on in the intimacy of our memories.

She was slim, and so astoundingly young, both attributes emphasized by her tight black jeans and equally close-fitting white sweater. I could hardly believe that this was the same creature I had bedded and lived with as my wife. No wonder at the consternation that domestic reshuffle had caused amongst my friends and colleagues. She smiled nervously and looked as if she was about to offer to shake hands. There was a certain clumsiness about her. Her face was soft and unwrinkled and the expression on it was more of bewilderment than of confidence; and above all she exuded sexual attraction. She seemed entirely unaware of the effect she was having on me, although that might be more rationally explained as a measure of my lifelong failure to understand women. So while I found myself succumbing to this intoxicating sexual allure there was another – sober – half of my brain that saw what was happening, wondered why, and advised against it.

Perhaps she realized that Morgan was in a nearby cubicle, for she lowered her voice almost to a whisper. 'I was going to come to California and rescue you,' she said with a grin. 'I thought they were holding you prisoner.' She'd had her blonde hair cut quite short and it was held with a cheap plastic clip. This added to the schoolgirl appearance. I wondered if she knew that.

'Not quite a prisoner,' I said, although upon reflection I suppose she was right. I don't think it would have been very easy to push my way out of there, shout goodbye to Bret, and depart.

'I sent a postcard. Did you get it?'

'No,' I said.

'Van Gogh: the postman in the blue uniform.'

'I didn't get it.'

'They're letting me work on the Hungary desk.'

135

'So I heard. I suppose you are making a name for yourself.'

'I work hard,' she said. 'But I've forgotten so much of my Hungarian. The grammar. My father is helping me.'

'You're living with your parents again?'

'You never wrote,' she said, without making it into an accusation or a reprimand.

'I'm sorry. I tried to write …'

'Wives come first, Bernard. "Other women" know that. Deep in their hearts they know it.' There was still no bitterness audible in her voice, but she tossed her head, and she pouted for a moment before remembering to smile. 'You went off on that Friday morning and said it was just for the weekend. Back Monday or Tuesday, you said … And you never came back. I still have suitcases with your clothes and all sorts of things.'

'I wasn't told that they planned to bring Fiona out that weekend. I had to go. They said she'd know it wasn't a trap if I was there.'

'I'm not blaming you, Bernard, I'm really not. It's the job. It's the men running this bloody rotten Department. They treat us all like dirt.'

'But you're all right?' I asked. 'I put money into your account.'

'You were decent enough, Bernard. But they were determined to separate us. First they reneged on their promise to keep me on full pay if I could get a place doing Slavonic Studies at Cambridge. No money, they said. When they saw that you and I were still together, they closed Daddy down.'

'What do you mean?'

'They bullied him about us. They hated you and me living together. You can see why, now that we know Fiona's defection was all a ruse. They knew she was coming back. They bullied my poor father about it.'

'Who did?'

'How can they be such hypocrites? What harm did we do to anyone? We were happy together, weren't we, Bernard?' She looked over the partition to be sure there was no one in earshot.

'Who did?' I said. 'Who knew Fiona was coming back and that it was all a ruse?'

'Daddy won't talk about it.'

'So how do you know?'

'He was happy doing work for the Department until you and I set up home together. Then suddenly he loses the lease on his surgery, and that workshop he had at home is closed down.'

'Why?'

'You don't know the lengths they will go to. And the power they have is awesome. Daddy got a visit from the local Environmental Health Officer or Inspector or something. He said Daddy's workshop contravened building regulations. It was in a residential zone, they said.'

'Didn't your father apply for planning permission when he built that extension?'

'The Department told him not to apply in writing. They didn't want any attention drawn to the way Daddy did secret Departmental work at home, in case the KGB noticed and came prying into it. The Department said: Go ahead and build, and promised to arrange some special permission through the Ministry.'

'It's not a conspiracy. It sounds more like some jumped-up little sod in some office somewhere. Does the D-G know?'

'They came into the surgery and removed everything; from plaster casts to his drills and lathe and tools and all the paperwork. Everything. My father won't pursue it. He took the compensation they offered. But they've ruined his life, Bernard. He's still young and he loved being a dentist.'

'He can start again.'

'No, that's part of the deal. He'll lose his Departmental pension if he works full-time.'

'That couldn't have been because of us living together,' I said. 'It's absurd.'

She looked at me, took my hand and held it. 'Perhaps not, Bernard. Don't blame yourself.'

'Seriously, Gloria. It doesn't make sense.'

'It makes sense, all right, Bernard. Your wife runs this Department. She couldn't have more power if they made her the Director-General. She has only to raise her little finger and everyone is running to fulfil her every wish.'

'Rubbish,' I said, and laughed at such exaggeration. But I could see it might seem that way to poor Gloria.

'It's not rubbish, Bernard. If you were some lowly clerk, or just a nobody like me, you'd see the sort of reverence Fiona gets throughout the whole Department. She's treated like a saint. They weren't going to have some silly little girl like me ruin all their plans. That's why they sent you to California to be with your wife. And as soon as you were there they took the children from me, victimized my father and made sure I was rendered powerless.'

'It's not a conspiracy, Gloria. You've met my father-in-law. You must see what an interfering old idiot he can be. He's got no connection with the Department.'

'You told me he was some kind of blood relation.'

'With Uncle Silas. Yes, a cousin but a very distant one. They are friends but not very friendly. There could be no collusion between them, believe me.'

Absently she fingered the keyboard and called up a directory of codenames. 'I wish I hadn't mentioned it,' she said. 'I wasn't going to tell you.'

'I'm glad you told me. I'll go and see Uncle Silas and tell him what's happened.'

138

'Don't rock the boat, Bernard. Daddy says it's better to let things remain as they are.'

'I'll ask Uncle Silas to give me his advice, without mentioning you or your father.'

'You'll get yourself into trouble; you'll get me into trouble, and you'll do nothing to help Daddy,' she predicted gloomily. She leaned down and picked up one of her books from the floor and turned to a marked page. 'You'll upset your wife too. She won't like it.'

'I'll go to his house in the country and talk to Uncle Silas,' I said. 'Are you down here every day?'

'Two days or more. I still have a lot to do.'

'And everything's okay otherwise?'

She looked at me for a long time before answering: 'Yes, I'm on a motor-rally team. I'm a navigator. I have a really super driver as my partner. It's fun.'

'Motor rallies? You were always a crazy driver, Gloria.'

'You were always saying that. But I never had a crash, did I?'

'No, I had all the crashes,' I said.

We lingered for a moment, neither of us having anything more to say, and neither knowing how to say goodbye. Finally I blew her a kiss, went to a work-station across the aisle and started digging into the mainframe. From where I was sitting I could see Gloria at work. I suppose I was hoping that she would turn, or find some way of snatching a glance at me. But perhaps she sensed I was watching her, for she never gave a sign that she knew I was there until the moment she packed up her books and papers and left. She waved as she passed me, giving me that same finger-waggling wave that she'd given me on arrival.

'Tomorrow perhaps,' she said.

'Yes, tomorrow.'

There was no way I could pretend to myself or to anyone else that I had forgotten to bring up the question of her visiting the children. It was in the forefront of my mind all the time as I sat at the console. I really tried to think of some way of asking her to stay away from them, but I couldn't do it. Anyone who'd seen her with the children would know that she loved them as much as anyone could. I suppose that is what had persuaded even my insensitive father-in-law that Gloria's visits were good for them.

It was not until Gloria left the Centre that I started my real inquiry. It took me only ten minutes to discover that the computer would not provide me with the information I sought. I booted up and responded to the menu request for program with KAGOB, the KGB data section. I brought up another menu and clicked the mouse on RED LAND OVERSEAS to get the biographies. But when I keyed in VERDI the screen responded with the message: 'All field use cover names now require password for access.'

Damn! There was never a month went past without the data becoming more safeguarded. Soon only the D-G would be permitted to come down here. I tried a couple of the passwords I'd used to get data on previous visits, but the machine was not fooled so easily. I knew VERDI's real name of course, I'd known it all along. But the first lesson I'd learned from my father was that supplying the real identity of a field agent was absolutely verboten. Even if it was an enemy field agent. I remembered VERDI only too well, just as Werner did. My father had arrested him back in the Seventies, but he'd claimed diplomatic immunity and been released within an hour. His family name was Fedosov and his first name Andrey or Aleksey or maybe Aleksandr. When I went back to the first menu and keyed in Fedosov and asked for a 'Global' the machine whirled for a long time and I thought I was going to be lucky, but then it said: 'File withdrawn in reference Transfer dated 1.1.1865.'

I pressed the Quit key. Okay computer: a good joke. You get the last word. And that mistyped date was not the only operator error to be found in the data. When the Data Centre was first built, there were no such things as optical read-out machines, so for weeks and weeks every vetted typist in Whitehall was down here at some time or other, transferring the typed and written files on to the mainframe computer. Typists were going home with bulging wage packets, as some of them worked seventy hours a week. I don't think Whitehall had ever seen such energy displayed in the workplace. But the price was paid in accuracy, and now everyone has become accustomed to such errors as dates being 100 years behind reality, along with most other things in the government service.

I remembered when some Jeremiahs were saying that there were millions of pages of typed and written material in those racks of bulging files, and predicting that the job of entering them into the computer would never be completed. They were wrong of course. Finally it was all on disk or chip or wherever words end up when the computers swallow them. And now all the old files were abandoned and gathering dust in the archives downstairs on the storage level. Of course nothing had ever been added to those old files, but perhaps young VERDI had secured a place in our records before the conversion.

I went down to the storage mezzanine. It was a gloomy place of bare concrete echoing with the constant noise of pumps and generators. Apart from the machinery it was only used for unwanted desks and chairs, dented filing cabinets, and packets of paper on racks as high as the ceiling. At one time they'd started shredding all these old secret documents, but when the index cards jammed the knives of the shredding machines the project had been temporarily halted. And then the shredders were needed upstairs and the files were conveniently forgotten. Now only the guards and engineers ever came down here, and even they did not stay long.

I didn't have to search for the old files. They were arrayed on the same metal racks that had held them when they were stored in Registry. All of them were dusty and torn. Some had burst open and been retied like waste paper ready for the recycling machine. There was none of that fancy silver-coloured anti-static carpeting that covered the floor of Level 3, and my footsteps echoed from the grey walls.

It took me a little time to find my way along the racks but I had used the files a lot in the old days. Here was the British Empire's postwar history written in blood. Palestine? No; Kenya? No; Cyprus? No; Malaya? No; Suez? No. I'd spent a year in London Central as a dogsbody, and fetching and carrying from Registry was the task everyone wanted to foist off on someone else.

I switched on another light. Berlin. Here were some files I recognized. Of course the bloody agent files would be on the top shelf. I went and found a ladder and climbed up to get them. As the dust rose from secret files that had not been touched in a decade or more I felt like Howard Carter breaking into Tutankhamun's inner chamber.

The files were arranged in alphabetical order. Not in the alphabetical order of agents, or agents' codenames. They were arranged in the order of the case officers, or more accurately the persons who ran the agents. I sighed. If I needed proof of the value of a computer, and the access it afforded, this task provided it. It was logical for the files to be arranged this way, because each agent-runner jealously guarded his agents – as policemen cherish their informants – and hid their files away from their colleagues and superiors. I looked at the long line of files I would have to go through to locate Fedosov, who might well prove not to have an entry at all. There were more than forty files there, and some were of back-breaking weight.

I took down the first one and put it on a table under the light. Peter Andrews. I remembered him, an amiable ex-SOE man who in 1944 survived Gestapo interrogation in Lyon. Even more surprisingly he'd survived the selection boards of the SIS; for the arthritic old Foreign Office diehards were determined to keep such 'wartime amateurs' out of 'their' service. It wasn't a very long file. He'd run four agents into East Germany but, as a child, what I remembered most vividly was that on the wall of his office he had the framed front page from a prewar satirical magazine: 'Arch-duke Franz Ferdinand Alive: Great War a Mistake!' In 1963 an order from Whitehall suddenly detached him to Iraq to take ten thousand Maria Theresa silver dollars to the revolutionary group led by Colonel Aref. Arriving as the rebellion began, he sent a message that he'd made contact. But Andrews was too old to be a revolutionary. The next message said his mutilated body was buried in the desert one hundred miles north of Baghdad, and would HM Government pay for it to be sent home.

As I went through the files I became more adept at finding the separate agent listings inside them. But there was no Fedosov as far as I could see, and no VERDI either, so VERDI must have been assigned a cover name after the data was transcribed. When I looked at my watch I found it had taken me two hours to search only half the files, but getting Dicky to agree to me coming down here again tomorrow would involve all kinds of silly discussions, so I continued with my self-appointed task and finished the last file at nine fifty-two p.m. I was hungry and thirsty, my hands were dirty and my lungs choking with dust and accumulated filth.

The flickering light had given me a headache, and the loud buzzing of a malfunctioning fluorescent tube drilled through my brain, as did the throbbing of the other machinery as I got to the end of the final file. Billy Walker, another man I remembered very well; always sleekly dressed in dark suits from London, with a diamond tie-pin and a heavy gold watch-chain. He was a little older than my father, and when the appointment as Berlin Rezident fell vacant he became one of my father's most dangerous rivals. Some people said afterwards that Billy Walker followed one of his agents on an impossible job, believing that some kind of award for bravery would assist in his getting the position he coveted beyond any other. Some said his conspicuous homosexual lifestyle was punctuated by quarrels with dangerous young men. Whatever the truth of that, Billy was fished out of the Landwehr Canal having died of multiple stab wounds. According to this file, Billy Walker's best agent was never seen again.

My head was spinning with memories as I carried the file back up the ladder and pushed it back on to the shelf. My head was brushing the cobwebbed pipes and tin ducting. Despite the lateness of the hour I couldn't resist getting down one of my father's personal files. To see his handwriting on all these stuffy old reports brought back memories of the letters he used to write to me. He felt guilty that he hadn't pushed harder for me to go to university. Had it not troubled him, perhaps I wouldn't have thought so much about it myself. I told him I wouldn't have enjoyed being away from home, and that I probably wouldn't have secured a place. But my father insisted that it was all his fault. He had allowed me to start work in the Department where a university education, no matter how inappropriate or inadequate, was the only way to get to the top floor.

I thought about all this as I flipped through the written account of my father's days in Berlin. Fedosov. Good grief! There it was: Fedosov. Not Fedosov the younger; this was Valeriy Fedosov, born 1910, a captain working in the Red Army headquarters at Berlin Karlshorst. According to these reports, he had provided my father with secret information from the Soviet files during the time that the Soviets blockaded Berlin. The US Air Force and the RAF combined to stage an airlift, their aircraft expanded by the addition of any other large plane that could be bought or rented anywhere in the Western world.

Here were photocopies of the Soviet assessments of the supplies arriving and their estimates of how long the airlift could be kept going. Knowing what the Soviets were thinking day to day was vital. Even London and Washington secretly believed the airlift could be no more than a brief easing of shortages before the city collapsed under the Russian stranglehold. The aircrews had been told to take 'enough kit for ten days'. In the event the planes brought enough to keep both the civil population and the Allied forces supplied. It was a triumph. It unified the Germans and the Anglo–Americans in a way that nothing else could have done. And it shook Russian self-confidence at a time when their confidence seemed unassailable.

There was no mistaking my father's signature on the payments card and no mistaking the name of his informant. It was good material too. No wonder my father kept it all to himself, running this agent in person. There was no Wall in those days and my father could walk across the city without attracting any attention and brazenly visit Fedosov in his Pankow flat. There was no need to wonder why this hadn't been put into the computer. On the front cover of the file there was a big black rubber stamp: 'Data not transcribed by reason:' Someone had provided the reason in handwriting: 'file ended December 1950 with no continuation' and under that in a box there was the scribbled signature of a supervisor. It was a legitimate reason for not entering all this material on the computer at a time when it was taking so much time and effort to get the up-to-date essentials into the machine.

The Soviet blockade of Berlin was lifted on May 12th 1949. Payments to Fedosov continued for another three months but then stopped without explanation. It was not unusual for informants to come and go in that way: most of them were mercurial prima donnas looking for love and money that they weren't getting from their own side. In those days everything was very casual. Fedosov had been run by my father personally, and as far as these records revealed, had never been given a cover name. I took the payments card, folded it and put it in my pocket. And I wondered if this Valeriy Fedosov, VERDI's father and the Soviet Union's Hero of Banner Party No. 5, was still living in his flat in Berlin-Pankow.

I reasoned that Dicky Cruyer would soon get around to deciding that my visiting Berlin was urgently necessary. And if Dicky didn't soon get around to deciding that, I'd have to think of some way of putting the idea into his mind.

9

On Tuesday morning, as if to confirm Gloria's theory – that the Department was secretly commanded by Fiona's every wish and whim – the whole top floor was in an uproar. By mid-morning desks, filing cases and other furniture had been heaved and carted around to provide her with an office next door to Dicky.

Compared to the miserable little place allotted to me, her office was magnificent, but being next door to Dicky was a high price to pay for such comfort. That proximity to Dicky was important to him and the reason why old Flinders Flynn, the Statistics wizard, had been unceremoniously relegated to a noisy downstairs room adjacent to the lifts.

'Aren't I lucky, darling?' said Fiona as I went in to see her and take her to lunch.

'You didn't say anything about this new job last night.' I knew she'd been helping Dicky with his work but I'd figured it as no more than a determined attempt to stay out of the clutches of the Hungarian desk.

'You were so late. Anyway Dicky only said he was thinking about it. I always like to be quite sure.'

'What's your official label?'

'Deputy to Dicky,' she said. 'But it won't become official until the first of next month.'

'In Operations?'

She smiled conspiratorially and glanced at the door that connected her to the ante-room where Dicky's secretary and assistant lurked, tirelessly alert for his next command. 'Artfully not stated,' she said.

'So Dicky is hoping to hold on to German Stations Controller and Operations too?'

'He told me it's just a temporary arrangement. If he gets pushed out, I go too.'

'Why didn't Controller Europe assign Harry Strang to hold the fort again, as he did during the summer vacation?'

'I didn't ask him, darling,' she replied loftily.

I supplied the answer: 'With someone as high-powered as you to prop him up, Dicky hopes to split the two jobs laterally and cling to both.'

'Exactly,' said Fiona. 'And you think he's a fool.' She screwed up her face, reached for a handkerchief and sneezed into it.

'Not in office politics,' I said. 'Have you still got that cold?'

'No, it's the dust.'

I looked around her office. 'Is that Bret's old desk?'

'It was in the store-room,' she said. 'Everyone was frightened to lay claim to it.'

I looked at the remarkable glass-topped desk and remembered one of the junior staff saying that Bret's desk was like his women: ultra modern, with shiny legs, black drawers and see-through top. I hadn't thought it very amusing at the time; perhaps because I hadn't eliminated Fiona from the list of Bret's possible amours. 'And the carpet too?' I said, looking at the expensive grey carpet that had contributed to the totally monochrome room that Bret had had designed for him.

'This is Bret's old office, darling. Didn't you realize that? The walls have been redone but the carpet has been here all along.'

'I see.' Just for a moment it gave me a curious feeling to be remembering Bret and all the things that had happened to me and to others in this room. The decisions taken, the operations okayed, the careers made, blood spilled and reputations blighted.

'Are you kidnapping me for lunch?' she asked.

From her new glass-topped desk she picked up a folder. Despite its plain cover I knew it was the one containing my revised report; Dicky's assistant had given it a big red Top Secret, and in the distribution box there were Dicky's initials and Fiona's too. I also saw the light circular mark of a teacup that I had left on its front. An old-timer named Riley once showed me that making a little fold or stain on one's own submissions was a useful way of identifying them, for instance when they were on the desk of a superior. In Riley's case, I suspected that he often used it as a way of retrieving things of his authorship which hindsight decreed better lost, so he could put them into the fine-cut shredder.

Fiona noticed me looking at it as she locked it away in a metal cabinet. 'Why do you fill Dicky's head with such absurd stories?' she asked as she pushed the drawer shut and turned the combination lock.

'Did you read it?'

'I mean what you told him about VERDI. The suit with nothing in the pockets,' she said mockingly. 'Have they eliminated all the dry-cleaners over there since I left?'

'I was just thinking aloud. I told Dicky that.'

'He's gone off to the Cabinet Office to give them his lecture and tell them the good news: the Permanent Secretary and all his acolytes and heaven knows who else.'

'Tell them what?'

'That the dead man is not VERDI. He's telling them that VERDI is still alive.'

'Oh, that's all right,' I said with unconcealed relief.

'If Dicky comes out of this looking a fool he will hound you.' Her warning was emphasized by her tone of voice and the expression on her face.

'It's all right,' I said again.

'How do you know that, darling? Just because the dead man's pockets were empty?'

'Don't be tiresome, Fi. I know because I know.'

'Then tell me how you know.'

'I know what VERDI looks like. I knew him in the old days. I'd recognize him. The dead man wasn't VERDI.'

Her face registered consternation. 'You said you didn't know him. You told everyone you didn't remember him.'

'I always like to be quite sure too,' I said.

She nodded soberly. 'Touché, Bernard. But seriously?'

'VERDI only got his name when he made contact with us. VERDI is a target name. That's how it's supposed to work, isn't it? Musician codenames for people vetted, recruited or enrolled but in any case tested for loyalty. But VERDI is no friend of mine: I have very strong doubts about VERDI. I'd need persuading that he really wants to come over to us. I knew him. And when I knew him he was working very hard indeed doing nasty things proving his loyalty to Moscow.'

'And you recognized the man in the Mercedes as VERDI? Is that it?'

'It was dark. But I'm guessing that it was VERDI from the context.'

'Why are you always so difficult, Bernard?' she asked with a sigh. 'Why does every single thing have to be dragged out of you?'

'I caught one glimpse of him on a dark country road when I was full-length on the ground, hiding my head under a radiator and aiming a toy gun at a wheel.'

'Dicky believes this could be a monumental step for us,' she said.

'What could?'

'This business with VERDI. This is off the record until Dicky tells you. Last year the Stasi started putting everything into a

150

computer. Stasi files and records; arrests, targets, their own personnel even. With VERDI to help us, we might be able to hack into their mainframe by phone ... without leaving this office.'

'I'm listening.'

'There won't be a big backlog of material. It will just go back as far as January but ... well, you see ...'

'But when VERDI comes over to us they'll change all the codes and electronic gimmicks, won't they?'

'They won't junk several million dollars' worth of computer equipment. They'll just change the codes and passwords. VERDI will have someone in place to provide the new ones. Now do you see?'

'Yes, I do see. It's the stuff that knighthoods are made of.'

'Not everyone is convinced. The D-G is very much against it. It was only when Dicky subjected the Deputy to a long boozy lunch at White's that he got permission to continue with it. He had to get in quickly because the Deputy will be leaving us before Christmas.'

'Who will notice?' I said.

'Don't be hard on him,' said Fiona. 'He has a sick wife. And he tries to run his law practice as well as his office here.'

'Why is the D-G so set against it?'

'He's too old be sympathetic to new-fangled gadgets like computers. He has never let his secretary have one; not even to do the mail. He is frightened that his lovely old-fashioned Department is being taken over by little black boxes.'

'I know the feeling.'

'Harry Strang is doubtful too. He keeps saying that electronic data can be tampered with. He believes that you can usually see if a printed document or photograph or something in handwriting has been altered, forged or faked. But the print-out from electronic data is always fresh and clean. It assumes an authority that is difficult to challenge.'

151

'What about you?' I asked. Although it was quite evident that her career was bound into the success of the new operation.

'I'm pushing the VERDI operation for all I'm worth.'

'Are you?' I said, surprised to hear a tone of commitment that went far beyond her loyalty to Dicky.

'The Stasi data will go back as far as January. That will be enough to give us all the reports and relevant material on Tessa's death.'

So that was still in the very forefront of Fiona's mind. 'Don't hold your breath,' I told her. 'Tapping into communications is the ultimate dream of the people who sit behind desks. Intelligence gathering without all the expense, trouble and bother that maverick field agents bring. What a lovely thought that must be for everyone on the top floor.'

'It's understandable,' said Fiona. 'People at the sharp end are always intransigent and difficult. But tapping into the flow is not without precedent. Didn't they dig under the road to Berlin-Karlshorst back in the Fifties and plug into the telephone land-lines of the Soviet Army?'

'Yes, Operation Prince. And in Vienna in 1950 when Red Army HQ was in the Imperial Hotel; Operation Lord.'

'And reputations were made?' I could tell she'd looked it up already.

'Except that getting the recording equipment needed in Berlin was the job given to George Blake, who, while working for us had been moonlighting as a KGB agent. He told Moscow.'

'And George Blake was a field agent; is that what you mean?'

'Fiona, please. Of course not. That would be in contravention of the "Praising the Enemy Act of 1836" wouldn't it?'

'We won't need recording equipment,' said Fiona, who could never take jokes about the Department's failures. 'We'll be getting everything along the phone line, and the print-outs will make it simple to assess and classify and evaluate.'

'But does it come into our Departmental authority? The people at GCHQ will say that communications are their job. They will be furious.'

'That will be a top-level decision, Bernard. That's what Dicky is doing right now. I've spent the last few days preparing his briefing sheets.' So I was right about Fiona having been reading the history books.

'And Dicky is going to make certain that our colleagues at GCHQ are permanently sidelined?'

'It's been approved at all levels internally: they even cleared it with Uncle Silas. This morning the Foreign Office Adviser is holding Dicky's hand while they put it to the Permanent Undersecretary and the Chairman of the JIC. If they give it the nod, it will go political.'

I was impressed. That was the way the big operations went. Instead of being subject only to internal decisions, they had to have the blessing of the Civil Service. That meant the approval of Permanent Secretaries, Deputy Secretaries, the Cabinet Secretary and all the babbling brass on the Joint Intelligence Committee. But only the really delicate ones 'went political', and had to have the approval of the politicians themselves. That's why there were many piddling successes, but so little of substance was ever achieved. 'Have you seen a sample of this material?' I asked.

'Not yet. But it will be good, really good, believe me.' Fiona had worked over there; she knew what sort of material they would be putting into the computer. But she also must have known that these were the most paranoid people in the world. It wouldn't have escaped their attention that modems provide ways of hacking into multi-million dollar computers by dropping a coin into any pay-phone in the high street. In protecting their intelligence material they were perceptive and efficient, frighteningly so.

153

'And that idiot Dicky will be adding this long-term operation to his official duties elsewhere, will he?' I said. 'God help us.'

She said: 'You could have been running this Department years ago if you had made a few concessions to people you don't like.'

'You mean now it's too late?'

'Everyone makes so many concessions to you, darling. I don't think you realize how many people here do that.'

'Next week I shall start taking vitamins,' I said.

'And you'll become Dr Jekyll. It sounds lovely, but I'll still be Mrs Hyde, won't I? Where shall we go for lunch?' She reached for her handbag and put it on the desk in front of her to rummage through it.

'We could go home,' I said. 'It's so close now that we live in town.'

She snatched a quick look at herself in the tiny mirror of her powder compact and snapped it shut. 'There's nothing to eat at home,' she said.

'Who wants to eat?'

Five minutes would have saved us. Another five minutes and we would have been in the lift on our way to the main entrance lobby. But as Fiona was reaching for her coat, Dicky came bursting through the connecting door shouting for coffee over his shoulder.

'Fiona, darling! And Bernard too,' he said as he looked at us. 'Magnificent! Exactly the two people I wanted to see.' He was carrying a large canvas artist's portfolio which he dropped on to a chair and rubbed his hands together. The portfolio was the one in which Dicky carried his presentations: large colourful cards with diagrams, pie charts, maps with arrows on, simple ideas reduced to slogans and itemized and numbered so that even the men he briefed in the Cabinet Office would be able to grasp them. Not that Dicky used these carefully prepared briefs to reveal as much as possible; on the contrary the object was always to sell the idea. Dicky had explained that to me many times when I had pointed out errors in his words and pictures.

'Hello, Dicky,' said Fiona dutifully as she put her coat back on the hook.

'Were you off somewhere?' asked Dicky, as if it wasn't lunch time.

'No,' said Fiona. 'I was just getting my handkerchief.'

'You've got a cold,' said Dicky. 'I noticed you sneezing.'

'It's the dust,' said Fiona and, using a handkerchief she'd retrieved from her coat, blew her nose loudly to prove we hadn't been about to go to lunch.

'It's a virus; everyone's got it. You should have a damned big Scotch and jump into bed,' said Dicky.

'Just what I was telling her when you came in,' I said. Fiona pursed her lips and glared at me angrily.

'What's the joke?' said Dicky, looking quizzically from Fiona to me, and then back at Fiona again. When neither of us answered, he shrugged as if proclaiming his bewilderment to the world. 'Well, I'm glad you're here, Bernard,' he said, smiling and nodding at me in the sort of uncharacteristic display of good will that sometimes resulted from high excitement. He paraded up and down in his new winter overcoat, a full-length woolly garment made from pale untreated sheepskins and surmounted with a big fur collar. 'It's damned cold outside,' he said as he unbuttoned his coat and, with both hands in its pockets, flapped noisily around the room like a baby albatross learning to fly. When he got as far as the connecting door without becoming airborne, he snatched it open and yelled: 'Bring the coffee in here: three cups and some of those oatmeal biscuits.' He closed the door and then opened it again. 'And cream,' he shouted. 'Mr Samson takes cream and sugar.'

155

'So it went well?' Fiona said as Dicky turned back to us. Neither of us was hanging on Dicky's reply, because it clearly had gone well. He was in that state of euphoria that I would have guessed only a knighthood or a new Lloyd Webber album could have brought about.

'Shall we tell hubby?' Dicky asked Fiona. 'Yes, they all think it's a wonderful opportunity.' He threw his coat across a chair and stood in a statuesque pose, thumbs hooked into his leather belt. 'In a way I have Bernard to thank,' he announced. 'After debriefing him in Berlin, I thought it only fair to circulate a memo telling everyone concerned that VERDI must be presumed dead.' He grinned artfully. 'That must have taken the wind out of the sails of my most garrulous opponents, because today, when I announced that we'd had a field agent come back with the news that VERDI was very much alive and kicking, I went through the same routine again. This time at the end I was practically given a standing ovation.'

'Well let's hope VERDI is alive,' I said.

'I'm exaggerating of course,' Dicky admitted. 'Our masters are keeping their options open. They always do; that's how they got to the top. But even if VERDI proves to be dead after all, no one is going to move me out of Ops while this one is on-going.'

Fiona looked at him with manifest admiration. He was right, of course. As long as he kept the VERDI operation on the boil, no one would want to disturb things by replacing him. And if he scored a significant success with VERDI during his probationary period they would have to confirm him. His growing confidence and power were evidenced by the clothes he was wearing: his tailored denim jacket and jeans. There was a time when Dicky confined his fancy dress to his office and his peers and juniors. Now he'd actually gone to see the stuffed shirts of the Cabinet Office in this worn and whitened denim.

He swung his head to me and said: 'There's a lot of work to do, Bernard. It's not just a matter of good old VERDI strolling through the Checkpoint with the Stasi phone number scribbled into his little black book. These computers are highly strung animals. They will have communications-security goons putting all manner of protection into the lines. There will be codes and challenges and a whole lot of electronic mumbo-jumbo. And it will be changing frequently. VERDI must have someone over there who will give us updates and details of changes to the equipment so we can go on with the scheme.' As Dicky's technological knowledge dwindled, his voice trailed off until he paused and looked out of the window as if he'd forgotten what he was about to say.

I said: 'The best way would be to get all the supplementary material and changes through your new man in the London embassy.'

For a moment there was that special kind of silence that tells you when you've dropped a brick.

'How do you know about him?' said Dicky.

'Because I've been sitting in on the Notting Hill meetings. Your written orders, Dicky.'

'Oh, yes, you're right. I forgot.' He wet his lips nervously. 'Well keep it under your hat, Bernard. "Five" are still whining and whingeing about the last time we went into an embassy. "Five" claim all embassies and consuls in the UK are their territory. And anyway our new boy from the embassy is too nervous for something big like this.'

'He's nervous because he's frightened we are going to bungle things for him.'

'He's just inexperienced,' said Dicky.

'We've used that safe house too many times,' I said. 'It wasn't originally intended as a safe house; it was just an overnight bed for overseas staff and people we didn't want to bring in here.

157

It's never been really secret. The other side are bound to know about it, and your new boy has reason to be nervous.'

'I'm not using him,' said Dicky petulantly. 'So let's drop it. I want to do it through Berlin. It's better and cleaner if it goes directly to us in Berlin.'

'I'm too well known in Berlin,' I said hurriedly.

'Don't worry, Bernard. I wasn't thinking of asking you to set it up. It must be someone who will be there all the time. Someone who knows the city and has an instinct for when things go wrong. You are needed for other things, Bernard. I want you free to go backwards and forwards. And anyway you should be here with your wife.' He smiled at Fiona.

'We could bring Werner Volkmann back on to the payroll,' said Fiona. 'He answers all the requirements.'

'No, no, no,' said Dicky. Then the coffee arrived, brought by Jennifer, a nervous, gangling young woman whose venerable landowning family had protected her against learning to spell, type or take dictation. With commendable haste she'd mastered the art of making coffee the way Dicky preferred it. Today she had quickly decided that the note of triumph Dicky had broadcast merited the Spode china and the silver creamer. 'That's good,' said Dicky, examining the tray. 'Ten out of ten, Jenni.' She beamed.

'Smells good,' said Fiona.

'It's only Nescafé,' I said, annoyed that Fiona too should join in these absurd games to warm Dicky's heart. 'They ran out of Higgins coffee,' I told her in a quiet conversational voice. 'Jennifer borrowed instant from the canteen.'

'No, it's not instant from the canteen,' said Dicky calmly. I had played such games too many times before for it to have the desired effect. 'It's lightly roasted chagga. Your husband likes juvenile jokes, Fiona.' Then turning to me he reached out and ruffled my hair and said: 'But we love him just the same. Don't

158

we, Bernard?' I suppose I glowered at him and pushed my hair back into place. 'No matter, Bernard. It will soon be Christmas,' he said. 'Think of all those jokes you'll find in the crackers and in the kiddies' annuals.'

'Thank you,' said Fiona as Dicky passed a cup of coffee to her.

'You had best pour your own, Bernard,' he said. 'Since you like putting so much cream and sugar into it.'

I didn't want his lousy coffee, but to refuse it would look childish, so I poured a cup and sat down on Bret's old buttoned sofa and took a deep breath. Unlike the glass-topped desk, Bret's sofa had taken quite a beating since he left us. It had been put in the waiting-room, and that was where the duty night officer hid, and bedded down, in the small hours when all was quiet. Half the buttons were missing and there were scars and burn marks on the arms where neglected cigarettes had toppled out of ashtrays.

I said: 'It won't take them long to tumble to the fact we are reading from their mainframe. They'll seek VERDI out. They'll search to the ends of the earth to find him and he'll get it in the neck.'

'I don't think so, Bernard,' said Dicky, who was ready for that one and had perhaps faced the same question at his meeting. 'When they discovered that we'd run a cable under the street in Berlin to get their Karlshorst secrets, they circulated it as propaganda to all their friends and allies, and enemies too. This will be the same. It will be used all around the world to show what wicked things we do.'

Fiona looked at me before saying: 'It sounds good, Dicky. It's going to be a big breakthrough.' I suppose any other reaction would have made it look as if her concern for me would stand in the way of her doing her real job of supporting Dicky through thick and thin.

He looked at me and waited for my response. 'It's ingenious, Dicky,' I admitted. 'It could work.'

159

'Well, thank you,' said Dicky. 'That's praise indeed coming from you, Bernard.' He waggled a silver coffee spoon at me.

'We should let Bernard think about it,' said Fiona. 'He might remember more about who this VERDI person is.'

'For instance?' said Dicky looking at me. 'What is it about VERDI that you don't remember?'

'You'd better share the true facts with me, Dicky. All this stuff about VERDI being desperate to come over to us doesn't ring true. These stories about him wanting to talk to some old buddy he knows, and that he's just itching to defect with a box full of floppy disks. All that stuff is bullshit, Dicky. Admit it! The truth is that you've targeted VERDI because he has all this electronic know-how. Maybe he is showing no interest in defecting. Maybe he's got a better offer from the Americans. You've been sending him boxes of chocolates and polishing his apples and whatever else you do for these jerks, but it's not VERDI wooing us, it's us wooing him. Admit it? I need to know.'

Dicky became very agitated; I was asking all the wrong questions. He went over to his canvas folio as if he was going to get out his charts and diagrams, and give me an off-Broadway rendering of his whole presentation. 'He's wavering,' admitted Dicky, shifting ground a little. 'He's paranoid. He'll only deal with people he recognizes.'

'I see,' I said.

Dicky said: 'He's frightened the KGB will send a couple of goons around to see him, pretending that they're our people.' He turned to Fiona and said: 'Didn't you tell me that's the standard KGB tactic if they want to test a man's loyalty? That's why he was asking for Bernard.'

'Is that what he's been selling you?' I said. 'Listen, Dicky, a man like that, a Moscow-trained senior Stasi officer, has on his desk every morning a list of all the contracted employees, contacts, informants and hangers-on used by Frank's office. Names and addresses; sweethearts and wives; habits and preferences. Complete with photos and medical sheets.' I was exaggerating of course. Dicky had gone pale at the thought of it. 'He doesn't have to worry about us sending someone to call on him that he doesn't recognize,' I said.

'He's nervous,' Dicky persisted. 'We've been through all this before, haven't we?'

'You bet we have,' I said. A hard-nosed KGB man named Stinnes had come to us with a bag full of Spielmaterial, and everyone had taken it seriously. So seriously that MI5 sent a K-7 search and arrest team to pick Bret up. There is no telling what mischief would have been made, except that Bret escaped to Berlin and, helped and protected by Frank Harrington, we provoked a showdown.

I suppose Dicky guessed what was going through my mind. He said: 'VERDI is the right one, Bernard. We've checked with the Americans: they aren't negotiating with him, and they are not going to. We'll share him with the Yanks. Believe me, he's what we want and he's ready to roll our way.'

'I hope you're right, Dicky,' I said. 'Because some people who know what's what tell me he's the sort of nasty little bastard who will bite juicy mouthfuls out of anyone who approaches him. I think he will lead us up the garden as far as he can, and then he'll blow the whistle.'

'I don't think so,' said Dicky.

'He'll take our money and laugh in our face. And anyone who is unfortunate enough to be on the other side of the Wall when it happens will be shipped back in a box.'

'It won't be like that, Bernard.'

'Not for you it won't,' I said. 'You won't be there.' I saw Fiona's face tighten. She hated rows, and I suppose she felt she was unfairly positioned in the middle of this one.

161

I thought Dicky was going to face me with a take-it-or-leave-it ultimatum. But Dicky doesn't precipitate showdowns that he might lose. Even ones he might only lose on points. 'Think it over, Bernard,' he said in a mild and friendly way. Then, as if the thought had suddenly come to him out of the blue, he added: 'I think you and Werner Volkmann working together would make a perfect team for this one.'

'How would that work, exactly?' I asked.

'You'd need a new network.' Dicky was obviously using off-cuts and out-takes from his lecture. 'But reliable people; people you and Volkmann know from way back.'

Dicky looked at me quizzically. What did he think I was going to do: leap up on to the table, stand to attention and whistle Rule Britannia? The idea of turning over my old contacts to Dicky was too horrifying to think about. I stared back at him without letting any reaction show on my face.

Dicky said: 'And Volkmann might be grateful for a chance to work for us again. He would be given a completely free hand.'

'Really, Dicky?' I said.

'In so far as anyone has a free hand,' Dicky corrected himself. 'And he'd be rehabilitated of course. Quite frankly he's not in a position to refuse.'

'I'll think about it,' I said.

'Good,' said Dicky, 'good.'

He knew I would agree. Quite frankly I wasn't in a position to refuse either.

10

Those grey and stormy days were, like my life, punctuated by what the weather men call 'bright intervals'. We were driving down to visit our children, and I didn't care that the rain was beating down from an angry sky.

'I think I fell in love with you the first time I saw you driving a car,' I said.

Fiona glanced at me suspiciously; she was always apt to suspect I was needling her when I said or did anything she wasn't ready for. 'Driving a car? Why?'

'I don't know,' I said. It was something to do with the calm way she did it. She drove fast but kept everything under control and was never flustered or uncertain. 'You drive like you do everything,' I added, but then became stuck for words. She drove as if she was guiding the Berlin Philharmonic through pianissimo passages of Ravel. I wished I could drive with that sort of restraint: my style was more like von Karajan winding them up for the end of the 1812 Overture.

'I prefer automatics now,' she confessed. 'That's a sign of getting old, I suppose. I used to say I'd never buy one.' She switched the wipers to the slower speed.

'You haven't bought an automatic,' I pointed out to her. 'You've borrowed it from your father.' It was an almost new Jaguar V-12 in metallic red with cream-coloured leather. Some might have thought it flashy, but my father-in-law considered it an example of his unassuming good taste. Now we were on our way to see him: and our two children who were in his care.

'Yes, but I've a good mind to give it back to him,' she said. 'I thought having a resident's parking permit would mean I'd find a place to park near home. Last night I had terrible trouble finding a space, and it gets worse the nearer to Park Lane you go. I wonder how George managed. I wonder how all those other people in the block manage.'

'Oh, the problems of the rich! They have chauffeurs, darling. Or take cabs.'

'I suppose you're right.' A few years back her father had given her a red Porsche for her thirty-fifth birthday, but he was so enraged when he heard that his daughter had defected that he seized the car and sold it. Now Fiona was a heroine and David Kimber-Hutchinson manifested his pride with an unhesitating generosity that was characteristic of him: he'd given her his wife's Jaguar.

'Are you sure you don't mind me driving?' she asked. I watched a bearded youth in a bread delivery van swerve across three lanes to pursue a mini-bus, drenching us with a spray of dirty rainwater as he went.

'No. You drive. I hate driving,' I said. It wasn't entirely true, but she was an obsessive driver and she hadn't had a chance to drive decent cars during her time in the DDR. And after that, at the house in California, Bret had become nervous whenever anyone decided to break out of prison for a few hours. Anyway this was Fiona's mother's car, and I didn't relish the prospect of explaining away any scratches the car might suffer while in my care. I was happy to be a passenger with nothing to do but look around. I toyed with a leather box that was between our seats. It contained audio cassettes. 'Are these yours?' I asked.

'Mummy's.'

164

'Wagner?' It seemed unlikely. Fiona's mother was a pinched pale-faced woman who seemed to have no role other than providing an awed audience for her husband's loud-mouthed and shallow-minded lifestyle. 'Boulez's complete *Das Rheingold* with Peter Hofmann's Siegmund?'

'You like to put everyone into little boxes, don't you? Then we have to comply with your classification.'

'Your mother and Wagner? They've been keeping it very dark.'

'She only plays it in the car, or on her Sony Walkman with earphones. Daddy can't stand Wagner.'

There must have been two dozen Wagner cassettes in the box, and there was no mistaking the signs that they were well used. 'I had your mother down for something more like this,' I said, holding up the one interloper and reading the label aloud: 'The Best of the Mormon Tabernacle Choir.'

'Oh, good,' said Fiona. 'Daddy's been looking everywhere for that. In fact I think he's ordered another one from Harrods.'

I put it back and closed the box. 'I met an old man – a pastor – over there in Magdeburg. He talked of you as if you were a saint. He said you were a great woman.'

'And I'm sure you put him right, darling.'

'Don't be that way, Fi. No one can be more proud of you, and what you did, than I am.'

'There's still so much to do over there.' We had never talked at length about her work in the East; she always managed to evade questions or make everything into a joke.

'He knew you. Wrinkly-faced old man with steel-rimmed granny glasses and one of those strong South Saxon accents that make even a sermon sound like a funny story.'

'I met so many pastors.' I glanced at her and she looked back at me without expression. Her double life in the East had provided an enigmatic overlay to the cool English serenity.

165

'He talked about you in a hushed voice. You taught them how to fight, he said. His flock regularly say prayers for you.'

Fiona shivered. 'I know.' Evidently she would have preferred not to know.

'Fight the government? Outwit the Stasi? Is that what you were preaching to those poor bastards over there?'

'Mobilizing the churches was the major part of the project.'

'It won't work, Fi. They'll be pulverized.'

'Do you think I don't worry about what I did? And about those people?'

'You won't bring the Wall down using only the trumpets of the Church. Joshua took an army with him.'

'You underestimate the Church. Everyone is underestimating it. Bret was the one who first saw the possibilities – that the Church was the most powerful force for change.'

'Bret? The Church?'

'They were Lutherans. Bret pointed out that of the twenty million people living in the DDR, more than ninety per cent of them were still members of the Church.'

'Even so …'

'I know what you're going to say. I heard it from everyone when we were trying to get permission for me to do my defection trick. Everyone here thought the DDR is the same agnostic chaos of materialism that we have in the West. It is not. You know that, Bernard.'

'*Chaoten*,' I said. The radicals, the squatters, drug addicts, serial killers, bomb-wielding terrorists of the Baader-Meinhof persuasion – these were the aspects of Western life that even the most repressed Ossis feared.

'Churchgoers in the East are a powerful, cohesive force, armed with their deeply held faith.'

'Deeply held faiths leap out of the window when the Stasi knock on the door.'

166

'No, Bernard, no. You have your faith just as they have theirs. You've faced nameless horrors bolstered only by your faith in the rightness of your cause. Give the Germans the benefit of the doubt. To each of those members of the Church, a promise has been made at baptism that they should be brought up in the Christian faith. And for a German, a promise is a solemn commitment.'

'I don't see it, Fi. I wish I could believe that the Churchmen could orchestrate a vast ground-swell of popular revolution that would sweep through the land and knock the Wall over. Is that what you truly hope?'

'Yes, it is.'

'Drip by drip, perhaps. A gradual process of liberalization. But that's not going to knock the Wall down before the end of the century. If ever.'

'We'll see,' she said.

'There's no denying that you've lit the fuse, Fi. But this new world of freedom is not waiting just round the corner. Anyone who thinks it is will be sticking their necks out.'

'They won't be risking anything for themselves that I didn't risk on their behalf.'

'Take it easy, Fi. I know Jesus Christ was a woman, but don't pull rank.'

She gave me a vicious jab in the ribs with her elbow. I gave her a kiss on the cheek in response. She said: 'Don't work against me, Bernard. That's all I ask.'

'I would be the only one,' I said.

'What do you mean?'

'Don't pretend you haven't noticed, darling. They roll out the red carpet for you. They hang on your every word. Dicky is courting you. Your secretary brings you fresh-cut flowers. The juniors give themselves hernias carting furniture to give you a lovely office. The Department is yours for the taking.'

'I wish it were true. But you don't see the opposition to my ideas that comes from those on high.'

'This business with Dicky – trying to tap into the Stasi mainframe computer and having Werner set up a network to collect the updates. Is that something you are really and truly pressing for?'

'Why do you ask?'

'There's something damned odd going on,' I said. 'Dicky went and did his stand-up comic routine in the Cabinet Office without anyone else there.'

'He's being groomed for stardom. Didn't you know that?'

'No one from the Department was there, except Dicky and the FO Adviser, who is not really one of us. That's unprecedented. Last year when the D-G was sick, and the Deputy was tied up with his law practice, the Cabinet Office refused to set up a meeting with the Controller Europe in the chair.'

'Perhaps they are becoming more easygoing.'

'Ha-bloody-ha.'

'What then?'

'Perhaps the D-G and DD-G are determined to keep at arm's length from it.'

'From what?'

'God knows.'

'Don't be so cryptic.'

'I really don't know,' I insisted. 'But judging by the lousy rotten things we know they are prepared to countenance, it must be something damned murky.'

'And Dicky is a part of this Machiavellian contrivance?' It was her way of scoffing at my cynicism, but I answered seriously just the same.

'I hope so,' I said. 'Because if he's not a party to it, he must be putting his head on the block.'

'Is this your devious way of telling me to stay clear of it?'

'I wouldn't presume.'

'Well, thanks anyway, darling. But if the Stasi mainframe computer can shed some light upon Tessa's end, I shall be standing up and giving three cheers for Dicky.'

Fiona's parents lived in an old house set in woodlands near Leith Hill in Surrey. The rain gods were packing up their act as we arrived, and a repentant sun scattered gold coins over my father-in-law's house and surrounding trees. Fiona got out of the car, stamped her feet and hurried inside, blowing on her hands. But I stood there for a moment, tasting the clean country air and looking at the landscape, no less haunting for being almost colourless. Winters were so much more severe here than in London. The ornamental fish pond was covered in ice, and in the shadows where the sun never reached, the grass and plants were spiky with frost. 'Come along, Bernard. You'll freeze to death if you stand there gawking at the pond.'

'Can the fish still be alive under that ice?'

'Daddy says the ice keeps them warmer.'

My father-in-law sometimes called it 'the farm' on account perhaps of the outbuildings: the stables, the kennels, the gardener's cottage and the lovely old box-framed barn that he had converted into an artist's studio. He'd torn down its roof to install a large overhead window, complete with electrically operated sun-blind. The walls, lined with polished wood, had been adorned with a few of his best canvases, and there were carpets on the floor except around the easel where they might have suffered drips of paint. Here he painted the pictures that were to be seen hung in unduly prominent positions in the houses of men who did business with him.

He was at the easel when the housemaid showed us in. He wasn't painting, he was inspecting a plain white canvas, flicking dust and lint from it and checking that its stretcher was precisely at right-angles. 'Darling!' he called in the theatrical baritone voice he could summon at will. 'And Bernard. How splendid.' He was dressed in a white cashmere turtleneck with a colourful neckerchief tied loosely at his throat. Dark corduroy trousers and monogrammed velvet slippers completed the effect. He seated us, and sat down on the sofa while Fiona itemized and admired the improvements he'd made to his studio. 'You've worked wonders, Daddy.'

He hadn't put any lights on and it was gloomy, a Rembrandt chiaroscuro from which the burghers had fled. The barn had gradually become David's 'den', complete with sofa and easy chairs and a cupboard always well stocked with wine and spirits. The ruthless modifications he'd wrought upon this old building, like the meticulous attention to detail and the high quality of the workmanship, were a tribute to David's energy and determination, and a key to his character. So was the way in which he now allowed family and business colleagues into his sanctum with the tacit implication that it was a privilege that brought with it unspoken obligations.

'It's a place I come when I have to think,' said David.

'Do you spend much time here?' I asked.

Fiona glared at me but it went right over David's head. He was concentrating upon pouring the drinks.

'No,' said David. 'Not much time for painting nowadays. Too busy trying to put a few pennies together.' He handed out the glasses: ginger ale for Fiona and mineral water for me. 'I wish you'd have a real drink.'

'He mustn't have a real drink,' said Fiona. 'He's on the wagon; trying to lose five pounds before he goes away.'

He stood back to look at me. 'You don't need to diet, Bernard. I've never seen you looking fitter. Have you taken up boxing? I used to be a rather useful fighter myself in my young days. How does he do it, Fiona? Tell me his secret.'

170

'Anger,' joked Fiona, but said it so promptly that an element of sincerity was evident in this judgement.

'Anger? What kind of anger?'

'Fierce and unrestrained anger at the world around him.' She laughed to make it a joke.

'Anger? If that was the secret I would be as thin as a rake,' said David grimly. 'This damned government have got no idea of what they are doing; they couldn't run a fish and chip shop. I'm serious when I say that: they couldn't run a fish and chip shop.'

'Was that the children arriving?' said Fiona, looking towards the door.

'Didn't the maid tell you? They went to the cinema with your mother.'

I felt like asking him why their outing to the cinema had to coincide with our visit and the first time we'd seen them in months, but I held my tongue. 'Here's health,' I said, holding up my glass.

He held up his gin and tonic, drank some and nodded before saying: 'I'm a socialist. You know that, Bernard. I always have been. It's my nature. That's why I took your children in. Can't bear to see anyone in trouble.'

In an attempt to head off another diatribe, Fiona said: 'And you're both well; that's wonderful.'

'I could go to Switzerland,' said David, still occupied with his own thoughts. 'And if the government tighten the screws any more, I will go.'

'Would Mummy like living in Switzerland?'

'Business has to come first, Fiona. You know that and so does she. Where do you think your trust fund comes from? You've noticed that I've topped it up, I suppose?'

'I phoned you,' she replied.

'It's always nice to get a little note. Better than all the talk in the world: a little thank-you in writing.'

171

'Yes, I should have written.' Fiona was totally dominated when she was in his presence; it was hard to believe that this was the same woman who had the Department in thrall.

'George is in Switzerland,' said David. 'Now there's a husband for you.' He said it to me as if George's journey to Switzerland was something I could learn from. 'He's determined to get to the bottom of Tessa's accident. Says he'll spend every last penny, if that's what it needs to do it. Count me in, I told him.'

'Yes, I spoke with George. I went there,' I said. 'But what is the mystery?'

David looked at Fiona. Sitting well back in her armchair she was almost lost in the gloom, but her head swung round and I saw her become attentive, as if the mention of Tessa's name had sparked some alarm in her.

'Where's the body?' David asked me, and then looked at Fiona: 'Now, now, Fiona, I know this distresses you; it distresses me. But it has to be dealt with.'

He waited for me to answer. I said: 'I suppose it's with the DDR authorities. Wasn't there a burial or post-mortem or anything? What have you been told?'

'We've been told nothing,' said David resentfully.

'Just that she died in a car accident on the Autobahn,' said Fiona.

Fiona knew all about it. She had been there at the Brandenburg Exit that night when Tessa was killed. But wisely Fiona had not shared her memories of that experience with her father, and it wasn't something I was inclined to embark upon. In any case Bret had got me to sign an official letter acknowledging that the events of the night when Fiona escaped from the DDR were all covered by my terms of employment. Taken literally, I wasn't allowed to talk about it, not even to Fiona.

'So where's the body?' said David. He finished off his gin and tonic and got up with a movement that emphasized his frustration.

'What time does the film end?' Fiona asked him as he rattled through the drink bottles.

There was a hiss as David snapped the top from a can of tonic. I could only just see him standing at the cupboard that held his paints and linseed oil and turpentine. 'I really don't know,' he said and then, turning to look at her, he added: 'Your mother usually takes them for tea and cakes, but I don't suppose she'll do that today.'

'It's just the snail's pace of their bureaucracy,' said Fiona.

'So what's happening meanwhile? Is she buried? Or is she rotting away forgotten in some refrigerator in some filthy little German mortuary?'

'Please don't, Daddy,' said Fiona.

'You've got to face it, Fiona. You can't hide your head in the sand.'

'I'll see what I can find out,' I volunteered. 'I'm going over there next week. I'll see what I can discover unofficially.'

'I wish you would, Bernard. George has hired a Berlin lawyer, and some investigator at zillions of dollars a day, but I don't hold out much hope that anyone can get those swine moving. I've heard nothing from him lately. Have you heard anything, Fiona?'

'From George?' said Fiona vaguely.

'From anyone,' snapped her father with that special wrath that parents save for inattentive children.

'No,' said Fiona. 'Not from anyone.'

All of a sudden the door opened and the children came bounding in, shouting and laughing. Billy was fourteen now, the time when children undergo great physical change. Sally was two years younger. No matter how many times I'd tried to explain to her that both of us still loved her, Sally had never accepted and adjusted to the idea of her mother going away so suddenly and without a goodbye or explanation. 'Why are you

173

sitting in the dark?' Sally asked without receiving an answer. But pragmatic Billy went round switching on the lights.

Billy was wearing a dark blazer and grey pants, but Sally was in a pretty dress. 'Long trousers,' announced Billy when there was enough light for us to see what he was wearing. This was why he was wearing school uniform on a weekend. He pointed to the badge on his pocket. 'And this is the school motto in Latin. I do Latin now. And French. I'm third from top.'

'That's good,' I said. 'You need Latin for languages.'

'Sally won't be doing Latin for a long time,' he said.

'But I'm in the swimming team,' said Sally. They were both standing close to me and waiting to be embraced in the way I always greeted them. But I didn't grab them. I could see that Fiona was tense and frightened of this confrontation. 'Go and kiss Mummy,' I said. 'You haven't seen her for a long time, have you?'

They turned to look at Fiona, but didn't move towards her. 'Hello, Mummy,' said Billy diffidently. 'Was it nice?'

'No,' said Fiona and smiled. She'd dreaded this first meeting and done everything to put it off.

'Are we coming home to live with you?' Sally asked her mother in a whisper.

Fiona glanced for a fleeting moment at her father and then at me.

I answered: 'Yes, of course. I'm going to cook spaghetti in our new home in London. I've made the sauce already. And you'll try out your new bedrooms. Then I'll bring you back here to Grandpa's tomorrow night.'

'Why?' said Billy, his voice a wail of disappointment. 'Why can't we stay with you always?'

'Just until the end of term,' I said. 'We think it might be bad to pull you out of school so close to the exams.'

'I'll do the exams,' promised Sally. 'I'll do anything.' They were wonderful children; uncomplaining and trusting; and

174

resolutely cheerful despite the constant upheavals they'd been subjected to. One day soon, when they were judging us for what we had done to them, could we plead extenuating circumstances? They were big now; very big. Suddenly I realized that they were so big that I would never again pick either of them up in my arms, throw Sally into the air or carry Billy pick-a-back and gallop upstairs with him. This realization gave me a pang, a deep and desperate feeling of loss.

Fiona's mother came through the door. Her coat and dress were almost ankle-length, and she was wearing a broad-brimmed hat with silk flowers on it. Her pastel-coloured clothes made her look like someone from a Victorian photo, and that perhaps was her intention. Behind her there was a maid in starched frilled apron carrying a tray. The Kimber-Hutchinsons had lots of local people working for them; they arrived from the village each with their assigned individual tasks. One made the beds, another cleaned the baths, another did the washing-up and so on. They provided a house that constantly teemed with women of all ages coming and going, and gave fitting reason to seek refuge in the den to which such labourers were denied access.

'Ah, there we are,' boomed David, looking at the tea-tray. 'This is what you children like, isn't it.'

The tray was arrayed with a Staffordshire bone china tea service, and two huge glass goblets inside which ice-cream of primary colours had been doused in brightly coloured sauces, whipped cream, chopped nuts and other confectionery. Stabbed into these sundaes were two wooden sticks: one bearing a coloured cut-out of Mickey Mouse and the other of Pluto. Solemnly David handed the ice-creams to the children. 'This is their favourite,' he told us over his shoulder in a conspiratorial voice.

'Don't eat it all; it will spoil your dinner,' said Fiona, who had spent many years restraining her children from eating sweets and biscuits and chocolate bars.

'Don't ruin the fun, Mummy,' David admonished her as he used a teaspoon to savour the concoctions. 'Eat up, children. You're only young once.'

Mrs Kimber-Hutchinson smiled wanly and took off her hat and coat. Catching Fiona's eye she mouthed the question: 'Did you bring the tapes?' Fiona nodded.

David smoothed his hair with the flat of his hand and said. 'What did I hear you saying, Bernard? Spaghetti? That's not a proper meal. We can't have you racing off again as soon as you get here. That Kingston bypass is a dangerous stretch on a Saturday night. "Murder mile" they call it. There was a TV documentary showing all the fatal pile-ups last year. You're staying to eat a real dinner. It's a celebration in Fiona's honour.' He was facing me now.

'We must get back,' I said firmly.

'But Fiona promised you'd be staying,' he insisted. 'We've made all the arrangements. We have friends coming all the way from Richmond. The food is being cooked and your bedroom is all prepared.'

I looked at Fiona in alarm. Defensively she said: 'That was when Uncle Silas was expected too. I thought you might want to say hello to him, Bernard.' Was it supposed to be a chance for me to ingratiate myself with Silas Gaunt, and thereby get a decent promotion? Jolted back to life, I found I'd been glaring at Fiona without even seeing her.

David corrected her: 'Silas hasn't said he wouldn't come. He said he would try. He is at some important antique show in Guildford. And there's a dealers' get-together afterwards. It's only a stone's throw from here. He'll come; we're expecting him. He won't want to drive all the way home from Guildford. Did you bring your things, Fiona?'

My glaring must have had some effect, for she was looking at me, her expression more contrite than I can ever remember, and her voice so hushed as to be almost inaudible: 'I did tell Daddy we would stay, Bernard. I packed a bag for us. Perhaps I forgot to tell you.'

'That's the spirit,' said David, jovial now that he had won the day. 'And tomorrow we'll go to church.' To me he said: 'We go to church every Sunday. I hope you'll join us, Bernard.'

'Yes, I will,' I said. 'I've got a whole list of things I want to take up with God.'

11

I've often suspected that my father-in-law had sold his soul to the devil. How else could he have arranged that everything he wanted came so easily to him? I was unpacking the bag that Fiona had hidden in the back of the car, and selecting a tie and shirt suitable for the sort of dinner party David liked to give, when I heard a car arrive. I looked out of the window in time to see the driver of a very muddy Range Rover holding a door open and helping the Falstaffian figure of Silas Gaunt as he climbed laboriously out of the front passenger seat. Silas was wearing a short military-style khaki waterproof. On his head he had a floppy-brim fisherman's hat of checked cloth.

Trying to describe Silas Gaunt's role in the Secret Intelligence Service would be like trying to describe Irving Berlin's role in the history of popular music. Gaunt had lived a long time and had seen the British Secret Service through thick and thin. Mostly thin; there hadn't been much thick; some said it had been nothing but one disaster after another. Now Silas was retired to 'Whitelands', his farm in the Cotswolds, but the influence he still wielded ensured that few major decisions were made in London Central without Silas's blessing.

Silas was seated at the end of the dinner-table. There was little alternative, for his girth and his gestures precluded him from fitting in between other guests. Once in position, he assumed the demeanour of host as he ordered the other guests to pour the wine or pass the vegetables and commanded their silence when he related one of his anecdotes. Instead of the country tweeds that were his uniform, he seemed to have gone to a great deal of trouble for this rare excursion into the outside world. He was wearing a dark pin-stripe suit, whose seams had succumbed at places to the weight he'd added since buying it. He had a dark blue pullover that I knew had been knitted for him by his adoring housekeeper, Mrs Porter. Now it was beginning to become unravelled at the hem. His shirt was freshly washed and pressed but the overall effect was marred by his worn and well-fingered necktie, its repeat pattern the neat coat of arms of some school or college he'd attended.

David was at the other end of the table. He was wearing a dark blue worsted Savile Row three-piece with a pink poplin shirt and a very brightly coloured necktie. Perhaps he'd forgotten about the clamorous behaviour for which Uncle Silas was famous, for David never entirely relaxed, and he quickly instructed the girl waiting at table to move some of the more valuable items of china and cut glass, so they were not within radius of Silas's exuberant gesturing.

There were other guests at the dinner party: a retired insurance tycoon, the owner of ten racehorses, and his magistrate wife. A son of a duke, looking down-at-heel as sons of dukes are expected to look, with long hair in a pony-tail and a shrill wife who shamelessly plugged her pony club and the titled people who sent their daughters there. There was also a very quiet Australian couple who had made an unexpected fortune from a marina built on the site of their alligator farm. They seemed to be constantly circling the world in an earnest attempt to spend the proceeds. Now they were considering the purchase of a luxury Monaco apartment in which David seemed to have a financial interest.

Soon after we sat down, a common theme emerged: horses. There was enough talk of point-to-points, 'accumulators', 'yankees' and Lipizzaners to leave me silent and confused. Even Uncle Silas joined in, contributing an old story about the horses of the Berlin fire department that were sold to the breweries when the motorized fire engines arrived. Every time they heard fire-bells these massive creatures galloped in the direction of the sound, taking the loaded drays with them on frenzied errands that shed barrels and teamsters too.

The menu was an elaborate one of pheasant and all the trimmings, with caviar to start, an oyster and bacon savoury to end, and crispy apple charlotte somewhere in between. On some other evening I might have found the food and conversation amusing, but I couldn't help remembering that while I was enduring this pretentious ritual, my children were upstairs having sausages and mash with one of David's many servants before being packed off to bed.

It was midnight when the racehorse people got up and went for their coats, and began the rites of thank-yous and good-nights. The Australians went racing after their coats too, skilfully resisting all David's urging to stay and look at his colour photos of Monaco. It was then that I noticed that Uncle Silas had also slipped away. I went upstairs and caught him as he emerged from the bathroom.

'Are you leaving, Silas?'

'Alas I must.' He opened the door of the room next to the bathroom, and switched on the lights. It was a bedroom, and from the clothes cupboard he took a hanger bearing his ancient waterproof coat. 'Alas, I must, Bernard,' he repeated. This bedroom had obviously been assigned to him for an overnight stay. The expensive soap on the wash-basin was new and unwrapped, the bedclothes had been turned down, and there were half a dozen of last year's hardback best-sellers and half a dozen freshly cut pink roses arranged on each side of the bed.

'I was hoping for a word with you,' I said.

He was still nursing his coat, scarf and hat, but now he draped them over the back of a chair and pushed the door closed. 'You open the batting, Bernard.'

'They've kicked someone out of the Department. And I think it's because of me.'

'Who was that?'

'A man named Kent. Outstanding record.'

'The Hungarian dentist. Yes, I know. Why should you think that was anything to do with you?' He turned to the window. The curtains had not been closed. I turned my head to see why he was looking at the walled kitchen garden. It was ablaze with light. I suppose they were anti-prowler lights; David had an obsession about prowlers.

'I was living with his daughter,' I said. 'Some people think that he came under pressure in order to break up the relationship.'

'The daughter?' He frowned as he thought about it. 'Is that who suspects that the Department applied pressure, and interfered with her love life?' There was a mocking brutality behind his words; he wanted me to know that I was stepping out of line.

'No, *me*,' I said. 'I suspect it.'

He stared at me for what seemed like ages. 'Don't be a bloody fool, Bernard. You've got a fine wife. You should be down on your hands and knees to her.'

'I am, all the time,' I said. 'But I keep splitting the arse out of my trousers.'

'Your dentist friend's usefulness came to an end,' said Silas. He pulled the curtains together with an angry jerk. 'I don't want to bore you with the minutiae of the Department's projected dental needs, so I suggest you just take my word for it.'

'Bore me,' I said.

'Very well.' The curtain was not completely closed, and through the gap in it he looked down again at the garden. 'There's something forlorn about a floodlit cabbage patch,' he pronounced. 'Walled. Looks like a prison yard.'

'Then don't look at it,' I said, and pulled the curtain completely closed.

Forced now to look at me, he said: 'We brought Kent and his family out of his homeland when things were very rough. He had a curious hobby: he colleeted old dental tools, and studied the history of European dentistry. He wrote a paper for one of the scientific journals. A smart young man in Coordination noticed it and told me. Here was a man whose handicraft could ensure that one of our agents sent into Hungary, East Germany, Poland or even the Soviet Union's more remote regions could arrive there with dentistry appropriate to his cover story.'

'That was useful,' I said.

'It was amazing. Of course it also meant that Mr Kent spent a long time with quite a number of our most important field agents. Unavoidably he knew when they were off, and where they were bound.'

'You should have recruited men with better teeth.'

'You're right,' said Silas. 'And that's what we have done. The false teeth and bad teeth that were so prevalent in my youth are now a thing of the past. Young men nowadays seldom have more than a filling or two.' He took a quick look at his wrist-watch. 'Cash is tight, Bernard, and we have to examine every penny of our expenditure. We decided to close the Kent operation down, and paid him off. Is he complaining about the money?'

'No, I believe he's content.'

'The girl?'

'Doesn't want to rock the boat.'

'She didn't ask you to take this up on her behalf?'

'She asked me not to. She's one hundred per cent reliable and dedicated.'

'Good. The work she is doing is very important. Hungary may be converting to capitalism, but we have to have people watching what's happening there.' He scratched himself and yawned, as if discovering the lateness of the hour had suddenly exhausted him. 'And what about you, Bernard? Are you one hundred per cent reliable and dedicated?'

'I thought I'd proved that on several occasions.'

'Of course you have. That night when we pulled Fiona out … You were there, Bernard. I don't have to tell you what happened.'

'It was a muddle. I grabbed Fiona and drove away.'

'You killed two of their people, Bernard.'

'It's in my report,' I agreed.

'And the only copy of that report is under lock and key. I don't want them to know that you killed those two men. Two senior KGB men. You know what rotters they are, and how they feel about fatalities to their own people. If they ever discover what happened …' He fixed me with those cold grey eyes that seemed so out of place in that chubby avuncular face. 'Well, they won't appoint a defence attorney for you, and warn you that you have the right to silence. I don't have to tell you what happens, do I?'

'No,' I said.

'And speaking from a purely selfish point of view, there will be hell to pay for us in London if the Stasi people decide your impulsive action was a gratuitous execution. Repercussions I mean. You've thought about all this sort of thing, I'm sure.'

'It has crossed my mind.'

'Expunge the events of that night from your memory. There is nothing on paper to say you were ever on that section of Autobahn. You and your wife were in a diplomatic vehicle with bogus diplomatic passports. At this end you were picked up in an army car and put on to an RAF transport to go to America. All without names. There is no document anywhere that places you at the site of the shooting that night. I suggest you never admit it. That you never talk about it or even think about it. Do I make myself clear?'

'You always do that, Silas.'

'It's you I'm concerned about, Bernard. The Department would no doubt weather a storm of that sort, as it has weathered such storms before. It's always the individuals who suffer.'

'Thanks, Silas.'

'Just forget the whole business. And forget the Kent family. Go to Fiona tonight and tell her how much you love her. Everyone in the Department wishes you well. Both of you. You know that, I'm sure. Me especially.'

'Thanks, Silas.'

'Fiona came out A-1 in the medical. You were pleased to hear that, I'm sure.'

'I didn't know,' I said truthfully.

'It was better that she was re-engaged and went through the regular enlistment procedures. Yes, A-1. Mind you, she's not the little girl we used to know.' He paused. 'The medical examiner thinks she would benefit from a few sessions with the psychiatrist. She became a bit angry at that suggestion: you know how touchy ladies can be?'

'Yes.'

'Of course you do. But she might change her mind. It would be much better if she did unwind with a psychiatrist. We have a top chap we regularly use: Harley Street specialist and all that rigmarole.' In a gesture combining friendly concern and authority, he grabbed my upper arm and clutched it tightly. 'I want you to watch her closely, Bernard. I don't mean spy on her, but if she needs help of that sort, you are to contact me immediately.'

184

'You are very kind, Silas,' I said. I pulled away from his grasp and wondered who were the 'we' who regularly used this top chap in Harley Street.

He gave a deep sigh. 'She'll soon be herself again. But meanwhile it frightens me to think she might go unburdening herself to some little doctor man she's gone to consult on account of not sleeping well. The Departmental secrets she holds in her head ...' He shook his head, as if thinking about that was too much to bear.

'Damn you, Silas,' I said without raising my voice. 'And damn your shrink, and your bloody medical examiner. Can't you think of anything but the Department and its bloody secrets? How many has it got left by now? I should think its secrets could be counted on the fingers of one hand. Fiona will never be herself again. Never, do you hear me? You sent her out there; you and Bret and the D-G and all the rest of you unfeeling bastards. And she's come back crippled. I know her better than anyone and I can tell you categorically: she will never be well again.'

He looked at me and sniffed. I had gone too far. 'Yes, well perhaps you are right, Bernard.' He wouldn't argue with me; that was a privilege reserved for equals. I was no more than the son of a colleague; someone to be indulged.

'Yes, I am,' I said. 'And another mistake you make is in thinking that Kent owes us a favour for bringing him out of Hungary. A more careful scrutiny of the record would reveal that he worked for us for a long time in Hungary. Damned dangerous work: we put newly arrived agents through his surgery so that he could positively identify them by means of their dental chart. It couldn't last: they were all going through that surgery. Eventually one of them was bound to be captured and talk. Kent was taken into custody and given the full treatment. They arrested his brother first – there was the confusion of the family name – and the brother didn't survive the first questioning in the police station. Kent cut his way out, through the floor of a

185

communist prison van, and escaped. He was on the run for two weeks. Then we brought him out.'

'Perhaps I was misinformed.' He smiled. He was a wonderful actor: the smile he gave was warm and friendly, as if he'd not heard anything I'd said. 'I'm off then.' He patted the belly of his knitted pullover and stifled a belch.

'David thought you were staying.'

'The roads are very quiet at night, and it's Sunday tomorrow. I like to have Sundays in my own home.' He searched his pockets to find a dented spectacle case. The cloth covering had completely worn away, so that its bared metalwork had become shiny like a bar of polished silver. After putting his glasses on, he snapped the case closed. 'Sorry to have missed the children. Bring them to see me some time.' He picked up his coat.

'Thank you. I will.'

He thrust an arm into the coat, raised it into the air and, with me tugging at it, dragged the garment on to his bulky form. 'There was some talk about everyone going to church tomorrow. I'll be sorry to miss that of course.'

'I'll say a prayer for you.'

'Would you, Bernard?' He reached for his floppy hat and put it on carelessly. 'I'd really appreciate that.'

After watching the lights of Silas Gaunt's Range Rover disappear into the distance I went up to our assigned bedroom, 'the pink room'. Fiona was sitting up reading. She had a whisky and water on the table by her side. Such was Fiona's most cherished time of the day: reading in bed with a drink at her side. *Buddenbrooks: Verfall einer Familie*, carried along with a pocket-sized German dictionary upon which her glass was now standing. She was working her way through the great German literature. Bret had compiled a list for her; he fancied himself as a connoisseur of German culture.

'What did Uncle Silas want?' she asked. As if suddenly remembering the whisky, she picked it up and took a sip. Hardly any of it had been consumed. She didn't really need the whisky: she just preferred to have it at her side. She was like that about the German dictionary too. She was like that about a lot of things, including me perhaps.

'The usual bullshit,' I said. She looked at me as if such sentiments about Uncle Silas offended her. But she didn't respond. She went back to *Buddenbrooks* while I undressed. She had even remembered to pack my new pyjamas.

'Why did Uncle Silas come here?' she asked eventually, without looking up from her book.

'Your father invited him to dinner.'

'Yes, I asked Daddy about that. He hasn't seen Uncle Silas for almost ten years. He says Silas phoned and invited himself, then said he couldn't come, and then changed his mind again.'

I went to wash and clean my teeth. When I returned I said: 'What's it about then? Did Silas want to see your father?'

'No. I was downstairs when he first arrived. I opened the door to him, and was with him while he had a drink with Mummy and chatted with Daddy. He took me in to dinner. Then after dinner, when the others were leaving, he went upstairs and I heard you ask him if you could have a word with him.'

'You've kept tabs on him very efficiently, darling,' I said. It was a joke, but Fiona had to rebut it.

'Of course not. I was dressed and ready before you were, so I went downstairs. Perhaps Silas just wanted to visit Daddy and Mummy again; they are family. He obviously didn't want to say anything in particular to anyone.'

'Obviously,' I agreed.

She looked at me, as together we reached the only possible conclusion about why Silas wanted to come here. 'What did he say to you just now?'

'Nothing I haven't heard a million times before,' I said. 'Keep the faith, keep the secrets, keep hard at work.'

'Is that all?'

'Forget the past, and the usual claptrap about keeping my head down when I'm in the East.'

'Perhaps he simply wanted to avoid the rubber chicken at the convention dinner,' said Fiona.

'There was no antique dealers' convention in Guildford,' I said. 'I checked it this afternoon; I phoned. I thought an antiques show might be an amusing outing for us. There was no antique show. Silas made a special journey to be here.'

I looked at her and waited for a reaction, but she made none. She continued reading for a moment and then, keeping the place on the page with her finger, she said: 'Doesn't *Weib* also mean wife?'

'Only in the Bible and other fancy writing. Or "old wives' tale" – *die Altweibergeschichte*.' I pulled back the duvet and climbed between the sheets.

She read on to the bottom of the page, put a marker in and put *Buddenbrooks* on the bedside table. I suppose her question had been a way of changing the subject, she was adept at that.

As she settled her head on the pillow I said: 'It might be better to let Tessa be buried over there.'

'Darling. How could you say such a thing?' She was very calm and seemed ready to talk sensibly about it.

'Bringing her back will simply get everyone hysterical,' I said. She grunted.

'George will ask for a post-mortem,' I persisted. 'Or your father will. You can see that coming a mile off.'

'I don't want any part of it.'

'You were there, Fiona.'

As if in answer she reached for the master switch on the bed-head and turned off all the lights. The room was in darkness, apart from a trace of light filtering through the curtains from somewhere down in the grounds. I turned on to my face and tried to go to sleep. I left everything unspoken. I really didn't know what construction Fiona put on the events of that night, but I knew that bringing Tessa's body back to England would tear the family apart and I wasn't sure Fiona could handle that amount of family discord.

'You didn't want to read?'

'No,' I said.

I didn't go to sleep. I was thinking of everything that had been said. Sometimes it's better to leave things unsaid; once spoken, ideas start hardening and eventually become memories. It was a long time afterwards when she spoke again. Her voice startled me, for I had felt sure she was asleep.

'What was she like, Bernard?' Fiona said suddenly and without warning. 'Was she like me?'

'Don't let's talk about it.'

'We have to talk about it. I lie awake all night thinking of her in bed with you.'

'Well, take sleeping tablets,' I said, and then regretted my short temper. In measured words I said: 'It was a situation of your making, darling. Your choice, your plan, your decision. I was totally unprepared for it. My dismay and consternation were a vital part of the plan. Don't blame me because it worked so well.'

'Were you in love with her?'

'I don't know.'

'Are you in love with her still?'

'No, no, no.'

'Did you tell her you were in love with her?'

'Perhaps. I don't remember. It's all in the past.'

'It's not the past for me, Bernard.'

'Fiona, it's all over between me and Gloria. She's not a bad person; and I wish you'd accept that she had no animosity towards you or anyone else.'

189

'I loathe her,' said Fiona. 'She's determined to get you back. You know that don't you?'

'No, I don't know that. Neither do you.'

'She's young, and young people have instinctive cunning.'

'You should try Uncle Silas.'

'Of course you are flattered by having a young girl's attentions, and a loyal wife too. Why shouldn't you be? You're human.'

I counted to ten, debating whether to ask her if she'd been unfailing in her marriage vows. Then I said: 'If you keep on putting us both through the wringer, everything we cherish will drain away.'

'Don't threaten me, Bernard.'

'There is no threat. You are destroying yourself with all this unfounded jealousy and suspicion and hatred.'

She sighed. 'They are my children, Bernard.'

'No, Fiona,' I said. 'They are our children. And soon they won't be children any more; they will be grown-up people. They'll be asking us both questions that might be difficult to answer without telling them they were relegated to a lower priority than our work. This possessiveness towards them, and your possessiveness towards me, is unnatural. And it's eating you up.'

'They are my children,' she said. 'And I can't have any more.'

'How do you know?' I asked. There was something in her voice that told me what she was about to say. 'How can you say that with such assurance?'

'I saw my gynaecologist on Thursday. He's doing tests and so on. But he said it would be unwise.'

'I'm sorry, Fi.'

'You're sorry?' she laughed bitterly. 'What the hell do you care? I thought you'd be delighted.'

I felt the movement of the bed-springs as she moved as far away from me as she could. I suppose I should have reached out and comforted her, but I didn't. I hadn't sufficient emotion to be able to spare any for Fiona.

Right now my mind was filled with anger at the realization that I'd played right into the hands of Uncle Silas. His reputation for being the most cunning and devious man the Department had ever had would not be eroded by the way he'd handled me tonight. He'd gone through an elaborate scenario to come here, bare his long fangs, and tell me to back off. Had I not gone racing upstairs after him, he might have been forced to take me aside and bully me back in line. But Silas knew me, and knew I'd want a private word. I had to bury my head deep in my pillow in order to block out the sound of him laughing his head off.

12

I ordered a car to collect me from the office at 6.30 p.m. but it had still not arrived at 6.45, and I was standing in the bitterly cold underground car park, marching round on the concrete in circles, trying to keep my blood circulating. Somewhere out of sight, at the far side of the floor, I could hear an engine turning over repeatedly but showing a melancholy disinclination to spark and start. Finally I walked along to see who it was.

It was Gloria. She had the car hood open and was bending over the engine of a little Peugeot 205. She flipped the starter motor and cursed to herself when the motor didn't catch. As she heard my footsteps approaching, she stood up straight and looked at me. She had taken off her suede coat but her big fluffy fur hat was still on her head and there was a furious scowl on her face.

'Bernard. Is your car on the blink too?' She was in sweater and skirt, and now she rubbed her arms to warm up.

'I'm waiting for a car from the pool.'

'Transport have some kind of crisis. Everyone had trouble getting a car today.'

'Can I use your cell phone?' I asked her.

'Haven't you got your own?'

'Dicky says phones are only for staff permanently assigned to the London roster. That's why I haven't got a proper office or a secretary.'

'Poor Bernard,' she said, without sounding too concerned. 'I don't carry my phone any more. I left it in a pub last week. I was so relieved to get it back that I've locked it up in my desk ever since.'

'Damn.'

'They make you pay for them if they are lost. Fifty-five pounds.'

'Shall I try it?' I said, getting into the driving seat of the Peugeot. I could guess what had happened. When she had her souped-up Mini she was always flooding the carburettor. 'Just leave it alone for a couple of minutes,' I said. I could never make her understand that you could have too much petrol. I could never make her understand that you could have too much anything. I suppose that's what had appealed to me when I first met her. She had a childlike determination to prove the truth of Oscar Wilde's axiom that nothing succeeds like excess.

'I'll give you a lift,' she offered.

'I haven't got it going yet.'

'You will, Bernard. Cars seem to like you.' She got her coat and put it back on.

After a suitable interval I turned the key and, with a couple of hesitant coughs, it roared into life. I stabbed the pedal to make sure the juice was flowing and then let the engine tick over as I got out of the car.

'Wonderful!' she yelled and clapped her hands. 'Jump in, Bernard. Where do you want to go?'

'I'll wait for the car I ordered.'

'Oh, yes? You'll be here all night.' She got into the car and switched the lights on.

I weakened as I saw that my sole chance of escape was about to disappear. 'Maybe I'll ride along with you until we spot a cab.' I climbed into the Peugeot beside her.

'Bayswater any good?' she asked, driving at a hundred miles an hour to the ticket machine, raising the barrier and going up the slope with a scream of burning rubber. She plunged into the evening traffic without hesitation while using one splayed hand to discover if the heater was dispensing warmth.

'You look like hell, Bernard. What have you been doing over the weekend?' She grinned wolfishly.

'I'm fine,' I said.

'You're not fine. Several people have remarked that you are not looking well.'

'I wish you wouldn't discuss my apparent state of health with all and sundry.'

'With your friends,' she said. There was still a measure of teasing.

'I've never felt better,' I said. 'How would you like me to start an inquiry into how you spend your weekends?'

'I told you what I was going to do. I was on a car rally in Shropshire. We came ninth out of fifty-three cars.'

'Why weren't you first? Have trouble starting?'

'That's a mean gibe, Bernard. I'm not the driver; I'm the navigator.'

'I forgot.'

'The competition's fierce. Some of the teams do almost nothing other than rallies; some of them were professionals. I think we did fine.'

'You did, Gloria. I was only kidding.'

'You've got to have a good driver; I just sit there and shout directions.' We were on Westminster Bridge going over the Thames now. 'Where are you heading?'

'I'm meeting someone in that safe house at Notting Hill Gate.'

'Is there a safe house there?'

'We were there. Don't you remember that night? The radio was on and we danced together.'

'When?'

'I don't remember the date. A nice apartment up at the top of the building. There's a view right across London. It was moonlight. You said how wonderful it would be to live in a penthouse like that.'

'Do you know, Bernard, I think I must be getting prematurely senile or something. I can't remember anything these days. My mother says I should take one of these memory courses that she sees advertised in her kitchen and bathroom magazines. Do you think they do any good?'

'I don't know.'

'Don't go bitter and twisted, Bernard. I can't help it if I can't remember going to a safe house in Notting Hill with you.' She jammed her foot hard on the gas pedal and the engine roared as we streaked down the wrong side of the road while she was tapping the clock to see if it was still working. 'Is that the time? I have to just call in to a garage in Bayswater, Bernard. Two minutes. Would that make you awfully late?'

'That's okay.' I had been looking out for a cab, but all the ones I'd seen were either carrying passengers or too far away to intercept. In the circumstances, accepting Gloria's offer seemed like the only way to reach my appointment on time.

'I have to collect the rally maps for next week. We're going to drive the route and do a reconnaissance before the rally.' She turned off Bayswater Road and, after going round a leafy square, found a narrow arched entrance. It gave on to a street of crippled little two-storey dwellings that had once been coach houses for the grand mansions they backed on to. The street was dark, its cobbled surface lit only by a couple of low-powered orange-coloured street lights. She pulled up in front of one of a row of lock-up garages. Discreet painted signs and brass plates indicated that the coach houses now housed repair and maintenance specialists for drivers of high-powered cars or fussy owners of ordinary ones. 'Come in if you want.'

Gloria got out and, using a key she took from her handbag, unlocked a brass padlock to enter one of the garages through a wicket-door that was part of a larger one.

Ducking my head I followed her through the door and waited until she had switched the lights on. Half a dozen blue fluorescent tubes pinged into life to reveal the sloping back of a turbo-engined Saab 900 of indeterminate age, painted with all the numbers and adverts that rally cars wear. On the far side of the garage stood a work bench and metal-working lathe. On the wall there were spanners, wrenches, saws and other tools. Shelving held tins of various spare parts, labelled and arrayed with commendable order across the width of the wall. A locker was decorated with a coloured photo of a shapely oiled nude hugging a spark-plug; the sort of calendar without which no workshop is complete. Impaled on the nail from which the calendar was suspended there was a sheet of oil-stained paper and scrawled upon it: 'Gloria darling, maps in kitchen. Take one set and the application form. I will deal with the insurance queries – It will be a tough one – Love P.' Gloria took the message and folded it carefully before throwing it into the waste-bin. She smiled at me.

'Whose workshop is this?'

'My driver owns the place. A really good fitter works here full-time. He pays his rent by fixing the car without charge.'

'And this Saab belongs to your driver?'

'It's getting old,' she said. 'In summer the Porsches can make rings around us, but in winter a Saab stands a good chance of winning.'

'It's serious, this rally business, is it?'

She smiled. 'I'm not giving up the day job, if that's what you mean. Wow!' she said as she looked at the bench. 'Look at what he's doing.' She switched on a bench light.

The car's engine was totally eviscerated; its oily entrails scattered piecemeal along the benches. Pistons, connecting rods, nuts and bolts were arrayed in such a way that they would go back in the same places from which they had come. Mysterious springs and small metal objects had been placed in tin lids and immersed in oily marinades.

It was a strange old place. Marks on the walls showed where the horse stalls had been fitted, and there was damaged brick-work from which the troughs had been removed. The floor was made from bricks worn smooth, with a gutter going to an orna-mental central drain. Everything was almost exactly as it had been when these same premises held a coach and a couple of horses.

'I'll get the maps. Do you want to see upstairs?'

'Sure,' I said, and followed her up the steep wooden stairs which creaked under our combined weight. These houses were getting on for 150 years old. The kitchen was just big enough to hold an unpainted table, two chairs and a square-shaped 'but-ler's sink' with a fearsome-looking gas water-heater above it.

'Does your friend live here?'

'Of course not. It's just store-rooms for engine spares and so on.' She picked up the maps that were arranged on the table together with a big envelope holding letters and application forms from the rally organizers. 'Have you got time for a per-fectly foul cup of coffee?'

'No,' I said.

'It won't take a minute,' said Gloria. As she filled the kettle with water from the gas heater it gave a soft bang and then roared into life with a furnace of blue and orange flames. She reached into the cupboard for an opened tin of thick gooey condensed milk, a jar of powdered coffee and two decorated pottery mugs. Then she sat down and waited for the electric kettle to boil. 'You didn't talk to anyone – Silas Gaunt or Dicky or anyone – about what I told you … about Daddy?' She began spooning the treacle-like milk into the cups.

'Mind your coat,' I said. 'Suede coats and condensed milk don't go well together.'

'Because it all worked out all right.'

'In what way?' I asked.

'For Daddy. They voted him a prestigious job at the university. He's leaving in a day or so.'

'Leaving? To go where?'

'Budapest. The university in Budapest. It's what he's always wanted, Bernard. He's so happy.'

'When did this happen?'

'They sent the official letter a month ago. The wrong address. It was returned to them. Luckily one of the Senior Fellows ... a man Daddy used to know, decided to phone. They haven't got used to making international phone calls for things like that. He'll have a lot of things to adjust to.'

'They phoned?'

'Last night. They tracked him down.'

'That's wonderful.'

'Just think: they might have simply asked someone else when their letter came back to them undelivered.'

'It's dentistry?'

'Yes. Research, teaching and so on. He's part of a programme the Americans are financing. He'll have control of his own budget, they said on the phone. Of course it won't be much of a budget, but that doesn't matter.'

'No, of course not.'

'Not when you think you are all washed up. You should have seen him.'

'What about your mother?'

'She's pretending it's what she always wanted too. I know she's a little scared of going back, but she can see how much it means to Daddy.'

'You'll miss them.'

198

'It's not so far away as once it was. And they won't sell the house here until they're quite sure.'

The kettle boiled. Gloria poured hot water on to the milk and coffee powder, and stirred the mixture furiously before passing one mug to me.

I sniffed at it. 'It's delicious,' I told her.

'Do they still XPD people?' she said without warning.

I stiffened. It was one of those taboo questions that I thought everyone at London Central knew better than to ask. Expedient Demise, the deliberate killing of an enemy operative, is an action never officially acknowledged or referred to in spoken word or writing. 'No,' I said firmly. 'That all ended many years ago, if it ever happened at all.'

'Is that your way of saying Shut up?'

'What's worrying you, Gloria?'

'Nothing. Why should you think that anything is worrying me?'

'This business with your father ... You don't seem so pleased about it.'

'Of course I am.'

'I know you too well, Gloria. There's something on your mind.'

'Did you speak to anyone about Daddy?'

'Yes. Entirely by chance I saw Silas on Saturday evening. I mentioned your father. Perhaps I tackled Silas in a bad mood, because I got no change out of him.'

'Saturday evening?' she said. Her face stiffened.

'And your father got the phone call on Sunday evening?'

'From the university in Budapest, yes. Just time enough for Silas Gaunt to make the arrangements,' she said cynically.

'What do you mean? You think there wasn't any letter that went back to them?'

'I don't know,' she said.

'But what's bothering you?'

'I'm frightened for him, Bernard. If he was in some remote spot in Hungary … It can be desolate there. And they said it would involve travelling and lecturing.'

'You've got to tell me what this is really about, Gloria. What are you keeping from me?'

'I know I'm not supposed to use the computer for anything but assigned tasks, but I was worried about Daddy. That day I saw you down there, I brought his file up on the screen and it all looked normal at first: the usual listing of operational files and continuity files and cross-referred "personals" and so on. So then I began looking at all his files, one after the other. It was all in order until I got to an operational reference dated this summer … It had been cleared, Bernard.'

'So what?'

'So what? Bernard, files are never cleared. This file has been emptied. And the file number has been entered on the list for re-use.'

'Why should that worry you so much?'

'You don't understand what I'm saying, Bernard. If you worked with those computers in the Data Centre you'd realize that that is unprecedented. And you'd know how much work is involved in wiping the files, and every single cross-referred file too. They've even wiped each numbered message referred to in each and every file.'

'If they are wiped, how can you tell? You can't see them, can you?'

'Because all the reference numbers – file, personals and so on – have been listed for reassigning.' She sipped some coffee. 'Let me explain this to you, Bernard. When you open a file, or even send a simple message, the machine provides a number automatically. Automatically; you don't select it. At present I can see what they've been up to, because I can call up the empty files on the screen. I load the file but there is nothing to be seen but a number; the screen is blank, all the back-ups are blank, including the master back-ups in the mainframe. But the worrying thing is the way in which those file numbers are listed for reassigning. One by one the computer will provide those numbers to new documents, and there will be no way of telling that anything has ever been wiped.'

'Okay, I don't know anything about computers. But doesn't each file number have a date? These newly assigned file numbers will have dates that are not chronological.'

'That won't mean anything. Lots of files are opened prematurely. They are dated as from the time that money was allotted, that someone gets permission to start work. No operator ever goes down into the Yellow Submarine trying to trace anything by means of a date; it would be hopeless. Nothing is chronological. No, once those files are reassigned there will be no way to see the join.'

'But how does this concern your father?'

'Three of his operational numbers are wiped.'

'Why are you telling me all this, Gloria?'

She hesitated and opened one of the maps on the table. 'You're not going to report me, are you?'

'Of course not.'

'Four of your files are wiped too. One of them was an ongoing operational file with a Category A prefix. The same reference as one of Daddy's files, so it was something you and Daddy did together.'

'Except that I've never worked with your father.'

'I shouldn't have told you.'

'Perhaps there is a rational and innocent explanation,' I said. 'Maybe they are just weeding the electronic data, the way they do with paperwork. Maybe it's just an error; there are plenty of those.'

'Forget it, Bernard. Forget I ever said anything to you.' She stood up and drank her coffee hurriedly.

'Look, Gloria. If what you've found out proves there is a plot to kill your father, then wouldn't it also mean there is a plot to kill me too?'

The effect of my question was dramatic. 'Oh, go to hell, Bernard!' she said, with a flash of that truly terrible self-righteous wrath she could muster. Then she picked up a map from the table and quietly said: 'Look at this route.' She spread it across the table. It was one of the large-scale Ordnance Survey maps showing all the contours, footpaths and every last cottage. 'We'll drive over the whole route next weekend. Then perhaps do it again the following weekend. Knowing the course is what makes the difference.'

'Will that Saab be put together in time?'

'In my car, silly.' She got out her handkerchief and dabbed at her eyes and blew her nose. 'I'll get you to Notting Hill Gate,' she said, picking up the maps and forms.

Before I went downstairs I used the bathroom. With its ancient taps, stained bath and cracked linoleum it was as cramped and timeworn as the rest of the little house. But Gloria had left her unmistakable mark here. The mirror was spattered with make-up, there was a long grey smear of mascara in the sink, and half a dozen balls of cotton marked with eye-shadow and rouge. But any last doubt I might have had that this was a habitat Gloria shared was removed by the perfume hanging faintly in the air. What reached so deeply into my memory was the almost comical absurdity of the heavy, spicy and totally unsuitable fragrance that she insisted upon wearing on special occasions – she called it her Arabian Nights perfume.

'Let's go, Bernard,' I heard her call from outside the building, and by the time I got down to the cobbled street she was standing with the brass padlock in one hand and the key in the other, waiting to lock up.

The short drive along Bayswater Road took only a few minutes. We talked banalities until she pulled up at the front door of the apartment block. 'Here we are,' she said. 'You are delivered safe and sound.' We sat in the car for a moment. I could smell the Arabian Nights perfume now. I wanted to kiss her but I knew I would not.

'Thanks for the lift, Gloria.'

She looked at the entrance to the apartment block. 'I told you a lie; I'll never forget that night. We danced. I remember every note of the music. I was only pretending when I said I'd forgotten.'

'I know,' I said.

'You'd better be getting along,' said Gloria. 'Take care of yourself, Bernard.' Like a small child, she reached out and slowly ran a finger down the sleeve of my coat. We both watched it moving as if it had a life of its own. I shivered as it was about to touch my wrist, but she lifted it away.

'Yes,' I said. 'I'd better be getting along.' But neither of us moved. 'Good luck with the rallying. Good luck to you both.'

'Thank you, Mr Samson. That's very sweet of you.' She smiled a brief nervous smile and I opened the door and got out. I slammed the door shut and waved goodbye. But she couldn't have seen me; she was five blocks away by then.

I'd collected the key to the Notting Hill apartment, so I let myself in. I suppose that someone had tried to decorate the place in a style that was warm and comforting but there was an all-pervading theme of kitsch, from the gilded mirrors in the hall to the electric candle wall-lights and the tassels on the curtains.

When I went into the drawing-room, Fiona was standing by the window wearing a mink coat. It was a legacy from her sister Tessa. 'I didn't see the car arrive,' she said.

'The car didn't show up. I got a lift.'

'That was lucky,' said Fiona. 'I had to get a cab from Hampstead; I had terrible trouble getting here. Is it still raining?'

I hung up my raincoat, sank down into an armchair and sighed. Fiona looked at me quizzically. 'No,' I said. 'It stopped raining a long time ago. Where's Dicky?'

'The meeting is cancelled. Our man couldn't make it. I hung on for you. I thought you'd have a car.'

'He's nervous,' I said. 'We're going to lose him.' The man we had been due to meet was described on the Diplomatic List as a Third Secretary of the East German embassy. But his real job was assistant to the codes and ciphers chief. He was a good catch but he wasn't landed yet. I'd been in at the previous meeting and I could tell he was having second thoughts.

'What you told Dicky was right,' said Fiona. She was angry because Dicky had not told her of the cancellation earlier and had caused her a wasted journey across London. But she didn't rail against Dicky; she blamed the house instead: 'It's this damned safe house. It's compromised. It shouldn't be used for operational meetings any longer.'

'It's the money,' I said. 'There isn't enough money for new safe houses. Not even enough to heat this one properly.'

'I didn't switch the heating on. I thought you would come here directly from the office.'

'I wondered why it was so cold in here,' I said. 'Would you like to go out for dinner?'

'I don't want fish and chips from Geale's, if that's what you mean.'

The Notting Hill safe house was conveniently close to one of London's finest fish and chip restaurants, but I suppose Fiona wasn't dressed for it.

I went to the phone in the hallway and ordered an official car to take us home. While on the phone I inquired from the car pool desk why my car hadn't arrived.

'Your car was cancelled, Mr Samson,' said the duty transport officer.

'Cancelled? I don't think so.'

'A lady phoned …' there was a pause and I heard him as he turned the pages of his booking register. 'Here we are: six-thirty. Car to Notting Hill Gate – cancelled at five minutes past six. I took the call myself. It was a young lady's voice. I thought it was your secretary. Is that where you are now?'

'I haven't got a secretary,' I said. 'Yes, that's where I am.'

'I'm sorry, Mr Samson. It sounded official. I'll send a car right away.' He'd recognized Gloria's voice of course. He knew who'd cancelled my car.

'Thank you,' I said and rang off.

So Gloria had pretended she couldn't get her car started, to provide a chance to tell me about the wiped files. She reasoned that anyone going to such elaborate trouble to eliminate the files would also want to eliminate everyone who knew what was in them. What she told me seemed like a persecution theory, but Gloria was a smart girl.

So had she been about to tell me more? Had my slowness to understand what she was driving at caused her to abandon an attempt to explain a more elaborate theory? Or were Fiona's suspicions, about Gloria wanting me to marry her, the real motive? Was this 'persecution' invented as a way of seeing me regularly?

'What's happening?' Fiona asked when I stepped back into the drawing-room. She was standing near the window, still wearing her mink coat, framed by the elaborate floral curtains and the ridiculous flouncing that topped them.

'The car pool will send a car right away,' I said.

She looked at me, and, using both hands, smoothed the big fur collar up around her head as if she didn't want to hear any more.

I knew the transport officer. He was a young red-haired Scotsman. I liked him – he always laughed at my jokes – but how long would it take to go around the Department that I was getting together with Gloria after work? And how long would it take for the rumours to get back to Fiona?

13

'Your new hair-do looks nice, Tante Lisl,' I said, in that feeble confused way I always delivered such compliments.

She fluttered her mascara-laden eyelashes and touched her dyed and lacquered hair. She was sitting in her study. This had always been her special retreat; she took her breakfast here – on the tiny balcony with the French window open if the weather was warm – and did the accounts, checked the bills and took the cash from her hotel residents. A stirring portrait of the young Kaiser Wilhelm was on the wall where it had hung in her father's day, when this was his study. And on the mantelpiece, over the stove, there was the old ormolu clock that measured the night hours away with chimes more audible than most within earshot wished.

She was no longer confined to the stainless steel wheelchair that had occupied the centre of this room on my last visit. The wheelchair was relegated to the cobwebbed basement store-room, along with a trunk of my father's possessions which I'd not so far disposed of, and Werner's cherished golf clubs for which Lisl, upon finding them, had expressed picturesque contempt.

Her knee and hip operations had made her surprisingly ambulant, so that she was occupying a comfortable wing-armchair under a reading light. Some of the light struck the lower part of her face and revealed the powder and rouge without which she felt undressed. On the floor beside her chair there was a magnificent leather photo album with a hand-written label: My Caribbean Cruise. 'New hair-style, new hips and knee, new hotel, new life,' she said, and gave one of her inimitable full-throated laughs.

'Yes. It was a quite a surprise walking in here,' I said with unalloyed sincerity. I'd known Lisl Hennig and this shabby old hotel off Kantstrasse since I was a child, since I was an infant I should say. And when I walked in that morning I had almost shouted out loud. It wasn't that there was anything here that I didn't remember seeing before. But the last time I was here Werner Volkmann was taking over the management of the hotel. He had just married Lisl's niece – the one-time Ingrid Winter – and a complete refurbishing was being undertaken.

But now Werner's brief spell as manager, and his marriage, had ended. The tasteful furnishings that the dedicated Ingrid had lavished upon the hotel had been swept away. Back behind the bar, arranged around the old spotty mirror, were the shelves filled with dozens of bottles of rare and remote liqueurs and spirits that no one ever ordered. Huge prehensile potted plants, that endlessly shed leaves but never flowered, were once again helping to block the narrow entrance at the bottom of the stairs. Lisl's collection of signed photos of people who'd visited the house as guests in the old days or as hotel clients after the war – Albert Einstein, Von Karajan, Max Schmeling and Admiral Dönitz – had been reinstated on the wall. The complete set of 'Scenes of German Rural Life' prints were back on the walls of the dining-room along with the priceless original George Grosz drawing. Lisl's hotel was now almost restored to the place it had been for half a century or more before she handed over to Werner. The old bentwood chairs in the breakfast room, the dusty aspidistra plants that seemed to flourish in the salon's dim light, everything was back the way I remembered it from my childhood. Even Tante Lisl had turned the clock back. The joint replacement operations had restored to her the ability to stride slowly around the whole premises, go unaided up and down stairs – albeit with deliberation and care – and to pounce upon anything that was not exactly to her liking; anything that seemed to have originated with the mild-mannered Ingrid.

The legal reversion, and the exhaustive reinstatement of furnishings that followed it, was understandable when one remembered that for Lisl this was not just a hotel. It had been her home; she'd grown up in this house. So had I; that was something that I shared with her. My father had been posted to Berlin at the end of the war and billeted in this house together with me and my mother. The salon had become a smart little teashop by that time, with Lisl's concert pianist husband playing Gershwin tunes on the Bechstein, missing a chord now and again because of the arthritis that was slowly transforming his hands into claws. My family remained here even when all manner of lovely houses were available to the 'rezident' – a man who was running the only reliable Allied intelligence organization probing the Russians. I suppose all three of us Samsons became sentimentally attached to this house, its shell-pocked façade, its interior decoration – like a museum of old Berlin – and became bewitched by wonderful crazy old Lisl too.

'Did you eat? The plat du jour is Eisbein.' She was wearing a vivid emerald green wrap-around dress, a convenient garment for someone on a drastic weight-loss programme with some way still to go.

'I've eaten already,' I said.

'You used to adore Eisbein.'

'I still do.'

'I'm sure there will be one left. A little extra cooking time doesn't hurt an Eisbein.'

'This evening perhaps.'

'You've seen your room?' she asked.

'Thank you, Lisl,' I said. 'You're a darling.' In fact I knew that it was Werner and his wife I had to thank for preserving the accumulated squalor of the cramped attic room I always used. But Lisl was not above taking credit from others when affection was at stake. I went to her, leaned down and kissed her on the cheek. She was heavily made up with the sort of paint and mascara job that was more usually seen on the other side of the footlights. Her perfume was almost overwhelming.

'Two kisses in Germany, Bernd. You are not in England now.' She lifted her head and turned the other cheek to me.

'I love you, Lisl,' I said. 'It's wonderful to see you so fit and well.'

'I look after myself,' she said complacently. 'You should stop drinking, lose some weight, take exercise and get more sleep.' She said it automatically and without much hope that her advice would be taken. She'd always enjoyed mothering me, and like a mother she repeated always the same advice. Even when I was eighteen years old, and as thin as a beanpole, she would tell me to stop eating dumplings and avoid any but German beer, because of the chemicals. 'You promised that next time you would bring family photos,' she said.

'I'll send some,' I said. 'Fiona is looking wonderful. And the children have grown so tall you'll not recognize them.'

'Stay with your wife, Bernd. You'll not regret it in the long run. She's given you those two wonderful children. What more could a man ask?'

I smiled and said nothing.

'That girl you were with on the night of the party. She was no good, Bernd. That's why she got killed. She was no good.'

'That was Fiona's sister. I wasn't *with* her,' I said, trying hard to remain unruffled.

'I heard differently.' She looked down to admire the silver boots she was wearing. They were high–sided shiny ones intended for party wear. She wiggled her toes and then grinned at me. I suppose she hadn't seen her toes in a long time.

Her distraction was intended to stop the conversation, but I was determined not to let it go at that. I said: 'Dicky Cruyer booked a double room at the Kempi or somewhere, using my name. Tessa was with Mr Cruyer.'

Lisl waggled a finger at me. 'That woman left with you, Bernd. Don't deny it. She got into your car and you drove off with her.'

'It was a van with diplomatic plates. And it wasn't mine. I couldn't persuade her to get out. I had to leave. It was an official job.'

'Cloak and dagger,' said Lisl slowly in her execrable English. She liked sprinkling her speech with English and French words and phrases. That was why people had trouble understanding her.

'Yes, cloak and dagger.'

'Her man came looking for her. He was angry. She was no good, that woman. You only had to look at her to see what she was.'

'It wasn't like that,' I said.

'Crime passionnel,' said Lisl. 'He was furious, the man who came to collect her. He roared off on his motor cycle with a terrible look on his face. I could see there was trouble ahead.'

'What man on a motor cycle?'

My question gave Lisl instant and profound satisfaction. She smiled smugly. 'Ah! You don't know it all, Liebchen. So they didn't tell you about her man following her. I was frightened for your safety, Bernd. If he'd found you together …'

'Tell me more about the man. How do you know he was looking for Tessa?'

'He was her boyfriend or some sort of paramour. He was asking everyone where she was.'

'What did he look like?' I asked her.

211

'Oh, I don't know: older than you, Bernd, quite a lot older. Plumpish, but strong-looking, with trimmed grey beard and American-style glasses. He kept saying he was late. He was carrying two of those big shiny helmets. Two of them! I suppose one was for her to wear while on the back of the bike.'

'You're right, Tante Lisl. I didn't know about him.' It was a man named Thurkettle. So that was the missing link. It all started at that damned fancy-dress party at List's hotel. Until now I'd never been able to believe that Tessa's death was part of a conspiracy, for I'd taken her to the Brandenburg Exit, that place on the East German Autobahn where she met her death. And since then I'd been blaming myself for everything that happened. When I set out from the party to meet Fiona, in her escape to the West, I'd let Tessa climb into the van ... or at least I'd not dragged Tessa out of it, the way I should have done. But now it seemed more likely that Tessa had deliberately got a lift with me, perhaps because Thurkettle had not turned up to collect her.

'Detectives came next day. They said there were reports of drug-taking at the party. I said I didn't know half the people who were there. They spoke to Werner too. They didn't come back. Were there people taking drugs that night?'

'I don't know, Tante Lisl. I didn't see anyone who looked particularly high.'

'Not even that woman – Tessa?'

'Perhaps.'

It was a trap: 'She was on drugs, Bernd. How can you deny it?'

'You may be right, Lisl. She was behaving very strangely.'

'I hate drugs. You don't take anything like that, I hope.'

'No, Lisl, I don't.'

'You've got to think of your family, Bernd.'

'I do, Lisl. I don't take drugs.'

'Neither does Werner I hope.'

'No, I'm sure he doesn't,' I said.

'Have you spoken with Werner?'

'I always come to see you first.'

She smiled. She knew it wasn't true. 'Werner is backwards and forwards. Doing things over there. It's dangerous, Liebchen. Can't you stop him?'

'You know what Werner is like,' I said. 'How could I tell him what to do?'

'He respects you, Bernd. You are his closest friend.'

'Sometimes I wonder if that's still true.'

'Yes, it is,' she snapped. 'Werner thinks the world of you.'

'He's back with Zena,' I said.

'He told me.' She rolled her head and stared at me in a wideeyed grimace that signified that the world was a strange place in which outspoken judgements concerning such partnerships could be hazardous. 'Perhaps it's all for the best.'

Poor Ingrid. So that's how the situation had played out. I suppose she was the focus of Lisl's displeasure for changing the hotel. It was too inconvenient to blame Werner. 'I liked Ingrid,' I said cautiously. 'Zena is just out for what she can get. She doesn't care about him.'

'You can't tell people whom they must love, Liebchen. That's something I learned many years ago.' Lisl's upper body swayed, and then using the strength of both arms she got to her feet with admirable agility. 'I shall now have my afternoon nap. The doctor says it's important for me. You go and find Werner. I think I heard him come in.'

'There's nothing wrong with your ears, Lisl.' I hadn't heard Werner or anyone else come in.

'He has that room with the hard mattress. I think his spine is bothering him again; he's always suffered with his back. The door squeaks. And you must tell him to stop going over there.'

'I'll try, Tante Lisl.'

'It's lovely to have you back here, Liebchen. Just like old times. But if your people in London want to find the killer of that woman …' she paused. Her tone of voice expressed considerable doubt about this being our wish. 'Look for the man on the motor bicycle.'

'Yes, Lisl.'

Werner must have had hearing as acute as Lisl, for no sooner had I left Lisl's study to find a seat in the salon than he came in carrying a vase with a dozen long-stem red roses in it. 'Has she gone?' he asked.

'For a nap.' Werner always remembered to buy her flowers.

'I'd better not disturb her,' he said, although we both knew that Lisl's naps were convenient fictions, contrived to enable her to do the crossword in *Die Welt*, or drink a glass of sherry without the distraction of polite conversation. 'I'll take them to her later.' Werner put the flowers on the piano.

The piano was open and Werner couldn't resist fingering the keys while standing over it, but in deference to Lisl's notional nap he stopped after a couple of bars. Still at the piano he said: 'She keeps nagging me about exercising and losing weight.' His tailored tweed pants and custom-made shirt were obviously Zena's doing, and he was looking very trim despite Lisl's recommendations. It was certainly a change from his usual outfit of baggy corduroy trousers and old knitted shirt.

'She does that to everyone,' I told him.

He closed the piano. 'It's the hip replacement. She's suddenly discovered good health. She is fired with all that evangelizing zeal of the newly slender.'

'You need have no fear of anything like that from me,' I said.

'She treats me like a small child.'

'She worries about you.' Werner pulled a face. 'She worries about you going over there,' I said and pronounced *drüben* – over there – in the slurring exaggerated way that Lisl always said it.

'I haven't been over there,' said Werner in the same voice.

'I thought you were there doing Dicky Cruyer's bidding.'

'Bidding?'

'A network for VERDI.'

Airily he said: 'You're losing your grip, Bernie. You don't go over there when you are negotiating that kind of deal. That would tempt them to lean upon you heavily, or even arrest you on a charge of suborning a servant of the People. No, at the very first contact when you are enrolling a first-rate Moscow-trained bastard like VERDI, you make him come over here and talk.' There was a certain restrained relish to the manner in which Werner delivered this lesson. Playing at spies for London Central was to Werner what batting for England represented for Dicky Cruyer: a dream so precious that it was usually referred to only by means of bad jokes.

'So VERDI came here?'

'It's the rule isn't it? The first contact must be on home ground?'

'What do you want me to say, Werner? Do you want me to ask you to lecture at the training school or would writing an instruction manual be enough?'

'VERDI came here to West Berlin. I showed him the written enrolment contract that Dicky sent to me. VERDI locked himself into a room the Russian Army keep for the soldiers who guard the memorial, and read it carefully three hundred times. I sat outside in the car and got a chill.'

'And he agreed?'

'I think so. Yes.'

'So you'll set up a network?'

Werner gave a mirthless little snort. 'Set up a network? How would I do that?'

'Isn't that what Dicky wants?'

'It's early days. Let's see what VERDI can provide.'

'I thought Dicky was in a hurry,' I said.

'Yes, he is,' said Werner cryptically.

'What did the contract offer?'

'It was a contract – a sealed pack.'

'But what did it say?' I persisted.

'Dicky said I was just to be a messenger. He said it was safer for me personally to stay at arm's length from the deal. VERDI doesn't know that I'm the one who is supposed to set up the channel to handle his material. No danger of VERDI expecting answers to his questions if I am just the messenger.'

'So what was in the contract?'

'I thought I'd better have a quick look through it,' he admitted, shifting uneasily. 'You won't say anything in London?'

'You know me, Werner. I'll go back there and tell Dicky everything you say. I've already promised him to have your room bugged.'

'The usual contract,' said Werner, and gave me an uneasy smile. He wouldn't budge. He didn't believe I would spy on him but simply hearing me say it was enough to have him give all his attention to picking imaginary cotton threads from his dark shirt.

I watched him for a moment and then I said: 'I used to know someone named Werner Volkmann. A nice kid: four beats to a bar. Maybe not always straight and level but I knew his rate-one turns would have just enough bank and rudder. Do you see anything of that kid nowadays?'

'What do you want from me, Bernd?' I was Bernd now; no longer Bernie.

'You've changed,' I said. 'I don't know where I am with you any more. Back in the old days you would never have told me

216

not to go back to Dicky and spill anything you told me. We were partners. So what's the deal nowadays? What did I do, Werner? Or what did you do?'

'Zena was reporting on me. Reporting back to London.' So it hurt that much.

'So she told me.'

'On me!' he said. I obviously had not reacted energetically enough to his cry of pain. I scowled. 'Checking on me while I was living with her,' he added, just to make it clear.

'I got it, Werner. So how does that have any bearing on why you won't tell me what was in VERDI's contract?'

'Why didn't you tell me what Zena was up to? Did you think it was smart to play with me like that?'

'Come along, Werner, you don't think I knew that she was on the payroll? London doesn't tell me things like that.'

'You're one of them.'

'One of what?'

He shrugged. 'You're British; I'm German.'

'Go and take a cold shower, Werner. Then come back and tell me what was in that contract.'

'Why?'

'Because tomorrow I'm going over there to talk to VERDI's dad.'

His eyes fixed on mine as his brain searched rapidly through the computer. 'Yes, I heard the old man was still alive. Is he still in Pankow?'

'Sure to be. You don't move out of one of those pension houses in Pankow. Not when the alternative is living in an unheated barracks in Moscow. None of the Russians want to go back.'

'Watch your step with him,' Werner said. 'He's sure to be a believer of the old school.'

'He was on the payroll. Our payroll. Do you know that, Werner?' I could see that I'd surprised him, despite his trying to hide it. 'Dad paid him right through the Berlin airlift. Wonderful stuff about the Soviet estimates. Dad was running him personally.'

'That explains a number of things.'

'For instance?'

'Those gold sovereigns we took to Zurich – remember?'

'No, Werner. That was years and years afterwards. We were only kids at the time of the airlift.'

'Your dad wouldn't let a contact like that go cold. How many agents did your father run? Run personally, I mean? I'll bet your dad kept paying him. I'll bet the monthly payments we used to make to Madame Xavier were a Swiss bank account for him.'

I'd never thought of that. 'It's possible,' I agreed finally.

'Madame Xavier,' he repeated.

'Maybe.'

'You thought your dad had a woman over there,' said Werner. 'You thought Madame Xavier was his fancy woman.'

'I never did.'

'You never said it; but that's what you thought. Admit it, Bernd.'

'It crossed my mind.'

'VERDI's old man is probably still living on the money he earned from your dad. Things are tough for Russian army pensioners these days. Even the Guards regiments are weeks and weeks behind with their pay. A few Swiss francs would go a long way over there.'

'I'm going to see what I can get out of the old man, Werner. But I need to know what it's all about. Does VERDI's contract provide for him to come over here to live? And if so, when? Or is Dicky going to keep him over there as long as possible? Is the old man coming over too? Or is the whole thing bullshit – just one of Dicky's dreams?'

'Reading the ashes of that contract Dicky offered him won't help you figure out any of that.'

'He didn't keep it?'

'He burned it.'

'Is he on the level?'

'If he goes through with it, his people will spend a lot of time and trouble trying to find him and kill him,' said Werner. 'They would have to. If he got away with a big one like this, others would try.'

'Perhaps we both have spent too much time with devious people, Werner. I almost feel sorry for VERDI trying to decide which way to jump.'

'Don't feel sorry for VERDI,' said Werner feelingly. 'He's a nasty piece of work and always has been. You know that. And you're his meal-ticket.'

'You said you didn't think he would come over to us.'

'No, I said his people will seek him out to kill him. But that won't stop a man like VERDI. He'll ignore Dicky's contract. He'll wait for you to make contact and then he'll start the real bargaining.'

I sighed. What a prospect. 'And his father? Is he a part of the deal?'

'He must be a hundred years old. Forget about the old man. Watch out for VERDI. He's not the same greasy little thug we used to know, Bernard, hanging around in the Polizeipräsidium with his hands in his pockets and nothing to do. He's been to the Military Diplomatic Academy and spent some years behind an Area Desk before being transferred to the Stasi. He's acquired a polished arrogance you'll never believe.'

'But isn't he a codes and ciphers man?'

'He was, and that's why Dicky needs him, but since going to the Stasi he's a big shot. All the Russian-trained senior staff are big shots.'

'Do we know why he moved to the Stasi? Wasn't he better off with the KGB?'

'Who said he volunteered? They always get rid of them, Bernard. Even the Volga Germans are not permitted to serve in Germany, lest they become too pally with the locals. Having a German mother put VERDI in that same doubtful category. If he volunteered to move, it was only because he knew he would never get the *papakha* in the KGB.' The papakha was the peaked hat with the oversize top that is worn by Soviet colonels and above. It sounded right, and Werner had an instinct that I always trusted.

We sat there in that dark room watching the sun go down. Berlin was cold, as cold and grey as only Berlin can be. There was not a breath of wind, and the unusual calm added to the strange unreality. Summer had gone but winter had not arrived.

Strangers who hated the city complained about the wide streets and the larger-than-life stone apartment blocks that dwarfed the people below. And on days like this even Berlin's most loyal inhabitants were tempted to ponder ways to escape. The sun was low, its last rays dribbled down the top of the next apartment house like rich German mustard on a boarding-house dumpling. The trees were bare, and on Tante Lisl's cherished rose-bushes just one large white bloom survived: brown-streaked with frost, and drooping, it hung by a thread. 'But I'll see the father too,' I said, breaking a long silence.

Werner seemed not to have heard: 'Remember the days when hotel staff over there turned away tips, haughtily telling us that that was not the way things were done in their new socialist State? Remember when they were all so proud and condescending? Remember when spying was done by patriots? That's not so long ago, Bernie. Now those same bastards will sell their own mother for a Black and Decker power drill and a Rolling Stones album. It's dog eat dog and getting worse every day.' I could only just see him in the darkness but I knew he'd turned to look at me. Perhaps I wasn't registering the appropriate rage. My capacity to hate VERDI was limited. He had after all let me get away at a time when there was an arrest-on-sight order on his desk. Even being thrown off the Warsaw–Berlin Express was better than what was waiting for me at journey's end. 'Why are you doing this anyway?' Werner said, and sighed.

'For Dicky.'

'For Dicky,' said Werner scornfully.

'I'm not in a position to argue with London Central,' I said. 'And Fiona thinks that tapping into their records will tell us what happened that night Tessa was killed.'

'You were there, weren't you?'

'I was there on the Autobahn,' I admitted. 'We were at a section of road that was being rebuilt. It was staked out. It was dark and the rain was bucketing down. And all I could think about was getting Fiona out of there in one piece. So I don't know what happened. Not what really happened.'

'You're in one piece, and so is Fiona,' said Werner. 'Does it matter what really happened?'

'I'd like to sort it out, Werner. I'd like to have an explanation that eased Fiona's mind.'

'Let it go, Bernard. Just do your duty the way the book says. Screw it all up. Invite VERDI over here and say hello to him and make sure he doesn't like the offer. Let him say whatever he wants to say but then forget it. Scribble one of your famous reports that take five pages to say nothing. And go back to London and tell Dicky that it won't work. Dicky will believe you. And I'll back you up one hundred per cent.' I knew he was pulling the funny face that he kept for situations very serious. 'This is heap bad medicine, pale-face.'

'Fiona and George Kosinski … they won't let it go, Werner. They loved Tessa – I did myself. She's my family in a way. And bereaved families won't let go until they are satisfied. People are like that when they lose a relative; somehow it brings them a crumb of comfort to know who did it and why.' Werner nodded. No need to tell a Jewish Berliner that about the mysterious deaths of relatives, but I could see he hadn't given up on persuading me to drop it. I wondered if he had some motive that I wasn't party to. 'It's better to get it sorted out,' I said.

'You know best, I suppose. And you've got to live with the family.'

'Yes,' I said.

'I'm pleased it's all worked out for you,' Werner said. He was almost back to being the old Werner now. 'I hear Fiona is looking beautiful and working in London Central.'

'Yes, and the children are coming home in a week or so.'

'And you have a new home.'

'The Kosinski apartment in Mayfair; furnished with antiques and deep pile carpets. It's like a museum. Fiona just wallows in the luxury of it. I could never have done anything like it out of my salary.'

'And you are comfortable there too?'

'It's spectacular, it's London and I can walk to work.'

'So life is perfect?'

'Except that I love Gloria.' I couldn't believe that I'd said it. I was saying to Werner something I'd not even admitted to myself.

Werner looked at me and said nothing for a long time. Perhaps he was wondering if he'd heard aright, or he was waiting for me to retract this admission. 'Have you told Gloria that?' he said eventually.

'No.'

'Fiona?'

'Of course not.'

'So why tell me?' said Werner, as if he didn't want to be burdened by my secrets.

'Because I felt that if I didn't tell someone soon I would turn into a frog.'

'A prince,' said Werner. 'You're already a frog.' He was making light of it while he wrestled with the implications. The sun had finally disappeared now. The street outside was dark, Werner only the faintest shadow against a glimmer of light that was coming from somewhere down the hall. Tante Lisl's ugly old clock struck the hour. I wondered how she ever got a full night's sleep with that chiming all the time. 'I'm sorry, Bernie,' he said finally. He coughed and turned his head as if avoiding my eyes. Werner had been through all this with Zena and Ingrid. He knew the implications. 'When I saw you together – you and Gloria …' He stopped. I'll never know what he was about to say.

'I suppose it will pass,' I said. 'I hear that everything passes in time: the pain of love, death, failure, humiliation, hatred, bereavement … the pain of everything fades eventually.'

'No,' said Werner.

'Becomes an endurable ache.'

'Perhaps,' said Werner.

'But is it fair to Fiona?' I said to myself as much as to him. 'I mean, suppose I make sure I never speak with Gloria again, and smile a lot and make like a loving husband and perfect father? Is that enough?'

'Is this a rhetorical question, or are you going to sit there looking at me and expecting an answer?'

'Tell me, Werner.'

'Who am I to advise anyone?' Werner said calmly. 'Zena drives me crazy. She spied on me. I'm beginning to wonder if she didn't get me kicked out of Berlin. She thinks of nothing but money. You think she's a bitch; maybe she is, but I can't live without her. What do you want me to tell you? You'll do what you have to do. There is no such thing as decision-making, that's just a gimmick the gods provide to refine and add to the torment.'

'I know that old man Fedosov is the key to it.'

'You mean you have a hunch?'

'Yes, that's what I mean.'

'Your hunches have been wrong before, Bernie. Let me come with you tomorrow.'

'No. I might need you here.'

'Okay. Anything else?'

'Yes. Would you by any chance still have the keys to the bar, Werner?' I said.

14

Whatever trauma may have been troubling the deeper recesses of the collective communist mind in the Politburo, it did not mean that the gun-toting bureaucrats manning the frontier were any less obnoxious. It might even be felt that the contrary was true; that the more that Gorbachev conceded to the restless masses of the USSR the more vicious became the stranglehold that East Germany's communist dictatorship exerted upon its long-suffering proletarians.

I travelled to East Berlin by train, alighting at Friedrichstrasse station in the hope that the crowded concourse would mean faster processing through the control point there. I should have known better. The grey-faced men of the Grepo were at their most obdurate, sitting behind the bullet-proof glass, examining every passport and travel document as if they were learning to read. In the baggage hall bodies and bags were examined with the same malevolent scowl. I stood in the long line of passive travellers and waited my turn.

The railway station was a huge glasshouse on stilts with the trains echoing through it on their way around town on elevated tracks. It was all just as magical as it had been when I was a child, its glass-filled metalwork curving high into the grey sky above. But you were never alone on Friedrichstrasse Bahnhof. Here was the Kafka show as Busby Berkeley might have staged it. Dancing their slow ballet on walkways high in the air, a grim chorus line was silhouetted against the grey light of the sky, twirling sniper rifles and machine pistols and staring down at us menacingly.

It was bitterly cold that day, and the wind came through the station like a blast through a wind-tunnel. I couldn't help reminding myself how quickly and conveniently an army car would have taken me through Checkpoint Charlie. As an officer of the 'occupying power' I would not have been subject to the prying fingers and hard-eyed hatred of the Grepos.

But in a car marked with all the trappings of the British Army I'd have been conspicuous. They would have picked me up as I went through. And, with those abundant facilities always provided to East German secret policemen, they would have followed me wherever I went, difficult to detect and even more difficult to throw off.

So I lined up on the cold platform and waited my turn to go across as Peter Hesse, construction company's site-clerk and native of Hanover. It was an identity I'd used before. There was back-up from a builder's merchant in Düsseldorf and an address where the residents were ready to swear that Peter Hesse was their neighbour.

Once outside in the dirty Berlin air, I breathed freely again. Friedrichstrasse was busy with buses and bicycles and cars – some of them stinking and noisy with their rattling two-stroke engines. Friedrichstrasse station has always been the very centre of old Berlin; what the Westies called Stadtmitte, and the Ossis called the Zentrum. It was a popular crossing point, and always busy with Vopo cops and soldiers and the Grepo border police.

Back in the Twenties Friedrichstrasse was the busiest street in the city, its commercial centre and entertainment section too. Here some of Berlin's famous old theatres – the Wintergarten, the Apollo, the Metropol and the Admiralspalast – had provided the most outrageous entertainment in the whole outrageous city. Fight your way through the grotesquely painted hookers that crowded these streets, and, for the price of a drink, you could have seen Richard Tauber sing 'Dein ist mein ganzes Herz' or watched a youthful Marlene Dietrich croon 'Naughty Lola'. In those days the songs of the cabaret had been biting, topical and wicked, and in the audiences could be spotted everyone from Brecht to Alfred Döblin; from Walter Gropius to Arnold Schönberg. This was the Berlin you read about in the history books.

Stand outside the station and look towards Weidendamm Bridge and the narrow River Spree. On the night of the 1st of May 1945 Martin Bormann and a furtive band of Nazi big shots crept along this street and under this railway arch that is a part of the elevated station. They'd emerged from the dank safety of the Führerbunker, just down the street, where Hitler – married for only a few hours – having then killed his wife and committed suicide, had been doused with fifty litres of aviation spirit and ignited for a funeral pyre. The escapers were trying to get to Rechlin airport, which was still under German control. An experimental six-engined Junkers Ju 390 was parked there. It was capable of flying to Manchuria, and Hans Bauer, Hitler's personal pilot, was with the party and ready to prove it. But they had little chance of getting that far. Half of Berlin was on fire and the other half was thronging with trigger-happy Red Army soldiers, and even if most of the Ivans were hopelessly drunk, that did not mean that such a conspicuous bunch of Nazis could escape unnoticed. Some Tiger tanks of the SS Nordland Division were on the far side of the River Spree, and shell-fire from them dropped among the escapers. Bauer was carrying in his pack Hitler's favourite painting of Frederick the Great, and Bormann was carrying his Führer's last Will and Testament to proclaim it to the world. They got across the river and sheltered in a well-known brothel that stood on the corner of Friedrichstrasse and the Schiffbauerdamm. After a discussion with the brothel-keeper and her daughter the two men set out along the same S-Bahn railway embankment that my train had followed, past the hospital, to where the Wall has now been constructed to block off the Invalidenstrasse. A few more steps and perhaps they would have escaped, but Bauer was taken prisoner by an alert Red Army man and Bormann bit hard on a cyanide capsule and died. Hitler's last Will and Testament was never seen again.

Now I walked across the Weidendamm Bridge and nodded at the spot where the brothel once sheltered its much-sought visitors. I loved this filthy old town, and while away in California I'd sorely missed its inescapable allure. It wasn't just practical reasons that made me choose to walk to Pankow. I wanted to feel the hard pot-holed paving under my feet and sniff the brown-coal that polluted the air, and see the irrepressible Berliners go about their day.

Pankow is a Bezirk; a borough that comes complete with Bürgermeister and council. It's on the north side of Berlin, and is one of the larger ones. To get there from Friedrichstrasse station I walked right across the Prenzlauer Berg. It gave me a chance to be sure I wasn't shadowed. The Department's instruction manuals insist that a man walking is a perfect target, but I'd joined the Department as a Kellerkind – a street-wise Berlin kid who played in the city's postwar rubble – and I believed I could spot a tail within five minutes of the first contact. I knew the city streets and I knew the back alleys. I knew the big apartment buildings, many of them no more than gutted shells by war's end, that I'd watched as they were rebuilt to the original cramped specifications of their nineteenth-century designs. I knew which ones had courtyards and second courtyards – Hinterhofs – and exits that emerged on the far side of the block.

I carried in my pocket a letter to post. This provided an excuse to go to a post-box and then turn about and go back the way I'd come. It is often all that is needed to totally disorganize even a skilled surveillance. I was there in twenty minutes.

VERDI's father lived just round the corner from the Rathaus at the top of Mühlenstrasse, near the eye clinic. Berlin is not a very old town, compared with London or Paris. At the beginning of the century it was not very extensive. Fifteen minutes' walk from the city centre you can already spot here and there the remains of grand country-style mansions, built by men who wanted to be well away from the Alexanderplatz and the hustle and bustle of city life. Now most such mansions had been demolished by urban planners and replaced with apartment blocks, their grounds and gardens swallowed up by sports centres or parks or Volksschwimmhalle like the one that could be seen from the apartment where Fedosov lived.

I knew these streets. This block was conveniently close to Pankow S-Bahn station, Pankow U-Bahn station, and to the police station too. These were the places chosen to house VIPs, senior security officers, a few Red Army veterans like Fedosov, and retired Stasi staff. At one time there was a permanent police patrol around the block, but even here the economy was being squeezed and today I could not see a uniformed officer.

Apart from an ugly modern block of apartments this was a street of old buildings. Single-family dwellings right up until Hitler's time, they were now divided into spacious apartments like the one that Fedosov occupied on the second floor of number 16.

'Ja?' said a voice through the plastic grille at the side of the door.

'Colonel Fedosov?' I said, making a guess at what rank he might have retired with.

'Captain Fedosov,' said the voice. 'Who are you? What do you want?' It was the petulant voice of a capricious old man.

'I want to speak to you. I'm a friend of your son. Can I come in?'

'Come up.'

I stood there shivering in the cold. There was some grunting and groaning and eventually a loud buzzer sounded and the door lock snapped open to admit me. As I pushed my way inside the warmth met me. No matter what you didn't like about German communism, its heating arrangements were always extravagant to a fault. Heating was provided by the State as a part of the rental and they did not stint.

The lobby was grand, its floor black and white marble in elaborate patterns. Pankow had escaped from the war relatively intact. The Red Army's artillery bombardments, and the air attacks, had concentrated upon the Mitte, the Reichstag, the Chancellory, Wilhelmstrasse and the Palace. After an initial few days of raping and looting, the best houses of the still intact bourgeois boroughs like this one had been commandeered for the military and political occupiers.

Even the marble staircase was original, with an ornate balustrade, although there was an unmistakable institutional look to the dull colours of the paintwork and the austerity of the repairs and fittings. Fedosov emerged from his front door above and looked down the staircase-well to see me. 'Second floor,' he called. His voice was hard as it echoed off the marble and brick. He didn't seem to care who I was.

'Can you spare me ten minutes of your time?' I asked as I came huffing and puffing to his landing.

He nodded. He was a small man with one of those ferocious moustaches that you see generals of Stalin's Red Army hiding behind in old photos. I wondered if he had some circulatory problem, for despite the comfortable warmth provided by the central heating system he was wearing layer upon layer of garments: a long sleeveless padded coat over a white roll-neck sweater from whose collar a blue shirt was trying to escape, brown baggy trousers, thick woollen socks and zip-sided red velvet slippers bearing his initials VF in gold embroidery. He looked like a marginally more prosperous version of one of the vagrants who are nowadays to be seen sleeping in the streets of most large towns of the affluent West.

'Come in. Hang your coat on the hook,' he said. He no doubt thought I was a writer asking him once more to plant the red banner on the roof of the Reichstag. Fedosov's apartment was large and comfortable. His long-term residence here was evident on every side. It was a strange collection of treasures and keepsakes: ancient books, a pendulum clock, a crucifix, photos, badges, medals and souvenirs of a long military career.

'I'd like ten minutes of your time,' I said.

'Go on through,' he said.

The second room into which he'd shown me was a neat little den with a view of the street. Outside, on the window-sill, there was a wooden bird shelter fitted with a shallow water-dish. The carpets, like the armchairs, were old and large and run-down. They looked as if they might have served a generation or two of Berliners prior to the arrival of Fedosov and his comrades in May 1945. 'Sit down,' he said. I had the feeling that Fedosov would have willingly given ten minutes of his time to anyone who happened by. Thirty minutes perhaps.

On a side-table there was a pile of library books, copies of the Russian Army weekly newspaper and some Party magazines, all printed in Russian script. You have to be very bored to be driven to such reading matter. I looked around. 'What a lovely apartment,' I said. It was a shrine to Stalinism. The old brute's framed portrait was in a place of honour. Arrayed round it were countless enamel souvenir plaques. A thousand rippling red flags celebrated endless Party events: rallies, conventions and anniversaries. Facing the window, where it got the best light, there was a large framed print of the action of May

Day 1945 when Fedosov and the men of Banner Party No. 5 took their flag to the top of the Reichstag amid the bullets and shell fragments. The artist had improved considerably upon the well-known heavily retouched re-enactment that the Red Army photographers took in full daylight after hostilities ended, a photo in which sightseers could be seen in the streets below. In this painting the bullets were flying. It was dawn, with a very red sun prising its way through golden clouds. The men were tall and strong and handsome and had disdained such things as steel helmets and bayonets and guns. Their well-tailored uniforms were only slightly stained and their hands grasped a gigantic banner that floated in the wind so that its golden hammer-and-sickle device was well in evidence. This was war the way the propaganda service fought it.

'Your son used to know me,' I said. He moved a book from his armchair and sat down opposite me. I produced a pack of Philip Morris, took one and offered them to him. He took the pack and looked at it carefully before putting a cigarette into his mouth. 'Back in the old days.' I leaned forward and lit his cigarette for him, using a cigarette lighter that had belonged to my father. 'Keep the packet,' I said. I'd hoped that the lighter, a distinctive one with a double-headed eagle design, might provoke a memory, or even a comment. But he gave no sign of recognizing it.

'Old days? When?' He didn't look like a soldier. That is to say he didn't look like any of the retired military men that I knew in the West. My idea of a soldier was a fit active man with a ramrod spine, military haircut and brisk voice. But Fedosov wasn't that kind of soldier: he'd been just one man of millions and millions who had hacked their way from Moscow to Berlin on foot. He served under generals who openly affirmed that the quickest way of removing an enemy minefield was to send an infantry company to advance across it. Fedosov had survived three years of Eastern Front fighting armed only with an obsolete submachine gun and his quickness of mind. Never mind his battlefield commission and the artist's interpretation, such a man was not likely to be of the type who recklessly exposed himself to enemy fire. I reasoned that the law of averages said Fedosov would have learned to let others jump over the parapet and go to kill a hundred Germans single-handed; Fedosov, I decided, was going to be a man of caution and resource. He was hardly likely to resemble the men who presented arms outside Buckingham Palace. 'Do you speak Russian?' he asked.

'A word or two.'

'Old days when?' he said again. He kept to his German; if he was going to relate his war experiences he wanted more than a word or two.

Fedosov got up to find an ashtray for me. I could look at him more carefully now. He was small and muscular and inclined to be hunched, perhaps as the result of some injury. He had a furtive manner and a dark-complexioned face that almost hid the scars of an unstitched wound that disfigured his cheek and extended to his ear.

'The days of the airlift,' I said. 'Back when you worked with my father.' I had given up smoking; I hadn't had a cigarette in over a month. But, sitting there with a cigarette in one hand and a lighter in the other, I found that in Europe it is not so easy to maintain such embargoes. Everyone smokes, and the air of every restaurant and café, every train compartment and every home, is hazy with tobacco smoke. I lit up and he placed the ashtray at my elbow.

'Air Lift. That is a long time ago,' said Fedosov, his face betraying no sign that he might be guessing the identity of my father. I watched him carefully. I was in no hurry. One of the windows had been fitted with wooden shelves so that potted

233

plants of all shapes and sizes – mostly cacti – filled the entire space. More plants crowded the wooden bench in front of us, and on the floor under it there was a bag of plant food and some empty pots. The light coming between the plants backlit his wispy white hair, making a fluffy halo.

'Nineteen forty-nine,' I said. I flicked ash into the large chinaware ashtray in the base of which the flags of the DDR and the Soviet Union were bound together with a scroll bearing the slogan: 'Freedom, unity and socialism.'

'You were not even born,' he said.

'I was very young,' I admitted. 'But I remember the planes going over – one every few seconds.'

He smoked the cigarette, letting the smoke trail from his mouth and nostrils, savouring it with eyes half-closed, as Dicky Cruyer did when he was showing you how to judge claret. 'Do you know who lives in the apartment downstairs on the ground floor?' he said.

'No,' I said.

'Klenze. Theodore Klenze, the famous conductor.'

'Oh, yes.'

'The Bruckner specialist. He conducts at the Opera and works with all the big orchestras. Leipzig, the Brno State and in London too. I have all his records.'

Why shouldn't the old man be proud to live so near him? As with every regime in the East, the earning of hard-currency royalties was the ultimate achievement in this hard-pressed communist land. Such earners were cosseted and given the best of everything, including comfortable houses. To be Klenze's neighbour was to have shared that pinnacle of success. 'Yes, he's world-famous,' I said.

'When did you last see my son Andrey?' asked Fedosov.

'He's important now,' I said, rather than reveal it was to shoot at him on a country road near Magdeburg. 'He runs his own department. Or so I heard.' It seemed like a way of getting the old man started.

'His pension will be twice mine,' said Fedosov. 'Mind you, he works hard; very hard. Did you know his wife?'

'No,' I said.

'I wish he'd get married again, but he says it's none of my business and I suppose he's right.'

Perhaps he was still hoping that, by some miracle, I would start asking him about the Red Banner and forget his former indiscretion with the British Secret Intelligence Service. I nodded to show that I had no strong feelings about VERDI's nuptial ambitions and we sat there staring at each other and smoking and thinking and nodding and watching the sparrows come to the window-sill, find no bread there and peck at the ice that had formed in the water-dish. He watched them solemnly as they flew away chirping angrily. I could see his mind was racing. All this small-talk was just a way of providing time enough to get my sudden appearance into some sort of perspective, to decide if I represented a threat or an opportunity. Or both.

'He lives downstairs. Klenze, I mean. Not my son. The door with the brass knocker.' He smiled.

I flicked ash upon 'Freedom, unity and socialism' and looked at this friendly old man so happily ensconced in his gemütlich little home. It was easy to forget that this white-haired pensioner and his hard-working secret-policeman son – helped by dedicated Party workers, apparatchiks, writers and intellectuals and musicians like Herr Klenze, who all were provided with equally comfortable environments – were propping up the whole rotten and corrupt system. It was men such as Fedosov who built the Wall and patrolled the electric fences around the work camps, and kept the communist world subdued at gun-point.

'Who was your father?' he said suddenly.

'Brian Samson. The British resident-director in West Berlin.'

He nodded sagely. Rezident-director was a KGB concept and not an accurate description of my father's job, and still less of Frank Harrington's role, but it was enough. 'I remember him,' he said soberly.

'You worked for him,' I said. 'All through the Luftbrücke time, and long after.'

'No.'

'You gave him good and accurate accounts of all the important meetings in Karlshorst that were concerned with the air bridge and Moscow's plans to counter it.'

'Do you know what you are saying?'

'You reported to the British SIS,' I insisted.

He got up and came to stand over me, his hands clenching in anger. 'I'll send for the police,' he threatened.

'Send for the KGB,' I said. 'Send for the Stasi; send for your son.'

'What are you after?' He walked away as if he would not wait to hear my reply.

'I was in the rezidentura,' I said. 'I was just a child, but I knew my father came regularly to Pankow all through that time. And even after the Wall was up. My mother even suspected him of having a mistress here. But it was you he was meeting. I remember my parents, their voices raised in anger about him going to Pankow once a week.'

'No.'

'I've seen the documents. They are still on file in London.'

'You are lying.'

From my pocket I took the payments card. Exposed to the bright light coming through the window the card looked very old and tattered. Its yellow colour was faded almost to white, and some of the ink signatures were faint. Only the pencilled entries were unchanged. Fedosov peered over my shoulder

236

to see exactly what it was. I passed it back to him. He looked at it for a moment before going to fetch his spectacles from a case that was alongside his library book. With his glasses on he looked again at the card.

'You bastard,' he said. 'Why wasn't this destroyed?'

'Destroy it now,' I offered. I didn't say there were plenty more where that came from, I let him figure that out for himself. He had worked for us, been paid well for his services, and now he could not deny it.

'Get out,' he said.

'I'm not getting out until we've had a proper talk.'

'I said get out!'

'Not yet, Madame Xavier,' I said.

His face froze in horror and he got to his feet and began moving about in that restless way that is a symptom of sudden shock. I hadn't fully anticipated the profound effect that my visit was likely to have upon Fedosov. He'd kept his secret for half a lifetime. Comfortably settled in his Berlin apartment – accommodation of infinite luxury by the standards of the East – he was using his ill-gotten nest-egg to furnish himself with all the little comforts that the despicable West could offer. Suddenly a bombshell had been thrown into his world. I had arrived, not just with an accusation, but with a signed piece of cardboard that had been wrenched from his shameful past.

I had not allowed for the old man's distress, his anger and his desperate resource. He went to the other room and I heard him busy in the kitchen, as if making coffee. I was sitting with my back to him when he came up behind me. I was expecting a hand on my shoulder, and the opening words of an angry scene. I was not prepared for the strength of the blow he delivered with some hard and heavy object. He hit me on the side of the head and the pain was awful. I clutched my head and toppled forward to fall into the stacked flower-pots and bags of plant food that were under the bench. My weight caused the bench to collapse, and all the potted plants arrayed upon it slid to the floor with a resounding crash. I blacked out for a moment, and I think the way that I remained full-length on the floor, eyes closed and limbs still, made the old man think his blow had killed me.

I tried to open my eyes. I could see his feet as he backed away from me, treading the spilled earth and broken pieces of cacti into the carpet. 'Bastard!' he called again and his voice revealed his fears. 'Bastard!' he said again as if it was a plea to some jury that was pronouncing on his unprovoked assault. 'You deserved it. You deserved it.'

I couldn't see properly, or hear properly either. My head was too filled with pain to leave much room for thinking. I wanted to stay where I was on the floor and be left alone until suppertime.

I heard the sound of him lifting the phone and dialling. 'Andrey? This is your father,' he said when the connection was made. 'I've had a visitor. The Englander. The one you know about. I hit him; I think he's dead.' There was a silence and then his son at the other end must have said that it was better for them to speak Russian, because the old man said it all again in Russian. Before ringing off, the old man said 'As quick as you can then' in German and I guessed that VERDI was on his way. 'Goodbye.'

Until that moment I had been hanging on to consciousness, but the finality of the farewell seemed to make my resolution dissolve. I floated for a moment and then drifted slowly upwards into darkness.

15

I don't know how long it was before I was aware that my father was standing over me. He was wearing a fur coat and a fur hat. He had a stethoscope hanging loose around his neck. 'His pulse is strong,' my father said in German with a powerful Berlin accent. 'I think he's coming round. Look, his eyes are opening.'

It was not my father. He didn't even look like him except for the moustache. A voice belonging to someone out of sight said: 'Will he need stitches?'

'No. It's not bleeding very much. It's in his hair. The scar won't notice. He's got lots of scar tissue already.'

I was full-length on a sofa in the inner room. They must have carried me there. Far away I could see the room in which we'd been sitting. The light filtering through the plants in the window was green and shadowy. My head hurt; it really hurt.

'Are you in pain?' asked the man with the stethoscope. I tried to answer but no words came. 'He's not in pain,' he said, with that robust stoicism with which physicians confront their patients' suffering.

'Thanks, doctor,' said a man I could not see. 'Can he hear me?' It was VERDI's voice.

'I don't know. He's not fully conscious but he'll be all right. He's not badly hurt; just concussed.'

The second man came nearer. It was VERDI. I would have recognized that voice anywhere. 'Can you hear me, Samson?' It was a loud domineering voice suited for addressing the infirm and demented. 'Nod if you can hear me.'

The hell with you, VERDI. Your father has already tried to beat my head in. Nod it and it will fall off and roll under the table and I'll get it back covered in cobwebs.

I suppose he decided to give me a few more minutes to recover, for I heard him walking with the doctor to the door and saying that he wouldn't be needed any more. And then he used the phone to order an extra car. It should come immediately to Pankow he said, and the driver should have Russian Army credentials in case he had to go to the West Sector.

When the doctor had gone VERDI was less restrained: 'Why did you hit him, you bloody old fool?'

'We had such fun together when you were small,' his father said sorrowfully. 'I loved you then.'

'I said, why did you hit him?'

'Do you ever think of those days, little one?'

VERDI sighed. 'Can't you ever keep to the point? I am asking you a simple question.'

'It was the Military School,' said the old man, as if he'd never hit upon this solution before. 'You changed after that. You came back on vacation. But you were never the same. You became a little German.' There was a lifetime of resentment and regret behind that choice of words – little German – by a man who'd battled against the Germans, and then chosen one as a mother for this cherished only son.

'Mama died. You were always working.'

'Not always.'

'Or drunk. Working or drunk. That's what I remember of my vacations. You never had time to spare for me.'

'You know that's not true, little one. I gave my whole life to you. I refused jobs overseas, I lost promotions. I devoted all my life to you.'

'If only that was the truth,' said VERDI.

'It is true, little one. You just don't want to face it. You don't wish to feel an obligation. You were always like that. You even pretended you didn't like your toys.'

Perhaps the word 'toys' brought on the anger. 'Don't call me little one. I'm not your little one.'

There was a long silence then suddenly the old man said: 'The Englander was threatening me. I gave them … This was many years ago. I gave them some papers. Useless waste paper. I was short of money. It was for you and Mama that I did it. This one came threatening me about it all.'

'What did he say?' said VERDI very quietly and calmly. I knew he was looking at me. I kept my eyes closed and remained very still.

'He brought an English payments card. I'd signed for my money. I thought they destroyed the receipts. I only did it the once.'

'You did it for eleven years,' said VERDI. 'DO you think it wasn't reported?'

'Reported?'

'In those days we always managed to get someone planted in the Berlin SIS office.'

'Just the once,' insisted the old man.

'I tell you we had someone there.'

'Who? I knew them all. It was my job building our material about the Berlin rezidentura. Who did we have there?'

'A flashy creep named Billy Walker. A homosexual. He reported on you. There was a written report sent to your battalion commander but no action was taken.'

'I was lucky.'

'Walker and Samson were at the top. The rezident was this one's father. They hated each other. Our people processing the report on you probably decided that Walker was trying to make trouble … that it was a part of the vendetta between the two Englishmen.'

'How long have you known?'

'I saw you with the elder Samson. You were careless.'

'You didn't report me?'

'You're my father.'

'Thank you, little one. You are a good boy.'

'William Walker. The English called him "Johnny Walker" after the name of the Scotch whisky. They like that sort of joke. Smart suits and signet ring and gold cigarette case: not very English: too gaudy.'

'The bastard reported me.'

'We had to get rid of him finally. I was in the office when it was decided. We chose our most gorgeous male prostitute to do it.'

'I'm sorry, little one. I was stupid. It could have made bad trouble for you.' And then, in another voice: 'What are we going to do about this one?'

'Samson?' VERDI called loudly, bending over close to me. I pretended I was just coming round. I slowly opened my eyes and groaned and acted like one in pain. It wasn't difficult. 'Can you hear me and understand?' he said in German. He was comfortable in German; he liked the predetermined order its syntax demanded. I recognize that preference in myself at times.

'Yes? Yes? What?' I said slowly in a slurred voice. VERDI walked into view. Werner was right: I wouldn't have recognized him without a little prompting. The man I used to know was a hard-faced thug with bad teeth and frayed shirts. This one was soft and smooth and silky. Perfectly blocked soft felt hat, a dark cashmere overcoat slung over his shoulders, grey silk scarf

242

with tassels, and hand-made Oxford shoes, even kid gloves. All looking as if it had just come from exclusive West Berlin outfitters, which it probably had. He wore it with style too, parading up and down with all the sulky mannerisms Hollywood actors use when cast as East Coast Mafia bosses. Behind him, peeking at me furtively over his son's shoulder, there was the old man, his eyes glinting and a certain anxiety on his face. His troubles were not yet over, and he knew it.

'You take a message back to your people,' VERDI said softly. 'You leave my father out of this or the deal is off. You talk to your Director-General personally. Personally. Have you got that?'

He stroked his smooth talcumed face as if making sure he'd remembered to shave, and waited for a response. He was angry and upset. I had hoped that my unannounced confrontation with the old man would upset VERDI but it hadn't worked out the way I planned. 'Maybe,' I murmured.

'You should be ashamed of yourself, Samson. Coming here to frighten a harmless old man. My father has a heart condition. You might have given him a shock that killed him.'

'Your father can look after himself,' I croaked. 'Say what you want to say.' I tried to sit up, but the movement sent a bolt of pain through my head and I sank back again.

'I've already said what I've got to say. You get back to London and see Sir Henry Clevemore personally. Leave my father out of this. He's nothing to do with it. I don't want him threatened, do you understand? If your people have changed their mind, I'll take it to the Americans. You make sure he knows I'm serious. Got that, Samson?'

'They want it,' I said. By now I was beginning to guess that London Central would be grateful for even twenty-four hours of access to the new mainframe. Anything after that would be a bonus.

'Damned right they do,' he said. 'There is a lot of material on file over here, Samson. But it's not all good news. SIS disasters. SIS cock-ups, SIS betrayals. Heads will be rolling. And there are people in London who prefer to leave things the way they are. Right?'

'It's always like that,' I said.

'And perhaps Sir Henry Clevemore is one of them.'

'Say your say,' I told him. 'I'll handle the guesswork.'

'I've told Volkmann everything they need to know in London. I've been into the circuits and the programs. It's all possible; just as I said it was. I've prepared everything important at this end. It's up to your people from now on. But don't stall too long or I'll go elsewhere.'

'What did that old bastard hit me with?'

'Do you want a drink of water? He hit you with his crucifix,' said VERDI. I could see it now: the large cast-iron crucifix had been replaced on the wall at a slightly drunken angle.

'Scotch would be better,' I said.

'Schnapps?'

'Okay.' He went and poured me a shot of ice-cold Polish vodka; the one flavoured with rowan berries. I sipped it. It didn't get rid of the pain but it made it feel more endurable – more like a hangover.

Experimentally I touched my head with my fingertips. It was very tender and already swelling. I looked at my fingers; there was no blood.

VERDI watched me. 'You phone Clevemore,' he said. 'He'll see you, I guarantee that. This is the biggest operation your people have had in years. What's the problem?'

'The problem is – are you on the level?' I said, turning my head to watch the elder Fedosov kneeling by the window picking up the pieces of broken plant and pot.

'On the level?' he said, his voice raised in anger that may not have been simulated. 'You're the bastard who shot my driver dead. A good thing for you he wasn't one of my staff. I recognized you but I left your name out of my report. I just said that an unidentified British team came in and did the hit, and got away before they could be intercepted. We let the militia and the Vopos put out the net; I knew you'd have no trouble evading those dummies. So what else do you want me to do to persuade you that I'm on the level?'

'You're a lovely fellow, Andrey.'

'What's it worth in cash?' The old man turned his head to see us and hear better and watch my reaction to what his son had asked. 'The Americans would give me a great deal of money.'

'I have no authority to talk money,' I said. 'But you'd better know that there's not so much dough about these days.' The old man sighed and went back to putting his cacti back into their pots.

VERDI looked at me closely trying to decide if I was joking but seemed to think I wasn't. 'If it's not worth serious money, why send that stupid fat pig to pester me? And why send you after him?'

'I don't know any fat pigs except you.'

'Don't play the fool, Samson. Tiny Timmermann.'

'Timmermann?'

'Are you going to sit there and try and pretend you don't know the identity of your own field agent? The one you had sent to California so he could be briefed so carefully? Are you telling me you didn't know the identity of that stiff you frisked in the house in Magdeburg?'

'Timmermann? The dead man in Magdeburg?'

'Who did you think it was?' Now he was confused.

'I thought that was you,' I said truthfully.

'You thought it was me?' he said in a loud coarse scornful voice that took me back to when he'd been a small-time interrogator working the detention cells in the old Polizeipräsidium building in the Alex. He gave a mirthless laugh of derision. 'So who did you think you were shooting at on the road?'

'Timmermann? The dead man? Are you serious?'

'You sent him,' he said.

'I didn't send him. He doesn't work for us and never has done.'

'You got on the plane with him. In Los Angeles. You talked to him.'

I made no response, but I was impressed, and he probably saw that he'd scored a hit. Top marks, VERDI old pal. So I was under surveillance right from the time I left California.

'Just a coincidence,' he said in a pally aside, as if he wanted to reassure me man to man; agent to agent. 'Just luck. Someone I knew was on the same plane.'

'Timmermann? Who killed him? Your people?'

He didn't deny it. 'He stepped out of line, Samson. He went his own way asking questions about the Kosinski killing, and pushing his luck. That's dangerous. We don't encourage academic curiosity this side of the Wall.'

'You got the wrong man,' I said. He shook his head to show he didn't think so, and tugged his coat so it fitted more snugly upon his shoulders. I'd always wanted to wear an overcoat like these Germans and Frenchmen do it; without putting my arms through the sleeves. But when I tried it once, coming out of the Schiller Theatre with Gloria, it fell off and Frank Harrington's wife tripped over it and fell full-length in the street.

He looked at his watch. 'The car will be here by now,' he said, with the confidence that only a Stasi man in a police State would know. 'I'll take you as far as Checkpoint Charlie. Or through it, if you know where you want to go.'

'Okay.'

'Are you meeting your friend Volkmann somewhere?'

'No.'

'So London is employing Volkmann again. They blow hot and cold, don't they? I thought they had blacklisted him. Then all of a sudden I find I'm dealing with him.'

'They don't confide that sort of thing to me,' I said. 'I'm just an office boy.'

'An office boy married to the boss's daughter? Is that the way it is now, Samson?' Without waiting for an answer, he said: 'So where do you want to go?'

My head was singing and I didn't feel well enough to walk back across town. But I wasn't going to accompany him through Checkpoint Charlie in his official car. It would be noted and I'd never hear the last of it.

'Friedrichstrasse Bahnhof.'

'Whatever you say, Samson. But I think you mean Checkpoint Charlie. I can understand your desire to remain anonymous,' he said with a disdainful smirk. 'But you're not in the right state of health to go pushing your way through the unwashed Berlin proletariat.' He glanced at his father. 'And at this time of day that stinking train will be crammed full of grandads and grandmas returning from their day-pass visits.'

'Okay.' He was right: I wasn't in a fit state to go pushing anybody anywhere.

He'd brought a good car for us. Not a Trabbie or a Wartburg, nor even a Skoda: this was a metallic-silver-finish Mercedes 500 SEL with red leather seats and brand-new tyres. Even Stasi men need to show their colleagues that they have made good, but I think I'd seen it before. The only jarring note to our departure came from the old man: 'You mustn't go, little one,' he told his son. 'I only live for you. I couldn't bear it. You on the other side. I couldn't bear it.'

'Don't be a silly old man,' said VERDI, apparently unmoved by this request.

247

'I'm your father,' said the old man. 'I love you.'

'Then let me live my own life,' said VERDI quietly, and pushed past him to follow me down the stairs.

'You ungrateful little swine,' the old man shouted over the stair-rail. 'I hate you. Go. Stay away for ever. I might as well be dead for all you care.'

'I came, didn't I? I got you out of trouble yet again.'

Perhaps the exchange had embarrassed VERDI. He said: 'They become like children when they grow old.' When I didn't answer he added: 'He let his own parents die still living in the filthy little hovel where he was born. He only went back twice in all those years. He never even sent money.'

At the door a uniformed police lieutenant saluted. A sergeant opened the car door for us to get in. Nothing had been said about any favours owed to anyone. The time long ago, when his men had thrown me off the train instead of arresting me, had put me in his debt. Now the debt was doubled. There was no malevolence, nothing personal. He'd done it all very much the way it was always done when the other side misjudged things. I wasn't resentful. I figured that had he come into the West and browbeaten Tante Lisl I'd probably have treated him worse than he was treating me. There were two police cars parked in the street outside. Half a dozen men with guns standing around with conspicuous idleness. No handcuffs or rubber truncheons. Just a little show of force and then two cars with flashing lights to lead the way to the crossing point and make sure I would be humiliated in a way that I wouldn't quickly forget.

He rode with me. He had a plentiful supply of small-talk, larded with a few questions about Frank Harrington and Dicky and other luminaries of the Department, all contrived to demonstrate how much they knew about us. Fiona wasn't mentioned again, and Gloria not at all, and for that delicate

248

example of professional discretion I was grateful. Although it did leave me wondering exactly what they knew about my domestic problems.

At Checkpoint Charlie none of his tame Grepos, or the plain-clothes men, came anywhere near us. His driver took the car as near to the white wooden US Army hut as he could get without crossing over. Then the driver jumped out and opened the car door for me.

'Does Timmermann have family?' said VERDI as I started to get out.

'I've no idea.'

'If I don't hear in a couple of days I'll let them bury him here. Okay?'

I looked at VERDI. He sat back in the soft leather, folded his arms and smiled at me. He knew what I was going to say, but he wasn't going to make it easier for me. He wasn't that obliging. 'What about the woman?' I said. 'What about my sister-in-law?'

'No, no, no. They might want another post-mortem. The coroner won't release that one.'

'There is a lot of bad feeling,' I said. 'You don't really want the body do you?'

'Evidence. They say she was decapitated,' he said. 'I'll let you have the post-mortem documents and the coroner's reports. The army took care of it. That's a part of the deal. Didn't Volkmann tell you that?'

'I thought she was in a burned-out car. Carbonized. I thought there was very little of her left.'

'Maybe that's was how it was supposed to be, Samson. Perhaps someone miscalculated. You'd better explain that to your Director-General too. Or maybe he can explain it to you.'

'Okay,' I said. I closed the car door. I could see I'd get nothing else from him. He was a pigheaded brute who'd seen everything. I'd caught him off-guard by tackling his father, but he'd recovered his composure now. Such men were difficult to surprise.

When I walked through the Checkpoint the American sergeant in the box didn't even look up from his paperback book. I went to the cab rank on the corner and got inside the first cab. It could have been one of VERDI's people staked out for me but I didn't think so. What else did he have to gain?

'Kantstrasse,' I said. 'Hotel Hennig.'

I looked back to the Checkpoint. VERDI was still in his silver Mercedes watching me. He hadn't moved, right up to the time we turned into Kochstrasse and he was lost to view.

While the cab was driving along the bank of the Landwehr Canal, I thought about what VERDI said. I remembered the day they'd fished poor old Johnny Walker from the oily waters of the Canal. My father came home that night and didn't eat his dinner. That was a most unusual development; my mother thought he was ill. He just sat at the table staring into space. Poor Johnny, he kept saying. Blackmailed by a choice seducer from the KGB's selection of male prostitutes, he was sure to yield. Johnny was always a pushover for a pretty face, as I knew from being in some of the down-town bars with him. They all recognized him and said hello. I wonder if Dad suspected Walker was selling out to the Russians. And from that I began wondering how long it would take before Werner and Frank Harrington got to hear about today's fiasco. And while I was thinking of that – in that curious way that one's brain keeps working 'background' while you listen to music or deal with everyday problems – the whole thing clicked into place.

Timmermann. Timmermann! Why had I been so slow to get it? Even when Bret's cryptic Bible message arrived I still hadn't understood. What did the message say:

Timmermann was of course the 'expert' field agent that George Kosinski, encouraged by my idiotic father-in-law, had engaged to go and investigate the death of Tessa. And because Timmermann was vain and stupid enough to go in without proper preparation or back-up, he said yes. Or maybe poor old Timmermann was so short of money that he had little alternative. That's how field agents, driven to such lousy freelance jobs, so often end their days: riskier and riskier assignments for less and less money until the trap closes on your neck. Sometimes I worried that I would end up like that. With the present penny-pinching atmosphere at London Central, and my tenuous employment contract, it was looking more and more likely every day.

VERDI understandably thought Timmermann was from London Central, and no doubt continued to think so despite my denials. But Timmermann was doing a freelance job; he'd been in Los Angeles to be secretly briefed by Fiona. Bret – no fool when it comes to watching what's going on around him – had tumbled to what was afoot between Fiona and Timmermann.

And that was why Timmermann had avoided getting into conversation with me. In line with Departmental standing orders for operational assignments, my seat on the plane had not been booked until two hours before I travelled; Timmermann must have been dismayed to encounter me on that same flight.

I noticed the way that VERDI said he had shifted blame for Timmermann's murder on to an unidentified British team. More likely he'd left his masters in no doubt that I had killed Timmermann; VERDI wasn't the sort of man who submitted don't-know reports.

Blaming me for the killing was obviously the true purpose of getting both me and Timmerman to Magdeburg that same night. He was devious beyond compare. There was no point in wasting any time wondering how VERDI had discovered that I was on the plane with Timmermann. VERDI was not the sort of man who killed people without squeezing them. And VERDI was an expert with the squeezer, as I knew from personal experience.

16

Had I persisted with my plan to return to the hotel, and to stretch out in my room, nurse my head and recover slowly, everything would have turned out differently. But as my taxi from Checkpoint Charlie turned off Kantstrasse I spotted Werner Volkmann. He was wearing his 'impresario's overcoat' with its large shawl-collar of curly astrakhan. He was outside the optician's shop that occupied the ground floor of the Hennig Hotel premises and talking to Tante Lisl. She was attired in a golden-coloured fur coat and matching hat, the highlight of the complete new wardrobe she'd bought to celebrate her successful surgery. They seemed to be arguing, and I recognized the way they were throwing their arms around as the frantic exasperation that precedes the hug of reconciliation. Lisl had lost weight, in compliance with the promise the surgeon had exacted from her. But fur coats didn't suit her figure or her style. As much as I loved them both, there was no denying that my first impression, of the pair of them gesticulating excitedly, was of a ringmaster trying to control his ferocious dancing bear.

I knew beyond doubt that if I got out of the cab at the hotel entrance they were bound to comment on my being dishevelled and nursing an injured head. They'd ask questions which unanswered would provoke jokes that I was not in the mood to share. I didn't want to encounter either of them at that moment.

I wanted a glass of warm milk, a couple of aspirins, and the chance of going to bed to sleep for ever.

'Keep going,' I told the cab driver. It suddenly struck me that it might be a good plan to tell Frank Harrington my version of the events of the day. Any other account of my spontaneous and extracurricular excursion – even an account from someone as well-meaning as Werner – might give rise to a lot of official questions.

I gave the driver Frank's address in the Grunewald district. Frank was certain to be at home. Even in normal times he was never in his office after four in the afternoon, and lately – as the construction work continued at the Field Unit premises – he'd been working from home all the time.

The door was opened to me by Frank's valet, Tarrant. I had never liked Tarrant and Tarrant didn't approve of me. He believed that Frank's close friendship with my father had made him too ready to overlook my informal and insubordinate manner. And Tarrant was a fearsome upholder of life's formalities.

'I have to see Mr Harrington. I know he's here,' I added quickly before Tarrant could proclaim that he was not at home and a battle of wills develop as it had done before.

'The master is dressing – preparing to go out,' said Tarrant.

'I won't need more than five minutes,' I said.

'Wait here, sir,' said Tarrant. He didn't believe I needed only five minutes; I always said five minutes.

As I stood in the hallway I could hear the murmured voices from somewhere upstairs. When I was permitted to go up and see Frank, he was standing in his dressing room, struggling with a stiff dress-shirt and old-fashioned wing collar that had gone out of fashion and come back without Frank noticing. Behind him there was a long closet, upon the rail of which hung dozens of suits and jackets and pants. Standing six feet high there was a purpose-built rack of shoes, and drawers for linen. One of the drawers was open to reveal more dress-shirts wrapped in soft white tissue paper: Tarrant's careful hand, no doubt. Frank was wearing his evening suit pants, patent shoes and a black formal waistcoat over a stiff shirt. He was struggling with his heavily starched cuffs and looking at himself in a large mirror while he did so. As I came in he watched my reflection without turning to face me.

'I'm sorry to interrupt you, Frank,' I said.

'Bring Mr Samson a big Laphroaig whisky and water, Tarrant. I'll have a small Plymouth gin with bitters: two or three dashes of bitters, Tarrant. Laphroaig and ice? Right, Bernard?' he turned and asked me this with a smile. He was always pleased to remember what I liked to eat and drink; it was Frank at his most motherly. Not wishing to spoil his obvious pleasure, I smiled and said that would be wonderful.

Tarrant brought the drinks on a tray and then hovered. Frank told him: 'Mr Samson will help me if I can't manage it.' Tarrant went away not hiding his resentment at being displaced.

'I've upset him?' I asked Frank after Tarrant had gone.

'He's getting old. We have to indulge him. He's frightened you'll leave finger-marks on my nice clean shirt.'

I smiled. It seemed an unlikely reason for Tarrant's surliness.

Frank went to his defence: 'You left finger-marks on the front of a shirt I lent you once; about three years ago. The marks never came out: faint brown patches. I think it must have been gun oil. I gave the shirt to Oxfam finally.'

'I'm sorry, Frank. You should have told me. I must replace it. Do New & Lingwood have your up-to-date measurements?'

'I've got dozens of dress-shirts,' said Frank, who'd been getting his shirts at New & Lingwood since he was at Eton. 'I'm still wearing some my father left me. How often do I need a dress-shirt these days?'

'Going to the opera?' I knew it was not very likely. Frank was not a keen opera-goer. Jazz was his first choice. It was a waste; his job gave him a chance to see a new opera production every night if he so wished.

'The garrison. The regiment's farewell dinner for the commander. I'll be the only civvy there.'

'That's quite an honour, Frank,' I said, because for Frank being with the soldiers was the ultimate joy. Sometimes I thought that it was the tragedy of Frank's life that he'd not been a career soldier. Frank loved the British Army, in all its many functions and guises, in a way that even its most dedicated soldiers could not have bettered. But Frank came down from university with a reputation as a Greek scholar, and someone on high decided that he would be wasted in the army.

'My wife couldn't make it.'

'Too bad,' I said automatically, although I knew that Frank's wife hated attending army functions. She was one of those English people for whom everything foreign is either alarming or inferior or both. In fact she hated Berlin in every way, and remained in their house in England as much as she could. But it was not unknown for Frank to console himself with accommodating young ladies, of whom he had a considerable selection. At one time he'd even bedded Zena. I suppose Frank's love-life was an important aspect of Tarrant's continuing employment; he knew enough to write a book, and was wise enough to resist doing so.

Frank always fell deeply in love with his young lady friends. That was Frank's style: devotion, sincerity and passion, but it never seemed to last. I sometimes wondered if he took his inamoratas along to any of these exclusive army functions. While Frank's more usual habitat – Berlin's Anglo-German fraternity – was a hotbed for gossip, the army could show exemplary discretion about such matters.

'I've plenty of time,' said Frank. Anyone who had dealings with the English knew that such a declaration was a polite way of saying that he was pressed for time.

'I went over there today,' I said. 'I spoke with a man named Fedosov. Does that ring a bell?'

'VERDI?' said Frank.

'And VERDI's father too. He of the Number Five Red Banner Party.'

'Oh, that Fedosov. Are you any good with cuff-links, Bernard? My housekeeper washes these dress-shirts herself; by hand. I think she must pour a ton of starch into each one. It's like wearing a suit of armour.'

I took the first of the gold torpedo-shaped cuff-links and stabbed it through the starched buttonhole. It was devilishly difficult. 'He was one of my father's agents,' I said very casually. 'Did you know that?'

'Not specifically, but it doesn't surprise me. He had a few people over there that he wouldn't pass on to anyone. Did you go over there and face the old man with his past then?'

'Yes, I did.'

'What happened?' said Frank. He gave me the second cuff-link and lifted his arm to offer the other sleeve.

'He hit me with a metal crucifix and knocked me unconscious.'

'Did he?' said Frank, poker-faced. He could display a caustic wit, especially in response to any of my demonstrated failings, but he restrained it now. 'And you saw the son? VERDI?'

'He brought a doctor to look at me. I was unconscious. The old man thought he'd killed me.'

'Yes, your head. I can see the swelling. Have you seen a doctor on this side?'

'I've only just come back.'

'I'll get one of the army people to have a look at you. You should have an X-ray. I say! Are you all right?'

257

'Just a nasty turn. I'll sit down for a moment,' I said. I had that stomach-turning nausea that often comes before a fainting fit.

'It's the reaction. Shock goes like that, Bernard. An hour or two afterwards ... I'll put you on a plane or London tonight. I don't like the look of you one bit.' He picked up the phone and dialled the internal line. When Tarrant came on the phone he told him to call the RAF and tell them to save a seat on their evening flight: top priority, Frank said. And get an extra car and driver this end, and a car and driver at the London end too. 'Tell London that I want Mr Samson in a bed in the London Clinic or some such establishment. He is concussed. A complete physical examination.' And Tarrant must go to the airport with me in case there was any problem of identification. The RAF people knew Tarrant.

'Don't finish that whisky,' said Frank, putting down the phone with one hand while using the other to move the malt whisky away from me. 'That might have been what brought it on.'

'I don't think so,' I said. At that moment the prospect of being whisked away by magic on the evening plane, and escape from any questions Werner might ask me, away from Frank and the bone-freezing cold in this bleak city, was an attractive proposition.

'You go straight to the London Clinic or wherever. The driver will have all the necessary documentation. I'll put a message on the machine for London Central and tell them your arrival time and that you are hurt.'

'Thank you, Frank,' I said. I let my head loll back and closed my eyes. 'VERDI seemed to think that the D-G was opposed to this scheme of Dicky's.'

'How did he get to hear of that?' said Frank, continuing to work on the other cuff. He didn't seem unduly alarmed at the leak, or even concerned.

'I thought you might know.'

'Werner Volkmann and VERDI have had meetings,' said Frank.

'Does Werner know the politics and arguments going on in London?'

'Don't sound so amazed,' said Frank. 'Werner's new job is on the line. He must be interested in its chances of getting approval.'

'Dicky will push it through,' I said, just to see what Frank would say to that.

'It's Dicky's chance of getting Operations permanently. That would be a major step up for him.'

'Next stop Deputy?'

'Let's not go through the ceiling,' said Frank. 'Look, could you help with the final bit?'

Frank had got his second cuff-link through one side of the cuff but the other side was completely sealed and resisting all his efforts.

'Lovely,' said Frank when I completed the job for him. He tugged at his cuffs as he admired himself in the mirror. 'It wouldn't hurt you if Dicky became Deputy D-G. By that time Fiona would be ready to take over Operations and there would be a chance for you as German Stations.'

'I've all but given up those sort of ambitions,' I said. There was a time when Dicky and I were running neck and neck for any promotions that came along. Now I was being talked of as a possible subordinate to him. And even that was unlikely if I was to face the truth of it.

When Frank turned to me and slapped my arm in some sort of gesture of commiseration it didn't cheer me up. I was hoping that he might provide me with a few encouraging lies. I got his jacket from the hanger and helped him into it.

'I'm sorry to have burst in on you like this,' I said.

He took a gold watch from his waistcoat to see the time. Frank was old-fashioned enough to believe that only waiters wore wrist-watches with evening suits. 'They will hold the plane; it's a priority seat. But you'd better be getting along.' He was fixing his miniature medals to his jacket. It was a rather meagre display of gongs. The intelligence service is rather sparing with them. It was at that moment that I understood why Frank so coveted a knighthood. He wanted to go along to drink with his soldier pals, and have on his chest a bauble to compare with all the glittering hardware they'd accumulated in a lifetime of soldiering.

'Thanks,' I said.

'I'm glad you came to see me, Bernard,' said Frank as he buttoned his waistcoat and tugged it down. 'But you have never asked me how I feel about the VERDI operation ... Werner's network and all that ...'

'How do you feel, Frank?'

'I shall do everything I can to screw it up.'

'Why?'

'Why don't we just say that I don't want any secret network formed in my bailiwick, unless I'm the one setting it up.'

I looked at him. I knew it wasn't the true reason. At least it wasn't the only reason. Frank wasn't the sort of man who strongly objected to others doing work for which he would be sure to receive a large measure of the credit. 'No,' I said.

'I've sent a formal objection to the D-G.'

'Was he pleased to hear that his wasn't the only voice raised in protest?'

'Yes. Every little helps,' said Frank. 'The fact is that I feel that this is the wrong time to mount a big operation that can only have a limited life. I'm too old to have another one of those blood-and-thunder confrontations, with tanks and guns sighting up across Checkpoint Charlie. And where will I find the field agents to handle it? Do you remember how many good people we lost last time?'

Yes, that sounded more like the real reason. Frank had settled down into a live-and-let-live routine that suited his lifestyle.

Tackling the Soviets in any practical way would run the risk of Frank's evenings being spoiled and his social life ravaged. 'Yes, I remember, Frank,' I said. 'But I thought that was what we got paid for.'

'That's because you were a war baby,' said Frank. 'But some of us remember life without cold wars, hot wars and any wars at all. We even cherish the hope that such days might come round again.'

No one really enjoys being in hospital I suppose. But two days of check-ups gave me a chance to sort out my thoughts. They couldn't get a bed for me in the London Clinic so I ended up in a small private hospital on the wrong side of Marylebone Road. It was an ugly little room, newly redecorated and smelling of paint. There was a small sink in one corner, and over it a mirror and a glass shelf holding a toothbrush glass and a comb. On one wall there was a light-box for examining X-ray photos and above that a TV set extended on a swivel arm. A large window gave a view across the crooked roofs of west London all the way to the elevated motorway.

My metal hospital bed was equipped with a personal radio, and plugs for intensive-care monitoring equipment that was not installed. On the wall beside the bed there was a phone and, on a hook beside that, a TV channel changer. All I had to do was sit there and watch TV, or work my way through a dozen or more assorted paperback books that were in the bedside cabinet behind the bedpans, and wait for my meals to arrive. It really wasn't too bad.

I had lots of visitors. None of them asked me specifically what was wrong with me but I gathered that some sort of rumour had circulated about me being injured during a daring foray across the Wall. I encouraged this misunderstanding by giving only vague responses to well-wishers, and hinting about the Official Secrets Act when regretfully refusing to reply to direct questions.

Dicky sent his assistant – who actually proclaimed herself as 'Jenni-with-an-i' – to visit bearing a huge box of crystallized pineapple. Since there was no conceivable reason for Dicky to think I liked crystallized fruit in such abundance, I suspected that it was an unwanted present left over from the previous Christmas, especially since the sticky label, from which the price had been torn, had a robin on it. I gobbled some of it and shared it with the nurses, and the consensus was that it was delicious. It was particularly tasty when dipped into the brandy I picked up at the airport.

I don't think Jenni-with-an-i had ever been inside a hospital before. She looked around with wide-eyed interest and asked me if I'd like her to read to me. I decided against it. There were flowers from Werner, two dozen tulips, and telephoned good wishes from Frank Harrington. There were get-well cards, including one, featuring a risque cartoon of an elderly doctor and young nurse in bed, which was delivered by motor-cycle messenger. It proved to be from Mabel, a girl in the office who did my typing rather than let me loose on her word processor.

There were no wishes – good or otherwise – from Silas Gaunt, the Deputy D-G or Sir Henry Clevemore. I believe this was a signal that all three had been informed that my excursion to the East had been entirely unauthorized, that I'd not informed Frank before going, and had made the Department look foolish by letting an old Russian peasant beat me about the head with an icon.

A young Chinese doctor from Hong Kong seemed to be in charge of my 'complete check-up'. He arranged the head-scan and the ophthalmology examination, and dropped in frequently to discuss the prices of second-hand motor cars, and eat the glacé pineapple. He was not unsympathetic at all. He said that

262

such bangs on the head should always be examined carefully, and gave me some yellow tablets that he said might clear up the head-cold that I think I must have caught in Berlin. He said they'd also clear up the nasal congestion, because that's what they claimed in the commercials on TV. But I suppose he was paid to be sympathetic.

Fiona came to the hospital the night I checked in. She was waiting for me in reception when I got there. Frank had phoned her directly from Berlin and told her to make sure I followed his orders and got a complete check-up and didn't just discharge myself next morning. She arrived looking calm and beautiful. As practical as ever, she brought with her an overnight bag containing my pyjamas and shaving things.

Fiona returned again on the second morning. She brought a bundle of work that Dicky wanted me to read and explain to him.

'The children send their love. I told them I was going to see you but I didn't say you were in hospital.'

'I was thinking. I will have a day to spare after this. Would they like a visit to the theatre, a matinee? A musical. We could have dinner and get them back, not too late.'

'We'll have to have someone to help, when they come home to live with us,' she said defensively. 'I'm seeing people at the agency this afternoon.'

'A nanny?'

'They are too old for a nanny. But there will have to be someone who prepares a hot breakfast for them, and takes them to school in the morning. Someone will have to be there when they get back in the afternoon, and do their laundry, and make sure they do their homework.'

'Almost like a mother, you mean?'

For a moment I thought she would react angrily, but she smiled and said: 'Like your mother, and like my mother. But

263

things have changed nowadays, darling. You wouldn't want me to stay at home all day, would you?'

'No,' I said. There was no need to remind me that her new job as Principal Assistant Europe would bring her a salary higher than mine, as well as guaranteeing her a permanent post and a good pension.

'Suggest the theatre visit when they come home for the weekend. I'm sure they'd love it.'

'Say I'm in here having a tooth fixed.'

'Yes, I will.' She gave me a smile. 'When Billy was born, I had a fear that you might want to be a tough-guy father. I wouldn't have blamed you. It was your right to earn their respect. But you've never portrayed yourself as a tough guy with them, Bernard. You've never told them stories of the work you do. They don't know about the dangers you've faced, or of the times you got hurt.'

'Idolizing your father is a tyranny from which few men emerge intact. The Department is full of examples.'

'But not many fathers can resist playing the absurd roles their children make for them, Bernard.' She looked at me as if she was about to cry. I wondered what she could see in my face.

'Tough guys get lousy pension plans,' I said.

She took out her handkerchief and blew her nose. 'Dicky wants to give us dinner on Saturday evening,' she said. 'Is that all right?'

'I suppose so.'

'And we'll see the children on Sunday.'

'What's Dicky up to now? He only invites people to dinner when he wants something.'

'He's awfully concerned about your crack on the head.'

'He sent Jenni-with-an-i in with a box of crystallized pineapple.'

'Did he? Where is it? I love it.'

'That Chinese doctor has eaten most of it,' I said. 'I think the Portuguese cleaning lady must have finished it and taken the box away. She was very smitten with the box. The lid had three men of Pickwickian appearance singing outside a tavern. She was going to frame it, she said.'

'I wish you would stop talking rubbish,' said Fiona. 'Dicky is trying to find a better office for you.'

'I'm quite content to remain where I am.'

'You can't. They're going to use that room for storing paper. There's so much paper now – for the word processors and the copiers and so on – that they need more space.'

'Frank doesn't like the VERDI operation,' I said, thinking it would surprise her.

'Yes, I know. He's put in an official objection.'

'That's what he told me. Why?'

'The Deputy is resigning.' She looked at me, waiting to see if I made the connection.

Even with an aching head I figured it out: 'And Frank hopes that a lack of enthusiasm for VERDI could get him shifted from Berlin to London?'

'Perhaps. And the only place to put him is the Deputy's job.'

'No. I don't think that's it,' I said. 'Frank isn't that Byzantine, is he? He'd just go directly to Sir Henry and ask to fill the Deputy's job.'

'But Frank is too old,' she said.

'Yes, but don't you see? Doing that, he would retire as Deputy. He's dying for a K. He's missed them time and time again. This could give him everything he wants: a K and a better pension. And Dicky could put into Berlin someone who will support the VERDI operation.'

'And have an anti-VERDI Deputy in London? How would that suit Dicky?'

'You're right,' I said. Fiona must have been talking it over with Dicky; she wasn't usually so attuned to office politics.

'Frank will have to play ball,' said Fiona. 'He's filed his objection. Now he'll have to just get on with it the way it's been planned.' It was the voice of London Central at its most inflexible.

'Yes,' I said. I wondered if she knew that Timmermann was dead. She must have been expecting him to report back to her. I decided it was more expedient to wait for her to bring it up.

'Why did you go over and talk to VERDI? It's not like you to be so foolhardy.'

'It's nice of you to say so.'

'Why?'

'I wanted to see if he's still the same strong-arm man I knew twenty years ago.'

'And is he?' said Fiona.

'Yes. He just has better suits and shirts. Strong-arm men like VERDI always find it difficult to adapt to a life of stealth. If Operation VERDI comes to grief, it will probably be because of VERDI's loud mouth.'

'Is that what you really think? That he's unreliable?'

'I just hope I'm not standing near him when he explodes,' I said.

'But he's coming over to us? He's genuine?'

'I think he's been on the payroll for years and years.'

'How is that possible? On our payroll and we don't know?'

'His father was certainly on our payroll. I believe his money was paid into a bank account in Zurich; name of Madame Xavier. It's possible that the Madame Xavier money still continues, but instead of paying the old man, it now gets paid to VERDI.'

'But he didn't say that?'

'Not him. He just yells at me and wants me to tell the D-G what an eager beaver he is. He's full of crap.'

'On our payroll?'

'I'd love to get into that bank account and see if Xavier's payments are still being credited,' I said. 'Maybe not on our direct payroll. Some of our Berlin agents were turned over to the Americans, some to Bonn.'

'I don't think I understand.'

'I suspect he's on the payroll of someone else – the Americans, the French, or Bonn. Now he's spotted a way of selling himself twice. He's dangled the computer scheme in front of Dicky's eyes, and Dicky's taken the bait.'

'You think we should break contact with him?'

'If we could find evidence that VERDI has been on some Western payroll for years, we could make him dance to our tune.'

'Blackmail him, you mean?'

'Damned right. We could have him in the palm of our hand. I wish I knew how much the father knows; he obviously doesn't know the full story.'

'Is that why you went over there?'

'I went to show the old man that we have evidence that could get him a death sentence. I was hoping that VERDI would get the message that he too could find himself behind the eight ball.'

'And were you successful?'

'Not in the way I planned. But yes, VERDI got it all right. He's used to hints and half-truths.'

'Well, let's start at the very beginning,' said Fiona. 'Let's assume that someone somewhere is still paying him. We should be able to trace the payments or the transfer. If we let an agent go elsewhere, there will be a record somewhere.'

'And even if Dicky objects to a search, you can find out,' I said.

'I'm not sure about that,' she said hurriedly.

'You're Dicky's attendant, assistant and hired hand, aren't you?'

'Why would Dicky object to the search?'

'Everything is going Dicky's way at present. If we find that VERDI is someone else's agent – the Americans for instance

– they will want a slice of him. Or even claim VERDI as their own and want us to back off.'

'Dicky keeps a lot of cards very close to the chest. But if you've got something definite to start me off, I'll try and dig it out without mentioning it to Dicky. There must be a record somewhere in Central Funding.'

'Not Central Funding; they deal in millions. This is just one secret account. It will be well hidden, Fi. It's not a small task.'

'But you have no hard evidence to start me off?'

'Only circumstantial evidence.'

'You mean it's just your hunch.'

'It's just my hunch,' I admitted.

'You have too many hunches,' said Fiona. She looked at her watch. 'I think you are due to have an X-ray,' she said, and put on her coat.

'I'm perfectly all right,' I told her.

She leaned over the bed and gave me a kiss. 'Of course you are, you're wonderful. I'll see you tomorrow.'

'I'll be home tonight,' I said.

'Now, be good,' she said. 'You have the blood tests tomorrow. You'll be finished by early afternoon.' She was rummaging in the cupboard among my clothes. 'I'll take your suit and send it to the cleaners. I'll bring jacket and slacks when I come to collect you.'

I knew that my relationship with Gloria Kent was over and finished with. I think Gloria knew it too. And I'd promised myself that it would not resume. Not now; not ever. Ours had never been a sensible relationship; Gloria was young enough to be my daughter. I was happily married to a wonderful successful wife.

So it was sensible and to be expected that no word, no flower nor greeting came from Gloria. I wasn't disappointed. She was a sensible girl and I was relying upon her to accept the situation for the thing of the past that it clearly was.

I'd come back from radiography and was dozing over a cup of tea and plate of chocolate biscuits when I heard the door open.

'Hello, iron-head!'

'Gloria.'

She came swaggering into the room with a bottle of wine and a warm cardboard box smelling of toasted cheese. She put the box on the table by my bed and opened it to reveal two large slices of hot pizza.

'I thought they might not be feeding you properly in here,' she explained, while getting a corkscrew from her handbag and then throwing it to me.

'You're right,' I said, remembering the miserable chicken salad I'd been served at lunch.

'Open the wine then.' She slung her brown suede coat over the armchair. Under it she was wearing a beige roll-neck, matching skirt and polished leather riding boots. She took one of the slices of pizza in its paper wrapper and started eating. Elbows out, she craned forward awkwardly, holding the pizza in one hand while protecting her sweater against drips with the other hand. Between swallows she said: 'Two Spanish brothers do them in Marylebone High Street. They're the best pizzas in London.'

'It's good,' I said.

She took the two glasses that stood beside my allocated bottle of Perrier water and set them before me while I extracted the cork from the wine. 'Hurry,' she said impatiently. 'I've got a cab waiting.'

'Why didn't you pay it off?' I poured wine for us.

'I've got things to do: work!' she said scornfully. 'I'm not checking into the ante-natal clinic.' She grabbed the glass and swallowed some wine between bites at the pizza. 'This is hot sausage with extra cheese.'

'Not very hot sausage,' I said.

'Not very hot,' she agreed.

I watched her as she loped across the room and looked through the get-well cards and sniffed at the tulips, while continuing to eat. She was tall, with long slender legs and slim arms, and she displayed the halting gawkiness of a young antelope. Yet she was never clumsy. She never actually dripped tomato down her sweater, she didn't fall over when she was running for a bus in that ungainly way, neither did she ever drive truly dangerously – she just looked as if she was going to. Or was my concern for her parental and protective in a way that a true lover's concern should not be?

'Show me your war wounds, bruiser,' she said. With her free hand she grasped my hair and pulled my head forward to see the place where my head had been shaved. I could smell the soap with which she'd washed her hands and her touch made me shiver. If she noticed the effect this physical contact had upon me she gave no sign of it: 'It's not much. How did it happen?' She let go of my hair and bit into the pizza and licked a dribble of sauce that was about to fall.

'What did you hear?' I said, secretly hoping that it would be some awesome feat of arms.

'Don't say you really did dive into a drained swimming pool?' she said. 'I'll bet you broke some tiles.'

'Where is all that tender loving care you used to bestow upon the weak and weary?'

'Spurned.'

'Ouch.' Oh, well. I held up the tumbler of heavy red wine to see the light of the window gleaming through it. Gigondas, a rich and heavy Rhone red. 'This is beautiful wine, Gloria. It must have set you back a fortune.'

'It's from my father's cellar. He said I could help myself to what I wanted.'

'Ummm. Is your father all right?' I doubted whether Gloria's father would have approved us guzzling his carefully stored old wine with a take-out pizza.

270

'We haven't heard from him yet. It's sure to take him a few days to settle down. I don't want to fuss, and neither does Mummy, but she runs to answer every phone call. You can imagine.'

'I hope it works out for him.'

She finished the last of her pizza and threw the paper napkin into the waste-bin. Then she licked her fingers. 'Listen, Bernard. That was silly, all that stuff I told you the other night.' I looked at her without responding. 'I was drunk.'

'You weren't drunk, Gloria. I've never seen you drunk.' She never had shown much liking for alcohol. Her wineglass was still more or less full.

'I can hold my drink,' she said sternly but, unable to sustain her serious face, she burst into a giggle of laughter. 'I was worried about Daddy going away. I was silly.'

'Yes, of course.'

'Did I tell you, I've still got lots of your clothes? I was going to leave them at the office for you but I didn't know who to leave them with. People gossip. And you know how the security staff get about unattended boxes and bags. They force them open if they think there might be bombs in them.'

'I'll send someone down to your home to collect them.'

'There are dozens of shirts. And there's that lovely old suede jacket. You always look great in that, Bernard. I loved you in that, you always looked so ...'

'Young?'

'Don't start that all over.'

'We mustn't start anything all over,' I said. Perhaps I said it too hurriedly.

'No. I know we mustn't. I try to avoid making difficulties for you, Bernard, I really do. In fact the real reason I popped in, was to ask you if it's okay about dinner.'

'Dinner?'

271

'Yes, I thought you wouldn't know. The Cruyers have asked me to dinner next Saturday. And I know you are going to be there with Fiona. Would it annoy her? Me being there, I mean.'

'I don't know. I don't think so,' I said, although I felt quite sure that Gloria's presence would in fact upset Fiona very much indeed. I was surprised that Dicky didn't know that too. Or was this Dicky's way of sowing trouble for me?

'Daphne phoned me this morning. They have an extra man at dinner, and she wants to make the numbers even. It was Daphne's idea.'

'Won't your boyfriend mind?' I asked, clutching at a straw in the hope she would suddenly decide not to go.

'Boyfriend? I haven't got a regular boyfriend.'

'Is it over so soon?'

'What?'

'Your driver. Your rally companion.'

'You pig! We're an all-woman team.'

'Your driver is a girl?'

'No, she's a forty-year-old woman. Do you think I need a man to drive a rally car?'

'No, of course not.'

A slow grin: 'You were jealous.'

'Don't be ridiculous.'

She was immediately angry. 'Ridiculous?'

'You know what I mean. It's all different now.'

'I know. Look, I'll leave the trade card of the pizza bakery on the side-table. They'll deliver if you phone them.'

'Thanks, Gloria. That's very thoughtful.'

'Bernard?' she stopped and gave me a fleeting grin.

'What?'

'It's not true … about us being taken over by the CIA, is it?'

I laughed. 'Who told you that?'

'Or that we are being merged with the CIA?'

'You can rest your mind on that one, Gloria,' I said. 'Who on earth have you been speaking to?'

'Some silly girl in the Registry told me months ago. I didn't believe it, of course. But then, when I heard that Mr Rensselaer was coming back to London, I thought there might be something in it.'

'Bret Rensselaer? In London?'

'He's coming back to work in the office. Didn't you know that?'

'Are you quite sure? Who told you?'

'That's who will be the extra man at the Cruyers' on Saturday. That's who I'm to be with.'

'Yes, but not living in London,' I said with waning conviction. 'Just a visit I should think. Or a meeting.'

'No, he's coming back to work for Dicky. He's already got a place to live and there's a secretary lined up for him. The problem is the office. There's nowhere for him on the top floor, unless they turf your wife out and give him his old room back. And Dicky Cruyer would never agree to that.'

'How do you know all this?'

'Girls' talk,' she said. 'Hang around in the ladies' wash-room and you'll find out anything you want to know.'

'I'll try it,' I said.

'So you don't mind about Saturday dinner?'

'I'm sure Fiona will understand.' My head was throbbing again.

'Daphne is in a state. You know what she's like. She's convinced that Bret Rensselaer is a vegetarian. She's thinking of giving him tomatoes filled with bulgur wheat as a starter, and cauliflower cheese as the main course.'

'No, not Bret. He wouldn't like that.'

She leaned over the bed to kiss me goodbye, but stopped before doing so. Poised inches above me she said: 'Can I tell her that, definitely?'

'Daphne? Of course.'

'Otherwise we might all be eating nut-rolls and great heaps of that bloody bulgur wheat and tabbouleh and all that muck that Daphne says is healthy.' She gave me a kiss on the lips, and then wiped the traces of lipstick off my face with a spittle-moistened piece of tissue. 'We don't want your wife asking you awkward questions, do we?'

'Fiona has already been in. She was here before you.'

'Yes, I know. I saw her in the office with your suit.'

'She wanted to be sure I wouldn't walk out of here.'

'She's clever,' said Gloria, with admiration that was unmistakably genuine.

'Yes, she's very clever,' I said.

17

I often thought that Daphne's life with Dicky must have been unendurable. It wasn't that Dicky was stupid or selfish; he was no more so than many people of his age, class and background. And I'm sure there were many husbands who had strayed far more often than Dicky had done, and done it more cruelly. It was simply that Dicky seemed unable to indulge in an extramarital fling, however fleeting, without Daphne discovering all about it. It may have been something in Dicky's subconscious, some need for attention, that caused these lapses that betrayed him. It may have been deliberately done to cause Daphne unhappiness. But, whatever the reason, Dicky Cruyer's character contained some flaw – or was it some virtue? – that made him quite unable to keep his indiscretions secret. Time and time again, a brave but tearful Daphne would be phoning Dicky's secretary asking about Dicky's recent evening appointments. To me such episodes only cast further doubt on the boundless confidence our masters had reposed in him as a custodian of the nation's secrets.

And over the years Daphne had become more and more adept at recognizing the high-spirited deportment that he displayed when these intrigues were in full flood. It was not difficult. I had learned to recognize some of the symptoms myself. So when, that Friday morning, I found Dicky in his office singing, I guessed that his life had taken some new and exciting turn. I wondered who was the lucky girl, and whether there was a clue to her identity in the fact that he was giving an animated rendering of 'You Ain't Nothin' But a Hound Dog' accompanied by Elvis Presley trapped in a small cassette recorder on the desk.

'Oh, Bernard,' he said, and switched the machine off. 'Come in. Head better now?'

'Yes, thank you, Dicky,' I said.

'Sit down, sit down.' He moved the cassette recorder to one side and tapped a finger upon the report I'd submitted about going to Pankow and talking to Fedosov. It said only that the elder Fedosov was a well-established contact I'd used for many years, and that I had visited him as part of my regular method of remaining in contact with informants. We'd had an argument, my report said, in which I was slightly injured. VERDI was not mentioned. Dicky knew it was nothing like the truth, but he wanted the whole episode to be forgotten as soon as possible, so he wasn't about to sit me down and interrogate me about it. 'There will be no repercussions in respect of your going off on your private errand seeing Fedosov the elder,' he said.

'Oh, good,' I said.

'Not unless something unforeseen happens.'

'What sort of something?'

'Well, you know … If there was some official complaint.'

'About me being attacked and injured?'

'Well, yes. That's what I mean. Not very likely, is it?' He moved my report an inch to one side and lined it up with a new digital clock that showed the time all around the world. Dicky bought it when he 'got Europe'. 'I'm pleased to say we've brought the D-G round to our point of view on the VERDI business.'

'That's good,' I said. Not knowing exactly what our point of view was, I artfully added: 'What did he say?'

'He's happy to leave it to me.'

'That's quite a change of mind,' I said. 'From what I was told, he was digging his heels in against it.'

'No, no,' said Dicky, 'not at all.' Then, deciding that such a disclaimer would deprive him of credit that was rightfully his due: 'At first he was. Yes, that's right. Very much opposed. But if there's one thing I pride myself on, it's being able to sort out complicated technical material so it can be understood by the layman.'

'Yes, you have a mechanical mind, Dicky,' I said.

'So why didn't you wind it up this week? Yes, I've heard that joke, Bernard. It's time you got some new ones.'

Naughty Bernard: no coffee for you today. 'And the D-G authorized the use of Werner Volkmann too?' I prompted.

'I told him that we would have to use people with a special knowledge of Berlin. I mentioned you and Volkmann and a few others, and I gave him a list of people on an official memorandum so he won't be able to say he didn't know afterwards. Volkmann will be coming over next week for a briefing. Yes, we're pushing ahead.' Dicky picked up a small sheet of memo paper. 'From the desk of Richard Cruyer' was printed along the top in ornate Saxon lettering. Upside-down, from where I was sitting I could see a typewritten list of names, with pencil marks down the margin. He put the paper at his elbow where he could refer to it.

'Is that why you wanted to see me?' I said. He had sent Jenni-with-an-i down to find me and get me to his office urgently.

'Ah, yes. No, that was in connection with staff changes. I thought you should be informed early that we're bringing Bret Rensselaer back into the office.'

'Really,' I said politely, injecting surprise, gratitude and on-going interest into my reaction.

'Yes. I'm not sure quite what we're going to do with him, to tell you the honest truth. You've seen him recently, Bernard. Off the record: what's he like?'

277

'You know what he's like, Dicky. He used to work here on the top floor.'

'Don't be stupid, Bernard. I mean what sort of shape is he in now? What's his health like?'

'Perfectly fit from all I could see. He does twenty miles on an exercise bike before breakfast every morning,' I said, improvising a story that perhaps went a little too far.

'Well, I know that's not true,' said Dicky, with a stifled chuckle that revealed his exasperation. 'He's been very ill.'

'He was shot,' I said. 'Yes, I was there. But wounds heal, Dicky. He's in fine shape.'

I could see from the crestfallen look on his face that my appointed role in this discussion was to provide Dicky with quotes that he could take elsewhere and prove that Bret was quite unsuited for a job anywhere in the organization.

'Fine shape? That's really your opinion?'

'Yes.'

'But you're not medically trained, Bernard. And I am inclined to believe that a man who was taken to one of the best hospitals in Berlin, and given up for dead – and that's not long ago – is hardly suited for all the stresses and strains of day-to-day work here.'

'Oh, I don't know about that, Dicky,' I said. My own unspoken feeling was that there were quite a few senior men working on the top floor whom I had long since given up for dead.

Dicky bit his lip and reminisced soberly: 'Bret's brother Sheldon came barging into the Steglitz Clinic in Berlin, and carted him off to Washington DC on some special plane that accompanies the American President on his journeys and is kept on call in case he suddenly needs top-flight emergency medical treatment. That's the kind of pull Bret's family has in Washington.'

'I was there,' I said, in case Dicky decided to relate the whole of that long saga from his own very personal viewpoint. 'I was

278

at the shooting; I was at the Steglitz Clinic when they rolled him out.'

'But that kind of influence cuts no ice in this Department. Not now that I've got Europe,' added Dicky with Napoleonic self-assurance.

'What is the arrangement going to be?'

'About Bret? We'll probably find out what he has to offer over dinner on Saturday night. He's coming to dinner; did I tell you that?' I nodded. 'But I can't play favourites, Bernard. Bret knows he can't expect me to push Fiona out so soon after her appointment.'

'And before yours is confirmed,' I said.

'What?' He permitted himself a sly grin as if surprised that my mind could be as devious as his. 'Yes, and before I'm confirmed. That's right.' He stood up and posed with his hands on his hips. 'This has all happened before, hasn't it?'

'What has?'

'It's *déjà vu*,' he said, 'seen before.'

'Yes, I have a little French,' I said. 'But I thought it meant something you only imagined the first time.'

'Bret Rensselaer hunting through the Department to find a place to build a nice empire for himself.'

'You must have thought of some job for him.'

'It's not sensible,' said Dicky. 'Sending a senior man like that over here, when it's obvious that I can't use him. No one checked with me. No one asked me if I wanted the fellow.'

'They couldn't make him German Stations Controller without your approval, could they?'

'He couldn't manage the German,' said Dicky. And then, less sure of this: 'Does he speak good enough German?'

'Good enough,' I said. Better than you, would have been a more precise assessment. Dicky's German had been put together in assorted bits and pieces, and stuck on to a few basic elements of grammar he'd learned at school. Bret, with that directness of approach that is characteristically American, simply went and did an intensive course at London University. He did it in addition to his five-day week at the office, something it would be difficult to imagine any of the other senior staff tackling. But it had provided Bret with a background of knowledge – literary, historical, and contemporary – that had surprised me more than once. As an amusement during his studies, he'd translated Schikaneder's libretto for Mozart's *Magic Flute* into English. I still remembered some little gems that he uncovered. 'Remember the *Magic Flute* he translated?'

'No,' said Dicky.

I reminded him:

'Die Worte sind von hohem Sinn!
    Allein, wie willst du diese finden?
Dich leitet Lieb' und Tugend nicht,
    Weil Tod und Rache dich entzünden.'

'You're gabbling much too fast,' said Dicky. 'You do that sometimes, Bernard. You must learn to enunciate more clearly. Tell me in English.'

'Those words sound fine and brave, I know.
    But say, how do you hope to find them?
For neither love nor truth is found
    By men whose hate and vengeance blind them.'

'Bravo,' said Dicky. 'You committed that to memory, did you? I wish I had time to go to the opera. It's one of the things I miss.'

'That wasn't opera you were playing when I came in?' I asked, as if it might well have been.

280

'Elvis Presley,' said Dicky, glad perhaps to confess it. 'But you always hit the nail right on the head, Bernard old man. You have an uncanny way of picking out exactly the most crucial part of whatever comes up for discussion.'

'Do I, Dicky?' I said, knowing that sooner or later he would tell me what he was talking about.

'What was it in that *Magic Flute* thing about truth and love? That's the sort of broad cultural landscape that Bret likes to occupy. He is a philosopher, not a man of action. While Bret is talking about truth and love, I am sitting up here making the decisions that end in blood and snot. See what I mean, Bernard?' He ran his fingers back through his unruly hair.

'Up to a point, Dicky.'

'Bret has always been appointed to positions where high-flown policy decisions were being hatched. He's simply not right for our sort of work. He's not an Operations man.'

'I suppose you're right,' I said in my usual cowardly way.

Dicky jumped in quickly. 'In that case I shall expect you to support me.'

'Doing what?'

'We must keep Bret right out of Europe. Why couldn't he have Hong Kong? That will be vacant at the end of the year.' He moved the memo with its list of names. I could see there were pencilled ticks and crosses alongside some of them.

'You couldn't put someone in to run Hong Kong who'd never worked there,' I said. 'And you could hardly expect Bret to go there in some junior capacity.'

'Umm,' said Dicky, and started biting the nail of his little finger. There was no need to add that the same problem was true of all the stations outside Europe.

'Bret wasn't born in Britain,' said Dicky. I'd heard him say that before. There was a strict rule that only British subjects born in Britain could be engaged to work here in the SIS office.

281

There had been only two exceptions granted to that rule; one was Bret Rensselaer and the other was George Blake, the KGB mole who was eventually uncovered and sentenced to forty-two years for spying.

'Bret was injured in action,' I said. 'He is a celebrated hero of the Department's secret history. Don't let's forget that, Dicky. The Department is bound to feel indebted to him.'

Dicky frowned and bit greedily into his fingernail. Dicky would have done anything to have something like that said about him, but Dicky knew that going into the field, to find action, was the quickest and most certain way of disappearing from the promotion lists for ever. And if he ever forgot that basic fact of life in London Central, he had only to look at my career to be reminded of it.

A tap came at the door and one of Dicky's young ladies poked her head round it and raised her eyebrows.

'Yes,' said Dicky. 'Run along and get him.' He made a mark on his sheet of names. When the door had closed again Dicky said: 'Well, I'll see you on Saturday evening, Bernard.'

I got to my feet. 'I'm looking forward to it,' I said. I could see now that the names on the piece of paper were Department employees. One by one they were being given a tick, a cross or a query. It was evidently part of an organized campaign to thwart the Rensselaer threat. I had been given a query.

Bret was the star of the show, of course. He had an instinct for drama, and had been keeping well away from the office up to the time he arrived at Dicky's for dinner. There was a certain demonic air to his appearance: smooth white hair brushed close against his scalp, a beautifully tailored black worsted suit, a white starched dress-shirt with a neat bow tie of natural-coloured raw silk. He remained slim, he'd always been slim. It was difficult to imagine Bret plump at any stage of his life. The only notable change was that the big wire-frame speed-cop glasses that he'd required for reading were now worn all the time.

Bret walked around the Cruyers' drawing-room as if he'd never been there before, admiring aloud their possessions in that accomplished way that only Americans can bring off.

'Now I like that painting. Adam and Eve, isn't it?' Unerringly Bret's eye had settled upon the Cruyers' most cherished artifact.

'We adore it,' said Dicky. 'And we got it for a song. Didn't we, darling?'

It was a naïve painting: two emaciated nudes by some myopic admirer of Jan van Eyck who had chronically neglected life classes. But Daphne had been to an art school, and had spent the rest of her life trying to prove that her training there was not a waste of time. She'd bought the painting in Amsterdam, in a flea market on Waterlooplein, when she got lost looking for Rembrandt's house round the corner. I liked Daphne. In one of her moments of candour she'd told me that on that same occasion she'd also bought three fake ship's lanterns and a lot of reproduction Dutch tiles, for which she was grossly over-charged. I suppose that's why antique dealers do so well; we boast about the bargains for ever and the swindles are conveniently forgotten.

Bret turned to Gloria and said: 'Wouldn't you just love a painting like that on your wall?'

'Yes,' said Gloria. She'd been upstairs admiring Daphne's doll collection. At one time there had been only half a dozen or so, and they cohabited comfortably in the china cabinet in the drawing-room. Then, as they proliferated, they'd been arrayed up the staircase, and now they had demanded a room to them-selves. There were china dolls and celluloid dolls, wooden dolls and 'piano dolls'. There were dolls in elaborate velvet gowns, Barbie dolls in miniskirts and festival dolls in kimonos. Gloria loved them all, I could see that in her face. She must have been able to read my thoughts, for she glanced at me and grinned self-consciously.

Once the dolls had gone upstairs, Dicky had started to fill the china cabinet with old fountain-pens. It was his latest diversion, and like all Dicky's diversions, the quantification of its growing value was a vital part of its interest for him. 'What did you do with your collection of paintings?' Dicky asked Bret.

'Sold them at auction,' said Bret, '... to satisfy the court. My wife wouldn't accept my assessments of value, so finally I put them up for sale.'

I suppose we all desperately craved to know whether Bret's assessments or his wife's were verified by the prices made at auction, but being English none of us was bold enough to ask.

'And this is your family home?' Bret asked, pointing at a colour photo of an extensive neo-Gothic mansion, framed by oak trees and with a well-kept front lawn.

'No,' said Dicky. 'That's my son's boarding school.'

'Is that so,' said Bret, looking at it with even more interest. 'Yes, I can see the kids now – quite a lot of them. Those at the back are standing on chairs, I guess. You must be proud of those little guys, Dicky.'

'Yes, I am,' said Dicky. 'One of them will be going to Oxford next year. My old college.'

'That's just great,' said Bret.

I glanced at Fiona, but she appeared to be studying Gloria's shoes. I had the feeling that I had been here on a previous dinner, visiting Dicky, with Bret present. I was wondering whether Bret wasn't going through an elaborate routine to irk Dicky, but that wasn't Bret's style. He worked hard to be Mr Nice Guy and he wasn't likely to sacrifice all that hard work in exchange for a little joke at Dicky's expense. Or was he?

Dicky was holding a couple of his most valuable old fountain-pens. He looked around the drawing-room to see if we were a suitable audience for him to explain how rare they were. He must have decided we weren't, for he put them back in the glass-fronted cabinet and locked it. His wife Daphne was in the kitchen. Fiona, me, Bret and Gloria were all Department employees. In the interests of security Dicky had even decided to manage without the man-and-wife team he usually brought in to wait table and wash up. 'Did you hear about the VERDI plan?' Dicky asked.

'I heard,' said Bret. He drank some of his Martini cocktail as if fortifying himself against what was to come.

'It will be Operation Prince all over again,' said Dicky. Operation Prince was the tunnel dug under Berlin to tap into the Russian Army's main telephone lines at Karlshorst.

'Not exactly like it, I hope,' said Bret drily, for Prince had been betrayed by Blake right from the start.

Dicky smiled. It was not a good beginning, and I could spy in Dicky's tense face his determination to see Bret stationed far away from anywhere where he could influence policy. 'No, we've learned a lot since then. This is the computer age that we're living in.'

'So I read in your report,' said Bret.

'You read it then?'

'The D-G thought I should get up to date on what is going on.'

'Yes, that's wise,' said Dicky. 'There have been profound changes since you were working here, Bret. Let me see, how long ago was that?'

'I left my Japanese pocket calculator in my other pants,' said Bret with a good-natured grin.

Daphne came in at that moment. She was looking very worried and, although she was trying to signal something to Dicky by mouthing it silently, this only engaged everyone's attention.

'What is it, Daphne?' said Dicky testily. 'We were just talking office talk.'

'It's the microwave, Dicky,' she said in a whisper, and then looked around to see if anyone had noticed her. Finding that everyone was looking at her, she gave a brief but all-embracing panoramic smile before looking at Dicky again.

'Well, I don't know about it,' said Dicky.

'The door's stuck. Shall I phone and tell them?'

'They've gone out to the theatre. Otherwise I should have had to invite them.'

'Do you know anything about microwave ovens?' Daphne asked Fiona.

'Bernard's awfully good with machines,' Fiona replied.

'Would you mind, Bernard?'

I picked up my glass of wine and followed Daphne into their newly refurbished kitchen. They were always changing it. On my previous visit it had been all cupboards, but now the doors of the cupboards had been removed so that the shelves, and the equipment on them, were exposed to view. Daphne must have seen the surprise in my face.

'Dicky could never remember where the dishes and things were,' she explained. 'And he left the cupboard doors open sometimes, and cracked his head on them.'

'Is this it?' I asked as I approached the microwave.

'I hope you don't mind that we invited Gloria,' said Daphne. 'Bret had arranged to take her out to dinner tonight, but Dicky persuaded him to change his plans. Dicky was very keen to have you all together tonight.'

'Bret's coming back to the office,' I explained. 'Dicky wanted to see him unofficially beforehand.'

'I knew it was something like that,' said Daphne.

'It's a child-lock,' I said.

'Oh, you've opened it. How clever you are, Bernard.'

'It's a child-lock. That red lever has to be in the up position. Then it works normally.'

'I couldn't do it.'

'You have to push the lever while you press the door button.' I sipped some of my wine. Dicky had provided extra-special wine for this evening.

'I don't know why they put these child-locks on everything these days,' said Daphne. 'The children are the only ones who can work them.'

'Smells good, Daphne.'

'Roast chicken. Dicky likes to carve and that's the only thing he carves really well. The microwave is only for reheating the sprouts. I cook them first and then warm them in butter. My neighbour insisted that I try their microwave, but I can't get on with things like that.'

'These Brussels sprouts look a bit overcooked, Daphne.'

'The hell with the sprouts,' she said, and in an uncharacteristically carefree movement dumped them into the waste-bin with hardly a glance at their going. 'They can bloody well have tinned beans.' She went to the shelf and selected a copper saucepan from a row of pans of varying sizes. Then she took a tin of baked beans, opened it with the electric machine, and tipped the contents into the pan. Some beans went astray. Not without some difficulty, she picked up each errant bean between thumb and finger until they were all in the pan. Then she smiled at me. 'I suppose I should have come and asked you to look at it before, Bernard.' She took a half-full bottle of wine and poured some into my glass and then carelessly slopped a lot into her own empty glass. She put the saucepan of beans back on the shelf with the other saucepans. Then she turned to me, lifted her glass – 'Salud! Bernard. Salud y pesetas!' – and drank.

'Yes, good health and money,' I agreed. 'Were you going to put the beans on the stove to warm?'

'Yes, I was.' She retrieved the saucepan from the shelf, lit the gas and put it on to the stove. It slid to one side but she grabbed it and put it back more carefully. It was only then that I realized that Daphne was totally plastered. I felt sorry for her. She had never been much of a drinker, and I knew how nervous she always became when Dicky arranged one of these dinner parties.

Daphne tucked an errant lock of hair back into the velvet headband she was wearing and said: 'I'm going to leave Dicky. You've always been nice, Bernard. Simpatico! That's what you are: simpatico. You're one of our best friends, I've always liked you. But he doesn't deserve nice friends. He's such a selfish bastard.'

'I'm sure it will all come right, Daphne.'

'He doesn't care about anyone but himself.'

'You've been through all this before, Daphne,' I reminded her. Most recently she'd endured watching Dicky enjoying a brief affair with Tessa Kosinski. 'He always comes back to you,' I said. 'You have your nice home, and he loves you.'

'I've had enough of him.' She finished her wine and poured more for herself. I covered my glass with my hand to show I didn't want a refill.

'And there are the children,' I said.

She came close to me and tapped my tie. 'All these years I've put up with him for their sake, Bernard. But now they are old enough to understand. I've had enough of him. I deserve a little happiness, don't I?'

'Yes, Daphne, of course you do. But is going off on your own a way to find it? You might be lonely.'

She laughed. 'Dear old Bernard,' she said, and reached out and patted me gently on the cheek. 'Am I so very old and ugly?'

'No, Daphne, no. But the right partner is hard to find.'

'You're telling me,' she said and laughed again.

'I'm sure he'll come back to you. These things are just infatuations.'

'Has Dicky got some new one in tow?' she asked, her mood suddenly darkening. 'Is that it?'

'No. Isn't that what you are telling me?'

'No, I'm talking about me. I'm talking about the man I've found. My Mister Right. It took a long time, Bernard, but you find the right partner eventually. I went to Gloria's fortune-teller and she told me I'd be happy, and that was ages ago.'

'Mister Right?'

'A young fellow in my Tuesday evening painting class. With Professor Belostok. Well, not too young; just right.'

Now I was stone-cold sober. Very casually I said: 'What's he do for a living?'

'Journalist. Newspaper reporter actually. He used to work for an agency that files stories for foreign newspapers. He's out of a job at present but he'll get another. Next year he's going to take a year off and write a novel. He's going to South America and live as cheaply as he can, while he writes. I said I'd go with him. It's the chance of a lifetime.'

'It certainly is,' I said. 'Is he English?'

'Czechoslovak. His father is a South African.'

The whole picture jumped into position. I had read it in a thousand case histories. 'Daphne!' In spite of trying to keep my voice down I said it much too loudly.

'Yes, Bernard?'

Next door I could hear the murmur of voices. My inclination was to scream Jesus Christ, Daphne, are you out of your mind? Are you too stupid to see when you are being targeted by a foreign agent? But I remained very calm. I said: 'Is he a good painter, Daphne?'

'Not very good. He's a dabbler.'

'Did he join the class after you joined it?'

'Yes, he's a newcomer. Never tried to paint or draw before. I've been helping him.'

Shit! I tried to smile. 'Well, let me drink to your health, Daphne,' I said.

We drank.

'Does he know what Dicky does for a living?'

'I told him Dicky works in the Foreign Office.'

'Good. You can't be too careful.' Already I was planning the next move. Would it be possible to get into this situation and maybe neutralize it before telling Dicky? Should I even try?

'You'd better go back to the drawing-room,' said Daphne. 'They'll wonder what's happened to you.'

When I got back to the other room, they were all sitting round the fire, watching the gas flames with everyone saying how like burning coal it was. Dicky looked up at me and said: 'Well, well. Here's the microwave engineer. Stay and have a drink, old chap. We have to suck up to the workers.'

I smiled and went and sat on the sofa next to Fiona. She was wearing her best black Chanel outfit and the gold Cartier watch her father had given her when she arrived from California. She touched my hand and quietly said: 'Are you all right, Bernard?'

'I'm fine.'

'You look as if you've seen a ghost.'

'Just a spook,' I said.

She smiled.

By that time Bret was saying: 'The people in Washington have long since abandoned all that telephone garbage. It takes for ever to translate and analyse it and, at the end of the day, what have you got? Junkmail. Know what I mean? It's all effort and no reward.'

'So what are the people in Washington concentrating on?' Dicky asked, with no trace of curiosity in his voice.

Bret said: 'It's all top-secret but it's been going on for years now, so I guess I can tell you. They are buying Soviet weapons technology. I'm talking about hardware: state-of-the-art Soviet electronics, Soviet air defence systems and advanced Soviet weaponry, and Uncle Sam is paying for it in greenbacks.'

'From Poland?' I said.

'Good boy, Bernard. Yes, Poland is the major supplier. But other Warsaw Pact countries are also trading in their weaponry. Helicopters, radar, torpedoes and self-propelled artillery. Hundreds of millions of dollars are being shelled out. But I'm telling you, when they open the crates they see what they are getting for their money. Not a lot of telephoned chit-chat.' Bret looked at Dicky, waiting for him to start arguing. But when Dicky held his fire, Bret said: 'When the Pentagon examine that material they figure how they can save billions of dollars. Billions are being saved by not developing weapons we'd never need.'

'Wait a minute,' said Dicky. 'Who is getting this money? Crooks?'

'No one is sure. The payments go through foreign intermediaries. They even send us price lists. The Pentagon experts and scientists go through the lists and select what they want.'

Dicky said: 'Shipped how? I don't understand.'

'Shipped by ship,' said Bret. 'By freighters. That's why Poland is the main supplier: direct access to the sea. Of course it couldn't happen without top officials in the Polish Defence Ministry giving it the okay. Some CIA studies theorize that the idea comes from the very top of the Warsaw government – General Jaruzelski himself – but we can't verify that. A lot of this Soviet weaponry is shipped to okay countries – such as Middle East states – and then on to the US. We have established letters of credit in overseas accounts so it all looks really kosher. There's an agency called Cenzin that handles Poland's military sales, and the money paid to them has to go to the government. It could be the whole scam is a way of easing the cash crisis in Poland's economy.'

'Have you been involved in any of this, Bret?' I asked.

'Just on the banking side. Some members of my family could help with the overseas commercial agents, foreign letters of credit and so on.'

'And now you're looking for another job?' said Dicky.

'Well there's not much more for me to do on that one. The lines of payment are all in position and working smoothly. And anyway I miss London. You guys just take it for granted, but I have this city deeply in my bones.'

Bret's little speech had completely pre-empted the pitch that I could see Dicky had been about to make on behalf of his telephone-tapping scheme.

Perhaps Bret could see that too, because he said: 'Why are we targeting East Germany anyway? Okay, so the country is governed by a lot of crooked bastards. But the Soviet Union is a basket case, dying cell by cell, Hungary has seen the light, Poland is on a life-support machine, and we're not about to invade Germany to teach them the error of their ways. At least Uncle Sam isn't; so you Brits are on your own if you have that kind of ambition.'

Dicky said: 'Maybe the Soviet Union is dying cell by cell. I don't know, and we get a lot of conflicting reports. But before you get too complacent, I can tell you that no one in the Kremlin has attempted to cut back the money allotted to the Soviet armed services, still less on the money going to the KGB. And the Soviets have their greatest concentration of missiles, long-range bombers, submarines and tanks – all of them armed with nuclear missiles, shells, rockets and bombs – in East Germany. Not in Soviet Russia or Hungary or any of these places where you say communism is on the verge of being defeated. They are all packed into East Germany. And your home town, wherever you say it is, Bret, is targeted by those jokers. Don't forget that, when you dismiss East Germany as being of no account.'

For a moment Bret was at a loss for words. 'Okay, Dicky,' he said, pausing to collect his wits. 'You've made a point and it's a good one. But is tapping into Russian Army landlines going to tell us what we want to know? And will we hear it soon enough?'

Before Dicky could answer, Daphne came through the door banging a saucepan with a spoon: 'Come along all of you. Sit down where you like. The food's ready. I told you it was pot-luck, didn't I?'

Dicky frowned. He liked his dinner parties to be run on more formal lines. As I later noticed, there were place cards telling guests where to sit but no one sat in their allotted place.

I suppose women are, for the most part, more effective than men. My deep dislike of Dicky meant I could never resist an opportunity to spar with him. But Fiona and Gloria that night wielded rapiers with polished decorum. They made my exchanges with Dicky look like drunken brawls in the mud.

In the impromptu seating that Daphne had provoked I ended up sitting in the centre, opposite Gloria, with Fiona beside me on one side and Daphne on the other. Gloria passed the bread rolls, Fiona declined, saying she was on a diet, and Gloria said what lovely rolls they were and ate two in rapid succession, coating each bite with butter.

The first course was not bulgur wheat, it was smoked salmon, and the main course was roast chicken with baked beans and potatoes in their jackets. There was no mistaking the change of menu; this was Daphne in full rebellion. Normally she would be slaving for hours to prepare one of her dinners. Elaborate recipes from her widely travelled neighbours were re-created using rare ingredients purchased from distant ethnic speciality shops. It was at Daphne's that I first encountered the Balinese Gado-gado, and but for Daphne, and her neighbours' travels, I would still not know that Finland had a cuisine, let alone that Kalakukko, a fish pie incorporating spiky bones and heads, was a cherished part of it.

So serving her guests smoked salmon followed by roast chicken was a signal that any husband other than Dicky might have registered with considerable alarm. But Dicky gave no sign of alarm.

He ate his salmon with gusto and made carving the chicken into a performance of considerable bravura, if not bravado.

Dicky was obviously rattled by the way that Bret had made his VERDI scheme sound like a side-show, and had done it by extolling the CIA's skills. It was not easy to counter that without bad-mouthing the Americans, and not even Dicky was stupid enough to try that. But Bret's dismissal of the scheme that Dicky had set his heart upon was causing considerable distress. Otherwise Dicky would never have held the carving fork aloft and asked Bret if he wanted leg, breast or thigh, and then added: 'I've always had you down as a thigh man, Bret,' and laughed.

I was watching Bret at the time. His face twitched and he managed a slight smile and said: 'I'm sure anything you choose will be delicious.'

Even through her alcoholic haze, Daphne could see that Dicky's noisy schoolboy routine was ill-chosen in the present company. She said: 'That's the most stunning dress I've ever seen, Gloria,' and put all her vitality into it.

Gloria's dress was of thin crêpe de Chine, almost see-through, with a high neck and long sleeves, and printed all over with a leopardskin pattern.

'It's lovely,' agreed Fiona. 'I almost bought one myself when I was in Oxford Street the other day.'

'It would suit you perfectly,' replied Gloria, and waited for a moment before adding: 'I think I'm far too skinny for it.'

Daphne, sitting on my right, said: 'You can't be too skinny,' and almost knocked over her wineglass, catching it before more than a spoonful of wine hit the tablecloth. 'Anyway you're young. You can wear anything when you're young.' She dabbed at the spilled wine but only succeeded in spreading it around. Becoming aware that I was watching her, she turned her head to me and beamed.

'Who wants stuffing?' said Dicky, who had noticed the wine being spilled. Dicky was angry and letting it show.

No one responded. Gloria took the antique dish with the herb and breadcrumb stuffing mixture from Dicky, delicately spooned a dollop of it on to her chicken and passed it to Bret. Bret passed it on to Daphne without saying anything. 'Don't you like it?' inquired Daphne, in a voice displaying no more than scientific curiosity.

'No,' said Bret.

Daphne didn't want any either. She gave it to me and I took a lot, in an effort to make her happy. 'Look, Bernard loves it,' she said.

Dicky had put the chicken carcass on the sideboard and, having sat down again, was starting to eat.

'Good health,' said Bret, taking his first taste of the wine that everyone else had started long before. There was a murmur of response from all present.

'Are they tinned baked beans?' said Dicky in horror, suddenly recognizing them on his plate, and probing at them with his silver fork.

'So they are! I haven't had baked beans since I was at boarding school,' said Fiona. 'And I adore them.'

'Don't they give you wind?' asked Gloria.

Dicky grabbed the wine bottle and poured more wine. Getting to his feet again he went round the table to serve some to everyone, although Daphne was given a very small measure.

'Sometime,' said Dicky, sitting down again, 'we are going to have to think about where we can put you.' He bent forward in order to look past Gloria at Bret, but Bret carried on eating his meal as if he hadn't heard.

'I'm in your old office,' said Fiona. 'I will of course move … I have your glass-topped desk and everything.'

'No, Fiona, no,' said Dicky, feeling that his authority was being undermined, if not ignored entirely.

'It's all right,' said Bret. He drank some wine. 'Lovely wine, Dicky.' He wiped his lips. 'No need to worry. It's all been arranged.'

'Share with Fiona,' said Dicky impulsively. I suppose he'd suddenly realized that making him share an office would not only severely limit all Bret's activities, it would also be a tacit implication that he'd added Bret to his staff. 'For the time being,' Dicky added, when the look on Bret's face made it clear that this was not an offer that would be warmly taken up.

'It's all fixed, Dicky. Thanks all the same.'

'Don't you like chicken?' Daphne asked, leaning forward to see Bret's plate.

'I'm not a big eater.' Bret had followed the official US dining code and pushed everything around on his plate after a couple of tiny bites at it.

'That's how he stays in such good shape,' I told Daphne. Bret never ate much, as I knew from weeks of watching him send almost-full plates back to the kitchen.

'Are you a vegetarian?' Daphne asked him. 'I've got bulgur wheat and cabbage dumplings if you'd like that instead. It wouldn't take a minute.'

'No,' said Bret, restraining a shudder.

'What's fixed?' said Dicky from the other end of the table.

'If you've all finished, pass your plates,' said Gloria, who had already piled up several dinner plates and put the used cutlery into the half-empty bowl with the stuffing. 'We'll help with the washing-up,' she added in her hockey team captain manner.

'Gloria! Please don't,' said Daphne. 'Because I'm not going to even fill the dishwasher tonight. Just put it all on the sideboard. I have a woman coming to do it in the morning.'

'I'm in the Deputy's room,' said Bret to Dicky, who was still leaning forward, head twisted, trying to see him.

Dicky craned forward so far that his ear touched the bowl with the jacket potatoes in it. I think I was the only person to eat

296

a potato, so they were still piled high. 'Ouch!' said Dicky, and straightened up and rubbed his ear.

'Just a temporary arrangement. By early next year they might want to replace me with a permanent Deputy.'

'You?' said Dicky hoarsely. 'You are to become Deputy Director-General?'

'As a temporary measure,' Bret said again, as if trying to placate Dicky. But the repetition seemed only to make Dicky more distraught.

'So you'll be in Sir Percy's office?' Dicky said, but as the office arrangements settled into his mind, he saw the implications of Bret's attitude. Bret was likely to throw a spanner into everything that Dicky was planning for Operation VERDI. 'Congratulations, Bret! I think this calls for a bottle of my best champagne.' But, belying his words, his voice slowed and deepened like an old wind-up record-player coming to a stop.

'Thank you, Dicky.' Everyone repeated the congratulations. Bret nodded modestly to each and every one of us.

Dicky got to his feet. 'I'll look in the cellar,' he said. 'I'm sure there are a few bottles of vintage champagne in the rack.'

18

When we were driving home from the Cruyers' that Saturday night Fiona said: 'All that smooth chatter. All that modesty and charm. It makes me sick. It really does.'

'Dicky, you mean?' I asked innocently.

Fiona struck me with her fist in a playful show of aggression. But I knew her well enough to know that she'd spent the evening seething more with indignation about Bret's opposition than with anger about Gloria.

'He's going to stop VERDI. YOU see that, don't you?'

'It sounds likely,' I agreed.

'He more or less said so.'

'I don't know that he did that, Fi. But getting it past Bret will challenge all Dicky's well-known powers of intrigue and influence.'

'For Dicky the evening was a disaster,' pronounced Fiona. It was an epitaph, and it came from someone who had spent many gruelling hours with Dicky and listened to his confident plans to get Bret safely tucked away in obscurity.

'There's a car following us,' I said. 'It's been with us for at least five minutes.'

'Which one?'

'You'll see him in a moment. He's not keeping close.'

'Is not keeping close a bad sign, darling?' said Fiona in a sweetly mocking voice. She had had sufficient wine before Dicky suddenly decided to serve the vintage Dom Pérignon and then stand around consuming it in a celebration that was more like a wake.

'Maybe,' I said.

Fiona twisted round in her seat to peer out through the rear window. 'Where?'

'With the dipped headlights. The big one.'

'That's Bret, darling. That's Bret's Bentley.'

'Are you sure? Did he come in a Bentley?'

Fiona tutted. 'Where is your boy detective outfit tonight, darling? Didn't you see the turbo Bentley and the chauffeur in full uniform and cap?'

'I can't say I did.'

'I wondered if Gloria would go home with him, didn't you?' said Fiona. I didn't respond. I'd seen Gloria arrive in her own car. It was obvious from watching Bret and Gloria that evening that they would not be going anywhere together that night. Fiona must have seen that too. She said: 'I watched them both when they said goodnight. That's how I noticed the Bentley. That's who it is. Bret. You can relax, darling.'

'Where is he staying?'

'His cousin has a big house in Marylebone.'

'That Bret is amazing. Wherever he goes in the world, he always has a relative with a big house in the most fashionable neighbourhood, countless servants and a chauffeur-driven car or two.'

'Or was it Belgravia?' said Fiona, still turning to look at the traffic behind us. 'A cousin in Belgravia.'

'That sounds more like it. We've come right through Marylebone. Look, he's flashing the lights at us.'

'What does he want?' said Fiona. 'Don't invite him up, Bernard. I'm absolutely dead, and we're going to Daddy's to see the children tomorrow. I want to get there early before they go off on some damned trip.'

'I promise,' I said.

We were almost outside the entrance to our block of flats by that time. I stopped the car and Bret's Bentley pulled alongside us. With the window down, he called: 'Sorry to bother you, Bernard. I wonder if you could clear up a few points that came up this evening?'

'I'll park the car,' Fiona offered, and I got out and climbed into the back seat of the Bentley.

'I won't keep him more than five minutes, Fiona,' Bret called.

But once I was inside the car, Bret's mood was more businesslike. 'I must talk to you, Bernard.' The driver pulled the car closer to the kerb and then got out and paced up and down smoking a cigarette and left us alone. 'Timmermann's dead.'

'I got your message, Bret.'

'I knew you'd figure it out. Did you tell Fiona?'

'About Timmermann being dead? No.'

'About the message? The Bible?'

'No.'

'That's good. He was working for her. And for her brother-in-law. He went over there trying to find Tessa.'

'So I figured,' I said.

'She's not even convinced that her sister is dead, do you know that?'

'She needs more time.'

'It was a good thing that I tumbled to what was going on. She was meeting Timmermann in Santa Monica on those afternoons she went to the beauty shop. You didn't know that, did you?'

'I did not.'

'She's obsessed; and Timmermann isn't the type who turns money away.'

'But why the Bible and the secret code, Bret? Wasn't there a simpler way of keeping in touch with me?'

'That wasn't for you and me, Bernard. That was a hastily figured code for Timmermann to keep you informed.'

'It was?'

'That was the deal. I paid him even more than he was getting from Fiona. I bought him. We had to know what was going on, so I just paid what he asked.'

'He earned every penny,' I said.

'Yeah, you found him dead. That was tough.'

'I thought it was VERDI.'

'I know. Everyone did. Dicky was milling around out of control, and wailing to Frank about it. I couldn't tell you, or him, what the real story was without showing my hand.'

I looked at him. 'Yeah,' I said. Bret was the epitome of the desk man. Real stories were the ones written in ink, not blood.

'I'm talking to the D-G tomorrow. A policy meeting. You want to be along there?' Like all Americans, Bret dressed his orders up in the syntax of polite and tentative inquiries.

'Tomorrow is Sunday,' I reminded him. 'Monday you mean?'

'I mean Sunday, Bernard. Remember what it says on the first page of the indoctrination manual? The enemy never sleeps.'

'But I do, Bret. And tomorrow I plan to visit my kids.'

'Well, take a day off during the week instead. Would eleven o'clock be okay? That will give me an hour with the D-G before you arrive.'

'Sure, Bret. I'll be there.'

'Fiona doesn't give a hoot about the VERDI operation,' he explained. 'But she's pushing it along for all she's got, because she thinks it will tell her what the Soviets did to her sister.'

'And will it?'

'Don't be stupid, Bernard. You were there.'

'And you, Bret? How do you feel about the VERDI operation?'

'Dicky would be very disappointed,' he said, as if this was the very first time he'd thought about the consequences of cancelling it. 'Making everyone sore as a boil would be a bad way to start my time as DD-G.'

'It's never stopped you before.'

A wintry smile. 'Resources are limited these days, Bernard. We can't run an operation just to keep up Departmental morale.'

'It must be worth a shot, Bret. Until we find what the Soviets are pumping along those landlines, we won't know whether it's worth having or not.'

'I'll think about it,' said Bret. He slapped my arm. 'You too, Bernard.'

'Did you plan tonight's foray?' I asked him as I was about to open the car door. 'Did you figure that by demolishing Dicky tonight, you'd have him over a barrel at the meeting tomorrow?'

'Son of VERDI, you mean? I horse-trade him down, so we've got a cut-price type of landline-tapping scheme?'

'Right.'

'With a mind like yours, Bernard, you are wasted as a field agent.'

'Does that mean Yes, you did frag Dicky deliberately? Or that you didn't?'

'Dicky is not even going to be at tomorrow's meeting, Bernard. Not Dicky, not Fiona, not Harry Strang nor Gus Stowe nor any of the other top-floor gorillas. Just you, me, the D-G and Werner Volkmann.'

'For a policy meeting?'

'We're not putting together a poker game. The old man is giving me his blessing tomorrow, and you and Werner will be my number one project.'

'Blessing to do what?'

'I'm going to kick butt, Bernard,' said Bret. 'The whole damn Department needs a shake-out.'

'Am I allowed an inkling about where the first kick might land?'

'No, you're not. But I'm bringing that bright Kent girl out of the Hungarian desk and giving her something more important to do.' He saw the look in my eyes. 'No, nothing like that, Bernard: strictly business. I'm going to make her my personal trouble-shooter. Anyone who doesn't like that arrangement can go find another job.'

'Okay, Bret,' I said. 'I'll go upstairs right now and tell her.' I thought he would reach out and stop me. I thought he would say, no, that wasn't what he meant at all. But he didn't; he just smiled and said goodnight.

I slammed the car door in frustrated anger, but it just closed with a soft, cultured boom. I suppose it was coming from a rich family that made Bret feel that he was the only one in step.

By the time I got up to the flat, Fiona was sitting on the sofa in the drawing-room engrossed in *Buddenbrooks*. It was still relatively early, Dicky's dinner party having shuddered to a standstill after Bret delivered the bombshell of his new appointment.

'I still can't believe it,' Fiona said as I came in and slumped down in an armchair with a deep sigh. 'There's not been the slightest warning, no rumours, nothing ...'

'You're right,' I said.

'Is he just going to hang loose until a proper Deputy is appointed? Or is he going to take it seriously?' said Fiona. I realized from her tone of voice that by going to sit in an armchair, rather than beside her on the sofa, I had failed the little test she'd set me.

I switched on the TV. 'Bret? Hang loose? Don't make me laugh. Bret will turn the whole place upside-down.'

'Are you going to watch TV?'

'I don't know what's on,' I said. 'Will it disturb you reading?'

'If it does I'll go to bed.'

I flipped through the channels. There were only four of them; a gangster movie, a brightly coloured Indian film with Hindi dialogue, a pop star being interviewed and an Open University lecture on the Binomial Theorem. I went back to the gangsters but kept the sound very low.

Fiona closed *Buddenbrooks*. 'Did Bret actually say that to you just now? That he was going to turn us upside-down?'

'I'm going to kick butt, Bernard,' I said in a passable imitation of his voice. 'The whole damn Department needs a shake-out.'

'You're not serious?' She clutched her book to her breast and hugged it.

'I am, and so is Bret as far as I could see.'

'I suppose it had to come,' she said, putting her book on the side-table. 'It's crude of them to use Bret; he'll get more flak on account of being American.'

'Look, Fi, the butt-kicking starts right here: he wants me in the office tomorrow at eleven. I doubt if I'll get away before two. You know how these things go on and on. And Bret's not the sort of honcho who stops for Sunday lunch.'

'Poor darling.'

'It's almost as if the gods want to prevent me seeing the children.'

'How philosophical you've become these days,' she said. 'And they enjoy seeing you more than me.'

'No, Fi, no.' I pressed the button and wasted the gangsters.

'It's true, Bernard. They resent me. Children can be awfully unforgiving. When they are older, they'll understand why I had to go away. For the present, they just tolerate me for the sake of seeing you.'

'Don't cry, darling. You did it for them. They will see that. They are very young.' But she was right. They would never see it like that of course, and there was no way I could contradict her and still sound sincere.

She got to her feet hurriedly. 'They hate me, Bernard.'

'Now you're being silly.'

'They hate me. I can see it in their faces sometimes.'

304

I got up and embraced her and kissed her tear-laden cheeks. 'Go to bed, Fi. I have to make a phone call, then I'll be with you.' I kissed her again. 'The children love you, you know they do. And so do I.'

'Do you really, Bernard?' she said in a sad and satisfied voice, as if she'd never heard me say it before.

She picked up *Buddenbrooks* and looked at it as if wondering why she'd started reading it. And then after a long time, she said: 'At least we know he loves England just as much as we do.' She put the book back on the table as if abandoning it for ever. I decided this was not the right time to reveal that Bret had decided to appoint Gloria his personal assistant.

'You're right, Fiona. He loves England. He loves the idea of England – its history and its culture and its people – almost to the point of self-delusion. He won't hear a word against it. But the people who love a country to such extremes are the ones most likely to commit bloody rotten crimes on its behalf.'

The next morning we both sat down to breakfast at a few minutes before eight. Orange juice, coffee, cornflakes and three Sunday newspapers from which Fiona had taken the supplements. We had a bathroom each in our new home, and that had completely revised our morning schedule. By nine-thirty Fiona, taking advantage of empty roads on this winter Sunday morning, was nearing her parents' home. I was sitting in Kar's Club, in Soho, with a man named Duncan Churcher.

'Still going strong, Bernard?' He was a man much given to meaningless greetings of that sort.

'Yes, I'm still going strong, Duncan,' I said affably. 'But only because I haven't found anyone to pay me a living wage for going weak.'

'Are you drinking?'

'No. Neither of us is drinking.'

'Bejays but you're a hard man,' he said in a stage Irish accent. 'Two coffees,' he called to Arkady the son of Jan Kar the proprietor. 'The tea is shocking here,' he added in a whisper.

'Were you watching the chess game?' I asked him. I had spotted him immediately. There are not too many 200lb rugby footballers in Kar's on a Sunday morning, even when there is a championship chess game. He'd been wearing that same grey double-breasted chalk-stripe suit at our first meeting a decade ago. The same tie too. Or did he just phone his tailor and say, same again? There were plenty of men in Whitehall who did exactly that.

'Not seriously. The champion always wins. It's the way the world is.'

Duncan's real name was not Churcher, it was Cwynar. His father was one of many Polish soldiers to marry local girls during their training in wartime Scotland. But Churcher's father went off to the war before Duncan was born, and he never came back. Thanks to some Polish scholarship fund, Duncan Churcher eventually became one of those rare creatures, a public-school and university-trained policeman. Sometime, in response to the social pressures of school or profession, he'd become Churcher and risen to the rank of detective-sergeant in Leeds. Had he stayed there he would no doubt have become one of those very high-ranking policemen from provincial forces, with tailored uniforms, silver-wire badges and golden tongues, who appear on TV chat shows, to pontificate about legalizing hard drugs and criminalizing car-driving.

The duties and working hours of a conscientious detective are incompatible with being a good husband, good father or good anything except good drinker. But Detective-Sergeant Duncan Churcher's refined English accent, his talent for languages and convivial bar-room manner – plus an old school pal in Whitehall – found a job for him in London. He'd become an 'arm's-length' operative, which is why I was talking to him in Kar's Club.

'It's a simple little job, Duncan,' I said. 'But it's very delicate.' He nodded. It was the usual beginning I suppose; all his jobs were very delicate. 'No paperwork. I will have to pay you under some separate pretext.'

Duncan Churcher had only his work to occupy him. He was lonely and divorced, with a thirty-year-old daughter, an only child who'd wasted her life, and his money, in a futile obsession about becoming a champion ice-skater. Duncan's only social life, as far as I could see, was the evenings he spent at the local chapter of Alcoholics Anonymous.

'It's like that, is it?' he said. There was no relish in his words. 'No paperwork; just money.' He wasn't poor, neither was he venal. He had never been pushed to tout for work, or resort to the sort of domestic jobs that keep most of London's little detective agencies afloat. Whitehall's various arms of government always had an assignment for men like Churcher, men who could charm a witness, force an entry, bribe a clerk or rough up a suspect in four languages, and get results without fuss, and without letting reporters get word of it. Most importantly, Churcher had proved that his police service helped him elude the clutches of the law.

'A shake-down,' I said. I wanted to reassure him. 'No more than that.' He'd aged since our last meeting, or perhaps it was this bare-bulb light that emphasized his lined and wrinkled face, and spotted hands. And the healthy pink face that I'd always associated with his Saturday rugby club games was in fact a ruby legacy of the drinking that came after them.

'No deductions required this time?' he said as if deeply disappointed. 'No Sherlock Holmes stuff?'

I smiled without replying. We both knew that Duncan Churcher was not a detective in the strict sense of that word. His solutions came from dialogue with people, rather than

307

deductive reasoning from premises to consequent conclusions. He kept to polite conversation as far as was possible, but I used him knowing he could be very rough.

'I like this place,' he said. Looking round it was hard to see why. The white-painted brickwork, schoolroom lights and uncomfortable little chairs and tables, each with their chessboard and box of pieces, would have been nothing without a magical ingredient, and that was Kar himself.

Kar's was one of the few such basement clubs that had survived in Soho. During the war there had been dozens, frequented by soldiers of all nationalities who, baffled and frustrated by the strange English laws about the drinking of alcohol, were driven to these 'dubs' where the freedom to get drunk was extended over longer hours.

Jan Kar, a Polish veteran of some of the fiercest Italian fighting in 1944, opened his dilapidated little cellar for his Polish army friends. Chess soon became its primary function, but there were still plenty of Poles who came in just to exercise their native tongue. One of them had brought back from Monte Cassino a photo of the Polish memorial on Point 593. Those who peer at the fuzzy amateur photo that hangs behind the bar can just read the inscription;

WE POLISH SOLDIERS
FOR OUR FREEDOM AND YOURS
HAVE GIVEN OUR SOULS TO GOD
OUR BODIES TO THE SOIL OF ITALY
AND OUR HEARTS TO POLAND.

I watched Kar's son Arkady as he poured the coffee. What did he make of it all, I wondered. Like Churcher, he'd never been to Monte Cassino, and never been to Poland either. Neither of them had any obvious connection to the land of their fathers.

308

When the coffee arrived at our table, Churcher paid Arkady with a ten-pound note from a crocodile-leather wallet where he kept a silver pencil and his engraved visiting cards. He was like that.

'I come here looking for my father,' said Duncan, as if in reply to my unspoken question. 'Don't I, Arkady?'

Arkady smiled.

A little crowd had gathered in the next room to watch the champion defend his title. It wasn't just the usual Sunday game, there was some sort of trophy at stake. We were sitting alone in the narrow lobby at the bottom of the stairs. I wanted to avoid the bar, which provided temptations to which Churcher was all too likely to succumb.

'No paperwork. That's perfectly all right, Bernard,' he said in a deep round perfect voice, like a BBC announcer back in the days when they spoke English. 'Your word is always sufficient for me.'

'Professor Belostok teaches drawing and painting from a private house in Hampstead. One of his students is a middle-aged woman …' I thought of Daphne Cruyer. 'Or make that youngish woman. A young fellow has joined the Tuesday evening class recently, not very talented … totally ham-fisted I suspect. Says he is Czech. South African father, that will be to cover his accent I expect.'

'Whom should I be looking at?'

'It's a boy-meets-wife story,' I said.

'Someone we know?'

'Wife of Dicky Cruyer … it might be nothing at all, Duncan,' I added hastily. 'Last night, when I first heard about it, I went bananas, but who knows? … I don't like these situations at any time but, from a security point of view, this one may be completely okay.'

'Ah, yes. The German Stations supremo?'

'He's Europe now.'

'Cruyer is? I say! And he's younger than you, isn't he?'

'Thanks, Duncan. I thought everything was going too smoothly for me this morning.'

'Awfully sorry, Bernard. Very well: I'll go and look at Romeo and avoid Juliet. Where do they meet? Regular assignations? Anywhere other than the painting class?'

'I haven't got the exact address but I can show you where it is. I gave Mrs Cruyer a lift there once.' I took an A-Z Street Guide from my pocket and showed him the approximate position of the house where I'd taken Daphne to her class, one evening when Dicky had wrecked his own car and borrowed hers without asking.

'May I ask what you plan?' said Churcher.

'I'd like to get rid of him. I want you to get rid of him. Scare him, I mean.' From the chess room there came the concerted noise of a couple of dozen people reacting to an unexpected chess move without uttering a sound.

'Even if it's all above board?'

'Above board? They're having an affair, Duncan.'

'How old-fashioned you are, Bernard. How does a puritan such as you survive in our big bad world?' He looked at me, trying to discern some motive in my face. 'Does Cruyer know what a good friend he has in you?' It was an exploratory query.

'Shit, Duncan. I don't want Dicky to find out what's going on. I want to break it up because that's easier than deciding who to report it to.'

'We all like to play God, Bernard,' he said, nodding as if in warm approval. He was a sardonic bastard; I'd forgotten that.

'How will you start?' I asked.

'I'll say I'm from Customs and Excise. I'll tell him he's been named in a confession by someone caught with hard drugs. That keeps all our options open.'

'That sounds okay,' I said.

'He'll probably leave the country eventually,' said Duncan. 'That's my experience.'

'Even if he knows it's a total fabrication?'

'Oh, yes, especially then. If he's a foreigner he'll figure he's being framed by whatever department of government he's most frightened of.'

'Suppose he's got a UK passport? Suppose he toughs it out?'

'Look, Bernard, old chap. If this Romeo of ours is likely to be packing an AK-47, this would be the appropriate time to mention it.'

'I wouldn't send you unprepared into a knock-over competition.'

'You are the one who put me into Guy's Hospital for three weeks last year!'

'Wait a minute, Duncan. That job didn't come from my Department. I phoned you. I stuck my neck out telling you to unload that one; you insisted upon doing it personally. And it wasn't last year, it was the year before that.'

'Ouch! Forgive me, Bernard, you're right. And I shouldn't be complaining; it's all part of the job. And I was careless. But you haven't answered my question.'

I could see all the hesitations. He didn't want to turn the job down, lest I crossed him off the list. But this was the sort of job that Churcher felt should be done cautiously, step by step. He didn't like being rushed, and in other circumstances I might have agreed with him.

'This is a quick little routine job, Duncan. I'm only using you because I'm in a hurry. Even if it's a probe by the other side, it will only be a pretty boy making first contact. Take him aside, grab him by the ankles and shake him until his teeth fall out. Then the other side will back off. Have you got the idea?'

'The customer is always right. I'll ship him off on the Tuesday night ferry boat, and bring you a lock of his hair at crack of dawn Wednesday morning,' said Duncan deadpan. Maybe he wouldn't have ended up in a senior post in the Leeds Constabulary.

311

'You may not like it, but we haven't got time to be subtle, Duncan.'

'I'm beginning to get your message, old boy.' He smiled. I recognized it as the sort of smile I gave Dicky when he was sending me off to do something he couldn't do himself. And that I couldn't do either.

I looked at my watch to see how close it was to my appointment with Bret. We both stood up. 'That's a good one, don't you think?' said Churcher. He was pointing to a framed cartoon on the wall. The drawing depicted a distraught old man writing on a postcard. The message said: 'White Queen to King's Knight 6 and Checkmate.' The old man was writing: 'Not known at this address' across the postcard.

'Yes,' I said. 'Checkmates don't work if there's no one answering the door.'

Churcher nodded and got his tweed coat and umbrella from the rack and handed me my coat. 'Message for the work-force. Is that what you mean, Bernard?'

'Maybe.' There were more muted noises from the chess room as the next devastating gambit began. The champion was going to win; everyone knew that, even the loser.

Duncan followed me upstairs and out into the lifeless street. Not even the Arctic offers a landscape more desolate than Soho on a Sunday morning. Stacked high outside the eating places were black bags bulging with last night's chef's specials, and in the hard daylight the glittering adult cinemas were exposed as tawdry little hovels.

'Charing Cross Road will be our best bet for a cab,' he said. As we headed in that direction he added: 'You can't bear it, can you, Bernard?' I smiled and waited for the rest of it. 'You can't bear passing this kind of job on to anyone, can you?'

'I'd just like to see what he looks like,' I admitted. 'But I can't do it myself, she'd recognize me.'

312

'Exactly. That's the only reason you're letting me do it.' While walking down Old Compton Street a cab came along. Churcher hailed it with the ear-splitting bellow that such public-school rugby players use when ordering beer. He insisted that I took it. Opening the cab door he ushered me in. 'I won't screw it up, dear boy. I'll waltz him around the floor with my usual exquisite delicacy. I won't get you fired, Bernard, if that's what's worrying you.'

'Let me worry about my job security,' I said. 'I don't want you inviting him to dance; stamp on his toes.'

'You have made yourself quite clear, Bernard,' he said with a sigh.

'In your spiked shoes.'

As the cab pulled away, I looked out of the window and saw Churcher holding up his rolled umbrella in a silent farewell that was not without a trace of mockery. I could read him like a book. Duncan had all the signs of being too old for this sort of job; I'd let my doubt about his capability show, and he was offended.

19

I got to the office a few minutes before eleven. When you spend all your life among Germans, you form the habit of getting to appointments ahead of time. The lower-floor offices were empty except for the security guards and the night staff who also fill in the weekend duties.

I found the other three in the D-G's room on the top floor. Werner was early too. He was wearing his best suit, sitting with Bret and Sir Henry Clevemore, balancing upon his knee a cup of the China tea that was Sir Henry's favoured refreshment. Sir Henry was wearing a well-worn Fair-Isle pattern cardigan and carpet slippers.

Bret was peering around the D-G's office as if he'd never been there before. It was in its usual state of total confusion. No matter how many secretaries Sir Henry employed, or how hard they worked, there was no chance that they'd ever keep up with the chaos that he created around himself. Unread reports; unanswered mail; discarded balls of paper that had failed to reach the paper bin; a bird's nest of shredded paper overflowing from the secret waste. Along one wall, and almost lost in the wintry gloom, there was a marquetry cabinet with an elaborate design of flowers and birds. I'd often wondered whether it was a priceless original or a nineteenth-century reproduction. One day I would muster the courage to go and examine it, but I sensed that this was not a suitable moment.

It wasn't a particularly large room: Dicky's was bigger. There were books stacked high on every side. The D-G's desk was covered with so many framed photos of his children and grandchildren that there was scarcely room for his blotter and pen set. Today the desk-top was also holding a large wooden tea-tray with a simple brown china teapot under a knitted cover, milk jug, sugar and cups. It was typical of the D-G that all the chinaware was of a cheap traditional design that one would find in almost any home in the country. In his choice of clothes, and domestic possessions, Sir Henry Clevemore exhibited that artless self-confidence that is the hallmark of the British land-owning classes.

'Find somewhere to park yourself,' the D-G commanded. His books were at the heart of the problem. With no room on the bookshelves, he customarily placed books on chairs. When a chair was needed, his visitors removed books in order to sit down, putting the books on the floor. For this reason there was always a barricade of books stacked high around the room. I now built the barricade a little higher and sat down.

Sir Henry sat behind his rather ugly kidney-shaped ped-estal desk. His big black Labrador sprawled under it with proprietorial nonchalance, so that Werner, Bret and myself – sitting facing him – had to take care not to kick the animal which, from time to time, stirred in its sleep and made disgusting noises.

'Ah, Collins! Good,' said the D-G, looking up at me when I was finally seated. 'Pour yourself some tea.'

'Samson,' Bret told the D-G. Bret could not bear misunderstandings, especially chronic ones. This made his job difficult, for our work depended upon them.

'No, you are Rensselaer,' the D-G told him firmly.

'Yes, but this is Bernard Samson,' said Bret.

'I know, I know,' said the D-G irritably, and cleared his throat as if about to cough.

'You said Collins,' said Bret, who never knew when to retire gracefully.

'No, I didn't,' said the D-G. 'Now can we please get on?'

'Yes, sir, of course,' said Bret.

'It is Sunday,' said the D-G testily. 'We all owe it to our families to get this meeting over as soon as possible.'

'Shall I brief Samson about the decisions we reached this morning?'

'I wish you would,' said the D-G, as if he had been fretting under Bret's delay.

I reached over to the desk, removed the tea-cosy and poured myself a cup of tea from the brown china teapot.

'The Director has decided that the operation based upon information passed to us by agent VERDI should go ahead,' said Bret.

'They know that,' said the D-G. 'Get on, or we shall be here all day.'

'The next stage is to bring VERDI into a meeting with our electronics experts,' said Bret. He looked at me and then at Werner, who was sitting there gaping. Werner had never been on the top floor before, let alone in its sanctum sanctorum, the room of the Director-General himself. The look on his face was of utter consternation and bewilderment. He simply couldn't believe that Britain's Secret Intelligence Service was controlled by this quixotic tea-partying Mad Hatter.

'Who are they?' I said. I drank some tea: it must have been brewing for hours, for it tasted like paint-remover. I poured a lot more milk into it but it wasn't much improved. 'Who are these electronics experts?'

'We'll have to bring GCHQ in,' said Bret. Having told Dicky that at the very beginning I merely nodded.

'VERDI,' said the D-G.

'Yes,' I said. Under the table, the dog half-awakened at the sound of its master's voice. It scratched itself lazily before making a loud moan and sinking back into a deep slumber.

'Bring him to London,' said the D-G.

'The Director is uneasy that this whole operation is at present dependent upon one person.'

'VERDI, you mean?' I said. The D-G nodded.

'Yes, VERDI,' said Bret. 'It could all be a crackpot idea in his head. Or just a way of gouging cash from us.'

'I thought most of the preliminaries had been cleared away.'

'No,' said Bret.

I looked past Bret to Werner, and said: 'I thought you'd talked about the technical problems?'

Werner glanced at Bret apprehensively before contradicting him: 'Yes, some of them.'

'Dicky said the ideas had been checked out. He said we know it could work,' I persisted.

'Yes, in theory,' said Werner. I could see he felt self-conscious about his English, as well as about arguing against Bret.

'There is no need to subject the whole operation to scrutiny,' said Bret in an admonitory tone. 'Your job, Bernard, is to get him to London.'

'Is he in danger?' I asked.

'He will be once the Soviets realize what he's up to,' said Bret. 'And that will take them thirty minutes at the most.'

'Something wrong with that tea?' said the D-G, glaring at me and then at my cup. He seemed not to have heard Bret's sardonic aside.

317

'No, sir. It's delicious.' I leaned forward to get my teacup again, and in doing so trod on the dog. It jumped up and gave a loud yelp.

'The only thing you need to know, Bernard, is that he's your pigeon.'

'Who is?'

'Getting VERDI here safely,' said Bret.

The Labrador was licking its foot where I'd trodden on it. I leaned down to stroke the dog but when I did, it growled and bared its teeth.

The D-G must have heard the dog growl. He said: 'C! Behave, C. Do you hear: behave.'

Was the dog really named C?

Bret, who was watching this exchange, looked at me without expression and said: 'There's one other aspect of this operation, Bernard. This man Fedosov has had direct involvement in the investigation of the death of Tessa Kosinski.' He let that sink in. 'The Director-General is most anxious that we should use his presence here to get to the bottom of that incident. He wants it cleared up once and for all.'

'Good,' I said.

'Werner will do all the contacting. No need for you to go over there, just in case it's some sort of trap. All you have to do is collect him from Werner and bring him here. Or perhaps you both should go. You and Werner can work out the details.'

Werner said: 'VERDI wants his father brought out too.'

I looked at Werner. It was a new development and I wished Werner hadn't sprung it as a total surprise.

Bret said: 'Any problem about that?'

'Is there some official line of contact with him that I'm not a party to?' I asked. VERDI was clearly in regular contact with someone who wasn't telling me what was happening.

318

Werner said to Bret: 'No. Bernard and I will work it out somehow.'

'It's a need-to-know situation, Bernard. Just for once, do it the way we want it,' said Bret. 'Just toss this goon in the trunk of your car and bring him back here, Bernard. Don't start opening cans of worms.'

We were right back to the beginning again. It was a full circle back to Kinkypoo offering me handcuffs and sticky-tape to bring back VERDI alive and kicking.

Fiona arrived back from her parents' house in the late afternoon. 'Werner is here,' I called. 'He's staying for dinner. How are the children?'

She came in looking radiant. 'It was such a gorgeous day, Bernard. Hello, Werner. You are looking well.' I gave her a kiss.

'You should have stayed longer,' I said.

'It was very tempting but I knew you'd be waiting for me. The children can be so funny. We laughed and laughed all day.'

'Where was your father?'

'He's been looking at horses. I think he'll be hunting again before the month is out. That bad fall shook him but I told him that if he doesn't get on a horse again soon, he may not ride again. What's that you're drinking? Beer? Uggh.'

'Shall I phone for an Indian take-away?'

'Oh, so that's why you are drinking beer. Yes, do. I'm starved. But would Werner like that?'

'If you order it,' said Werner. 'I don't understand the menus.'

'What are you drinking, darling?' I asked her.

'Nothing at all. I drank too much last night.'

'Sit down, darling. I'll order the curry.' But she preferred to order it herself. She had the names of the Indian dishes we liked best written in her notebook in the kitchen, and she hated some of the hot ones.

Our dinner arrived as a dozen mysterious tinfoil trays. Fiona stacked them into the fan oven for twenty minutes – just enough time to fill the entire apartment with the pervasive smells of hot curry – then tipped them separately into incongruous and expensive chinaware.

'Billy fell off his bicycle last week, and frightened Mummy half to death … he came running in with blood on his shirt. But it was only a few scratches. Perhaps I will have a beer. But Sally has amazed everyone at school by winning all the swimming races. I think some of the elder girls were not pleased to be outdone by a little shrimp. She might even wind up school champion.'

'Good for Sally. I'll phone her.'

'She's so like you, Bernard,' said Fiona as we ate the meal. 'So single-minded and tough.'

'Is that what I'm like?'

'And I'm like Billy … always stumbling and falling and getting hurt.'

'Really?' I looked at her with amazement. I'd always thought it was so obviously the other way round. Billy with his clumsy, ill-judged attempts to be a success was reliving my life, while cool calm and dedicated Sally effortlessly won all the prizes, and got all the praise, and was exactly like Fiona. But I didn't say that exactly; I said: 'But you are the tough one, Fi.'

'I wish it was true,' she said. 'When I was working in the East I was driven to inventing a fictitious personality for myself, a sort of Doppelgänger. It was a male named Stefan Mittelberg – I got the name at random from a directory – and he helped.'

'Helped? Helped how?' I said.

'I was all alone, Bernard. I needed guidance and I got it from a person I invented, a hard-nosed self-assertive male. Whenever I felt overwhelmed, I pretended I was this Stefan character, and did whatever he would have done.'

'Sounds like a desperate last resort,' said Werner, half in jest.

She smiled. 'Sometimes I pretended I was Bernard. But sometimes I needed someone even harder than him.'

'Even harder than Bernie?' said Werner in pretended surprise.

'There were nice people too,' she said, as if remembering it all for the first time, for I'd never heard her talk like this before. 'My assistant, at the KGB/Stasi command unit on Karl Liebknechtstrasse, was an elderly man named Hubert Renn. A dedicated Marxist but a thoroughly decent man. I planned to arrange everything when the time came for me to escape so that Renn would be completely eliminated from any suspicion of complicity. But when the time came ... it ... I wasn't ready ...' She got up from the table and hurried into the kitchen.

Werner picked up one of the dishes, still half-filled with chicken curry, and was about to follow her into the kitchen and help her. I took his sleeve and shook my head. He sat down again and sipped some beer.

When Fiona returned she was icily composed and seemed completely recovered. She sat down and asked Werner how he liked living in Zurich, and how early the powder snow was deep enough on the slopes. And eventually Fiona went to bed and left us to drink beer and talk.

'I think old man Fedosov has probably been marked for years,' I said.

'By their people?'

'Yes. You know how they work, Werner. They don't vet their people and give them a clean bill of health, the way our Internal Security does it. I heard VERDI say there'd been a KGB report on the old man, dating back to my dad's time. A serious report about betraying the State, not a complaint from the neighbours about playing the radio too loud. You know what that means, Werner. They will check him and double-check him. They'll do it again and again and again, for ever. When a suspect comes out of their vetting process with a clean bill of health, they just figure the investigators didn't try hard enough.'

'Would that affect us?'

'It might, if we brought them out together. Or even if the old man tried to cross the Wall alone and some suspicious Grepo checked the records and found VERDI was already in the West.'

'You think they would stop the old man crossing?'

'Of course they would. But that's the least of our problems. They can throw the old bastard into solitary in the Lubyanka and let him rot for all I care. But if they arrest the old man they might blow the whistle on VERDI too soon, and that would screw up the whole operation.'

'And VERDI wouldn't like it,' said Werner.

'Yes,' I said irritably. 'And VERDI wouldn't like it.'

'So what do we do?'

'I've nothing very clever to suggest, but let's bring the old man through a different checkpoint at exactly the same time. And let's take the old man to France or Belgium or somewhere. And maybe make it all very conspicuous.'

Werner said: 'You don't think the old man might be reporting on his own son?'

'The old man is a devoted Stalinist, but has a crucifix on his wall. Forget the fact that he sold out to my dad during the airlift. It's the lifetime of indoctrination that wins out in these cases, you know that, Werner.'

'And make it conspicuous? How do I do that?'

'There's a kid I was with in the Magdeburg fiasco. Get him to hold hands with the old man, and bring him through.'

'He's a cantankerous old devil.'

'And the kid is straight out of the training school and looking for action,' I said. 'They'll be conspicuous all right. Just stay well clear of them.'

'Could I have that last little bit of chicken korma?'

I collected together the left-overs, went into the kitchen and stacked them in the microwave. Werner followed me and watched. 'I didn't know you liked curry so much,' I said.

'The Indian food in Berlin is Sri Lanka style – too hot for me,' said Werner. The oven squealed. He scraped the various curries, and the rice, on to his plate and we went back to the dining-room.

'The samosas go hard in the micro,' pronounced Werner, savouring a bite from a pastry. 'But the nan bread is just fine. Sure you don't want some?'

'A little curry goes a long way for me,' I said, declining it.

When Werner had consumed the final morsels of curry he sat back, filled and satisfied, and looked at me. I could see by the nervous way he moved his lips and fidgeted with his glass of beer that there was something serious still to come: 'You must take into account the tremendous post-traumatic shock she has had,' he said.

'I don't speak psycho-babble, Werner. You'd better tell me in plain English.'

'You heard what Fiona was saying. She was in East Berlin long enough to develop strong feelings of friendship and loyalty. That old German fellow is on her conscience. When she was wrenched away, at very short notice, there was probably the guilt of the betrayer to add to all the natural anxieties she had about the risks she was running. About being caught and facing trial as a spy.'

'Go on, Dr Volkmann. Have you been working on this thesis for a long time, or are you just making it up as you go along?'

'You're a pitiless bastard, Bernard. You're my best friend, and my oldest friend. But you are a hard-hearted pig.'

'I said, go on.'

'A sort of Doppelgänger! My God, she must have suffered.'

'She's not the only one who went over there, Werner.'

'But Fiona had no experience of field work, Bernard. Can you imagine how she must have felt all the time she was working there? And then, in that terrible state of terror … when she's being brought out to that damned Autobahn site, she has to watch you killing people she knows. Then she sees her sister shot dead, and even gets spattered with blood.' He looked at me as if expecting me to deny it; I made no response. 'You told me you wiped spots of blood off her face before driving through the checkpoint, just in case one of the guards noticed it. I mean …' He stopped and caught his breath, agitated and distressed, as if it had all happened to him.

'Okay, Werner. Do you think I haven't thought about it? Not once; a thousand times. But what are you telling me to do?'

'I'm telling you to give her a chance. She needs help, Bernard.'

'She's getting better.'

'Maybe. Maybe not. But if you think – or she thinks – that she's ever going to recover from that experience you can think again. She'll come to terms with what happened, but she will never forget it or recover. I wish I could make you understand that. She won't get well. Stop waiting for something that will never happen.'

'Up to a point I suppose you are right, Werner,' I said. It was a depressing thing to hear, and desperately hateful to believe, and as soon as it was uttered I pushed it back into the recesses of my mind.

'At present, Bernard, her emotions are totally confused. She has to sort out her thoughts and memories and emotions. Some of them she will repress for ever. Maybe that's just as well. But what you must realize is that as she becomes adjusted, she will transfer her misery to some other person.'

'Why?'

'She needs a scapegoat. She'll blame someone. That's how she will recover her balance and adjust to normal life.'

324

'Me? Blame me?'

'The Department? George Kosinski? Dicky for taking Tessa to Berlin? I don't know. Such things don't follow logic. She just needs someone to blame. Don't make it so easy for her to choose you as that scapegoat.'

'You mean help her blame the Department?' I said.

'I suspect she's on the way to doing that already,' said Werner.

20

Werner went back to Berlin and began making all the arrangements for VERDI to come to London. I worked hard and soon cleared up the greater part of the backlog of work that Dicky had dumped upon me. On Wednesday, taking Bret at his word, I went off to visit the children in the depths of Surrey's stockbroker belt.

It started off as one of those beautiful winter days when the sky is almost entirely blue, with just a few scratches of cloud, and the wind is no more than is needed to make the bare trees tremble. Wednesday was the children's half-day at school, so I picked them up at noon and took them out for lunch at a fish and chip shop in the village. But by the time we got there grey misty cloud was speeding across the sky.

'Grandad doesn't like fish and chips,' said Sally. We were enjoying the English working man's traditional meal: fried fish in batter, fried potatoes, pickled onions, bread and butter, and hot milky tea. As a child, and coming from Germany, I'd found it a curious meal. But it was what my father liked best to eat whenever he visited England, and I grew fond of it too, although the fearsomely acid pickled onion was something I still denied myself.

'Grandpa says fish and chips is common,' said Billy.

'But look at what they've done to this place in the last few months,' I said. 'They even have printed menus, and the new sign outside says "Fish Restaurant".' We'd often called in here for a take-away supper on the way back from visits to their grandparents. Not so long ago it had been called a 'fish and chip shop', with scrubbed wood counters and bench seats, linoleum on the floor, and the take-away orders came wrapped in newspaper.

'I liked it the old way,' said Billy. We always tried to get a table near the window so that we could keep an eye on the car, and on predatory traffic wardens.

'No,' said Sally. 'It's nicer now, with the red check tablecloths, and the waitress wearing a proper apron.'

'She's not a real waitress,' said Billy. 'She was always here. The man at the fryer calls her Mum.'

'You'll wind up a detective,' I said.

'I'm going to be a museum curator.'

This was an entirely new ambition. 'Why?' I asked him.

'You just look after things,' explained Billy, as if he'd penetrated a closely guarded secret of the museum trade, as well he might have. 'And no one would know they weren't yours. You could probably even take things home for a day or two.'

'What sort of museum?'

'I'm thinking about that,' he said. 'Probably guns. A gun museum.'

'There's no such thing as a gun museum,' said Sally.

'Of course there is, silly Sally.'

'Don't call me silly Sally. There isn't, is there, Daddy?'

'Not many,' I said judiciously.

'I hate guns,' said Sally. 'Why do we have to have guns, Daddy? Why don't they make them against the law?'

'So that we can shoot bad people,' Billy said.

'Do you shoot bad people, Daddy?' Sally asked me.

Although they went on eating their meal with care and attention, I knew they were both watching me. I had a feeling they'd discussed it. 'Certainly not,' I said. 'Policemen do that.'

'I told you,' Sally said to Billy. To me she said: 'Billy said you've shot lots of people. You haven't, have you, Daddy?'

'No,' I said. 'I'd be no good for anything like that: I'd be afraid of the bangs. Would anyone like to eat my chips?'

'Billy would,' said Sally.

'Grandad is going to take me shooting rabbits,' said Billy. 'He's got a lot of guns; he even has a gun-room. I don't mind bangs.' He helped himself to my fried potatoes. 'Or a museum of cars. Then I could drive them home at night.'

'Cars are better,' I said. What kind of business were we in, when lying to our children was mandatory? One day I would sit them both down and explain everything, but with average luck I'd be hit by a truck before that day arrived.

After lunch we braved the misty rain and walked across the North Downs. It's impressive countryside, with Stane Street, forts and camps, and other remains of the Roman occupiers if you know where to look. Luckily most of them had been visited by the children with parties from school, so they were able to put me back on the right trail whenever I was about to go astray. In the more delicate matter of correcting the mistakes I made about the history of Roman Britain they were more tactful.

By the time I returned them to my parents-in-law they were both tired out, and so was I. On the way back, by Sally's special request, we bought currant buns at the baker's. After we'd all eaten toasted buns and tea, in front of the open fire with Grandma, they came out to see me get in my car to drive home. I was driving a Volvo that the Department had authorized as a purchase compatible with my grade and rank. Billy admired it and was already making a list of which cars he'd have in his museum. But when I kissed them goodbye, Sally smiled at Billy's museum plans and told me: 'Cars are better than guns.'

I simply said yes and let it go, but as I was driving back to London, listening to Mozart piano concertos on the tape player,

I had the uneasy feeling that Sally – younger than Billy but more perceptive, more cynical and more demanding, in the way that second children so often are – had seen through my fibs in the fish restaurant.

Early on Friday morning, old man Fedosov and the kid went through to West Berlin without incident. They drove to the airport and took a plane to Paris. At the same time, synchronizing their movements carefully, Werner collected VERDI at Checkpoint Charlie. They flew from Berlin to Cologne and then took an air taxi to Gatwick airport.

Dicky Cruyer and I met them at Gatwick, having arranged that the Customs and Immigration formalities for Werner and his charge would be minimal. He did well, for the formalities were done inside the plane and Dicky took the car through to the 'air side' and close to the aircraft where we waited for them to emerge.

'You can't use Berwick House,' said Dicky while we sat there in the car waiting for them. 'You got the message I sent?'

'No, I didn't,' I said. 'When did you send it?' I had difficulty keeping my voice level. I was furious that he should have been sitting alongside me for nearly half an hour before bothering to mention it.

'I asked Jenni to tell you,' he said vaguely. I knew he'd done nothing of the kind. I knew it was something that had totally slipped his mind until this very moment.

'We need Berwick House,' I said. The Berwick House compound consisted of seven acres of ground with a high wall around it, and armed guards and anti-intruder devices. There was no better place to put people like VERDI who had to be kept hidden and secure.

'It's closed down. No one is using it,' said Dicky.

'Why? When?'

'It's closed while they take the asbestos out of the ceilings or something.'

'Jesus Christ, Dicky. I can't believe it. Taking the asbestos out of it? What are we using in its stead?'

'Don't throw a tantrum, Bernard, it's not my doing. It's the "Works and Bricks" schedule. There's nowhere much like it these days, I'm afraid.'

'Where the hell are you going to put him?'

'The decision … the final decision that is … must be yours. But I've left instructions that your party should have exclusive use of the Notting Hill Gate safe house. I've arranged for a team to watch the front and rear entrances. You'll be safe enough there.'

'When is someone going to hear and understand what I keep saying over and over? The Notting Hill pad is compromised. They've even been using it for overnight stays by out-of-town visitors. You know as well as I do that it's a place that junior staff take their tarts for an afternoon. It's not safe and it's not secret.'

'Wait a minute,' said Dicky. 'I know no such thing. About … Who takes tarts there?'

'Then you must be comatose, Dicky. Haven't you noticed that when the key is needed, there are all sorts of worried looks and internal telephone calls and red-faced people running around the building to find it?'

'No, I haven't. I mean, that's pretty circumstantial, isn't it? It doesn't prove it's being used by staff to shack up.'

'I don't want to argue with you, Dicky. But Notting Hill was never a proper safe house, just a "Home Office notified premises". How can you think that's a secure premises to hide, house and protect someone like VERDI?'

'Where do you want to take him?' said Dicky. Some of the swagger had gone out of him as he began to see how right I was.

'It will have to do for tonight. But for God's sake get on the phone tomorrow and find somewhere properly protected to put him. The police or the army must have secure premises.'

'Do the junior staff really use it as a place to take their girls?'

'Ask Jenni-with-an-i,' I told him.

He looked at me to see if I was joshing him. 'You are a shit-stirrer, Bernard,' he said, not without a note of admiration in his voice.

So I took Werner and VERDI to the Notting Hill Gate safe house. Someone had given it a very thorough cleaning job since my previous visit. The thing that really annoyed me about Dicky's stupidity was that deprived of the guards and domestic staff that were routine facilities at Berwick House, I would have to stay with Werner overnight. We would need two of us. There would have to be someone awake at all times to keep an eye on things while VERDI slept. Even if VERDI was being very coop-erative we couldn't run the risk of him walking out of the door and disappearing into the busy streets of central London.

I called Fiona on the car phone and left a message to say that Dicky had assigned me an overnight job and that I would see her the following day at the office. It was vague, but Fiona would easily guess what was happening from that message. And if she didn't, she could check with Dicky.

'Look at this, Bernard. And this is just the beginning,' said Werner. Across the plastic-topped counter in the kitchen Werner was spreading out some of the material VERDI had brought out with him. 'Tessa Kosinski,' said Werner.

The fluorescent lights set in the work-counter shone down upon a set of large glossy black and white photographs. Brightly lit, a badly burned corpse was laid out on a mortuary slab. A close-up of the head frontal view, and another in profile, close-ups of the hands and views during the dissection.

'An army post-mortem?' said Werner.

'Yes, they have the best pathologists,' said VERDI, who was standing behind Werner drinking whisky. 'You must read the post-mortem and the coroner's report.' There were half a dozen pages; closely typed sheets of the usual sort. But the photocopies were poor and it was not easy to decipher the text.

'What was the verdict?' I asked.

'Not burning.' Still clasping his tumbler of whisky, VERDI shuffled through the pages to find what he wanted in the report. 'No smoke or traces of carbon in the trachea or the lungs.' He put his finger on the paragraph. 'There it is – death was caused by gunshot wounds. A 12-gauge shotgun was used at close range. Lead shot remained in the body … buckshot: large pellet buckshot … lots of pellets.'

'Wouldn't they have melted when the body burned?' I asked him.

'Yes,' he said. Again he shuffled through the pages to find the appropriate reference. 'There you are: forensic noted traces of metal from melted shot.' In the bottom of the wallet he found a file card to which a small plastic pouch was stapled. Inside it there were half a dozen pellets of buckshot, VERDI looked at me. 'No. 4 shot, I would guess,' he said.

'Yes,' I said. Jungle fighting during the Vietnam war persuaded the US Army that shotguns with No. 4 shot were the most lethal ammunition for use against human targets.

'But who did it? And why?' said Werner.

VERDI shrugged. He was leaving the easy ones to us. He went and sat down. He looked at us both and smiled. We all knew how it would go. Over the next few days VERDI would lay out his wares for us, like a peddler in an oriental market. We'd pick up each piece and inspect it closely and then we'd bargain.

'Satisfied?' VERDI asked.

'It's a start,' I said.

He nodded and sipped some booze. 'It's not the Kosinski woman,' he said softly. 'It's good, isn't it? Very thorough. It is the woman killed at the Brandenburg Exit but it's not Kosinski.'

I said nothing. I was watching VERDI very carefully. I knew then that I'd been wrong about him. I'd allowed my feelings to influence my judgement. VERDI had changed. He was no longer that stubborn thug I'd known in the old days; he was a resourceful and educated professional.

'Who is it?' said Werner.

'It's a female Stasi lieutenant. She was sent there that night when they heard that Fiona Samson was escaping down the Autobahn. Our duty officer phoned the Brandenburg office to go and get her back at any cost. That was the order: get her back at any cost. Brandenburg sent a three-person team from the duty watch. The woman was the senior rank.'

'I was there on the Autobahn that night,' I said.

'Well, you know what a muddle it all was. Everything went wrong. The message was modified twice as Berlin collected the facts. The Brandenburg team had been told to bring back Fiona Samson, who was escaping in a Ford Transit van with diplomatic licence plates. They arrived at the road-works and identified the van. There was a woman in the back of it. They grabbed her and put her in the trunk of their car and drove away. Except that the Stasi lieutenant remained behind. She said she would delay things. It was pitch-dark. She said she would make them think she was Fiona Samson while her men got away. She was looking for a commendation, I suppose. Women always want to prove themselves, don't they? She was armed and she was the senior person. The two men did as she told them.'

VERDI looked at me but I remained deadpan.

'What happened then?' said Werner.

'Ask Mr Samson,' said VERDI. 'He was there. There was a lot of shooting. I never discovered how many were killed. The

333

female lieutenant died. Samson survived. He got into the Ford van and drove away with his wife. Is that right, Samson?'

'I'm listening,' I said. I could guess what was coming next.

VERDI said: 'Someone put the female lieutenant into a car and torched it. I went out there first thing the next morning. It was a scene of devastation. I gave orders that the burned corpse should not be identified as the Stasi lieutenant and put a seventy-two-hour security clamp on the whole business. The security clamp was extended and still remains in force.'

'What happened to the Kosinski woman?' said Werner.

'I had her put into solitary confinement at Normannenstrasse. She wouldn't say a word to anyone. I'd never met Fiona Samson so she was fingerprinted and photographed as Fiona Samson. That's what helped sort out the mistake, but it took a couple of days before we could get Fiona Samson's papers sent to us. I knew Fiona Samson was a hot potato so there was no question of interrogation until I got it okayed from above. Eventually the prisoner was identified as the sister, Kosinski.'

'Where is she now?'

'She was moved to the high-security prison in Leipzig. They are waiting for a political decision about her disposal.'

'She's alive?' asked Werner.

'She's fit and well. I suppose that in due time she will be traded for one of our people.'

'Is that what you've come here for?' said Werner.

'Partly,' said VERDI. He turned to me and said: 'You've said nothing, Samson.'

'We'll go through it again in the morning,' I said. I would need a recorder and a video too if this was all going to be a part of the official record.

It was only a few minutes after that when the phone rang with a call from Duncan Churcher. At first his tone was supercilious.

'Pull up your trousers and tell her goodnight. I'm at the Praed Street address. Meet me where the cabs drive in to Paddington Station in thirty minutes. I take it you have some magic wand that will let you leave your car there without it being towed away. Okay?'

He was about to ring off. 'Wait a minute,' I said. 'I'm not sure I can get away.'

His frolicsome manner changed. 'Whatever you're doing, Bernard, it's not more urgent than this. And I can't hold the lid on this one for more than an hour.'

'What's happened?'

There was a long pause as he carefully decided how to phrase it. 'You'll need the clean-up team. Perhaps you'll want to alert them before coming over here.'

'Jesus Christ!'

'Where the cabs drop their fares. I'm wearing a white trenchcoat.'

'I'll be there.'

Perhaps I sounded doubtful. I suppose he wanted to reconfirm the arrangement. He said: 'Are you far away? I went through three different numbers. Doesn't even your secretary know where you are?'

'Did you try my wife?'

'Touché, Bernard. No, I should have thought of her.'

'Have you been drinking, Duncan?'

'Honest to God, Bernard. No, I swear it. Not for weeks.'

'Then don't start now.' I rang off without saying goodbye.

Werner was looking at me. I said: 'Werner – I've got to go out. Look after his nibs. I'll be back within the hour.'

'Where are you going?'

'I'm going out,' I said.

'If Dicky or Bret want to know?'

'Say I fell down the stairs, and I've gone out to buy Band-Aids.'

'Do you need a gun?'

335

'No thanks,' I said. 'It sounds like it's too late for noisy explosions.'

It was a mean little room in an old creaky building smelling of decay. The sort of seedy little hotel that the neighbourhoods near rail terminals and bus stations spawn. Such buildings, with only a short lease available before their demolition was due, were the favoured investment of predatory landlords. I followed Churcher up the stairs. Leading us there was a man with a bunch of keys, a stubbly chin and gin-flavoured breath that I suspected Churcher might have arranged. He was a lean fellow, the result no doubt of heaving his enormous bunch of keys up and down the stairs with frequent grabs at the stair-rail so that he did not lose his balance.

Poverty brings lack of choice, and thus urban poverty has a monotonous and melancholy quality that is common to cheap accommodation from one end of the world to the other. Vomit stains, cigarette butts and empty bottles: these cramped rooms could have been in a New York tenement, a Mexico City rooming house or a Berlin squat. The metal bed with its chipped paintwork and sagging springs, the dirty windows, the mattress old and stained and smelly, two kitchen chairs and a few bent implements alongside an ancient cooking ring to justify the 'apartments to rent' sign that overlooked the street.

'Come and look at him,' said Churcher, walking through the first room into the dingy little bedroom that adjoined it.

Leaning forward in a jack-knifed position with the grubby blanket kicked aside was the scrawny body of a man of some indeterminate age between twenty and thirty. He had long wavy hair to his shoulders and was wearing a grubby undervest and striped boxer shorts. Like an anatomical diagram, the injection sores followed the patterns of his veins along arms and legs. Against the bed-head there were a couple of pillows propped, where he'd been sitting up in bed until he'd taken a bottle of pills, retched – but not retched enough – and died. 'Is this what you brought me here for?' I said.

'I wanted you to see him,' said Churcher.

'Why?'

His face tightened with concern. 'Oh, no. I don't mean that, Bernard. You've nothing to reproach yourself about. Nothing at all.'

'Why then?'

'It was the quickest and most effective way of showing you that he couldn't possibly be what you thought.'

'Daphne Cruyer's lover, you mean?'

'A KGB probe … or Daphne Cruyer's lover. You can see. He wasn't anything, Bernard. He was just a fragment of big-city flotsam.'

'When did this happen?'

I watched Churcher as he pulled the body back into the sitting position for long enough for me to see the cadaver's white drawn face and staring eyes. As he let go, the weight of the skull overcame the stiffness in the neck muscles, and the head rolled forward as if coming alive. 'Several hours ago, judging by the rigor.'

'Have you searched?'

'I did that while I was waiting for you.'

'I wouldn't like an intimate diary to turn up in the coroner's court, and Daphne Cruyer feature in its pages.'

'Nothing like that. I talked to him at length on Wednesday afternoon. No pressure, Bernard, I swear it. No need. He'd just shot up. He was quite lucid and rational but there was nothing behind his eyes, Bernard.'

'So why not Daphne Cruyer's fancy man?'

'Look at him! Look at the sores and the veins. Would any woman with half a brain in her head get into bed with him?' He

337

twitched his nose as if smelling the air for the first rime. 'I met Daphne Cruyer once or twice, a couple of years back. I remember her at a cocktail party at the German Institute, or one of those freebie get-togethers. She was dressed in a long floral dress with beads and bangles and ballet shoes. Very artistic, isn't she?'

'I believe she is,' I agreed.

The body had continued to move and now, suddenly, it slid all the way to reassume its doubled-up position, like a man trying to touch his toes. Churcher saw it but didn't pause in his conversation. 'A very creative woman, I thought. Very imaginative.'

'She didn't make it up, Duncan.'

'I think she did, Bernard. A fantasy that she had to express, that's what I think. It helped her control her anger towards her husband perhaps. She didn't think you'd ever see him, did she?' When I didn't respond to this he said: 'Was she drunk? Was she angry? Was she jealous?'

'All three,' I admitted. 'Cause of death?'

'Take your pick, Bernard. He's got enough pills here to start a pharmacy. Half those bottles are empty; for all I know, he swallowed them all in one go. He was on crack and all kinds of filth. Even if he'd checked into a health farm yesterday morning, his life expectation wasn't more than a year.'

'So why didn't you tell me this when you first saw him?'

'I was checking his medical record, and that's a slow business. He walked out of a mental hospital about three months ago. You know how it is these days, no one wants to sign a commitment order and hold anyone. You could slice up some old lady with a chainsaw, and they'd still not put you under lock and key.' He looked around. 'Not that this one would ever do anything like that. He was polite and considerate and gentle with everyone. Doctors, patients, even the people living in this rat-trap said the same thing. The poor sod had just had all he could take.'

'They'll bring in a suicide verdict?'

'Suicide? Where do you draw the line, Bernard? In Russia they call alcoholics "partial suicides" and that's it, isn't it?'

'I don't know,' I said.

'Then you are lucky.' He looked at his watch. 'If you don't want your clean-up boys called in, I'd better get the law soon, Bernard. Have you seen enough?'

'So there was nothing in it, Duncan?'

'He went to the art classes. He didn't pay and it was warm and light: better an evening there than an evening here. Perhaps he wanted to meet people ... I don't know. He was lonely and broke and desperate. When I talked with him the other afternoon, he didn't even remember who Daphne Cruyer was. I asked him to tell me who was in the class with him; he could only remember three other students out of the twelve, and Daphne Cruyer wasn't one of them.'

'Poor Daphne,' I said.

'Perhaps she's lonely too, Bernard. You can't always tell by the way people seem from the outside. Loneliness is love spelled backwards, if you know what I mean. That same energy and power and passion that sends you sky-high into the rarefied stratosphere of love, when you are lonely drags you down to the sea-bed, and holds you there under a heavy rock until your lungs burst with misery.'

'Have you been on the booze?'

'No, I swear it.'

'Okay, bring the law in. I must get back to work. What about Hitler downstairs?'

'He'll be all right. I'll give the police a statement and he'll breathe gin all over them. They'll listen to what I tell them because I can save them a lot of work. Leave it to me. This is what I do for a living.'

'Any next of kin?'

'No one. The hospital tried to find the parents when he was first admitted, but he has no one, no relatives at all.'

'No worries on that score then,' I said.

'When I was tiny, I used to pray every night, asking God to make sure I died before my parents died. I just couldn't face the thought of being alive without them, you see.' Churcher was identifying with the dead youngster and it wasn't helping things.

'What about Belostok?' I said. 'Should he be told?'

'Don't blame yourself, Bernard. What you asked me to do made no difference. It would have happened like this even if Daphne Cruyer had never been born.'

'Belostok will be expecting him on Tuesday. Maybe Daphne Cruyer will be alarmed.'

'Bugger off, Bernard. This is what you're paying me to do and I'm bloody good at it. I'm not over the hill yet, no matter what they are saying about me.'

When I got back to Notting Hill Gate, VERDI and Werner were sitting in the dark. The curtains were wide open and they were drinking watery whisky and looking across London and watching the sluggish movement of the traffic along Bayswater Road.

There was enough light to see that VERDI was wearing a white roll-neck, and Werner was almost lost in the gloom wearing a black knitted shirt. They both looked as if they had adjusted to the idea of a long stay here. I was clinging to the hope that Dicky would find somewhere more suited to VERDI's incarceration so that I could escape from my role as jailer.

'One of us should turn in, Werner,' I said.

'Are you going to guard me?' VERDI asked with amusement.

'You sleep first, Bernie,' said Werner. 'You look worn out.'

He went into the kitchen and called: 'I'm making a sandwich and coffee. Anyone else?'

'No,' I said, but VERDI said he'd join Werner in the late-night snack.

Werner was still in the kitchen when it happened. I was in the front room with VERDI. I was kneeling on the carpet rummaging through my overnight bag to find my toothpaste.

The sound was no more than the sharp crack of breaking glass and a strangled cry from VERDI, the sort of gargling sound that is made by a man using mouthwash. I knew what it was. The glass was the window and the gargling the sound made as a man's heart explodes and he swallows several pints of his own blood.

Werner heard the glass break and recognized it too. He came rushing in from the kitchen. 'He's shot,' Werner said.

'Down! Stay still, Werner. Freeze. They'll be watching for movement.'

I was crouched over my zipper bag in the part of the room away from the window, and I remained down. 'Get right down. Don't try to look out of the window, Werner. Come to this side of the room and watch the door. Be very careful.' I waited while he did it, and then I scambled across the room on my hands and knees to look at VERDI.

'Is he dead?' said Werner from across the room.

'Yes,' I said. One look at his face was enough.

'He's moving.'

'Yes, but he's dead. It went right through the chest. Shit!' I said. I was putting my hand along his back to find the exit wound, and found a terrible gaping hole and a lot of blood still pumping out. His roll-neck sweater was saturated in it and it now covered my hands too.

'Could you see where it came from?'

'Don't go near the window.' I got my handkerchief from my pocket and wiped my hands. It didn't help much.

'But it's too dark to see.'

'A sniper,' I said. 'My fault. I should have thought of that. Someone out there on the rooftops with hand-loaded rounds, a sniper rifle on a bipod, and an infra-red nightscope.'

'You can't be sure how it was done.'

'It wasn't a lucky shot, Werner.'

'But you've been near that window. I've been near that window. But when they pull the trigger, they hit him. They must be able to distinguish him.'

'Yes. You don't set up that kind of hit and then leave it to chance which of the three men you get.'

'A nightscope.'

'This is a very expensive professional hit, Werner. Chest hit, with a round that strikes the heart and severs the spine. You couldn't do better than that if a surgeon had him on an operation table in the theatre.'

'I should have closed the curtains,' said Werner.

'Keep still and stay down,' I said. 'If it's some pay-by-result freelance, he'll be miles away by now. But if this is a KGB operation they may be ordered to wait and see what happens.'

'Even with all the lights off, they could see that white roll-neck as he came near the window?'

'Exactly, Werner.'

'But if we'd had the lights on we would have closed the curtains.'

'Life is full of maybes.'

'But even then … How did they know which of us was wearing the white roll-neck? That's what I'd like to know.'

'Maybe they're going to pick us off, one by one.'

Werner gave a nervous laugh.

I got to the curtains and pulled them closed. 'Maybe they watched us arriving,' I said. 'Maybe someone told them.'

'Do you think they'll wait at the front entrance for us? Shall I phone for the clean-up team? We'll need a Special Branch man and a doctor, won't we?'

'Maybe. Let's just wait here a moment and get our thoughts together.'

'Is he still bleeding?'

342

'One shot, Werner. They must have figured that there would not be time enough for a second round. Flat trajectory. Hits the glass, spreads a little and takes him out. Even allowing for an element of luck, how many rent-a-guns do we know with that kind of expertise?'

'No one.'

'I'll find him, Werner, I'll find that bastard,' I said, expressing my anger more than my considered opinion.

'Is this the end of Operation VERDI?' said Werner.

'It's the end of a lot of things.'

21

'Why have you got all this paper in your office?' Werner was not the first visitor to express surprise about the boxes that were stacked from floor to ceiling, scarcely leaving room for me to work.

'They can't think of anywhere else to put us,' I said.

'Who's up there on the top floor?' Werner asked nervously, and not for the first time. He went to the window and stood there looking out. The sky had become darker and darker, and now there came a rumble of distant thunder.

'Who isn't?' I said. We'd already been waiting almost two hours for the inquiry to send down for us.

'Number Two Conference Room,' said Werner. 'Not Bret's office. That shows they are really serious.'

'Bret is having his office redecorated. Haven't you noticed all the men in overalls, with ladders and transistor radios? They are stripping the paper off the walls, and putting in a false ceiling.'

'Don't you know who's up there?'

'I saw Frank arrive, and the D-G must be there too because I heard that bloody dog barking.'

'Does he take that smelly animal with him everywhere?'

'They've always said if you want a loyal friend in Whitehall, buy a dog,' I said.

'By the time we get up there we'll be the only ones left to blame,' Werner agonized.

'Yes, we're the ones chosen to be pushed out of the sled.' Werner shuddered at the thought.

'Do they all sit round a table?'

'I don't know, Werner,' I said sharply. His fretting was having an effect on me. These official inquiries were always unpredictable. It was difficult not to worry that you might walk in through the door and have them say: You are a KGB spy so why not confess? It had happened to others, and many of them had eventually proved totally innocent. The Soviets were always trying to make trouble within the Department, by sowing false evidence and disinformation. No one was safe from it.

There was a perfunctory tap on the door and Bret came in. He was jacketless, with dark pants and a waistcoat from whose pocket a row of gold and silver writing instruments were peering. 'What's going on? Why are you guys sitting here in the dark?' said Bret, switching on the lights without waiting to hear.

'It's energy-saving week,' I said. There was a crackle of electricity and a flash of lightning that lit the two men, freezing them into poses that stayed in my mind long afterwards. Werner was hunched, with furrowed brow, and looking out of the window as if waiting for the rain to start. Bret, head bent, was looking down as his fingers searched among the pens in his waistcoat pocket.

'We are taking a thirty-minute recess,' Bret explained. 'But I wanted to ask you your opinions about the killer, Bernard. We're trying to construct a profile, to decide if this was a Moscow-inspired hit.' From his waistcoat pocket he'd taken a piece of metal. He tossed it on to my desk, where it came to rest on the typewritten transcript of a diplomatic phone call. 'What do you make of that?'

I looked at it. It was like a silver dollar that had been chewed at the edges. 'Did this come out of VERDI's body?'

'In a manner of speaking,' said Bret. 'It was in a large chunk of flesh found near the body. What kind of gun fired it?'

I didn't pick it up. 'I left my crystal ball in my other pants, Bret. It's just a piece of metal that has distorted on impact.'

With manifest patience Bret said: 'It's what killed him, Bernard. It's the round that came through the window. Can't you say anything helpful about it?'

Werner reached over and picked it up to study it.

'It's some kind of factory-made soft-point or hollow-point round,' I said. 'They all collapse like that. In doing so, all the land and groove markings are effaced, along with any other characteristics, except maybe the weight.'

Bret looked at Werner, who was weighing it in his hand. Werner shook his head.

'So what shall I tell them upstairs?' Bret asked.

'Say it's probably a Remington Soft Point Core-Lokt. That's usually regarded as the softest dum-dum, and you couldn't get much softer than this one.'

'How many different ones are manufactured?' Bret asked, while writing in a tiny leather-bound notebook. I looked over his shoulder and corrected his spelling.

'Quite a number,' I said. 'And for a tricky shot like that one, it may have been hand-loaded to increase the propellant charge.'

'So it's a Soviet hit man?'

'No, I don't think so. It's not that it's too sophisticated, but it's not Soviet style. They go for short-range gimmicks like gas-guns used point-blank, or poison-tipped implements. Every way you look at this one, you see American sophistication.'

Perhaps Bret took it personally. 'It's a sniper-rifle assassination, Bernard. A good shot maybe, but surely nothing a Soviet army marksman couldn't bring off?'

'More than that, Bret. I know that in the movies huge cross-hairs fill the screen, pan to the villain's chest and we're in to the end-roller. But that's not the way it really is. Even if the technology was provided by a third party, this one was an expert job.

For a shot like this, the trajectory will demand a lot of correction – for wind and for gravity too. And it was a moving target that was probably only going to be in view momentarily.'

'Okay, a freelance hit man then.' Bret took the distorted metal round from Werner, and put it back into his waistcoat pocket.

'It's a six-figure assignment by a top pro,' I said.

'I'm going to let you into a little secret, Bernard. When this little old inquiry finally shuffles to a close, its report will conclude that VERDI's death was caused by a Stasi hit man. Or by a freelance sniper employed by them.'

'I see.'

'It's logical and conclusive that way, Bernard. We don't want to drag in a lot of complex ideas that just don't make sense and leave loose ends.' The thunder was getting closer. Bret looked at me and raised an eyebrow: 'Unless you have some wacky Samson theory to peddle?'

'Not me, Bret,' I said.

'So can I take it that the board will not have to listen to, and my report will not have to incorporate, the one dissenting opinion of Bernard Samson?'

'It was a Stasi hit man, Bret. And you can quote me.'

He looked at me sadly and said: 'I didn't think it would end like this. When I saw you off from Los Angeles airport I. told you that faith must be your anchor. Grab VERDI and come on out, I said. I thought it would be something an experienced whiz-kid like you could wrap up successfully in forty-eight hours or so.'

'Is that what you thought, Bret?'

'Okay, I didn't want the D-G to send you,' Bret admitted. 'Not because I thought you'd fail, but because I knew you'd want to do everything your own oddball way. I warned you that there were people in the Department gunning for you: looking for an opportunity like this. You ignored that warning. You went running off to see Werner.' A fleeting smile for Werner to show

347

it was nothing personal. 'And pulled every other provocative antic that caught your fancy.'

'What you call provocation, I call protecting my back,' I said.

'I wanted to send someone "hungry": a younger man, an unmarried probationer who would do everything the way the book says do it.'

'Wow! Poverty, celibacy and obedience. But that's only for monks, Bret.'

Bret put his notebook away, looked at us both without evident admiration, and went to the door. 'Dicky is next. I don't know which of you we'll want after him.' As he stood in the doorway he couldn't resist giving me a final volley: 'I wish you hadn't run off to see Werner and your brother-in-law. At that time they were both persona non grata. Now your capers have all blown up in our face. I'm sitting there, hour after hour, listening to all this stuff and wondering how I'm going to handle it in my report and keep you intact. And right now, I'm all ready to commit hara-kiri.'

'Let me know if you need a hand,' I said.

Bret went out and closed the door, being very careful that it didn't slam.

When Bret had gone, Werner resumed his worrying, or perhaps he'd never stopped. 'Bret is determined to dump all the blame on us. You could see that in his face. Did you have to make it worse?'

'Just stick to what you wrote,' I said.

'That's just it. I haven't even got a copy of my own statement. That girl from Dicky's office said she'd bring a copy back for me, and never did. The board will be asking me questions and I won't even know what I told them already.'

'Just tell them the way it happened,' I said wearily. 'It was all over in sixty seconds. He's dead. We can't resurrect him.'

'I should have closed the curtains,' said Werner.

'Don't find reasons to blame yourself,' I advised. 'They'll find enough lousy reasons to roast you, without you supplying them with good ones.'

'They are out for blood,' he said. 'I could see it in Bret's face. He's absolutely furious.'

'Well, Frank won't be furious,' I said. 'The wire-taps would have gone directly to England. Frank saw the danger of his precious Berlin Field Unit becoming sidelined.'

'Bret is writing the report,' Werner persisted. 'And Bret doesn't like being the butt of your jokes.'

'Bret had begun to see he was going to be the referee in a knock-down drag-out battle between Frank and Dicky. Is Bret the type to pitch his tent in no-man's-land?'

'Dicky was staking his career on it, you told me that yourself. What is he telling them?'

'Can't you see him, Werner? He's up there in the conference room right now, explaining in that wide-eyed sincere way that he practises in front of a mirror, that deprived of Berwick House we did the best we could. And that means he put me and you in charge of it, and we failed him dismally.'

'If he says that,' said Werner, trying to be cool, calm and matter-of-fact, 'we'll take all the blame.'

It was difficult to disagree with that prognosis, but I was determined not to join Werner in his mood of Teutonic self-pity. I said: 'He'll be confirmed as Ops supremo, and that's all Dicky cares about. He is not going to be crying salty tears about the collapse of the VERDI operation. He couldn't understand it for one thing. And it wasn't the sort of job that could be done overnight, and establish him as a Wunderkind. Tapping into the Karlshorst computer was going to be a long-term on-going slog. And when he had Bret over to dinner the other night, he was left in no doubt that Bret wasn't going to offer him much support. Dicky realized that he was going to be fighting Frank, while the D-G looked on unsympathetically and Bret yelled told-you-so. Dicky saw it was going to be a long stony path.'

Werner looked even more dejected. Like most such long-winded arguments it sounded unconvincing, even to me. 'This was Dicky's opportunity to become the most important man in the Department,' said Werner. 'And we screwed it up.'

'Yes, but do the minds of Whitehall apparatchiks work that way, Werner? The more success he had, the more he would be proving his superiors wrong. That's not the Whitehall style and it's certainly not Dicky's.'

'Why would Dicky care about proving the D-G wrong? The Director-General's past retirement age anyway. A shove like this from Dicky and he'd be toppled. And who would be the hero? – Dicky.'

'You don't understand the British, Werner. No D-G is ever going to be happy with a black box Department tapping into Karlshorst, and run by people from the wrong schools who have little screwdrivers in their top pockets. The old man always said that we only get our allocation of funds because we use humans as field agents. That's what keeps us in business, Werner. I heard him tell Bret once, that NASA wouldn't get a nickel from Congress if the rockets they fired into space contained sensors and measuring equipment instead of crews. You need men to get money out of politicians, he said. And he's right.' There was a drumroll of thunder, and Werner looked at the window furtively as if considering escape. 'And don't think the D-G is so easily toppled. He's not going to "lose" the VERDI operation, he's assigning it all to GCHQ and leaving them to pick up the pieces.'

'That will be impossible. It's beyond salvage.'

'I think he knows that, Werner. It's his subtle way of cutting GCHQ down to size, lest they get ideas above their station.'

'The D-G said that with VERDI's help we could clear up the mystery of the Tessa Kosinski death.' Werner studied my face to see my reaction. 'For once and for all, they said. You were there when he said it.'

'I don't plan to tell them that yarn about Tessa still being alive, if that's what you're fishing for.'

'It wasn't in my written notes,' said Werner.

'I noticed that.'

'I thought we should discuss it before we told them upstairs.'

'What have we got to tell them? A totally unsubstantiated fairy story with Tessa still alive as some mysterious prisoner who they might one day unveil. The woman in the iron mask? I mean … what have we got to tell them, Werner?'

'You can't be sure it's a fairy story. They could have got her out of the Ford van without you knowing. It could have been another woman who was shot.'

'Don't give me that stuff, Werner. What do you know? You weren't even there.'

'You didn't contradict him, Bernie. I know you; you would have slaughtered him with questions if there had been a flaw in that description.'

I sighed. 'You're showing me exactly what could happen upstairs, Werner. If we open a can of worms like that, we'll both be picked to pieces. Keep stumm. If there is any truth in VERDI's story, the boys in Magdeburg will find another way of airing it.'

'You didn't tell Fiona?'

'Fiona? That's a major reason for saying nothing. Can you imagine what an uproar that kind of wild rumour would create with Tessa's family?'

'But the D-G said he wanted VERDI's help to clear up the Tessa Kosinski death. The board are sure to pursue it.'

'That's what the D-G thinks he's already done, Werner. The D-G showed Fiona that post-mortem report, the coroner's verdict and the glossy photos, and the little plastic bag with the buckshot in it. None of them have any reason to believe that

351

the body is anyone but Tessa. Maybe in time the Germans will release a burned body. I'm not going to examine it and try and find out its true identity. We'll give it a proper burial and then maybe the whole miserable business will end.'

'What about a Tessa still alive?' said Werner. 'Suppose what VERDI said is true? Suppose she suddenly turns up here?' Werner never let go; that was his greatest virtue and his most irritating vice.

'Then that will be all right,' I said crossly. 'She'll live happily ever after.'

'Is that what you think?'

'Yes. Let's cross that bridge when we get to it.'

'But if Tessa is really alive it won't be like that.' Werner was not to be put off. 'If she is alive they will start putting the pressure on to Fiona and to George, and, for all I know, on to your father-in-law too.'

I looked at him. Werner was a clever and perceptive man who was reminding me that such pressure might have begun already. It was an ominous thought, as if the worst was yet to come.

'I have to look after her, Werner,' I said. 'You were right in what you said. Fiona is crippled by her grief. What would it do to her to be told that a dead man says Tessa is alive, but brought no proof of it?'

'So VERDI said nothing about Tessa? That's the way you mean to handle it when you are upstairs?'

'You don't have to back me up, Werner. If you want to tell them everything, I'll say I wasn't present when he said it to you.'

Werner said: 'I'll go along with it, Bernard. I'll say whatever you are going to say. We're in enough trouble already without giving them conflicting accounts of what happened.'

'Fiona wakes me in the middle of the night and asks me who did it.'

'What do you tell her?' said Werner.

'I tell her to go back to sleep.'

'It's your marriage, Bernard. I'll do anything … you know that.'

'I know, Werner. Thanks.'

'Will she continue working?'

'Everyone's been telling her that burying herself in her work is the best antidote to grief. But burying yourself in work, to the extent she does, is just a way of escaping from the real world. It won't help her. It wouldn't help anyone.'

'And in the long term?'

'With love and careful attention, and the children too, she'll get better. My guess is that they would like to have a female Deputy D-G, just to show everyone how democratic Whitehall can be. I think Bret will serve out his time, and if Fiona keeps her nose clean they will leap-frog her into the DD-G's office when Bret goes.'

Werner nodded. It was one of my cosy little fairy stories and he knew that. 'And is that what Fiona wants?'

'She is going to get domestic help to live in with us and look after the children,' I said. 'So she has no plans for early retirement. If they fire me today I suppose I could become one of these new-style husbands who stay at home and look after the kids.'

'I wish her well,' said Werner. 'We need someone like her up there on the top floor.'

I'd always figured they needed someone like me up on the top floor, but I suppose Werner was entitled to his opinion. I said: 'And I see they are giving you a proper contract at last. You'll have better job security than I've got.'

'No contract is signed. It was with the lawyers last week,' said Werner. 'They will cancel it now.'

'Why? It wasn't made "performance-related" was it?'

I heard Bret coming back down the corridor to get one or the other of us. And then I heard Gloria's voice greeting him. Just for a moment or two they talked and laughed together. I

353

couldn't hear what they were saying but Bret's voice was firm and friendly, and Gloria's laugh was so light and fresh and warm.

The sky was even darker now. The thunder came again. How could the sky be so dark without it starting to rain? 'What's all this about having Faith?' said Werner. 'What does Bret mean by Faith?'

'Faith is the substance of things hoped for, the evidence of things not seen. Hebrews eleven, verse one. I found that in a Bible I was given recently.'

Winter

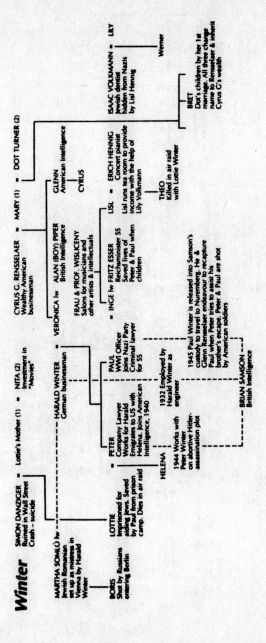

Game

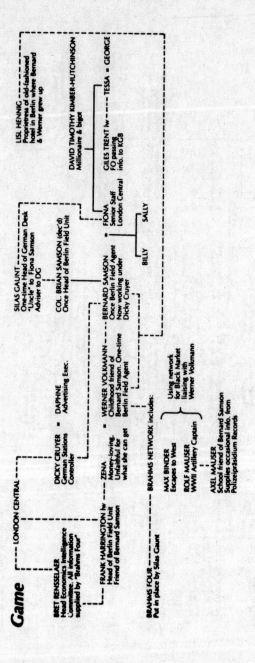

LONDON CENTRAL

BRET RENSSELAER
Head Economics Intelligence Committee. All information supplied by "Brahms Four"

FRANK HARRINGTON lw
Head of Berlin Field Unit
Friend of Bernard Samson

DICKY CRUYER = **DAPHNE**
German Stations   Advertising Exec.
Controller

ZENA
Money-loving.
Unfaithful for what she can get

WERNER VOLKMANN
Childhood friend of Bernard Samson. One-time Berlin Field Agent

BRAHMS FOUR
Put in place by Silas Gaunt

BRAHMS NETWORK includes:

MAX BINDER
Escapes to West

ROLF MAUSER
WWII Artillery Captain

Using network for Black Market liaising with Werner Volkmann

AXEL MAUSER
School friend of Bernard Samson
Supplies occasional info. from
Polizeipräsidium Records

SILAS GAUNT
One-time Head of German Desk
"Uncle" to Fiona Samson
Adviser to DG

COL. BRIAN SAMSON (dec'd)
Once Head of Berlin Field Unit

BERNARD SAMSON
Once Berlin Field Agent
Now working under
Dicky Cruyer

BILLY   SALLY

= **FIONA**
Senior Staff
London Central

LISL HENNIG
Proprietress of old-fashioned hotel in Berlin where Bernard & Werner grew up

DAVID TIMOTHY KIMBER-HUTCHINSON
Millionaire & bigot

GILES TRENT lw
FO passing info. to KGB

TESSA = **GEORGE**

Set

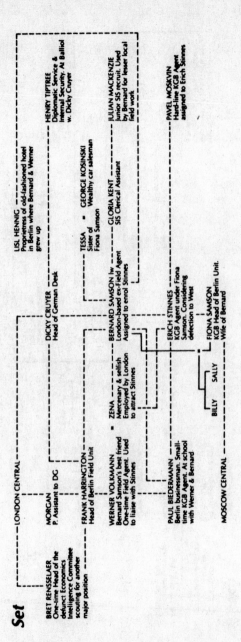

Match

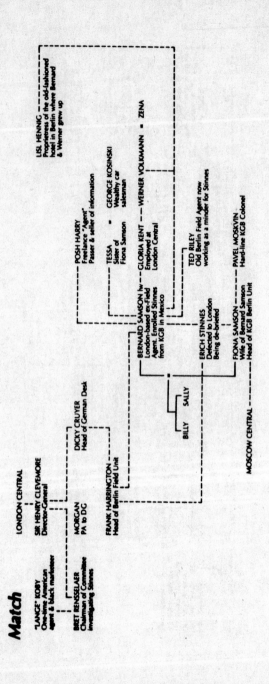

LONDON CENTRAL

SIR HENRY CLEVEMORE
Director-General

"LANCE" KOBY
One-time Armenian
agent & black marketeer

BRET RENSSELAER
Chairman of Committee
investigating Stinnes

DICKY CRUYER
Head of German Desk

MORGAN
PA to DG

FRANK HARRINGTON
Head of Berlin Field Unit

LISL HENNIG — — — —
Proprietress of the old-fashioned
hotel in Berlin where Bernard
& Werner grew up

POSH HARRY
Freelance "Agent"
Passer & seller of information

TESSA = **GEORGE KOSINSKI**
Sister of Wealthy car
Fiona Samson salesman

WERNER VOLKMANN = **ZENA**

GLORIA KENT
Employed at
London Central

TED RILEY
Old Berlin Field Agent now
working as a minder for Stinnes

BERNARD SAMSON Iw—
London-based ex-Field
Agent. Enrolled Stinnes
from KGB in Mexico

ERICH STINNES
Defected to London
Being de-briefed

FIONA SAMSON
Wife of Bernard Samson
Head of KGB Berlin Unit

PAVEL MOSKVIN
Hard-line KGB Colonel

BILLY

SALLY

MOSCOW CENTRAL — — — —

Hook

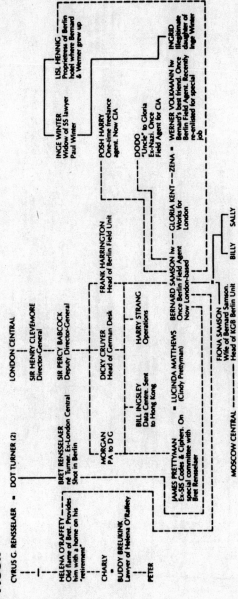

CYRUS G. RENSSELAER ▪ **DOT TURNER (2)**

LONDON CENTRAL

SIR HENRY CLEVEMORE
Director-General

SIR PERCY BABCOCK
Deputy Director-General

BRET RENSSELAER
né Turner. Ex-London Central. Shot in Berlin

HELENA O'RAFFETY —
Old flame of Bret. Provides him with a home on his "retirement"

CHARLY

BUDDY BREUKINK
Lawyer of Helena O'Raffety

PETER

MORGAN
PA to D-G

DICKY CRUYER
Head of German Desk

FRANK HARRINGTON
Head of Berlin Field Unit

HARRY STRANG
Operations

BILL INGSLEY
Data Centre. Sent to Hong Kong

LUCINDA MATTHEWS
(Cindy Prettyman)

JAMES PRETTYMAN
Ex-SIS Codes & Ciphers. On special committee with Bret Rensselaer

BERNARD SAMSON lw
Once Berlin Field Agent. Now London-based

FIONA SAMSON
Wife of Bernard Samson. Head of KGB Berlin Unit

MOSCOW CENTRAL

BILLY   **SALLY**

GLORIA KENT —
Works for London

ZENA

WERNER VOLKMANN ▪
Bernard's best friend. Once Berlin Field Agent. Re-enlisted for special job

DODO
"Uncle" to Gloria. Once Ex-Nazi. Once Field Agent for CIA

POSH HARRY
One-time freelance agent. Now CIA

INGE WINTER
Widow of SS lawyer Paul Winter

LISL HENNIG
Proprietress of Berlin hotel where Bernard & Werner grew up

INGRID
Illegitimate daughter of Inge Winter

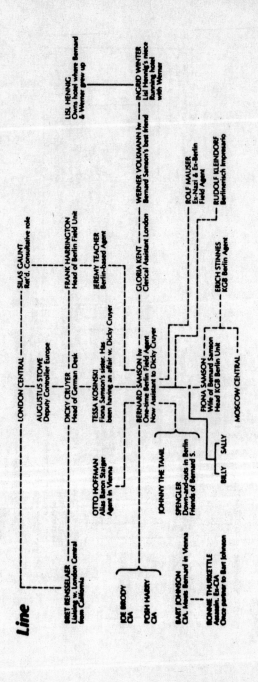

Sinker

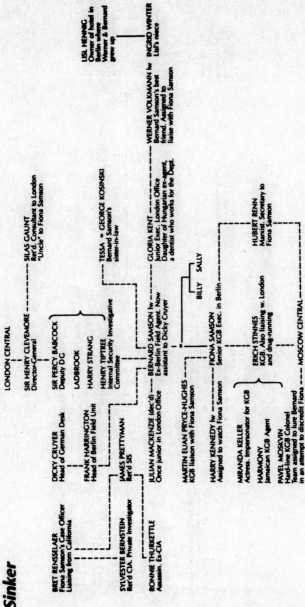

LONDON CENTRAL

SIR HENRY CLEVEMORE
Director-General

SILAS GAUNT
Ret'd. Consultant to London
"Uncle" to Fiona Samson

SIR PERCY BABCOCK
Deputy D-G

LADBROOK

HARRY STRANG

HENRY TIPTREE
Internal Security Investigative
Committee

TESSA = GEORGE KOSINSKI
Bernard Samson's
sister-in-law

DICKY CRUYER
Head of German Desk

FRANK HARRINGTON
Head of Berlin Field Unit

JAMES PRETTYMAN
Ret'd SIS

BRET RENSSELAER
Fiona Samson's Case Officer
Liaising from California

SYLVESTER BERNSTEIN
Ret'd CIA. Private Investigator

RONNIE THURKETTLE
Assassin. Ex-CIA

JULIAN MACKENZIE (dec'd)
Once junior in London Office

BERNARD SAMSON lw
Ex-Berlin Field Agent. Now
assistant to Dicky Cruyer

MARTIN EUAN PRYCE-HUGHES
KGB liaison with Fiona Samson

HARRY KENNEDY lw
Assigned to watch Fiona Samson

MIRANDA KELLER
Actress. Impersonator for KGB

HARMONY
Jamaican KGB Agent

PAVEL MOSKVIN
Hard-line KGB Colonel
Team assigned to lure Bernard
in an attempt to discredit Fiona

GLORIA KENT
Junior Exec. London Office
Daughter of Hungarian ex-agent,
a dentist who works for the Dept.

WERNER VOLKMANN lw
Bernard Samson's best
friend. Assigned to
liaise with Fiona Samson

LISL HENNIG
Owner of hotel in
Berlin where
Werner & Bernard
grew up

INGRID WINTER
Lisl's niece

BILLY   SALLY

FIONA SAMSON
Senior KGB Exec. in Berlin

HUBERT RENN
Marxist. Secretary to
Fiona Samson

ERICH STINNES
KGB. Also liaising w. London
and drug-running

MOSCOW CENTRAL

Faith

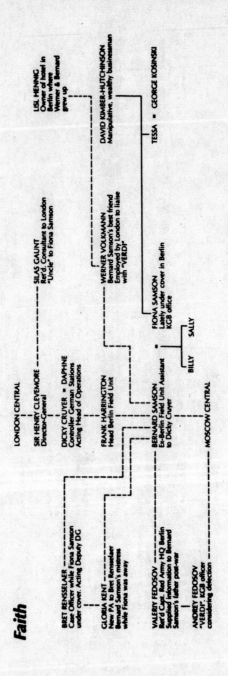

LONDON CENTRAL

SIR HENRY CLEVEMORE
Director-General

SILAS GAUNT
Ret'd. Consultant to London
"Uncle" to Fiona Samson

DICKY CRUYER = DAPHNE
Controller German Stations
Acting Head of Operations

FRANK HARRINGTON
Head Berlin Field Unit

WERNER VOLKMANN
Bernard Samson's best friend
Employed by London to liaise
with "VERDI"

LISL HENNIG
Owner of hotel in
Berlin where
Werner & Bernard
grew up

DAVID KIMBER-HUTCHINSON
Manipulative, wealthy businessman

FIONA SAMSON
Lately under cover in Berlin
KGB office

BERNARD SAMSON
Ex-Berlin Field Unit Assistant
to Dicky Cruyer

TESSA = GEORGE KOSINSKI

BILLY   SALLY

BRET RENSSELAER
Case Officer while Fiona Samson
under cover. Acting Deputy DG

GLORIA KENT
New PA to Bret Rensselaer
Bernard Samson's mistress
while Fiona was away

VALERIY FEDOSOV
Ret'd Capt. Red Army HQ Berlin
Supplied information to Bernard
Samson's father post-war

ANDREY FEDOSOV
"VERDI". KGB officer
considering defection

MOSCOW CENTRAL

Printed by RR Donnelley at Glasgow, UK